In the
City of
Fear

In the City of Fear

Ward Just

THE VIKING PRESS / NEW YORK

First published in 1982 by The Viking Press
625 Madison Avenue, New York, N.Y. 10022
Published simultaneously in Canada by
Penguin Books Canada Limited

LIBRARY OF CONGRESS CATALOGING IN PUBLICATION DATA
Just, Ward
  In the city of fear.
  I. Title.
PS3560.U75I5   813'.54   82-70130
ISBN 0-670-39679-6   AACR2

Grateful acknowledgment is made to the following for permission to
reprint copyrighted material:
Farrar, Straus and Giroux, Inc., and Martin Secker & Warburg Limited:
An excerpt from *Terra Nostra* by Carlos Fuentes, translated from the
Spanish by Margaret Sayers Peden. Translation copyright© 1976 by
Farrar, Straus and Giroux, Inc.
Almo Publications: Two lines from "Bout to Make Me Leave Home,"
lyrics and music by Earl Randle. Copyright © 1975 by Irving Music, Inc.
(BMI). All rights reserved. International copyright secured. Used by per-
mission of Almo Publications, an affiliate of A & M Records.

Printed in the United States of America
Set in CRT California

To Sarah

But reason—neither slow nor indolent—tells us that merely with repetition the extraordinary becomes ordinary . . . what had once passed for a common and ordinary occurrence becomes a portent: crawling, sending carrier pigeons, eating raw deer meat, abandoning one's dead on the summits of temples so that vultures as they feed might perform their cleansing functions and fulfill the natural cycle.

—Carlos Fuentes, *Terra Nostra*

Peace is at hand.

—Henry Kissinger, at a press conference

I

The security system was on the blink. The console on the side-board next to the breadbox emitted a low annoying buzz, and the red light was out. It was an internal failure, Marina had checked both doors and the downstairs windows and nothing had been tampered with. Now she stood in her kitchen in the early morning wondering what to do about it. Obviously something would have to be done. At night the neighborhood was unsafe, a war zone, two burglaries last month alone and the ghastly rape of Jo McDonough Cather in June. That was when Marina insisted that Piatt buy a handgun and keep it in the bed-room.

Glowering at the console, she turned on the radio and the water for coffee, all in one fluid motion. From the refrigerator came a grapefruit and from the breadbox a muffin. She stood at the sink looking into the garden, slick with dew. The sun, blocked, caught only the far corner where honeybees were nuzzling into the roses. She squinted sleepily and sighed, defiantly refusing to look up at the redbrick structure that concealed the sun. She saw it as it always had been, Washington at dawn, the heat of the dog days of August had yet to reclaim the city, and her garden was as still and sunny and symmetrical as an old print.

She moved in time to the music. For two decades, until last winter, she had listened to the FM, Telemann or Bach at six a.m. Telemann and Bach began her mornings, as much a part of her routine as the grapefruit and the muffin and the symmetrical view from the kitchen window. But now she listened to popular music, adolescent voices in falsetto, the rhythm and blues better suited to her own somber mood, and that of the city. She did a little two-step as the water whistled. It was only a few minutes' worth because shortly she would hear Piatt's step in the hall and his absent-minded turn of the dial to the all-news station.

On the breakfast table were the three morning newspapers, five pounds of information from Washington, Baltimore, and New York. She thought of the newspapers as she thought of ensembles, the New York paper a full symphony, the Baltimore paper a string quartet, and the Washington paper a jazz band. Piatt listened to the news on the radio while he read the newspapers, the Washington paper, the New York paper, and the Baltimore paper, always in that order. To Marina he resembles the serious music buff who takes the score with him to the concert hall, or the sports fanatic who brings a portable television set to the stadium to verify what he sees; to have described what he witnesses with his own eyes, and then to watch it replayed, as if he had no reliable memory of his own.

Linda Ronstadt gave way to a report from the White House, and she knew he was with her in the kitchen. She smelled his shaving cream and felt his dry mouth on her cheek and turned to smile up at him. He was dressed in his gray gabardine suit. She noticed that he'd missed a spot on his chin, a little gray tuft that would grow ragged by mid-afternoon, causing him to shave again. His white shirt was dazzling in the early morning light. He stood, his left hand resting lightly on her shoulder, reading Page One of the Washington newspaper. The headlines parsed, he turned to the editorial page; fifteen seconds there, nothing of consequence. He glanced at the Op Ed, his eyebrows rising once. Then he returned to Page One, something there had caught his eye. All of this with one hand on her shoulder, the newspaper open on the kitchen table, and the radio describing the President's preparations for a visit that day to a labor union convention in Puerto Rico.

Piatt? Pie-ut?

He grunted.

You missed a spot, Piatt.

His hand went absently to his chin, paused a moment—as if he had forgotten why it was there—then dropped to thumb the newspaper to Page Two. He tapped the page irritably, an item in the lower-left-hand corner, and muttered something. He shot his cuffs and bent closer to the newsprint, listening all the while to the radio broadcast from the White House.

And the security system's out, she said.

He said, The goddamned thing.

You can hear it, that buzz, and the red light is out.

You'd better call the guy, he said.

I think we need a new one, she said. This one's six or seven years old.

Well, it's supposed to have a guarantee.

He removed his jacket and hung it carefully on the back of a chair. He was moving into the interior of the newspaper now, "fishing the swamp" as he liked to call it. "The damn thing never does any good," he said, wetting his thumb again and rocking back on his heels. Piatt Warden, always well turned out. His shoes, polished to a high shine. The gold pin, precisely placed in his collar, lifting his tie just so. Senator Warden was exceedingly neat and orderly, he would change shirts in the mid-afternoon; if his suit became spotted, he would change that, too. This was not entirely disagreeable, having a neat man for a husband. But each morning in the kitchen she tried to imagine the racket in his mind as he read and listened at once, his own particular music, the brass of revolutions and terrorist attacks and economic collapse and the woodwinds of parliamentary maneuver, all backed by the drumrolls of lamentation, celebration, malediction, and threats, the usual carnal knowledge of the average news day in the federal city. She measured him, so tidy and respectable in his gabardine suit, indisputably a Washingtonian, one of those in charge. And when he looked at her, what did he see? A woman in a white cotton robe, worrying about the security system and a spot on his chin. Not a woman from the pages of *Vogue* or even the *New Republic*. She was a photograph on the cover of a respectable paperback novel, her head tilted at a becoming literary angle, dark hair falling carelessly to her shoulders, an amused look around the eyes, a hint of sexual tension, indisputably a woman who knew the score. She glanced over his shoulder at the newspaper's horizontal clutter. Piatt was shaking his head, evidently in disgust; a note was out of place. She saw it, an article concerning Henry Costello, an old nemesis, rumored now to be the President's choice for national chairman of the party.

She said, Coffee? He squeezed her shoulder, Yes. *Do not be deceived by this beautiful morning,* the radio announcer said. *Take your raincoat. A torrential downpour is expected by noon, according to the U.S. Weather Service.*

Marina let her robe fall open. She was not so badly turned out herself, red bikini pants and no bra, her own contribution to the atmosphere of austerity and reduction, so fashionable now among liberal people in the capital. She poured water into the Chemex, the heat of it warming her belly. In the garden a jay screamed, and flew away over the stake fence into the neighbor's yard. The sky was still brilliantly, gorgeously blue.

She started to whistle the Linda Ronstadt song, until his hand tightened again on her shoulder. The all-news station was broadcasting a summary of the day's events in Congress. It was a lengthy report; this was the last week before adjournment and the Senate would be in session late.

When it was over she picked up a banana and held it to her mouth, like a microphone. She intoned, "The day's events in Shakerville are as follows: Marina will be at home until noon, when she intends to lunch with a friend." He put his thumb to his mouth and turned a page. "Later, under the unanimous consent rule, she intends to sunbathe on the roofdeck. Later still, voting with the minority, she intends to dine with the Carneys down the street. Will you really be through this week?" She turned to face him. She was not a woman whose sexuality flowered in the morning. She was a night person, always had been. But the sunny fragrance of the garden and the heat from the Chemex and the jaunty red bikini—that, and his indifference—provoked and aroused her.

He shrugged, Probably. It was hard to say. The session could last through the weekend. She looked at him, concentrating so on his newspaper. Piatt was never randy in the mornings, owing to the newspapers to be read, the radio to be listened to, and the

6

long day to prepare for. If he had responded to her, she would have been surprised, perhaps even disappointed. She was not feeling sexy because of him, though their situation was provocative, he fully clothed, she nearly bare. The morning was wonderfully soft and damp, a Mediterranean morning; she could almost smell olive trees and feel a light mountain breeze. Her desire rose from within her, a part of her own memory and imagination and heat, her history, and Piatt was not necessary to it, though he was an undeniably attractive man, a shade over six feet, still slender, his face angular and unlined. He had the face of a boy, really, except for his eyes and the skin around his eyes: old gems in worn settings. He was usually humorous and many women found him attractive. He often gave the impression of a man in slight pain; that and his dry humor went together. She moved closer to the warm counter, leaning over it, her hands one over the other, waiting for the water to drip through the filter. The light fell in a certain way through the elm tree, coloring the garden with yellow bars. She loved the smell of coffee and looking now into the warmth and sunlight she felt herself swell, the bikini tightening pleasantly. She smiled ruefully as he removed his hand from her shoulder to pick up the New York newspaper.

He said, "I'll be late tonight, for sure." He stood a little straighter and frowned, as if to prepare himself psychologically for facing the vertical order of New York: a precise rationality, each block of news carefully arranged according to subject and specific gravity.

Grinning, she hummed the first few bars of *Thus Spake Zarathustra*. Then she poured coffee. "Do you mind if I listen to music?"

He looked at her, confused. He was deep into the financial section of the newspaper. The Congressional summary was over and a commercial message filled the kitchen. Then the announcer said there would be a special background report from a correspondent in Hanoi, evidence of a breakthrough in the latest effort to locate and identify American missing; the correspondent would be reporting live— Piatt looked quickly at his watch and, apologizing, turned off the radio and switched on the tele-

7

vision set. It was seven a.m. precisely and he wanted to see if there were any special interviews. He wanted to know who would gain a step that morning. She watched him, his long reach across the table to the shelf that held the TV. His shirt stretched across his shoulders, the light catching the hairs on his hand as he touched the dial. She blushed, turning slightly away, moving languidly into the sun; the sun warmed her breasts and belly. She lined herself up so that the ray of sunlight was exactly even with the top of her bikini pants. She watched her belly swell and then contract, brilliant in the yellow light, the down of her skin rising like a meadow swept by a warm breeze. She stared self-consciously at the ceiling and shook her head from side to side, feeling her hair bounce and then brush against her shoulders. She handed him his coffee, crossing her arms across her chest. A mistake, as it turned out.

"Not a thing," he said, turning off the television set. He almost added, "Thank God," but did not; it was obvious to anyone that no news was good news. He flopped the New York newspaper on top of the Washington newspaper and drew the Baltimore newspaper toward him, sighing dispiritedly.

She turned the dial of the radio to the station she wanted. The voice was either Carla Bonoff or Bonnie Raitt, she could never tell them apart. One of them was a songwriter and the other had gone to Radcliffe. He shifted position, moving away out of the sun; Piatt did not care for popular music. She was sweating under her arms and breasts, her skin slippery and hot in the sun. The sunlight was across her back now as she watched him bend over the Baltimore newspaper.

> . . . one more night like last night,
> I might have to pack my bag . . .

Abruptly she wheeled and left the kitchen. In the darkened living room she flopped on the couch, face down. The music followed her. She began to giggle, how had she gotten into this fix? Well, she knew well enough. That was not a mystery. It was absurd and crazy, she was so hot now.

"Marina?"

"In a minute, honey bunch." She turned on her back, her legs apart, laughing soundlessly. She covered her mouth with her hands. *Honey bunch,* an endearment from the old days, when they never addressed each other by name. It was honey bunch or lamb or darling or lovey or sweet or lover.

"Where's the grapefruit?"

"On the counter next to the toaster."

"What are you doing?"

She laughed out loud. "Making myself decent."

She heard him grunt.

"I'm coming," she said, rising.

She heard the rustle of newsprint. He had given New York awfully short shrift, she thought; not like him. The living room was cool and dry, but it did not ease the pressure inside. That was where it was, inside; she thought she would burst. Marina stood up, light-headed, and struck an exaggerated model's pose. She was in good shape for a woman her age, of course no match for the young women her son brought home, but . . . Well, that was not quite true. She was more than a match for the current one, except for the breasts. She always had wished that she had more on top, her legacy from the 1950s; that was what they all worried about, twenty-five years ago. The girls that Tommy brought home, they were uniformly buxom. There must've been a change in diet. She hadn't seen a flat-chested young woman in years; she used to worry that because she was flat-chested she would never be attractive to men. Once, in prep school, her roommate had looked at her in the shower and laughed. You and me, the friend had said. Look at us, two fried eggs on a plate, that's what we're offering. Marina had turned away, the water hiding her tears. The pressure had eased now. She snapped the elastic of her red pants; it left a little mark.

She could hear Piatt on the telephone now, his morning call to his administrative assistant. She listened from the living room, it was the usual call. The business that morning, a hearing in the afternoon, a particularly troublesome piece of legislation that placed him at odds with the leadership. He did not like to be at odds with anyone, but he hated opposing the leadership. There was that to sort out, and other matters as well. It was a ten-

9

minute phone call, and when he was finished he was ready to leave for the Hill.

"Do you like Leslie?"

He bent over the table, giving the editorial page of the Baltimore newspaper a last glance. "Isn't she like all the others?"

"There's a." Marina paused for a moment, wrinkling her nose. "Wanton quality about her."

"They're different than we were," Piatt said.

"She isn't all that attractive," Marina said.

"Well, she doesn't appeal to me," Piatt said.

"She's got awfully big tits," Marina said. "Probably that's why Tommy likes her."

"That kid," Piatt said absently.

"Tits," she said again, louder. Upstairs she heard the shower, Tommy. Piatt hadn't listened to a word she'd said. She was leaning against the door jamb, her white robe tight around her again. She looked at him in silent protest. His lips were moving soundlessly, his fingers drumming on the sideboard. He had begun to do that lately, talk to himself.

"He's a good kid." She knew he was thinking of something else, and presently she would learn what it was. It would be something to do with the Senate and his future there. He said, "I think the Mosquito is stepping down next year, the polls show him in a hell of a lot of trouble and so forth and so on." In their shorthand "the Mosquito" was the deputy floor leader, the whip. She moved into the sunlight again and poured coffee into both their cups. "I think I'll make a run for it, Marina."

She nodded. "The last time, you didn't think you had a chance."

"Situation's changed."

She waited, but he said nothing more. "How has it changed, Piatt?"

"I've mended some fences."

"Your fences have always been in good repair."

"Not lately," he said. "Well, actually . . . " He smiled crookedly and turned toward her, looking her full in the face for the first time that morning. "Actually, in a strange way you're right.

What I've done lately is not mend fences but bust a few. Image stuff."

"Yes," she said.

"It'll mean longer hours."

She nodded.

"I'll really have to start right now." He said, "I have as good a chance as anyone."

"Remember when you wanted to be President?"

"I never *really*," he began.

"Yes, you did," she said quickly.

"As you wish," he said.

She said, "I don't mean to make an issue of it, really."

"The President thing," he said. "Hell, we all wanted to be President then. Back then. That was our indoor sport. That, and betting who would be first on the cover of *Time*."

Two sides of the same coin back then, she thought. She said, "Well, you won that bet."

"It was a group picture," he said. "Anyway, in retrospect. In retrospect, the President thing . . . " He did not finish the sentence because Marina knew the rest of it. How many times had he made the point in the last fifteen years? A hundred times? Two hundred? Obsessed with it five years ago, he believed the country somehow bewitched, all the furies unleashed at once, the war and the scandals and the obese economy, cowardice and moral bankruptcy; God shrugged and looked the other way. If he had only known what would happen, had foreseen the calamity, he could then have been different, wiser, less timid, tougher, more resourceful, more *certain*. If he had known how high the stakes really were. He was a better man than those Presidents and more popular where it counted, in the Senate of the United States. But he had not wanted it badly enough, and had not had support in other ways. That must be the reason, his own desire. What other reason could there be but a lack of simple ambition? A refusal to bet all his chips on a single turn of the wheel. But he did not say any of that to his wife. He finished his grapefruit and bent down to pick up his briefcase. He stood quietly a moment, as if uncertain what to do next. He was a young-looking man, she thought, her husband the would-be commander in chief. Once an unfriendly journalist had written that he was younger than Springtime. That was the same journalist who had described him as "handsome as a boxtop." What was that one's name? Jessel. He was the one Max Cather had hated so. And of course he was not Piatt's favorite either.

She said suddenly, "Sam's worse."

He was fussing with the combination lock on his briefcase and did not look up.

"So I'm going over there around noon and again at six, so I won't be home until late, most likely. It means a lot to him, Piatt. And to me, too. I mention it on the off-chance that you get home early."

"No, I'll be late too. We'll be in session until midnight, maybe later."

"Poor Sam," she said.

He said, "Well," consulting his wristwatch.

"He's sort of in and out," she said.

"Remember, it's going to rain." Then, "You didn't say what you thought about me running for whip."

"Sometimes he's as lucid as ever, then he'll go off, and God alone knows where it is when he goes away, but he's not here or anywhere like here."

"It's a hell of a big decision."

"Yes," she said.

"I'm sorry about Sam," he said.

"I said 'Good luck,' " she said.

He shook his head firmly. "No, you didn't."

"Didn't I?" She thought she had wished him good luck, after he'd said—what was it?—that the situation had changed. She'd meant to say that, it was on her mind. "Well then," she said. "Good luck, *buena suerte*. You'll make it this time."

"I want it, Marina."

She looked at him fondly. "I know you do."

"I want it so badly I can taste it."

"I know."

"This goddamned country—"

"Maybe, Piatt, this time." She leaned toward him, hesitating; she let her robe fall open again. "Not quite so aggressive. Not quite so single-minded in the *pursuit* . . . " The last time he had played a fair hand badly.

He looked at her, his face closing. She knew the look. He felt always that she did not support him in the right ways, at critical times.

"But you'll get it this time, I know it."

He nodded, tight-lipped.

"All luck, really."

He said, "I'm sorry about Sam."

"Let me know if I can do any missionary work." She smiled hopefully.

"You never know about them, they're such pricks sometimes. Or should I say 'we'? I'm one of them. Maybe in the fall, we could have a few small dinners, here. It can help, that social contact." He looked over at her. "Well, you're looking very pretty today." He finished his coffee and bent over the sink to wash his hands of printer's ink.

She smiled again. "You're not so bad yourself."

"Say hello to Sam," he said.

"You ought to go see him, he'd like it."

Piatt said, "No." Then, softer, "It's such a busy time now. And he doesn't want to see me. And I don't particularly want to see him."

"Well," she said.

There was a step in the hall, Tommy.

"I don't want to belabor this," he said hurriedly. He looked at the briefcase. "But what do you *think*? What do you think about the idea? I mean, besides 'good luck.' "

"You'll be very good at it, whip. I've always said that."

But that was not what he meant. She knew it and he knew she knew it. He nodded pleasantly and said, "I'm off."

"Good luck," she said again and then, in conscious parody, "Have a nice day."

"You really don't mind?"

She remembered suddenly the Watergate thug, the one who

put his hand in fire to demonstrate his physical courage. When asked the secret of his abnormal tolerance for pain he'd replied, "It's not minding." She said, "Why should I mind?"

He leaned across the counter to kiss her. Her robe fell open again and she closed it. He glanced at the console, still buzzing, and shook his head. Tommy was behind them now. Piatt looked up and rumpled the boy's hair. There were general farewells and Piatt left through the back door. She watched him go through the zone of sunlight, swinging his briefcase. He'd forgotten his raincoat and she moved to call after him, then didn't. It was such a beautiful day, the sun higher now, peeking over the new block of condominiums down the hill; it was a large, redbrick, squarish structure and in this light resembled one of the newer gentrified government buildings housing the smaller commissions. Just a year ago it had been a vacant lot, where the neighborhood children used to play; except each year there were fewer children, and now there were the condominiums, $300,000 for a one-bedroom apartment. She watched Piatt close the gate, and thought she saw his lips moving soundlessly. She backed away out of the sunlight and felt cold and then, thinking of Sam, warm and sad again. She spun to kiss Tommy on the cheek, but he maneuvered around her, bending over the kitchen table to read the sports pages of the Washington newspaper. She turned again, preparing to leave the kitchen and mount the stairs to her own bedroom to dress. She would call Piatt later in the day, give him some encouragement. Everyone needed encouragement. She hurried out of the kitchen because her eyes were filling with tears and she did not want the boy to notice.

A few minutes before noon, from the window on the topmost floor, he saw the birds wheeling, their black wings flaring like capes. The birds soared in and out of his vision, undisciplined actors entering helter-skelter stage left and right. He envied their freedom, a chaotic ballet that moved him to smile. He watched them organize and turn their attention to an object partly hidden in the cornices of the building opposite. This was a very old building, weathered from decades of killing summer heat, with a proud frieze running along its crown. The frieze seemed to be a representation of anguish, a wretched column of bent and wounded men tended by a nurse—perhaps Clara Barton! The cries of the birds now sounded to him like a bugle's soft tattoo at reveille. In twos and threes they reconnoitered the defenseless object in the tucks and curls of the frieze, warily approaching it in squads, pecking and biting, worrying it, then flying away to bicker again.

Suddenly they were all in on it, attacking in murderous formation, their shrill cries rising in a martial tattoo. The object of their desire was concealed in shadows, a rodent or dove, some small night creature that had lost its way, sought refuge, and died. His eyes moved from the frieze to the monotonous rooftops to the window and then to the opposite wall, and the mirror and below the mirror the dresser with its vase of day-old roses. So it was true after all. With repetition, the ordinary becomes extraordinary.

Unexpectedly the sky began to darken, a heavy, lowering southern sky, humid and oppressive. Rain commenced and the birds dispersed. He lifted himself on one elbow and looked down at the street. As the rain increased he fancied the street a boiling cauldron, tendrils of steam rising from under parked cars, shrouding the street lamps. It was humorous to think of all Washington as a boiling pot, the stench of sulphur everywhere, and innocent creatures menaced by scavenger birds. Rain fell heavily now, darkening the frieze, drenching the nurse and her casualties. Below, a mother hurried along the sidewalk, pushing her little boy in a stroller. The child was laughing wildly, raising his eyes joyfully to the downpour while Mom navigated the puddles and the steam. It was 100°F, normal for the torpid days of August. He narrowed his eyes now and gazed toward the Capitol, his vision skidding over the low commercial buildings to the great dome. So familiar, the surroundings ached in their familiarity, Washington rooftops so square and secure, gray, durable in their utilitarian symmetry. *Form follows function.* He thought the city as neat and orderly as an army garrison, the federal buildings as humdrum as barracks. The city was a study in oblique geometry, all the angles converging on the Capitol building, the epicenter. He imagined Lincoln staring at it from the other end of the Mall, Lincoln's bronze eyes fastened on its decorative porches and plump summit, as across the Tidal Basin, a nineteen-foot-tall Thomas Jefferson looked south, his back to the city. As in the middle distance the river beat slow and muddy, gleaming in the heat, empty of vessels—and how gloomy late at night to walk along its banks, listening to the hiss of the current, the water's surface so benign and unruffled, yet dark, black as ebony. The river was a great ragged fault line, cleaving the district diamond.

The wind and rain intensified, the houses of Congress disappearing behind a tropical curtain. The woman and her little boy disappeared. The sky disappeared. It was all rain now, rain gray as ashes, smothering the steam. Streetlights blinked on and a bell began to toll, the Catholic church around the corner.

At noon, exhausted by his efforts, Sam Joyce lay back, breathing heavily, laughing in little gasps. Rain banged against the windows, steady and insistent. Then it was silent and his nerves froze, his body contracted once, then again, the sweat cold against his skin, the panic uncontrolled, his body heaving as if caught by wind. His vision blurred and his mind shut down for an instant. He reached instinctively for a cigarette, lit it, and waited, listening carefully for enemy activity. Almost immediately Sam felt him advance another stride—his voracious enemy, so silent, pig-dumb, and self-possessed.

A stupid army has invaded him, an army with no imagination and led by clumsy captains. It followed a scorched-earth policy, advancing on all fronts simultaneously, its commander in chief as slow-witted as Custer or the butcher Foch. *Mass*, Clausewitz said; mass directed at the vulnerable point. A swift, concentrated strike; mass, surprise, speed, economy of movement, dependable intelligence. His enemy—dull, oafish, obdurate, thick—followed none of these sound principles except the first, mass. It expanded like the tide, careful never to outrun its supply lines. It moved at precisely the same speed each day and in-

16

tended to kill him by attrition. That was what he believed during his bad moments. During his good moments he believed his enemy would overreach, and perish in a foolhardy invasion: an icy Moscow winter would close around him and he would die, exhausted and famished, frozen where he fell.

There were a few bad moments each day, always following some agreeable distraction—birds, the frieze, the mother and her playful son, the architecture of Washington. He described this enemy as a puritan army, determined to punish his lapses in discipline. Soon it will purify him out of existence, he'll be too pure to fight. He wondered, What has this cost me, this diversion into the feeding habits of birds? My sympathy for a night creature? Mr. Lincoln's angle of vision? The cost is five minutes or one hour, perhaps a full day. Whatever it is, it is too much, too dear a price for so ordinary a purchase.

When he sank back into the pillows, Sam was more exhausted than at any other time that week, a week worse than last. But he believed it important to think constructively, so he decided that his enemy had not, in fact, attacked. This relapse was his own fault, he had sinfully retreated and his enemy had merely filled the vacuum. He closed his eyes when the pain began, in the occupied territories—the present and its vicinity. He always had had a high tolerance for pain so this was bearable, a dull disagreeable ache that served to remind him of his enemy's ignorance of Herr von Clausewitz. The great strategist counseled a counterforce campaign, stressing military targets and avoiding civilian casualties. This, in the name of elegance—economy of means—and expedience. But in the enthusiasm of his advance, the enemy does not discriminate.

No doubt, he concluded—no doubt it is the spirit of the age, but his situation is profoundly ironic. He is ambiguous toward his enemy, inside him always, a living thing. He *is* me, Sam insists, some part of me gone berserk and vengeful. My doppelganger, he wants it so badly; he has a young lover's lust. Both armies are feeding off my body, I sustain them both. Truly it is war itself that is evil, the fact of the struggle and its mayhem rather than the combatants. The combatants are only following orders. How can I hate my enemy, this uncontrolled part of myself? Not aggression, no; a civil war, a war of national liberation. At another time, and in another country, might it be heroic? A dubious heroism certainly, but I encourage his maladroit spirit because if he were not maladroit, I would be dead. He need only strike at a vital point, a vulnerable organ; any one of several would do.

But he did not want to die a moment before it was necessary and was cunning during this siege, falling back, retreating in order and good discipline, *excellent* discipline following the agreeable distractions, successfully stifling the growing panic. He thought, I know him so well, this enemy. If he had wits enough to pause and organize, to attack and attack again, to concentrate on a single objective, to seize and *hold* . . .

He slept, lulled by the tap of the slackening summer rain. The rain receded as he did, leaving a dull, sullen sky. Slowly his mind emptied of all nonessential things, the birds, the heat—all save the order of battle inside his tortured nervous system. He avoided the consideration of motive. That was a closed book, not germane. There was no illuminating motive, assassins had no motive other than destruction, a general celebration of violence, and revenge. Violence itself was the motive, and that was a concept so convenient that it was not worth thinking about; in that way, it resembled the etiology of suicide.

"Colonel?"

He opened his eyes cautiously and looked right, irritated. Edna the day nurse stared at him. Her thumb was on his wrist. She had heard him talking out loud; only a few words were intelligible but they were enough to inform her that he was reprising his military theory of illness. He had explained this theory to the doctors and to the various nurses who attended him night and day. Being innocent of combat, they were politely unimpressed, none more so than Edna.

"Marina's here," she said.

A friendly hospital, everyone on a first-name basis, except for field grade officers. Of course he was no longer an active-duty field grade officer, he was Samuel Benjamin Joyce, U.S.A.

(Ret.), his last post a training command so obscure it was listed on no chart or table of organization. There was the suspicion that it had been created for him alone, and when he went out of business so did the command. Still, he liked the rank and did not mind being known by it. He had explained to Edna that a colonel commanded a brigade, five thousand men, the largest body of men that could be assembled within the range of one man's voice.

Sam nodded and patted the bedsheet. It was an effort just then to speak, and he wanted to conserve his strength for Marina. Sleep would have to wait.

"Lamb," she said, smiling. They were both smiling from the doorway, Edna and Marina. Marina cocked her head, hands on her hips, disapproving. She turned to Edna, who shrugged and disappeared. "Sam, you look terrible."

Indignantly: "I do not."

"Do," she said. "Edna agrees with me."

"He was talking to himself again," Edna said, her head popping around the corner. "War again, the advancing armies of the night. Male hysteria."

He said, "The last time, you called it paranoia."

She ignored that. "The Colonel was on bivouac, giving himself a briefing." Edna laughed and offered to delay lunch an hour unless they'd care to eat now together. Marina looked at her watch and shook her head. She could stay only a little while. She moved closer to him, bending over the bed, taking his hand. Her flesh was dry and cool. At first her perfume smelled acrid, but as she drew closer it became fragrant. Up close, her face was luminous.

"Dear Sam," she said. "How is it today?"

He said, "Hysterical."

She perched on the edge of the bed and talked, the small change of her life, this day not much different from the others. She described the garden in the sun, though not the way she felt in it. Then she talked about Tommy's new girlfriend. The morning seemed very far away to her.

"Is it true what the paper said, about Henry Costello?"

"I guess it is," she said. "From Piatt's reaction."

He shook his head. "It's unbelievable." Then he brightened. "Well, it's not unbelievable at all. That's the point, isn't it? It couldn't be more believable. Or inevitable."

"Piatt's going to run for whip," she said. "That's what he says anyway. He says he wants it so badly he can taste it." She put her tongue between her teeth and tilted her head, her eyes suddenly bright. "Can you imagine that?"

He laughed. "Yes."

"Well, that's what he says."

"And what about Tommy?"

"Tommy's going to California. Remember, we talked about that. That's what *he* wants so badly he can taste."

"Hungry crew you've got over there."

"Ravenous," she said.

"He has so much talent he'll do well in . . . Where?"

"California," she said. "And I don't think he will do so well there. And I don't want to talk about it anymore."

"The girlfriend's a good sign."

She looked at him silently.

He said, "Okay," and took her hand and kissed it.

"What about you?"

"I had a visitor." He looked at her mischievously. "Sol was in this morning."

She bent toward him, puzzled. He often slurred his words.

"Henderson," he said.

"How did he get up here?"

Sam moved his shoulders. "Wandered off."

"Oh, Sam," she said.

"Shit," Sam said, turning away. "All dressed up. Full kit. Christ, he looked like he was going on parade, which he thought he was, by the way. He thought there was going to be a review outside, he and I reviewing the troopers. He came to get me up." He looked at her, at her face in profile; her hand grew tight on his. "I think what he did was get into his uniform and walk out. Those stupid bastards downstairs probably thought he was the chairman of the Joint Chiefs of Staff, for Christ's sake. Anyway, he was here for about an hour. Outstanding. It was just outstanding, Marina."

"Sol Henderson," she began. Her eyes had strayed to the window and she found it hard to concentrate.

"Is a good friend," he said. "Will always be a good friend. Got Sol in my memory always, but Sol as he was. He isn't Sol anymore. He's been taken over by somebody else, and whoever he is now he's a goddamned nuisance at five in the morning. What are you going to do about it?" He looked at her grimly.

She smiled. "Hire an exorcist?"

"Good idea. You volunteering?"

She twirled the tiny gold cricifix she always wore at the base of her neck and made a face. "No," she said.

"He hasn't got any hair anymore. He used to have a nice head of hair, what you could see of it; he wore it about half an inch long. But what with the malnutrition and all the other good things, the beatings and the interrogations, and the worry. Never forget the worry. And the wounds, two of them in the last year alone. There's no hair. So the hat, the one with all the egg salad, the one he's had from '75 or whenever the hell it was that they were all released. Falls over his ears. Do you know who he looks like?"

She was back with him now. "Who does he look like, lamb?"

"Stan Laurel."

"He's too big to be Stan Laurel."

"Looks like Stan Laurel, Marina." Sam was silent a moment, staring at the mirror on the opposite wall. It looked to him like a window revealing another room, and a man in a bed being tended by a woman. The woman was seated, her back to the window, the man's face visible in the space between her arm and her body. Thus framed, it resembled a portrait, blurred at this distance, except for the deep lines in the face and the shining dark eyes. It was not a face to attract attention, in a gallery or anywhere else, but for the eyes and the voice. Sam Joyce had an actor's diction. He said, "Sol had the two stars on his shoulders, though, the ones he got after the release. 'Conscience stars,' he called them; they couldn't give him anything else, so they gave

21

him two stars. That was well after the time when peace was at hand." He smiled and then sighed, staring at the man in the window; the woman moved and his face vanished. "He wanted me to go on parade," Sam said. " 'Rise and shine, Samuel! Drop your cock and grab your socks!' " He paused to collect himself. "Very disappointed when I didn't climb out of bed. But he knew where the stuff was. Went right to the cabinet, got out a bottle, and poured a glassful. Offered me one, which I accepted. Then he started to talk, specifications mostly; stuff from the manual and the U.C.M.J. I didn't say a goddamned word. I was going to buzz for Edna, then I remembered that Edna wasn't on. It was that other bitch and I didn't know what they'd do to Sol. Probably lock him up again or, worse, give him a lecture. Anyway, after he got through with the U.C.M.J. he was back in War Zone C and doing pretty well so I thought the hell with it, and sat and listened while he talked. Faster and faster and faster, like a phonograph record being speeded up. The words were coming out so fast, they just fell all over themselves." She shifted and he saw his own face in profile in the mirror. It was no longer a window.

"I know, Sam."

Like hell she did. "That sad face."

"Yes," she said.

"He was just all shot to hell, you know, then the time in the camp. And when he got back he was like me, scared to death." Sam paused. Enough of that. "Then someone came in, I guess it was around six, and the shit hit the fan."

She smiled. "The shit hit the fan, did it?"

He smiled back through his tears. "Yeah, it did. As a matter of fact."

She kissed him on the mouth.

"I'd like to go back to Virginia, Marina."

"Tell me what happened to Sol."

"Right now, today."

"What did they do, call the gendarmes?"

"They don't know anything here, this is the wrong place—"

"Sol," she insisted.

"He told the nurse to get the fuck out, but to stand by so she could clean the hootch when we commenced operations." Sam began to laugh. " 'Di-di, mama-san,' Sol said. So she left, not un-pissed. Came back a moment or two later with one of the doctors, big bastard. New man, I don't know his name. But the sawbones was no dummy because he addressed Sol as 'General' and said he was needed urgently in the G-2 section. Sol looked to me for confirmation, which God knows I was happy enough to give. Yes, I said, we had a new defector, a commissar from Moc Hoa. A major, no less. So Sol marched off with the doctor and the nurse and I suppose he's back in his room now, up to his ass in chemicals. Like me. When?"

"Soon," she said.

"Christ, Marina."

"When they finish the tests." She smiled. They both knew that the testing would go on forever. "There isn't any room right now, that place's more popular than the Waldorf. They'll have to add a wing, or an annex . . . "

He turned away. Arguing was useless and of all people he did not want to argue with her. It didn't matter where he was, but he was more comfortable with his own kind. In the old days he would've wanted to be at Walter Reed but these weren't the old days. In Virginia, at The Farm, the doctors knew the score. You could recruit a first-rate general staff from the sick people at The Farm, even though most of them were civilians. Most of them were civilians because it cost a hell of a lot of money, but when he was there last there were two general officers and a colonel; the colonel and one of the generals were old friends.

She said, "I can come for dinner tonight."

"Do you think we can buy them off?"

"No, Sam. Did you hear what I said?"

"Dinner, yes. Good. Where's Piatt?"

"I don't know. A hearing. Something."

He said again, "Good."

She said, "Max and Jo sold their house." A titanic sum of money, she said. Jo and Max were going to move into one of the condos down the hill and take the profit and put it into one of the new government securities, the interest rates were sky-high; of course money was not a problem with Max Cather, he had money both here and abroad. Odd, she said. She and the Carneys were certain the buyer would be the chairman of an oil company or a lawyer or senior senator but he turned out to be a middle-level bureaucrat with the World Bank, a Brazilian. The house had a certain architectural interest and had been beautifully maintained, and of course Shakerville was superb. The Brazilian thought he had a steal at $450,000. Changing times, she said. He was a bureaucrat who lived with a woman and her two children. "It was always a neighborhood of married people, except you," she said.

"Not many of us left now," he said. But he was thinking of his own house, the tiny two-bedroom row house painted a ludicrous pink. Upstairs, the one big bedroom and the guestroom that doubled as a study. A narrow room at the rear of the house, it had no view and was crowded with his father's old desk and the gun cabinet containing the two shotguns and service .45 and the other souvenirs from a lifetime in the army. One large bookcase held his military books, and there wasn't a better private library in Washington, even a first edition of *The Guermantes Way*— the pages uncut except for the section on tactics and strategy that was as good as anything in Clausewitz. No accounting for genius: he suggested once that they line COMUSMACV'S office with cork . . . And on the wall facing the gun cabinet, the huge poster of Mistinguett, a rose between her teeth, her mouth wide in a gorgeous smile.

"Well, they'll still be here."

"That's the thing," he said, "government securities."

"Piatt bought some," she said. "The short-terms . . . "

He had bought that house so long ago. What had he paid? $40,000, $50,000. Highway robbery, he'd thought then. Remembering . . .

In the corner next to the daybed, the grandfather clock. The clock had a history, it had stood in the parlor in Genesee. A good deal went back to that parlor and its heavy furniture. His own father had stared at the clock, following the second hand, as he,

Sam, was being born upstairs. And when his father heard the first cry he'd noted the exact time, 2:03:05 a.m. His father had told him the story and insisted that he, too, must watch the clock when his own son was born. It was the link between them, physical evidence that they marched to the same drummer or anyway similiar rhythms. But he'd never had a son, being married to the service and in love with another man's wife. So he listened to the tick of the grandfather clock while he wrote in his diary. This was when he came back after his last tour, going to ground in the study, writing all day long, trying to heal himself. Soldier, heal thyself. The clock kept perfect time but he was out of synch. The pink house was empty now, though Marina stopped by once a week to verify that it was secure and undisturbed. There had been an epidemic of burglaries in Shakerville.

"Should've gone to live in Paris," he said suddenly. "That's the other thing I regret. We should've gone to live in Paris, the Île Saint-Louis."

"Oh yes," she said. "A terrible mistake."

"You could've worked something out with Piatt, I could've sold my place. My place isn't large enough for more than one person."

"Sam, cut it out."

"Too small for more than one, too large for one."

She looked at him, alarmed. His face was the color of ashes and his eyelids were fluttering. She bent over him and whispered in his ear. After the first few sentences he began to smile. Then he reached for her hand, less dry now. She was recalling a golden day in Spain, noontime at a plain country café near Madrid. They'd gotten lost on the road to Cuenca, stopped to ask directions, and instead stayed for lunch. It was a brilliant autumn. She remembered excitedly how hungry they were and what fun they had with the locals, he talking and she translating. No matter that this was two decades ago, her voice was so delighted and seductive it could've happened the day before yesterday. As, in a way, it had. *Sam,* she said, *remember . . .*

Memory, more diverting than morphine. They were driving to Cuenca, the cliffside city, in a red Volkswagen. The windshield wipers were askew, broken. Later, after the café, they parked the car and ran into a field and made love again and again in the dry grass. Even from this distance he was able to remember the field, its slant, the trees that bordered it, the smell, and the sounds they made in the grass. In Cuenca that night the waiter seemed amused at their appearance and they did not know why, until she turned and he saw the loose grass in her hair. They laughed all night long.

He said to her, I am more at home in countries other than my own. I love Asia. I know more about the Spanish Civil War than the American. Why is that?

She laughed. It's because you don't speak the language.

Say again?

You are happiest with an interpreter.

Later that night she asked him to marry her. They sat cross-legged on the bed, facing each other in the dark. The windows were open to the night and in the corner of his eye was a sliver of moon. She spoke softly to him. His was not an ideal life, she knew that; she did not approve of the way he made his living, and she knew he knew. Leaving Piatt would not be easy. But she had to do it and it would have to be now, not next year and not in five years. No decent intervals. He was inside her. He had occupied her and now he had to take possession and, she added with a smile, vice versa. She said, I am not a rental property. He remembered her nodding at her own words, as if hypnotized by them. He had rocked forward and kissed her, not daring to speak; he knew that in a month he would be in the Zone, *back* in the Zone for a second time. He knew it now as well as he knew her. So after a long silence, as she pulled back to the head of the bed, he began to speak. He talked first of his friends, Laurence and Henderson and the others, then of the men in his command; a number of them were dead. He thought she did not understand about the war. It was incomprehensible from this side of the ocean, from this hemisphere; not from the other. When you were there, it was real; you had to do what you could to help. You were obligated to do it, this was the promise that went with the commission. He watched her slip away from him, curl in a

26

ball at the end of the bed, her eyes looking at him through her hair. No matter how much he wanted this, wanted *her*, the other came first. The other was a matter of life and—

But it's so *stupid*, she'd said.

Oh, no, he'd replied, pleading. No, it was a lot of things. But when you were there, it was not stupid at all. At least it was no more stupid than any other war. The reasons might be stupid but they were someone else's responsibility. Reasons were not his command responsibility. His responsibility was fighting the war in such a way as to lose the fewest people, and gain the objective. Winning cost fewer lives than losing. Did she see that? Soldiers' *lives*. Against those, this—he'd gestured around him, at the old wood and the canopy above the bed, and the sliver of moon easing out of sight now, and her dark accusing eyes. And he knew that he'd gone too far, said more than he'd meant to say.

I'm a fool, he said at last. But I can't break this promise. I've broken others, but I can't break this one. . . .

She moved to the window and stood looking into the wet. They were reading each other's thoughts. He lived almost entirely in the past now, and so much of that invented. He watched her lean her forehead against the glass. His memory allowed him to forget the night in Cuenca and his present enemy and make love to Marina. It was not love the way it used to be, but he had the memory of himself then and the reality of Marina now. His invention removed the barrier of pain and fear and let him feel her emotion. Sensing her, he sensed himself. She told him that it was as good now as it had ever been and he believed her. Why should she lie? She would never lie to him about a matter of importance. And he knew without being told! He knew what he felt and surely she must feel the same. Lying together in the narrow bed, the room lit by the creamy glow of street lamps, he felt her desire and excitement. She never changed and he saw himself as a boy of twenty-five, hungry all day long and hoping to God she would never stop loving him, and that one grand day they'd awaken together— He'd believed then that they were one person, each living in the other; they cast each other's shadow. It was necessary for him to remember earlier times, young men's

27

dreams; he did not want to think of himself as he was now, confused and exhausted, his body torn to pieces by the warfare within. She was as magnetic now as the day he had met her, had taken her gloved hand in his and kissed her on the mouth, at the same time shaking hands with Piatt, his friend.

She'd said, Piatt talks about you.

He'd said what was expected. Nothing good, I hope.

Yes, she'd said brightly. All of it's good.

Then they, bride and groom, had turned away to greet the next guest in the receiving line, Piatt winking and leaning over to whisper something in his ear. But he could not take his eyes from the new Mrs. Warden. He was reading her thoughts from the first moment, had caught even the skeptical look she'd given his uniform with its shiny new lieutenant's bars. Now, with so much history behind them, he lived for their moments together and that was why he did not want to die, and fought with such stubborn skill. In order to live, he had to hide in the darkness.

He said, "We've been lovers for twenty years."

"Eighteen," she said from the window.

"We've lasted longer than most marriages."

She smiled. Every marriage but one.

"But Shakerville has always been stable, hasn't it?" The image of his pink house and its furnishings floated into his mind, and out again. "Still, we haven't done so badly."

She shook her head, No. She would not have said that eighteen years ago, but times and expectations changed. At any event it was what they had and many people had less. She was leaning over him again.

Sam squeezed her hand gently and closed his eyes. It was an enormous effort just then to speak, so he retreated again into his memory, Cuenca, a drive once to Toledo, the two of them so close in the little red car. There were other occasions in London, and once in Paris, and on the West Coast. And of course at various times and places in Maryland and Virginia, and in Shakerville. There was only the one long interregnum, when he was in the war and unable to leave it.

She smiled and said something he could not hear.

"My mistake," he said.

She did not answer that, and did not want to believe it. It was not a mistake. She refused to owe her life to a mistake. It was not his mistake and not hers, it was the spirit of the age. He had his duty and he performed it, and if it had nearly destroyed him, well then—

"Is he a Senator now?"

She looked away. Piatt had been a Senator for six years, and would be one for another six. He would be a Senator for the rest of his life, as she would be a Senator's wife.

"Does he like it?"

She said, "It's what he's always wanted." Then, in conscious parody of an old joke: "And what I've always wanted for him."

He looked at her, his eyelids fluttering, back in the present now. "Of course, I'm crazy as a loon. I'm crazy as Sol Henderson. It's been so long since I've seen him, it seems like forever. Remember Dennis's funeral?"

"Yes," she said.

"It's where we began, you and I."

She said kindly, "It's ancient history."

"Not so ancient." He closed his eyes against the shadows, then welcomed them. "Everything's like yesterday. Dennis is, Cuenca is, all the places we've been together. All the places we planned to go to and never did." He opened his eyes. "I must've had a hell of a good life because I've got great memories, I can tell you a few more if you've got time—" The years bunched up on him now, clothes that fit too tightly. It was difficult to move, or to distinguish one year from another. They were arrayed in his mind's eye but he could not sort them out. Perhaps they were all one year, that dreadful year; the year that was part of every day and every night, a continuous reel of film.

She leaned close to him, whispering.

"Say it again," he said.

She continued to whisper, her arms around his head.

He said, "Yes, that's wonderful." He said distinctly, "They haven't forgotten, have they?"

She shrugged. Then she shook her head, No, not wanting to

dispute whatever it was he meant. He nodded, unconvinced. They would forget all right. This was a country that specialized in the destruction of memory and the manufacture of myth. A gimcrack culture, pliable as paper currency. He looked at her, her face suddenly rearranged in his vision, a Picasso woman— profoundly modern, he thought, except there were tears in the corners of her eyes.

She said, "Sam."

It was not for lack of effort or industry, God knows. We worked to put it behind us. Everyone cooperated. No one doubted that there had been mistakes, thousands of them; millions literally. The nation resolved to forget and everyone assented. Assent was general in the capital. A confession of error would surely result in forgiveness. In Washington they imagined a great sign of relief from a multitude of throats. But it never came, neither relief nor forgiveness. The war ended, but there was no consolation. The dead continued to accumulate like so many bad debts. They were joined by the survivors.

She said, "Sam?"

He rose on one elbow, staring into the mirror on the opposite wall. He said to her, staring clear-eyed at her rearranged face: We lived off them for a very long time. We fed on them, our nourishment. Our tables were crushed by the weight of them.

There was a stir in the room, a shifting of feet, some murmuring.

She took his hand. She adored him so, looking at him, hearing nothing, reading his thoughts. The man who knew too much, the last romantic in America. He had gone to the war in the beginning and had stayed almost until its end. He was a rebuke to them, he and Sol Henderson and the others; so it was necessary that they be removed. In any disgraced and defeated army fighting a scandalous war, the warriors were the first to go, always. They were the despised witnesses, their memories fresh and unedited.

He said to her, or no longer to her but to himself, We closed its eyes as one does with the dead. But the time was late and it had seen everything there was to see. As we had done everything there was to do, and more. We did it for ourselves, we could not bear to look this corpse in the face, seeing ourselves reflected in its wideopen eyes.

She bent close to him but she heard nothing.

He opened his eyes.

He said, "What happened?"

She said, "You went away, but now you're back."

He was thoughtful for a moment. Then, "What do you think, do we want Piatt to get it?"

She smiled. "Sure. Why not?"

"Okay," he said. "They're all dead anyway."

She said, "We're not dead."

"*They* are," he said. "They're dead."

Her mouth touched his ear. "Who, lamb?"

One shadow moved, and then another. There were so many of them.

She held her breath.

"Dennis," he said. "My old man." The shadows crowded around his bedside, shutting out the light and the air. "Revdoc Laurence. Even Sol. How many do you want?"

"Not us," she said.

He nodded, apparently in agreement. She closed her eyes with relief. He was coming back to her now, she could see him rising from the depths slowly, as if oppressed by a great weight. Perhaps it would be all right after all, perhaps that one year would not crowd out all the others. . . .

"It just scared the hell out of me," he said. The words were out before he could recall them. He was missing parts of his sentences now and she was moving in and out of his eyesight, now clear, now vague. He wished he was at home, wherever that was. It was not the Zone and it was not The Farm. It was the pink house, the library, the gun cabinet, his diaries, the grandfather clock in the corner, and Mistinguett on the wall. They had never lived there together, it was a bachelor's house. He searched her closely, this slender woman dressed in clergy gray, a stylish suit, a going-out-to-lunch suit. The waters of the past washed over him; the darkness remained. No one would ever,

ever, know the truth of the last lunatic tour. Dwarfs, freaks, black boxes, pacification. The cavorting of clowns. He tried to reach for her but his fingers were as thick and unwieldy as tree trunks. She seemed to merge with the anonymous walls of the room, and the damp, somber, threatening afternoon, twilight in Washington.

II

The district they called Shakerville was located high up the hill near the cemetery. Teddy Carney named it for their half-joking description of themselves in the old days, "movers and shakers." Tourists crowded in on weekends, peering into their downstairs windows, giddy with envy at the exquisite houses, many of them dating from the formidable federal period. Slave quarters, the guidebooks said. There were wrought iron fences fashioned from the barrels of muskets in oval ceramic plaques stating that this house was the residence of so-and-so who served in the administration of Benjamin Harrison. Shakerville was a commotion of inquisitive strangers during the day and in the evening became as serene and secure as any residential neighborhood far from commercial hurly-burly, yet only a brisk walk from the iron triangle itself. On summer nights the cemetery collected drunks and lovers in equal measure, a circumstance the residents accepted as the inevitable burden of living in the bosom of a historic district, in a capital lately become glamorous.

One would not have been surprised to see Aaron Burr in tricorn, a lady in crinoline on his arm. In Shakerville the pedestrian walked a little more slowly, admiring the fine flowers and old wood and polished brightwork and cobblestones worn smooth by two centuries of use. The houses were as pretty and meticulously appointed as yawls, the front doors fire engine red or lacquered ebony, glittering brass knockers catching the eye. Fierce American eagles crouched above the doors. Outside, gaslamps flickered in the evenings and each house possessed its own rosy glow, as warm and inviting as an English pub. Thick curtains parted a quarter of an inch allowed an aggressive passerby to peek inside, the downstairs disclosing: flowering plants, photographs in silver frames (these are family people), oil paintings, a Steinway, and books. The books mark the room as a Washingtonian's and lend it a subtle allure, confirmation of knowledge received and stored. Useful knowledge, news you can use. This is a room whose occupant is at ease with conflict and discord, Marx touching Mark Twain; a Baedeker between the *History of the Jews,* volumes I and II; the diaries of Ickes, Forrestal, and Virginia Woolf; the memoirs of U. S. Grant, Sherman Adams, George Kennan, and Nan Britton; the parliamentary novels of Anthony Trollope and the Dreiser canon. Books of history and political science: *The Republican Ascendancy, The Rise of the Vice-Presidency, The Rise and Fall of the Third Reich, The Economics of the Political Parties, De Gaulle and the Anglo Saxons.* There are books from floor to ceiling, on coffee tables, framing fireplaces, obscured by ferns and screens. Unoccupied, the room looks somehow restored, as properly historical as the morning rooms at Mount Vernon or Monticello. It is redolent of history, though the newspaper on the hassock and the television set in the corner remind the passerby that this Washingtonian is not an academic or scholar, remote from the common culture. This is the room of a native, not a businessman in from Chicago for a tour as secretary of commerce or an academic down from Cambridge for a spell with the National Security Council.

The original houses were tiny, having the dimensions of vertical dungeons. In the months following the Second World War a newly retired ambassador and an investment banker, close friends, bought three each, six houses in a row, and converted them into two. That part of Georgetown was not fashionable then and the houses came cheap. The new owners did not interfere with the façades but gutted the interiors and made comfortable five-bedroom houses of them. The retired ambassador and the investment banker, both widowers, died within a few months of each other in the 1950s, and the Carneys and Cathers learned through the grapevine that the houses would be available. Bids were made and accepted, and many residents marked the Georgetown real estate boom from that moment. At any event, Shakerville became the jewel in the crown. Over the years the Carneys and Cathers between them purchased three more houses, which they resold at ever-higher prices, mostly to young foreign service officers, family people who bought houses to live in, not as investments. Max Cather handled these transactions, referring to the properties as "grace and favour" cottages. A few years after the Carneys and Cathers settled Shakerville, Piatt and Marina Warden, acting on timely advice from Teddy Carney, bought two houses in the next block. A year later Sam Joyce, then a major, bought a house down the street. They were all permanent Washingtonians who became close friends, their careers intertwined no less than their lives. They were always on the watch for new properties. Thus did Shakerville renew itself.

The houses were uniformly two stories high, the upper floor impenetrable through curtains and blinds. At night, light leaked around the edges but no movement was ever seen. Free of tourists, the cobblestone sidewalks were deserted and a footfall could be heard a block away—luckily so, for the neighborhood had become less secure each year. But in the glow of gaslamps, Shakerville was cheerful and steadfast, its defiant American structures facing the present with serenity and confidence—old buildings, young occupants. Yet the atmosphere was strangely European. That was what struck the passerby, the similarity to parts of Chelsea or South Kensington. A glance told the ambivalent visitor that the district was American, authentic American structures fronting the cobblestoned street, but still there was something foreign. Even the children seemed better behaved. The ambience was Old World, a district where well-off people lived and where the houses stayed in the family. Shakerville's manner was imperious, the look of a prewar aristocrat in homberg and furled umbrella, conveying the pride of heredity, of like begetting like, and of the continuity of authority: in sum, European genetics inside the American dream.

The Carneys were having a dinner party. They entertained frequently, usually eight at table, always including at least one Shakerville neighbor and one visitor—a diplomat or journalist on home leave, or a European intellectual. Piatt and Marina had been told that there would be only one outsider that night at dinner, Sheila Dennehay—and she had been around for so long that she was scarcely an outsider. Max Cather, his new wife, Jo McDonough, and Sam Joyce would complete the party.

Carney was speaking—a monologue, really, that began in Delhi, detoured briefly to Bonn, and was now bogged down in Paris. Dressed formally, his bearing almost ecclesiastical, Carney had regaled the table for an hour in his high-pitched voice. He was saying that his man in Paris was a lazy oaf but useful when the "proprietor" came for a visit. That was Carney's name for the publisher, Sloane. His man in Paris possessed unrivaled knowledge of restaurants, had known every "serious" cabinet minister since the government of Mendès-France, and could assemble them at a moment's notice to dine with Sloane. Once—a brilliant coup!—he had secured an audience with Charles de Gaulle when it was known that de Gaulle received no American except Lippmann. It was true that the audience was canceled at the last moment, immensely relieving Sloane, but the wonder was that it had been arranged at all. The proprietor had no interest in French ministers but acquiesced out of courtesy to the oaf, who took his position as chief foreign correspondent seriously. Paris stood "in contrahst" to his man in London, a merry-andrew who knew no one of importance and seemed bewitched by tarts and musicians. However, London's production was high and his expense account low, altogether an agreeable arrangement. Useful man, Carney said grudgingly, and popular with Sloane's two daughters. Nairobi remained a mystery, Carney did not know where she was at that moment, Nairobi had disappeared into the bush a week ago, nothing heard from her since.

Looking for King Solomon's Mines, what? Or Jomo's boodle, huh? Send her dispatches by forked stick, ha-ha.

Carney plunged his spoon into the mousse, amid a general tinkle as his guests did likewise.

Then he looked up and smiled maliciously. Teddy's face was round but his skin taut and ruddy as if from windburn, and in the candlelight he fairly glowed. Now he was in the mood for gossip and observed that everyone "on Desk" was intrigued by Jessel. Jessel and his dark lady of the sonnets, haaaaaa. The

Cathers looked at each other, then at Piatt and Marina. They all knew Jessel, who had been on the Shakerville circuit one year. Carney grinned. The reports were incomplete, he said to Jo, but it appeared that Jessel was walking out with "your Sonia." They traveled together in the countryside and were generally inseparable in the capital. "It can't be true that Sonia's in love?" Carney asked mischievously.

"She's of age," Jo said.

"Yes," Carney agreed. "And God knows, so is Jessel. But—"

"Teddy," Max said mildly.

"—I wouldn't've thought *there*, though Sonia's always had a mind of her own."

"She's her father's daughter," Jo said quietly. Dennis McDonough had been dead for seven years, or was it eight now? His name often came up in conversation, and people would remember his brilliance and vitality. At the time of his death he had been a member of the White House staff. "She was fascinated by that memo of Dennis's," Jo said. "Been fascinated by it for years. It was part of the buried past. So it's logical, her going out there. I didn't try to prevent it. Why should I? She said it was where the action was, and where she wanted to be. So she went."

Carney said, "You've missed the point." He pronounced it "pint." "The point is Jessel, all washed up. Everyone knew it. He knew it. I did. He wanted the assignment and I gave it to him, told him it was the last turn of the wheel. *Rien ne va plus!* If this didn't work out he'd find himself sous-correspondent in Richmond. However, I had a hunch. Jessel needed a dangerous mission far, far away. And he's never performed better. We're out front and no one's touching us. The government's fit to be tied. The President himself . . . " He laughed gaily. "I think it's little Sonia, Jo. Inspirational Sonia."

Max cleared his throat, then spoke directly to the foreign editor. "You were right a moment ago, Sonia has always had a mind of her own. She's an extraordinary young woman, thanks largely to her extraordinary mother." Jo smiled fondly at her husband and made a little self-deprecating gesture. Max's devotion to Sonia was what had brought them together after Dennis's death. His own marriage was breaking up and when he began to court Jo he had made it plain that he intended to step in for Dennis, to the extent that Sonia would let him. Jo was moved by his sincerity and he made good on the promise, though as it turned out Dennis was fully alive in Sonia's mind and she needed no substitute father. "Sonia has more good sense than anyone at this table, she'll get along fine."

"Jessel's a cavalier," Sheila Dennehay said.

"More Roundhead than Cavalier," Marina Warden said.

"He's very nice," Jo said.

"That's true," Max said loyally. "Delightful character, very charming, and good to Sonia. Though no better than she deserves, and naturally it's only a temporary infatuation. And she is not in any way an 'inspiration.' I wish she were. I wish he were a better correspondent. We've talked about him before, Teddy. Your man Jessel's not *sound*. He loves defeat, he's attracted to it, a night creature—"

"Jessel loves wars," Carney corrected.

"Same thing," Max said.

"*Au contraire*," Carney protested.

"—sees defeat everywhere, if it doesn't lead to defeat it's not real. Connoisseur of losing battles, he's like a wine snob at a fancy tasting. Algeria and the Congo, good nose, thin body; Korea, no character; Cyprus, no finesse. World War II, the European theater of course, the Haut Brion of wars, even though we didn't lose it. But Indochina, *voilà!* Superb! Best in a generation!" Cather flung down his napkin. "Losing battles. And if they're not lost in fact, he'll see to it that they're lost when he gets there. He thinks he's the ultimate authority. If we could bottle them we could market them with his name. 'Indochina Blanc de Blanc, Selected by Alex Jessel.' Just like Alexis Lichine. You can sure pick 'em, Teddy. Your foreign service."

"I stand behind my man," Carney said loudly.

Cather shook his thin face, an emphatic no. "Jews make lousy war correspondents."

"Except of course for Jeremiah," Piatt said.

Cather was unruffled. "Baptists and Jews make terrible war correspondents, it's well known. The one's self-righteous and the other's guilt-ridden." He warmed to the theme, drawing up close to its familiar fire. "They expect too much from texts, are too quick to criticize, and are meticulous in their search for error, and the exact distribution of blame. They don't understand the one big thing and never will, never have. Texts are always *merde* and everything's assimilated. It's not holy, for Christ's sake, and it's not moral either. And guilt doesn't come into it. It's *political*. That is to say, *nationa*." He thought it over a moment. "What you want is a middle-class Presbyterian. Middle class, mind you. Otherwise you've got Dulles. You want a man with a pessimistic temperament, conservative in his personal habits, who doesn't hope for too much but still's got faith and some *zeal*. You want a man with a certain respect for authority. And a man with a willingness to believe that God helps those who help themselves."

Piatt looked at Marina and winked.

"Of course he's too old for her," Jo said.

"Sonia has the wisdom of the ages," Teddy Carney said.

"So does Jess," Jo said. "But he's still too old for her."

"Jessel is not *wise*, dearest," Cather put in. "A delightful character, as I've said. Good to Sonia, so far's we know. Not a shit, by no means a shit. But not a capable correspondent. And not *wise*."

Jo turned to Sam. "Did you ever meet him out there?"

"Once," Sam said. "Maybe twice."

"And is Teddy right?"

"I never had any problems with Jessel," Sam said.

Marina said brightly, "Tell us more about Sonia. And her decision to go to the war. I thought she was still in college. When did she leave? What is it, a junior year abroad? I haven't seen her for a year—" Marina was struggling to prevent a landslide, to halt the pebble called Jessel. Jessel could dislodge the entire evening and send it spinning into acrimonious avalanche. It looked normal enough, the men in black tie and the women in long dresses, the silver glittering in the candlelight, the wine subtle and abundant, the food rich and ceremonial, Carney presiding with the formality of a bishop, his table a microcosm of the fed-

41

eral city. Things were composed and in their place, a worldly civility—that was Washington's metabolism—within and without, Mr. Lincoln in his temple, Mr. Jefferson in his, and the old mansion itself so pretty in snow. But emotions were very close to the surface that year. Lately Washington had come to seem to her like a Potemkin village, a façade maintained for the sake of the authorities, a city nervously preserving its good grooming— a gallant mustache, a confident pompadour—for the Crown, on those rare occasions when the Royal Train took to the boulevards. Washington now was like a family suffering terrible, unspeakable illness. It was an illness that could not be described to outsiders, so the family, once so cocky, was now subdued and defensive. It was family trouble, and they were all part of it.

The mood at Washington dinner tables could go from light to dark in an instant, without warning, though Carney had deliberately provoked this. Then he prodded the fire again. "Sam's seen him. How does he look?"

Sam Joyce smiled. "Jess? Fine."

Carney said slyly, "Did you see Sonia?"

"No," he said shortly.

"How odd," Marina said. "I would've thought if you'd seen Jess, you'd've seen Sonia too, since they're inseparable."

"Well, I didn't."

Max said, "A vulture feeding off carcasses." When Jo turned toward him, her mouth gaping in distress, he said hastily, "I don't mean Sonia, of course. I mean Jessel. Jessel and all the rest of them, but particularly Jessel."

"We all are," Marina said quietly. "One way and another."

"No, we aren't," Piatt said. His tone matched hers, he had no wish to precipitate a general conversation on the causes of the war or its accomplices. But he hated it when anyone indicted Washington, as if it were all one piece; simplistic nonsense, and the more irritating coming from Marina, who knew better. She did not look at him or reply and the others seemed not to hear the exchange.

"The real war is here." Cather said. "And there's nothing secret about it. This is where the war will be won or lost, right here. Your goddamned Jessel—"

"If your people would tell the whole truth there'd be no need for a correspondent as aggressive as Jessel," Carney said. "Lies, that's the style out there. Jessel only reacts to the facts, and the lies about the facts. What is there about this war, Maxie? The need to lie in the reports and the projections, victory, it's always victory around the corner—"

Sam turned away, concealing his smile. God, if it were only that simple. If it were as simple as lying. And Piatt, with his superior little Congressman's face . . . .

Marina leaned forward, her mind racing. Piatt could see it in the tilt of her head and the unconscious gesture, hand to neck. The tension was palpable now and she did not want to sit through another ugly hour. If Jo had not been present, Marina would have tried to get them talking about sex, Jessel and the girl. *Tell us more about Inspirational Sonia and her romance in the rice fields. Can you imagine them together, Jess and Sonia? Do you suppose it's true what they say about war and passion? Do you suppose he reminds her of her father, the worldly Dennis? How old is he, anyway? Forty? Forty-five? A hundred and forty-five? Are they compatible sexually? Do they make love in the afternoon?* It would be impossible for anyone at the table to believe that Jess and Sonia were having a love affair like anyone else. In the rancid atmosphere of the capital even a love affair was a substitute for something else.

Carney laughed, "Max wants to run his little war in secret, and Jessel won't let him!"

Ambition, a purchase on the future. So Inspirational Sonia allowed the correspondent to write excellent journalism, his florid dispatches required reading in Shakerville and elsewhere in the federal city. He was denounced privately by the secretary of defense and the President and his adviser. He "owned" Page One. However, Sam Joyce had not thought him troublesome. Marina wondered what it was that Sonia gained from the arrangement, aside from the obvious things and the experience.

Marina said she always managed to confuse Jessel with that other correspondent, the one who couldn't stay married, the one—what *was* his name?—who drank so. Applies to all of them, someone said, it's a prerequisite for employment. Hopeful laughter. Perhaps she could turn it around after all; in Washington women were regarded as the civilizing influence.

But the foreign editor said nothing, merely smiled and spooned the last of his dessert from the cup.

Sheila Dennehay snapped her fingers, saying she knew the one Marina was talking about, what *was* his name, when she and her former husband had been stationed briefly in Beirut he came to dinner and collapsed in the foyer, smashing a vase. Vase from Baalbek, pretty vase . . .

"He works for television," Marina said.

"Harris," Max Cather said.

Marina nodded. "That's the one. He's over there now, you see him every night. Always lying in a ditch, bullets overhead." She looked at Sam. "I saw him the other night, he was interviewing your friend Henderson."

"Some interview," Sam said.

"He's one of Jessel's sidekicks," Max said. "A rummy."

Sheila said slyly, "Alex Jessel's an attractive man."

"He's a little less attractive when he's walking out with your daughter," Jo said. "But I take the point."

Max said, "Who cares? Who in hell cares?" He looked belligerently around the table, as if expecting an answer. When none came he said, "It isn't Jessel's love life that interests me, you want to know, but the drivel he writes. Lies. He doesn't understand something. This is a *war* and we've arrived at the critical point. He has the opportunity to declare victory." He turned to the foreign editor. "Teddy, we've known each other a long time. Agree on most things. Not on Jessel. Jessel's more dangerous than a battalion of troops, except his effect is not on the battlefield. It's here, in Washington. This is his target, opinion *here*. And we can't compete. What do you want us to do, declassify every cable we have! Talking the other day to Henry Costello. You know Henry, Henry's got a damn good head." His voice rose. "Reminded me of Canning, what Canning said. You ought to read Canning sometime, Teddy, man in your position. Beware, Canning said, 'Beware the fatal artillery of public excitation.' That's what that bastard Jessel does with his burlesque. Excites the public. Titillates them, a little raw meat every day, a whiff of disaster. That Jew is a regiment of bad news."

The table was dead silent in the face of the avalanche, upon them at last. Carney bumped back his chair and laughed helplessly, his high tinny laugh that was half resignation, half provocation. He moved to the cabinet behind him and withdrew two decanters and a brass humidor. Eyebrows raised, humidor in one hand and decanters in the other, he smiled benignly at his guests. He lifted his arms in mock benediction, and the women rose slowly to their feet. Even civilization must have its interregnum so they were being dismissed. Each woman seemed intent on smoothing something, hair or skirt or merely the rancorous air. They waited for Helen Carney to lead them out of the dining room and to the sitting room upstairs, where they would take coffee together, leaving the men at table.

Sheila Dennehay paused, and looked back at Cather. "I don't care much for the anti-Semitism, Max."

Cather smiled triumphantly. It was not the first time he'd gulled them, nor would it be the last. In Washington, everything was assimilated, gentile into Jew, Jew into gentile; cosmopolitan people, they left their origins behind, Southerners, Northerners, rich, poor, connected or not, everything blurred, he thought, even the differences between the sexes.

"Am one," Max said. "Can say any damned thing about the Jews I please."

The women filed self-consciously from the room, disregarding the martial chronicle unfolding on the long wall behind them. A gaudy display, intrepid grenadiers and riflemen, Redcoats and Minutemen, surging in ragged lines, closing fast. Cannon boomed. A bugler and standard-bearer struggled in tandem up the slope of a low hill into the fiery maw. The wounded lay where they fell. It was so intimate the combatants could almost touch each other. A twisting line of Minutemen ran at the resplendent Redcoats, already breaking ranks despite the conspicuous gallantry of their plumed commander, astride an enormous stallion, laboring to rally his ranks. The stallion

45

reared, was rearing, falling backward; the commander's sword was still high but his effort was doomed. One more county family minus its baronet, and no war poet could doubt that as he fell his thoughts were of the realm (it was not yet an empire), the mad king, peaceful greenswards, the lads, cousins, and spirited women. The Minutemen were disorganized, yet riding an obvious tide of victory, yeomen fighting in familiar surroundings—their farms, fields, and villages, their country, their war. All this was observed by a solitary figure in black britches and soft hat who stood, arms folded, on a little ridge out of range of the guns. He was bent at the waist, leaning forward, his right hand pressed to his temple as if to assist his memory. He watched the Minutemen push in in democratic disarray, advancing across a clear field of fire. The objective was concealed behind a portrait, the enormous oily face of Thaddeus Carney, lieutenant governor of the Commonwealth of Virginia two generations after Mr. Jefferson. It was lost altogether in the folds of Mrs. Thaddeus Carney's black bodice and its bonewhite cameo, though in the two-inch interval between Mr. and Mrs. the observer could make out a rough wooden bridge, Redcoats sprawled behind it, firing in disciplined fusillade. Two dead men floated face down in the placid river beneath. The bridge would lead to the objective, a barracks or a town and beyond it another town and another barracks, armory, field hospital, headquarters; it would end at Yorktown, months or years later. This skirmish, so meticulously narrated, lacked a hero. Where was the American field commander? Were these troops so driven and disciplined that they needed no captain, some French or Polish aristocrat on loan from the Old World? Whoever he was, he too was concealed, apparently behind the lieutenant governor's steady right eye—of course he would be ahead of his men, an exemplary leader. Sam Joyce wondered: What possessed Carney to hang his ancestral portraits precisely at the climax of the narrative? Now Helen Carney, reversing direction, disappeared into the kitchen and the prologue stood revealed: a bland and sunny pastoral valley, cows at rest in yellow fields, rotund shade trees, barns, haystacks, and a pretty village dominated by a church with its towering white spire.

Of course it was his editor's sense of humor: ancestors concealing that which was central to the narrative. Carney's historical
determinism: enhance the present, obscure the beginning, confuse the end. Journalism has no memory! The more exotic and
confounding the details, the richer the sum, the more mysterious
and suggestive the experience. Detail piled upon detail, a disorganized militia of details, all of them marshaled in service to
. . . the moment. A scarlet-sleeved commander astride a rearing stallion, a "piece" written on "deadline," the moment seized
in mid-air, an exercise in elementary calculus. No heroes and no
villains, either. In Teddy Carney's aggresssively random world,
they were the same.

Max Cather accepted a snifter of cognac and turned it in his
slender fingers, watching the liquor slide up the sides of the
glass. He listened to the desultory pre-coffee conversation with a
half-smile, observing the protocol of small talk after which serious business could begin, now that the women were safely upstairs. Piatt watched Max, admiring again the durability of the
little man's friendship with Carney. It was a genuine friendship,
though so tangled in the fabric of the city that it was difficult to
know where affection began and intrigue ended and vice versa;
probably it was all one. At times they behaved like rival suitors
campaigning for the hearts and minds of the American people.
A gentlemanly rivalry early in the decade, the promiscuous public enamored of them both, two sides of the same glittering coin.
Now it was not so gentlemanly, Max insisting that if journalism
succeeded, the government would fail; in fact, that was the definition of journalism's success, and its only objective. So it was
important to Max that he let Carney know that his editor's version of reality was not accepted at Highest Levels. Max wanted
Carney to know that they in the government were watching him
with care, exactly as any suspicious board of directors would
watch the behavior of a subsidiary which, while not exactly
wholly owned, was not entirely independent either. Carney
had to be made to understand that journalism was not a game,
and that there were limits; there were no absolutes in a dangerous world. He could put one Jessel into the field. Two Jessels,
three. Three Jessels and three bimbos to keep their rocks off and

inspired but in the end journalism must founder and history survive. A melancholy commentary on the times, he thought, when the critics were as important as the actors. Goddamn Jessel.

Of course (Max would grudgingly admit this, if pressed), in a crunch Teddy would cooperate. He was not naturally seditious. Teddy was a *provocateur*, loving loose screws and the roar of the crowd. But he was a loyalist and a Virginian first and foremost and behind the façade of dapper mischief he was a man of principle. Still, he was not running the foreign policy of the United States, and he had to be reminded of that obvious fact and be made aware that his provocative acts had consequences. The main thing was, there was no free lunch.

"Piatt?"

In the skirmish of Teddy's mind—

"Take a look at Page Two tomorrow."

Piatt nodded.

"Fine dispatch from Salisbury. Six paragraphs as clean as a plain pine box. You'll like it."

Sam Joyce said, "What's this about?"

Teddy smiled. "Piatt reads the wire-service stuff, says it gets him going in the morning, like Stendhal sitting down after breakfast to read the Code Civile, then turning to the Charterhouse of Parma. Isn't that right, old man?"

Piatt nodded. Of course with him it was the other way around, he read wire-service dispatches in order to write civil codes. He admired clarity above all things. In the House he was known as an excellent draftsman, though he was not a lawyer.

Teddy said, "Piatt doesn't read our correspondents, who are rather fonder"—ratha funda—"of writing than reporting. Doesn't read my man in London or the oaf in Paris or even Jessel—"

This produced a fresh outburst from Cather. Scapegrace, he said, lowlife, neurotic, tosspot . . .

"And everyone reads Jessel, even Max."

Piatt turned again to the cognac. Alex Jessel was a perfectly competent newsman, no more and no less; some flair, and it was true that he found some inspiration in his own disorderly life, as

Stendhal found inspiration in the formal language of the Code Civile. As he himself found inspiration in wire-service dispatches. Jessel was attracted to danger and people at odds with themselves, but many men are; in his own way Dennis McDonough had been. And now his daughter was.

Cather was off again and Piatt listened without much interest. Journalism fascinated them so, the observation of the action somehow more "interesting" than and potentially subversive to the action itself. He supposed it was subversive; it certainly was not helpful. Thank God the House was relatively free of outside interference, a man could go about his business in relative anonymity.

Cather said he'd offered Jessel a letter of introduction to the chief of station, furnishing cooperation within limits. Saigon station had been very generous, offering to vet anything that looked suspicious or out-of-the-way, no obligation, a sort of informal entente cordiale. In your shooting gallery of facts, Mr. Jessel, give us a carbine. Station told Jessel the simple truth: My lads are not stupid, and we never load the dice. But of course Jessel knew that. He was an experienced correspondent, but now for some reason had got the wind up. He drank half a bottle of Station's best Scotch, retailed a salacious anecdote concerning the business activities of the minister of defense, and that was the last they'd seen of him.

Max said to Sam, "That damned interview with Sol Henderson, for example. He's a friend of yours, isn't he? Irresponsible, damned irresponsible, malicious—"

"I didn't hear any complaints from Sol," Sam said mildly.

Cather opened his mouth to say something, then thought again.

"No complaints of misquotation or anything else," Sam said.

"Not the way I heard it."

"Then you heard wrong, Max."

"I don't trust them," Cather said. "Never have. I don't trust their motives. Maybe I don't trust Henderson's either."

"You don't know a goddamned thing about Sol Henderson. And he's on the scene, and you aren't."

49

"A blind man at the ballet," Cather said.

"Sol Henderson?" Sam leaned forward.

"Jessel," Cather said shortly.

Piatt looked at Teddy Carney, expecting a riposte, but the foreign editor was not listening to them. He was staring at Sam Joyce, waiting for a break in the conversation. Cather was on another tangent now, and Piatt tuned out, bored and irritated. He tried to imagine Jessel and the station chief sparring over a bottle of PX whiskey. Then he tried to imagine Jessel and Sol Henderson, whoever he was. That was a more difficult imagining, though Sol Henderson had a story to tell and Jess was in that business. Piatt thought it was probably an attractive life, journalism. Journalism from the box seats, though, not the general admission. Jessel seemed to find it agreeable, and now he had a young woman to share it. Dennis's daughter, no less. They'd nicknamed her Dennis's Menace. Only her petite figure reminded you of Jo, everything else was Dennis, the wide mouth and the mocking laugh, and the recklessness. Specifically the recklessness. She was also Piatt's goddaughter, a fact he did not brood upon. Sonia was not in Jo's control and not in his. The bishop's charge had been to provide for her spiritual well-being and he had not forgotten the moment during the ceremony when Dennis had looked at him in mock alarm, and winked. Then just a year ago he'd brought her to the House for a morning, introducing her to the Speaker and the chairman of the committee and the majority leader. She'd asked naïve pointed questions, smiling all the while, as if at a private joke. Piatt had been defensive, but patient.

She'd smiled most broadly at the motto he kept under the glass of his office desk. *One man can make a difference, and every man should try.* He was embarrassed when she read it; the homily was not there to impress visitors, it was for his eyes only. Then, seeing her smile, he'd become irritated. What right had she to criticize? Her smile reminded him of Dennis. Dennis would've smiled in that way—You and I, the smile would say, who are we kidding?

"Tell me," Carney said to Sam Joyce.

"It's hard to do," Sam said. "It's hard to explain, you have to be there, to see it first-hand."

"I've heard that before," Carney said. "That's Jessel's line."

Sam's sober expression did not change. He had recently returned from two weeks in the Zone, having attached himself to a delegation led by the under secretary of defense. The under secretary was happy to have him, a man with experience; he would know the questions to ask. Sam Joyce was a man with a memory. Sam told the under secretary that he wanted to see for himself how the war was going, but that was a cover story. His principal was Mundelein and he was going at Mundelein's request.

Now he tried to explain to Carney what he meant. There was a creepy theatricality about it, beginning with the moment they arrived at Andrews in the limousines and boarded the C-135 transport, one of the shuttles; there were two or three a week, from capital to capital, twenty-two hours in a bucket seat and a cramped bunk, the lights as dim and the atmosphere as raunchy as a càbaret. Drinks were served with meals. When the jet banked steeply and commenced its approach into Tan Son Nhut the under secretary's party moved to the center of the aircraft, crowding around the two small windows. They wanted to see it for themselves, the war revealed in the contours of rice fields and villages and the sprawling capital. Looks peaceful enough, someone said; looks like any French colonial enclave. All of them were standing in the aisle, feet wide apart, gripping seat-backs as the aircraft heaved and banked again. They all stood a little taller, seeming somehow bigger and more muscular, their faces taut; they were at the war at last, Washington's rear echelon was twelve thousand miles away. The week before, an official aircraft had taken a hit landing at Tan Son Nhut, so there was the smallest fear mixed with desire; they had made so many decisions from the safety of the Pentagon or the State Department. When the plane touched down the younger staff members broke into applause, but no one was prepared for the heat when the big door eased open, revealing the wide tarmac with its camouflaged buildings and aircraft. They exited blinking into the sun, thanking the crew chief who smiled distantly and said formally, "Welcome to hard times." And at the foot of the stairs, COMUSMACV himself with his suite, all of them grinning and combat-ready in starched and pressed fatigues. Sam had detached himself after the landing formalities, explaining to the under secretary that he could do more on his own; he'd rejoin them in ten days. It was important to get away from the official itinerary, he'd said; but everyone knew that, the war's most enduring cliché. The under secretary, recognizing the voice of an experienced insider, instantly agreed.

Sam visited friends in the provinces and the capital. The story was the same everywhere, once the charts and bar graphs were put away and once his friends understood that he was not quoting them by name, and was not on any mission that would require a formal report. Whose can are you carrying? they'd asked him. None, he'd replied, offended; they knew him better than that. And it was true; Mundelein was his patron but he'd have no directed verdict. His friends were happy to talk to him. There was no change. There was just more. Sam was on familiar ground, it was like running into a childhood friend and recognizing him instantly—prosperous, thicker in the waist, older, but unchanged, the same smile and gestures and stance and language. "I'd know you anywhere." There was more of everything, however. His friends had gone to extremes, the pessimists darker, the optimists sunnier, the soldiers more warlike, and the civilians more peaceable. What was search and destroy in one vocabulary was pacification in the other. Drinkers drank more and the sexually obsessed were pathological. So vast now, the American community lived on the margins; the Vietnamese seemed almost to disappear, irrelevant to their own war. Yet—this is what he wrote to Marina Warden—they were so admirable. That was what had bothered him from the beginning, from his own time there, and the thing he could never adequately explain. The best men were there. They were not quite so good as they had been last year or the year before but that was because there were fewer of them now and the supply of good men was limited always and as the war grew it took more men to manage it. But they were pretty damned good even now and it broke

52

your heart to watch them work, the eighty-hour week was routine. Every visitor returned from the war zone depressed and guilty because the effort seemed so unequal. You wanted to deny them nothing. You pulled for them, and in the company of optimists wanted to believe what they believed, and in the company of pessimists wanted to confirm their blackest imaginings.

He'd revisited his old station, two Americans and three Vietnamese in a neglected border province. This was when he was an adviser; his first tour. The war never seemed to touch this province though he never had the feeling he was in secure territory. His number two, a civilian, was still there after all these years, having refused transfer or replacement; the Department gave up on him and allowed him to stay where he was. The assignment was not a choice one. A Vietnamese had died and another had disappeared, so he sat around the dinner table at night with the American and the Vietnamese who remained. He thought they had grown into a kind of marriage. It was impossible to tell who was the senior man, or who the Westerner and who the Oriental; they both seemed French. They spoke French at table and the talk was as it had been in his first year, rice delivered, roads repaired, reports certified, inspections conducted, births, deaths, the stupidity of Saigon. The acronyms were different, USAID had become CORDS and was now OCO. The estimate of the situation was unchanged and at the end of it Sam felt as if he had never left. But he felt obliged to inquire if the road from the provincial capital to the Cambodian border was secure in the evenings, open to traffic? Oh, *oui*, his American friend said. *Oui, oui, pourquois pas?* Any rumors to the contrary were false! Put nothing in your report that calls the road into question. The road is formidable, secure as the Avenue Foch *après-midi*. As Pennsylvania Avenue at dusk! For God's sake, Sam . . . Yes, the Vietnamese agreed, of course it was. He put his tiny hand on the shoulder of the American, so distressed at this turn in the conversation. He poured a glass of wine and put the glass in his hand. *Chéri*, it is all right. Do not disarrange yourself. Colonel Joyce was an honorable man and would write nothing critical of the road. Colonel Joyce was not that kind of man, he was an officer and a gentleman, and not least an habitué in the Zone. Colonel Joyce was a friend, not one of the filthy scum from OCO . . .

They were sweet together. Their office was filled with flowering plants.

He found Sol Henderson at My Tho. They had a long night together, reminiscing. An old enemy had just been named vice-chief of staff, and an even older enemy was rising at MACV. They raised a glass to Revdoc Laurence, dead now almost six months, then plunged into the details. This village, that province, this road, that "sector." Henderson told rollicking stories of fighting the enemy—everywhere, it seemed.

He said, It is very fragile and we are soon to be overwhelmed.

He added, The system rejects bad news.

In Washington, Sam said, they want good news.

Well, Sol said, they're getting it.

And you? Sam asked.

They've got something new in the works for me, Sol said.

A new command?

Something very far away, Sol said.

Do you want me to find out what it is?

I think I know what it is, Sol said. *You* take care. *You* be careful, it's worse where you are than where I am. They're out to get all of us, you first and then me.

Sol—Sam began.

Mark my words, Sol said.

No mysteries, please, Sam said.

It's shifting daily, Sol said mysteriously.

Next night he spent a long evening with Sol and his aides, enjoying the rough talk and the behind-the-lines atmosphere. They wanted him to go on patrol the next day, a neutral observer from the World, ha-ha. But Sam declined, excusing himself on grounds of a prior commitment. He had to rejoin the under secretary's party. He wrote Marina that he wanted to go and would have except that if anything had gone wrong there would have been hell to pay and it wasn't worth it. His death or injury would have made headlines, and Washington had automatic priority in the distribution of bad news. And they would have accused him of arranging it. It was not his mission to accompany patrols into no-man's-land, though he had done it often enough in the past. It was the sort of thing a civilian might do, in order to increase the weight of his testicles. Sam Joyce lived in safety and Sol Henderson did not, but an afternoon's walk in the bush wouldn't change that.

He and Henderson had gotten fearsomely drunk instead that night. The aides took them both back to Sol's billet. How could you not appreciate them? he said now to Carney. How could you *not* like them, those who were voluntarily present and paying the heaviest price? They seemed to want to win and how could you deny them support? You who lived safely in Washington. The truth was, the best of them—Sol, the late Revdoc, one or two others—reminded Sam of the Bedu, living strangely austere lives, fiercely resistant to change, humorous, hospitable, courageous, and soon to be overwhelmed. Of course they were not nomadic: once assigned a location on the margins, the dedicated Americans tended to remain, hanging on.

"Yes, yes," Carney said, "little Lawrences, all of them. How do you know anything about the Bedu, anyway?"

"I was once attaché in Jeddah," Sam said.

"Oh, yes, I'd forgotten."

"I was there to train them but they ended up training me."

"Yes, I remember. But what's the situation *on the ground* now? The fighting."

"I learned falconry."

"Yes," Teddy said impatiently.

"And swordsmanship, a little. I liked them, they're a hospitable people."

"On the ground," Teddy said.

"There's no agreed version," Sam said. "It depends on where you are and in whose company. And the time of year."

"Well, try us," Teddy said. "Try us with one version. Give us a plausible version, your favorite. Can you do that?"

Sam looked at the others for an objection. When there was none he shrugged. Then he rose and leaned over the table, his hands poised like a croupier's. He was conscious of an impersonation. For a few moments he would look and talk like a briefer, a Pentagon commando; they had the voices of anchor men, and the looks, too, white teeth and plenty of hair. Still, he had his voice. Smiling to himself, Sam collected coffee spoons and the two pepper mills and began to distribute them in the center of the table. This was Hue, that Danang, that Qui Nhon, that—he reached for a silver candlestick and plopped it down—Saigon, that Can Tho. Then up the western border, so many dominoes, beginning at Camau. The Parrot's Beak, Pleiku, Kontum, Khe Sanh. He dealt half a dozen butter knives, aiming them at the waist of the country. "The trails," he explained. He dug into his pocket and came up with a fistful of coins, placing them carefully here and there in the southern and western sectors. "Our strongpoints," he said and named them. Moc Hoa, Di An, Dak To. The four stared at the Joyce puzzle, rapt. The tablecloth had been transformed into a battle map. He dropped crumpled napkins, the mountains of the central massif. In the glitter of the chandelier one could imagine the facts of the war itself, air strikes at this point, a division-sized sweep here, a reconnaissance there. Off the coast at Camau, where Phu Quoc island would be, a crystal vase of daffodils reminded everyone of the serenity of Asia. So intently did the four men stare at Sam Joyce's map that an outsider, happening in the room, would swear they were the Joint Chiefs summoned from dining rooms all over the capital to resolve a military emergency—

"Mr. Carney?" the maid asked softly.

"What is it?" Carney looked at her, irritated. She gestured at the silent table. "No, no," Carney said impatiently. "We'll tend to it later."

But she made no move to go and in the awkward silence that followed, the men began to stir. What did this woman want? She said, "Shall I see Mrs. Carney?" Of course, it was her money.

"Yes," Carney said, relieved, genial now. "Do see Mrs. Carney upstairs and thank you very much."

But she remained, staring at the table. "My way home," she said.

Carney shook his head, bewildered.

"I have to get home, I thought—"

"Where do you live?" Sam asked politely.

She named an address in Southeast. Washington's quadrants were familiar to them so they would be able to locate the address on a map, in the same way that any of them could locate the Louisiana bayou. But none of them had ever visited the bayou, so they did not know what it looked like first-hand; the location would be theoretical.

"I think none of us is going in that direction," Carney said. He turned in his chair to face her squarely. "Mrs. Carney will arrange for a cab."

She said, "They don't like to go there. It's not so far from the Capitol, but they still don't like to go there." She thought about that a moment, nodding slowly, imperturbable as Buddha. Then she rustled out of the room.

And after an exchange of glances, immediately forgotten. Sam Joyce carefully swept crumbs from the perimeter of his war zone so that when he was ready to brief it would be plainly defined, a pristine sandbox in the middle of Carney's heirloom tablecloth. He had moved the Armagnac, cognac, and port to one side and worked patiently, with a soldier's eye for tidiness and the proximity of things. An inaccurate map was worse than useless. Finally it was done and he stood back a bit, peering at it. The doughty decanters stood to one side, sentries guarding the pepper mills, saltcellars, coffee spoons, butter knives, crumpled napkins, coins, the candlestick, and the crystal vase of daffodils—the hills, valleys, fields, cities, and garrisons of South Vietnam. Then with a sudden smile, as if he'd just had a welcome inspiration, he plucked three cigarettes from the oval dish and placed them just so, above Quang Tri province.

"The three divisions," he said softly, "in the North."

The table was hushed, mesmerized. Sam hesitated, then looked at Max Cather with a slight, inquisitive smile. Cather shrugged and smiled back. Sam jiggled his wrist, like a man shaking a dicecup. Coins rattled. Then he looked at each of them in turn, making no sign but inferring from the silence that they understood that what was to follow was private, family business.

He waved his hand over the Zone. "Look here, then." He took the coins from his palm and began to thumb them at various locations along the western border. There were eight coins, dimes, and he took his time about placing them. He reckoned that one inch of tablecloth equaled twenty miles of Indochina but still he was careful: some coins were more exactly placed than others. Once he caught Cather's eye but Max only stared back, expressionless.

He explained that the dimes were approximate locations of American firebases along the border. He emphasized, close to the border; very close indeed. They were manned by mixed teams of Americans and Vietnamese, some 'yards and Nungs as well. He looked up, smiling. "Well-trained men. *Outstanding* men." Then he turned to Piatt, wondering what the Congressman was thinking, and how much he would choose to reveal. Piatt's subcommittee had some oversight in the matter, and he was involved in other ways. But the Congressman's expression betrayed nothing. In fact, he reached for the cognac, spoiling Sam Joyce's picket line.

"A word about the weapons," Sam said. He gave a precise description of the weapons available, which ones, how many, and their deployment. There were other "assets" at each firebase and these were less meticulously described. Sam spoke generally of artillery fans, sophisticated sensing devices, and "smart" explosives. Twice, Teddy Carney interrupted with questions but the answers were vague.

Sam touched the dimes, each in turn.

Really, he thought, war should be left to the soldiers. He looked again at his battle map, so neat and orderly. The map was as orderly as the language he used to describe it. He saw the firebase in his mind's eye, star-shaped garrisons with concertina wire and guardposts, mortars protected by sandbags, claymore

mines on the perimeter, the refrigerators filled with beer and
Coca-Cola and cigarettes, the base itself in wilderness, the
present threatened by the infinite future.

Cather cleared his throat.

Sam explained that the firebases were intended to interdict
the trails. The interstices of a sieve, he said dryly. There were
not knives enough in all Shakerville to represent each trail. The
firebases were useful, of course, making life marginally more
difficult for Charlie. He smiled. "But it is as if in Southeast we
had a police force of three, two of whom were asleep at any
given time. However—"

Odd analogy, Piatt thought.

"—it is what we have. We make do with what we have, like
any army . . . " When they said nothing, he smiled. It was an
army officer's standard complaint, not enough of this, not
enough of that, but (sigh) somehow we'll get by. He said, "However, we ought to have enough. If the situation is as it has been
described, we ought to have plenty, a half a million men and the
air force, the navy. And so forth and so on." There was a glim-
mer of interest from Piatt Warden, but the Congressman said
nothing.

Now Sam's hand hovered indecisively over the trails. Suddenly his fingers darted to the tablecloth and roughly swept
aside the firebases. Dimes rolled and tumbled to the edge of the
table. "Only trouble is, it's not working. *It's not working.*" He
collected the dimes and slowly replaced them, base by base. He
said, "Bankrupt strategy, too many enemy filtering down too
many trails. And our army is no good at defense. We're fine with
amphibious landings or pushing across Europe or bombing cities
to smithereens. We're not good at defense or containment or
interdiction, whatever you want to call it. Not enough of our
men to prevent it. Not enough *outstanding* men." He looked
around the table, his expression sour. He would not get into it
with them, because it was not anything you could predict, and
you needed a lifetime in the service to recognize the particular
qualities that made a good soldier. A man could be outstanding
today and a basket case tomorrow, or vice versa, though not

often vice versa. There were only a few of them, his contemporaries, whom you could count on absolutely. So much depended on the conditions of the moment.

"All the good men are in hiding," Max Cather said.

Sam looked at him sharply. What?

Cather spoke softly, his voice betraying but slightly its foreign origins. "They're taking medical degrees or law or business. They have consulted their family doctors and found disabling health problems. Asthma. Anopsia. Or psychological irregularities. Transvestism. Melancholia." He poured cognac into his balloon glass, his fingers purposefully steady. "But mostly they are in the graduate schools, these young men who in another time would be platoon leaders or company commanders. Give thanks to the humane policies of our government that allow the ablest to avoid the war while at the same time requiring the dullest to join it. The weak protect the strong, that's the way it's been since the beginning of our civilization. Or anyway of North American civilization. We're not going to change it. The officers leading these teams." He touched each dime in turn. "Damn fine men." He seemed to lose his way now, and took another swallow of cognac. "Best we have. We lose half a dozen a week, KIA or wounded or sick or section eight. It's dangerous work, gentlemen. No wonder, I suppose, that no one wants to be a soldier boy."

As Cather spoke Sam Joyce moved back from the table. Presently his shoulders touched the mural, obscuring the narrative. There were no wounded and dying Minutemen, no bugler, no standard-bearer; the rearing stallion, the doomed baronet, all obscured. To his right was the sunny pastoral field, cows grazing in a glade. And to his left were the portraits of Carney's Virginia ancestors. He stood quietly for a moment, swirling cognac in his glass, contemplating the theater of war, and listening to Cather. What the hell, why should they go? He wouldn't, if he were them; he went because he was a soldier and it was his business to go. There were no sons of Congressmen in this war, and no official had resigned to enlist. It was not a thing worth volunteering for, at least no one did. But, *God* the officer corps was thin. Cather was right about that, and the result was more casualties;

there were not enough professionals to go around, though there was plenty of cannon fodder.

"Some of them get along all right," Sam said, cutting Cather off. "My friend Sol Henderson gets along. I did, when I was there. And will do again, whenever I go again. But." He paused. "But the illusion of control is very thin, it's all sleight-of-hand, really. They need more—"

Carney said patiently, "We seem to have given you quite a lot over the years, how much more do you need?"

"We've never refused an appropriation," Piatt said.

Sam looked at Piatt Warden. "But it hasn't been enough, has it? We've put them there and required them to stay. They're willing enough, the professionals are. It isn't *that*."

"Yes," Carney said.

"And it isn't negligible." God, he thought, he could tell them a hundred stories.

"No," Piatt said.

"What are you proposing?" Carney asked.

"We have a team in Cambridge," Cather said. He turned first to Carney, then to Piatt. "It's a special group, I oversee it. The brightest analyst came to us from the physics department at M.I.T. Twenty-one years old and so smart. Soundest analyst of the bunch and good with materials. Not just theory. Good with theory but understands the hardware, too. He." Cather smiled suddenly. "Calls the team the Rude Mechanicals. Knows weapons, this boy does, has an instinct for them. Goddamned good with weapons, understands that each weapon has a place in the scheme of things. Compares weapons to the instruments in an orchestra, which is an excellent analogy though not of course original. Foch used it. Understands the new technology, too, he's working on something now . . . " Cather waved his hand, no more of that. " . . . I do hope you won't think I'm beating the dead horse. But. He's evading the draft, taking his doctorate in physics. Draft board excused him as it was bound to do. In any other war he'd be on the line himself, he's a well-set-up lad. Big. Soccer player, squash racquets. A theoretician of the first order, this one is; perhaps at that they would have excused him in Two to work in the squash court at Chicago. Who is to say? At

61

any event he is not on the line in Pleiku, he is at Cambridge working with a team of analysts who supports the man on the line at Pleiku. Tireless worker, this lad. Self-starter. Nights. Weekends."

Sam moved, revealing a little of the chaos behind him, then approached the table. He lit a cigarette and moved back again, listening to Max Cather. Max, so smooth and supple; he never missed a trick.

"So it has its point, doesn't it? The country can't afford the loss of its educated mechanicals, any more than Britain could in One. It's not wise and not cost-effective to kill the flower of our youth, etcetera. What's the use of growing up in a suburban paradise only to be killed or maimed in a Zone? They are the ones who'll make the weapons of the future! We can kill the niggers and the high school dropouts, it's expected. Weeds in our garden. But don't kill the flowers, the scientists, attorneys, physicians, and businessmen of the future. That's what Congress and the Administration have decided and who are we, the civil servants, to object to this policy. We do not formulate policy, Sam and me, we merely execute it. We are good soldiers. We fight with the army we are given and who could argue that my lad in the lab would be more useful in a foxhole? It is sentimental to argue that this army should be like that one, or should I say as we assume that army to have been." He pointed at the wall behind him, and the men at the table stared at it as if it were hieroglyphics containing a hidden message, Teddy Carney's Rosetta stone.

"And a waste of breath," Cather continued. "Can't afford to kill the conspicuous flowers, our future Adamses, Reveres, and Hamiltons. Our Burrs. Of course they fought not because they were drafted to fight but because they wanted to, most of them, feeling the necessity for it. That is the legend, anyway. And it seems that Hessians are not for rent or sale this season. Surprise! We'll have to do it ourselves." He paused, his gaze far away now. It was impossible to say how much of this was passion and how much mischief. With Max Cather you never knew, he had different speeds for different people, and often different speeds within the same tortuous passage. "So we'll do what we've done before," he said cheerfully. "We'll substitute money for bodies. No lack of funds in this prosperous land, this pig-happy democracy, freedom's first line of defense. Important, isn't it, to keep the beans and bullets flowing for the poor bastards on the line. Our niggers and shell-shocked colonels."

Carney said, "Welcome to the twentieth century." But he was startled by Cather's vehemence.

Sam said, "Get on with it, Max."

"At Cambridge," Cather said, his voice low and confidential again. "This lad I mentioned. He and his mechanicals have devised something quite new. We believe that if this idea were adopted the Free World Forces could at least halve Charlie's infiltration at only a modest increase in friendly casualties. An acceptable increase." He glanced at Piatt. "The telegrams home would not burden Western Union. The calls from the Hill to the Pentagon would not overload AT&T. The idea is tactically sound and politically alluring. Really, very alluring. Attractive, Piatt, as you'll see. Though not without cost, no. It won't come cheap."

"How much?

Cather said, "Plenty, but that's not the point. The point's *lives*, the lives of our young conscripts. And the political difficulties they cause, these deaths."

"Then why are you telling me about it?"

"Not just you, Congressman. You and Teddy. We need some help." He paused. "And so do our friends downtown. Too many casualties, too much heat. We've got to find a way to fight this war without so many dead. It's a question of resources only, where they're allocated. There are plenty of resources, it's just a matter of allocation. Where the money goes." He bent over the miniature war zone, surveying the trails and the firebases. He pointed at the three cigarettes in line, enemy divisions. "They come this way," he said softly, his voice just a whisper, his arm sweeping in an arc ending at the coffee spoons. "Think of it as a funnel, relatively narrow in the north and wide in the south. The trails begin just above the DMZ, like so. In Laos they commence to separate." He spread his slender fingers, a pianist spanning an octave. "You stop them at the point of assembly. Then stop them again in the Laotian cordillera. Then stop them a third time at the point of entry along the border. If the job is done properly, there won't be very many of them left by the third 'stop.' "

Carney said, "How?"

Piatt added, "And how much will it cost?"

Sam said, "They're something, Max's mechanicals. Really, a remarkable achievement. Extraordinary, considering the difficulties."

Max Cather winked, smiling at Sam. "Piatt isn't a politician, he's an accountant."

"But that's what it comes down to," Piatt said. "Money, you said so yourself. Allocation of resources. If half as much effort were put into negotiations—"

Sam looked away. They thought they could have it cheap, at a discount. They thought they could get out the way they got in, stealthily, under cover of night. "No one over there thinks it will work," he said.

"They never do," Piatt said.

"Over there, they think negotiations are the biggest illusion of all. What's there to negotiate about, except our own withdrawal?"

"It's a beginning," Piatt said.

"Yes," Sam said. "It would be convenient."

"Yes, Max. The cost." This was Carney, odd for him to miss the main point and go to the margins. But his voice was like an oboe. "How much on the bill, time and charges?"

Cather either did not hear him or was not interested. He said, "There has to be a control. There has to be a brains. Destroy the brains and you destroy the system, correct? Destroy the system and you've destroyed the revolution. Like everything else, the revolution is a *process*. And there are three likely targets, here"—he placed a coin above the cigarettes, in the vicinity of Hanoi—"and here"—he placed another in the south, along the border about three inches from Saigon—"and here." He dropped the third coin in Laos.

Piatt asked, "Who are they?"

64

"The personalities? We don't know, except for one or two of the obvious names."

"You don't *know*?"

"No," he said tersely. "They don't publish their officers' list. But we know roughly where they are. We don't need to know names, as long as we know locations. The Vietnamese know the names, we think."

"What makes you think they'll tell?"

"The point's the monitoring." Cather spoke in an undertone, as if to himself alone. "It's important that we *know* what damage is done. That's the real problem we're working on. What." He cleared his throat. "Works in the laboratory doesn't always perform on the battlefield, and of course the reverse."

"I don't quite—" Carney began doubtfully.

"We've got to secure our own lines. All it wants is money. Disrupt the process, that's the idea. Needs money, to assemble the materials and conduct the deployments."

"And support," Sam said.

"Uh-huh," Max Cather said. "I think, properly presented. With the proper presentations, it's an inspired idea politically. An outstanding idea, wouldn't you say, and worth support?"

"Laos and Cambodia become the killing ground," Piatt said.

"Yes," Cather said.

"Play the games out of town, as it were," Carney added.

"Yes," Cather said. "Well put. Not all of them, of course."

Carney asked, "Where is it now in the mill? Where is it inside the bureaucracy? Which station of the cross?"

"Gethsemane," Piatt said.

"No," Max said. "By no means. These are just talking points. We are not at Gethsemane yet. The prophet is still in the hills with a loyal band of followers but as yet, alas, no influence."

Cather was impatient now. "We're interested at my place. And Defense is interested enough to fund . . . certain portions of the first stage. I'd say we're more interested than Defense, though of course no one wants to let this one get away. You never know what might come of it, and there are so many angles. Viewed in a certain light it makes more sense for us to control it than the army or the air force, owing to the question of the personalities and the decision to target or not to target. Army'll have a purchase because, hell, it's their men. And the air force because it's their aircraft that'll be doing the drops. But," he added after a moment's thoughtful pause, "whoever gets in first with the funding, that's it. If you fund the ground floor you tend to have a mortgage on the other floors as well, okey-dokey?" He lowered his voice. "This country owes a debt to Sam here, who's stuck his neck way out—"

Carney didn't buy. "Downtown," he said. "How do they feel about it downtown?"

Cather wiggled his right hand, a pilot describing an aircraft in distress. "To the extent they've focused, and understand what we're doing."

Carney looked at him like a man trying to peer around a corner. "I hope you've explained it to them in more detail than you've explained it to us, Piatt and me."

"Downtown, for example," Piatt said.

Cather was undismayed. "They have problems over there."

Carney nodded vigorously. "Problems of focus." He was on firm ground now, psychology; the President's mood. "His rooms are crowded. He wants to know all the details, submerged in details, submerged in subtext. No fact too small or insignificant. His rooms are filled to bursting. Man's preoccupied," Carney went on. The others listened carefully, this was Teddy Carney's specialty. He spoke from knowledge, or from the skillful culling of the knowledge of others. "Working inhuman hours, looks like hell." He tapped his cheeks. "Bad color, you can see it looking at him, he looks ten years older. Can't focus on any one thing. A soloist trying to conduct an orchestra, using the orchestra to soothe the beast, the public. Not succeeding." He shook his head sympathetically. "A flawed personality."

"Sam?" This from Max Cather.

"No," Sam said.

"Killing job," Carney continued. "But no one asked him to take it. He knew what the stakes were. Are."

"Sam?" Cather spoke again, softly. "I think so, Sam. I truly believe you could speak about the meeting and give us all a little clearer understanding of what we're up against. The situation over there and how it pertains. It would be helpful."

Sam Joyce shook his head.

Cather turned to the others. "Sam saw him the other day, the Man."

"Well, well," Piatt said.

"Goes without saying," Cather lectured, "any *talk*, anything pre*mature* . . ."

Carney smiled and refilled the balloon glasses in front of each man.

" . . . anything that might *hint*, what we've been saying here. This is confidential, strictly. Could give the game away, and aid and comfort to our enemies. What I'm saying is, anything now. Later, a week, two weeks, who knows what the situation might be at that time." Max rambled on, filling the room with his words, setting the stage for what would follow. "Tell them about it, Sam."

Piatt looked at Sam Joyce, whose eyes were bright with—what? Desire? Anger? Fear? His mouth stretched in a tight, mirthless grin. Carney was smiling in anticipation. It was not often that he possessed knowledge contemporaneously with the President of the United States, and at a point in the story before the climax. In Washington, knowledge was power but foreknowledge was superpower. It did not matter what it was, only that one had it. It was knowledge of weaknesses and strengths, mostly weaknesses. Weakness determined strength and was therefore the more important knowledge. Max Cather's dry run, he'd done it well, tantalizing them with the seriousness of the mechanicals, and his vague plans for resolution of the war—or anyway the casualties.

Cather said, "Sam?"

Candles cast their romantic glow over the war zone, forgotten now as the soldier prepared to speak. Carney moved to the sideboard to fetch more bottles, framboise, poire, calvados, an ancient Napoleon brandy, kirsch; and whiskey—Scotch, Irish, and Kentucky. He placed these next to the decanters, together with glasses, ice in a bucket, and an old-fashioned siphon. There was a brief buzz of conversation, as at the interval at the theater. Then they fell silent, waiting for Sam Joyce to begin.

Sam had taken a leather chair in the private lobby and waited easily, idly swinging his left foot. He watched the spitshined shoe, moving like a buoy, believing it was the slow motion of a man at ease. Aides and messengers hurried in and out of doorways, carrying blue folders. He liked the atmosphere, which was always special and self-contained, like a ship's. The pace differed depending on whether the vessel was leaving a port or entering one or suspensefully in mid-passage. It was a place where shoes were always polished to a high shine and speech seldom rose above a whisper, except when someone laughed. Not a barracks laugh either, but an intimate laugh; the laugh of the bedroom. Laughter was the best aphrodisiac, in the bedroom or in the government. This laughter was infectious, though of course you had to watch it, as in any seduction. Laughter either arose from a fact or concealed one. You had to know which. In the government it was nearly always the latter.

He had two attaché cases. The boy from the adviser's office would supply the easel and map. There would be supplementary charts if they were needed, but Sam was confident they would not be. He would speak without notes, as he had done many times in the past. He was not familiar with this Man but he thought he understood the office, and after a time the two, the Man and the office, merged and it was impossible to say where the one ended and the other began. No one could separate them, least of all the Man himself. He had known this for years, from the time of his first encounter with the Man—an earlier Man but the same Man—ill and careworn at the end of his second term. Sam was then attaché in Saudi Arabia, accompanying the ambassador to the White House. The ambassador wanted a spear carrier and thought it would be an excellent introduction to diplomacy inside the government. The ambassador briefed for a full fifteen minutes, surrounded by charts, bar graphs, a vice admiral, and the under secretary of state (the secretary himself being absent on one of his frequent journeys). The Man had sat glumly listening, then turned to a civilian aide; Sam didn't even know who he was. They spoke in whispers a moment, the aide leaning over the big desk talking into the Man's ear. At last he looked up and nodded. He never changed expression and the civilian aide had busied himself with a sheaf of documents. It was a nod of dismissal and the men in uniform, Sam included, saluted and left the office without delay. Outside, the vice admiral looked at the under secretary and grinned, then turned to the ambassador and complimented him on the briefing, a terse "well done." Sailor's language. The under secretary said nothing and the vice admiral exited whistling. The proposal was dead. Sam remembered every detail, and the care that had gone into the research and presentation, the under secretary's sympathetic handshake. That idea, it would be worthwhile to write it up for one of the professional journals, but of course the details were still classified.

He checked his watch. It was ten thirty-five, they were five minutes late, and that probably meant that the Man was receiving his pre-briefing. The briefing of the briefing: the talking points and Sam's own C.V. They would be interested in Sam's antecedents, though certainly the Man would know those. Sam believed he had them at a disadvantage, and was therefore confident. They wore so many faces and spoke to and from so many different interests and perspectives. The Man's world was a hall of mirrors. It was impossible for him to focus on any one issue, since they all cast back the same image.

"Colonel Joyce?"

He glanced up. A young woman stood a few feet away. She met his eyes boldly and did not smile.

"There will be a delay."

She did not wait for his reply but moved off briskly into an office to his left. He lit a cigarette, guessing that the vessel was in mid-passage that morning, sailing under sealed orders. That was why the young woman was dour. He put away his cigarette lighter, the one given him years before by a woman who reminded him of the young woman disappearing through the door. That woman had not been a working woman, however. But she had the same severity of expression. When he met her it was severe and it got worse with time, as he'd moved from capital to garrison and back again, from Jeddah to Fort Meade to SACEUR to the Zone to the Pentagon and back to the Zone. She left his life for good one weekend when he was attending a seminar at the National War College, "Perspectives on Revolution in Asia," taking her car, her clothes, her books, and the other *objets*. It was just as well, their lives could never fit. But for a while she was a diversion from Marina.

She had taken all the pictures except one. That was her note to him, her Dear Sam. It was an enormous poster of Mistinguett, a pink rose in her perfect teeth, her blue eyes flashing. A souvenir from the old days, a weekend escape to Paris. Piatt was attending a parliamentarians' conference in Geneva, and Marina arranged to escape for a weekend, she told her husband that she would visit her old college roommate, now living in Paris; that part was true enough, there was a roommate who lived in Paris and promised to cover for her. Sam flew up from Jeddah. They found the poster together in a shop in the rue des Beaux-Arts. It was expensive so they went around the corner for an aperitif to think it over. After an aperitif they returned to look at it again. It was still too expensive so they had another aperitif, and by midafternoon it was less expensive so they bought it and walked it the half-mile to their hotel where, propped on the bureau, it made a wonderful sight from the big double bed. Mistinguett was the symbol of all that was best in their . . . marriage. That was what it was, when they were together; a weekend here, a night there. When he got the picture back to Jeddah he put it in the living room of his billet. In Washington he hung it upstairs in the study, too private a work of art for a public room.

They looked alike, though, this young woman and Gretchen. He and Gretchen were reasonably well suited, but the problem was always that he had Marina. It was that, and no more than that; and no less, either.

"Colonel Joyce?"

He followed the young woman into the corridor. She talked over her shoulder, moving smartly as a sergeant. He noticed her thighs and rear, she was a good-looking young woman. She reminded him so of Gretchen, he felt a stab of desire. This young woman had long curly hair that fell carelessly to her shoulders, identical to G. The carelessness of her hair contrasted with her manner. The White House was a magnet to good-looking women, his father told him that and the old man was rarely wrong in matters of that kind. She knocked twice at the door, opened it, and stood aside so he could enter. She looked directly at him. His arm brushed her breasts as he crossed the threshold. She did not move. The door closed noiselessly behind him.

Mundelein was sitting on the couch, a telephone receiver against his ear. He glanced at Sam and winked, motioning him to a chair near the fire. A shaggy dog lay sleeping next to the window and at Sam's entrance it opened its eyes for a moment, sighed, licked its chops, and shuddered. The President was talking into the phone in a very low voice. The voice was directed into the mouthpiece and no word escaped. Abruptly he swung around, replaced the receiver, and glared at Mundelein. The adviser had been making notes as he listened. The President raised his arms and let them fall on the desk, continuing to glare. Neither man said a word, and it was as if they were communicating by telepathy.

Finally Mundelein said, "Imprecise."

The President nodded, apparently in agreement.

"No," Mundelein wiggled his index finger, "give."

"A little," the President said. "At the end."

Mundelein looked doubtful. "I'm tired. I have a headache. Maybe tomorrow night, darling."

The Man smiled, staring into the middle distance. He swiveled, again facing the window. The dog yawned. A light snow fell, he was staring into whiteness, a garden in exquisite winter balance. When he swung back his eyes were still vacant, obviously he had seen nothing; he was thinking about the telephone call. Sam sat quietly, waiting for the Man to acknowledge his presence. His left leg was crossed over his right but the toe of his shoe was not moving. He remembered reading somewhere that Generalissimo Franco demanded that his visitors sit with both feet flat on the floor. The sight of a sole was offensive to him, a sign of disrespect. He remembered now, it was a State Department cable. Unclassified.

The President sighed heavily and turned finally to look at Sam. His sour expression intensified. He said, "Now comes the army."

Sam stood. "Sir."

"Ever been here before?"

"Yes, sir," Sam said. "Years ago."

The President nodded and described the painting over the fireplace, and some of the bric-a-brac on the shelves. It seemed to be an inventory designed to validate his own presence. These were objects he'd owned for years, though one or two of them went with the room, in a manner of speaking. There were no photographs of the Man with other men, unlike every other official Washington office. Sam listened politely, concentrating. He could not force Gretchen from his mind, however. He remembered her in the mornings, naked in the heat. They had no air conditioning and would waken in a sweat, cooled only by ceiling fans. She used a particular oil on her body . . .

Mundelein said, "Coffee?"

Sam shook his head. Now he remembered Paris. He could see Mistinguett now in his mind's eye, the blue eyes following them, so amused. Reproachful eyes, as it turned out. He had not thought of Gretchen in months, what was there about this—

"Sure?"

Yes, Sam said. It was the young woman, the likeness was truly striking. He shifted his legs. Also, it was the room and its thick warm atmosphere, its tension and desire. The adviser poured two cups of coffee from the silver pot on the low table in front of him. He rose and handed one to the President, whose gaze had returned now to the middle distance. He gave the impression of a man trying to remember a simple thing that had eluded him.

Mundelein placed the cup and saucer on the edge of the desk, then dropped a lump of sugar into it, carefully using the dainty silver tongs. Sam noted these details while contemplating mornings at Fort Meade, the sunlight falling across her legs, the sweet fragrance of the room, and the down of her thighs damp in the heat. He noticed the flowers in a glass vase on the coffee table, and wondered where Gretchen was. He had not heard from her in years.

The President said, "You're a what now?"

"Colonel," Sam said.

"You've moved damned fast," he said.

Sam said, "Yes."

"You ought to be in uniform. Why aren't you in uniform?"

"Well, sir." He looked at Mundelein. "We thought it less conspicuous."

"Oh yes," the President said. "There's too much talk, much too much." Then, "You came back from there when?"

"I was in the under secretary's party."

The Man nodded.

"I arranged it," Mundelein said.

"So you've gone there and come back," the President said. "Pat says you've been there before, you've a long record." He did not wait for a reply. "So there must have been changes, lots of them. Everyone tells me there are substantial changes, the confidence of the troops, the security situation . . . " He looked away again, absently picking up a glass globe. He shook it and artificial snow swirled merrily in the glass. "One of the little kids gave this to me the other day. Isn't it cute?" He replaced it on the desk and the storm abated; flurries, then clear. He turned to Mundelein and said quietly, "Call Edward. Then call Harry. You, Edward, and Harry here tomorrow at ten a.m. sharp." Mundelein scribbled on his pad. "And that other one, what's his name, from Budget. We'll decide tomorrow at ten sharp. I want that fellow from Budget to have their recommendations *in one sentence*. With the supporting data, all of it."

The adviser looked up, a pained expression on his face. "He's in Seattle, I'm sorry to say."

"Christ," the President said. "O Christ on a crutch. Goddammit. Oh, dear," he said, simmering. "Get him back here. Send Air Force One if you have to. I want this thing out of my way tomorrow at ten sharp. Why is that so difficult?"

"He's getting the data there," Mundelein said. "That's where it is."

The Man looked at his adviser. "Is someone doing a job on me?"

"Next week," Mundelein said quickly. "Latest."

The President turned to Sam. "You better sit down, take a load off your feet."

"Yes, sir," Sam said.

"He's a little turd but he's dandy with numbers," Mundelein said. "We only have to squeeze him a bit—"

"It is a mysterious conflict," the President said to Sam. "Did you like it over there the first time?"

"Yes, sir," he said. Now that he was seated, the room seemed even more formal, the President elevated a little behind his desk. "Of course it was different then than it is now."

"You did a fine job," the President said. Then he turned back to Mundelein. "So he's in Seattle."

"I sent him," Mundelein said. "I take responsibility. We simply didn't have the numbers. They could've run all over us and would have, without the numbers. You know the particular—"

"Darn it," he said. "Seattle comes here. I don't go there."

"They wouldn't've brought the stuff you need. You know them. You know the way they tickle that. We had to have our own man, who understands the system and whose loyalty's not in question. Budget had to go to sources. The raw data as opposed to the evaluated data. The other way, we would've gotten screwed again."

"We're getting screwed now. We're always getting screwed."

"That's why I sent Budget out there."

"They want to screw somebody in this town, they go right to the White House. There he is! Let's give him a screwing!"

"Yes, sir," Mundelein said.

The President was silent for a moment, fondling the glass sphere. Then, to Sam: "How's your family?"

"Fine, sir." He had no family. There was only the delicious Gretchen, whom he hadn't seen in two years and then only at a distance. At times he thought of Marina Warden as family but this wasn't one of the times.

To Mundelein: "I don't like it."

"No," the adviser said. "I wish there'd been another way around it. But we had to have the raw numbers."

"Darned numbers," he said.

"They're bastards," the adviser agreed.

He said to Sam, "I'm glad to hear that."

Sam said, "Thank you, sir."

"All right then," the President said. "And for the meeting, I want Costello here as well, for the atmospherics."

"I'll see to it," Mundelein said.

He turned to Sam. "Your first tour," he began, then seemed to lose his way.

"Ten sharp Wednesday," Mundelein said, writing in the pad and nodding as he wrote. "I'll draw and quarter the little bastard if he doesn't have the goods. But he will. He's a dandy pencil man."

"You give them my regards," the President said.

"Yes, I will," Sam said. He must mean the nonexistent family.

"I knew this fella's dad," the President said to Mundelein. He smiled warmly, his voice softening. "A great lawyer and a great Senate man. One of the old breed. How old is he now? My God, he must be a hundred years old."

Sam said, "That's about it." This was true, his father would be a hundred years old in a few years. So the inquiry had been about his father.

"Oh, a hell of a man," the President said, his voice positively damp now. "He was over seventy when he ran for the Senate and won in a squeaker. A couple of thousand votes and those"— he laughed—"were in dispute, downstate votes. 'Landslide Joyce' we called him, but never to his face. We were on different sides of the aisle, of course, but Old Ben Joyce. You could count on his word, he'd lived so damned long, his word meant something to him. Wasn't he an old bastard when he married your mother? A late bloomer, he was, like Churchill!" The President paused, and when he spoke again the warmth had left his voice. "It's different now, of course, everything is. They're so selfish and stuck on themselves. Of course he only intended to stay for one term, so that makes a difference in how you deal and with whom, and what you expect in return. But Old Ben was one of a kind and that kind's extinct and I, for one, am sorry to see it, that kind, go. You give him my very best, Sam. He is a great man."

"Yes, sir," Sam said. The old man would like it.

"So Sam knows the score, you see," the President said to Mundelein. "He's familiar with this town, he's like one of the family. He's one of *us*, so we don't have to finish our sentences and cross every T and dot every I."

Mundelein nodded in agreement.

"He was something in the old days," the President clucked.

"I'll tell him," Sam said.

"You two talk. I've got to see a man about a dog." The President rose abruptly and left the room. Thus alerted, the animal on the floor opened its eyes and seemed about to follow and then—as if the effort were too great—settled again.

Sam smiled as the door closed. "It's good to see you again, Pat."

"You, too." He lifted his eyebrows. "But you look a little uptight."

"Things seem a little scattered in here today," Sam said.

"Bitch of a day," Mundelein said.

"Aren't they all?"

"Some aren't," the adviser said. "Some are all right. Some days, I wouldn't trade it for anything." He paused, looking away. When he turned back his face was slack and he had an unlit cigarette in his hand. Sam thought he'd aged in the past year but it was hard to tell. He had known Pat Mundelein since they were schoolboys, never very well; never well enough to know whether he'd aged or not aged. "Did you hear about Marsha?" Sam shook his head and it took him a moment to locate Marsha, a pretty, extroverted girl who had been at the National Cathedral School when he and Mundelein were at St.

Alban's. He remembered vaguely that she and Mundelein were engaged to be engaged, as the phrase then was.

Mundelein said, "She's dead. She was in and out of hospitals for years. When she was in Hartford I used to go and see her from time to time, when that asshole she married wasn't around. Then she went to Virginia and the asshole bailed out. It was easy for him to do, I guess, because Marsha had more problems than anyone ought to have. Maybe that made it tougher. But he was such an asshole. The notice said she died at home, no cause given. But I know the cause. It was suicide. Why do you suppose no one stays together anymore?"

Sam nodded sympathetically. He was trying to place her. All he remembered was a long-legged girl, very pretty with dark hair and a crooked smile. And she was fast. There was a rumor that she slept with upper-classmen. She had a reputation dating from the seventh grade. He remembered something else. Her father was a businessman who had come north to work for FDR in the thirties, and never went back home.

"She tried suicide at least twice before that I know about. Pills once. Another time she tried carbon monoxide, sat in her car with the engine running and the radio tuned to the good-music station. Made a hash of it both times. Told me once in Virginia that she couldn't even do *that* right, kill herself."

"That's the third or fourth suicide in our class," Sam said. "What's the trouble? What is it?" Sam Joyce refused to admit that he understood self-inflicted wounds.

"I don't know what the trouble is, Sam," Mundelein said wearily. "Or it is what it always is, or's supposed to be." What was that? Relations with Mommy and Daddy. Too much ambition or too little; unrealistic desires, or none at all. Disappointment in the conditions of the moral life of the ruling class. "Marsha," Mundelein said, "there was too much alcohol and too little sex, or sex of the wrong kind. And then she married the asshole, and everyone approved. Looked like a perfect match, they were a handsome couple. As handsome as orchids, both of them. I thought I'd tell you because you're the only one I see from the old days. There are a lot of us around, no one ever leaves this town, but I don't see them. There isn't anything to be done about it."

"It's a bitch," Sam mumbled.

"Aren't you seeing Sheila Dennehay? She's a good woman, smart."

Sam nodded. How did Mundelein know that?

"She married an asshole too,"

"I didn't know him well," Sam said.

Mundelein sipped his coffee. "She and Marsha used to be great friends. I'll miss her letters, too. She used to write me from Virginia, erratic letters. Howling wolves, that's what she thought she heard in Virginia."

Sam was only half listening. He was trying to pull Marsha into focus, but he confused her with other girls from NCS. Cashmere sweaters, Peter Pan collars, bobbed hair, and Capezios. He had not known that she and Sheila were friends. He said absently, "It's such a son of a bitch, sometimes." Their civilian lives were so far from his but of course there was stress everywhere now. He leaned forward in his chair, aware again of where he was and why.

"Yes, you said that. And it is." Mundelein hesitated, momentarily lost in thought. He'd write a note to Marsha's mother. She was still living in the big house on Prospect. He would write the note that afternoon, following the conference with the bunch from DIA. He would type the note and his secretary could correct the infelicities, then he would rewrite it in longhand on his personal stationery. Well, hell, it would be a short note. He only wanted to say how sorry he was and how fond he'd been of Marsha. She was someone he could discuss only with a person who went back, as he did, to the beginnings of the modern capital, Washington in the intense postwar years. The Creation. He did, Sam did, Marina Warden did. Growing up in Washington, one absorbed and savored the atmosphere. However, Sam Joyce was apparently uncomfortable with this reminiscence; it was obvious that he didn't remember Marsha, didn't know the family, and had never visited Virginia, "The Farm." So it was time he learned.

Sam cleared his throat. "Pat?"

"Damnedest thing, when I used to visit her in Virginia. There was a time, half the government was there. So it seemed to me. Mostly they were from the national security side of things, men who'd burned themselves out. There were maybe half a dozen of them, casualties of one sort or another. They were the permanents. Then there were the transients, in residence for a week or a little longer; sometimes they'd come for a long weekend, to get away, they said. I'd see them on the grounds, walking very slowly with their heads down. Dressed in dark suits and black shoes, talking to themselves, drying out; these were the ones permitted to leave their rooms. I was told never to speak to them, thought I knew one or two well enough to call by name. Pretty place, it looked like someone's horse farm. And that's what they called it, 'The Farm.' There were very few women there, it was a government of men then as now. Marsha had good days and bad. On her good days we'd take a picnic down by the brook and keep our conversation low because you never knew when you'd look up and see one of them standing alone, listening to you in their dark suits and serious expressions. Marsha would always give them a quick smile and they'd scurry away, frightened of her, frightened of me. I suppose they thought I was one of the doctors. They were frightened of themselves, really; they were men who were frightened of their pasts. They were living in the past tense. One of them was a psychiatrist who worked for one of the agencies. A special friend of Marsha's, they'd play chess every Saturday night. She admired him so, his competence and composure under fire. His stability. One night he jimmied his way into the clinic and administered an overdose to himself by IV. Knew exactly which chemical to use and the dose, and how to do it quickly. No fuss at all, he wanted to leave with a minimum of bother. He'd burned all his files, which was a considerable relief to the people in his agency, and left a note instructing the 'authorities'—his word—not to tell anyone of his death. He wanted his family to believe he'd disappeared while on assignment. An important, hazardous assignment for which he'd volunteered. An assignment necessary to the national security of the nation, and which would be disclosed in due course by the

National Command Authority. The President, in other words. He wanted the world to believe he'd disappeared with no trace, like so many heroes of the forties and fifties." The adviser shook his head and glanced out the window at the snow. Then he ground out his cigarette. "Be concise with your presentation, Colonel. We have a long day and this is only a small part of it."

When the Man returned he was all business.

"Let's begin now."

Mundelein said he would call the boy to set up the show-and-tell. They were silent while the adviser pressed a button on the console next to him. In seconds a marine captain appeared with an easel and half a dozen large charts. Mundelein said, "Just the map." The captain put the map on the easel and withdrew, saluting. Sam stood and moved to the easel. They were both looking at him. He knew he would have to begin with strength in order to get and keep the Man's attention. No obvious drama but he would have to make a little narrative of it, and leave some points unsaid. That he was divided in his own mind was not a handicap. He was not there to tell this Man how to win his war or end it, merely to describe its parts.

"Pat says you're smart."

"Pat is too kind," Sam said with a smile.

"He thinks you'll be better than the Joint Chiefs."

"Not better," Mundelein said. "Different."

"Let's begin then."

Sam began with a description of his sources, not their names but their positions and general reliability. He charted the change from the time he first went to the Zone. What worried them now, he said, was the infiltration. He described the situation along the border, giving equal weight to the opposite arguments: those who thought Charlie weak, and those who thought him strong. In five minutes he came to the crux: "The problem is that we never know how we do or where we stand. We play a quarter and we don't know the score at the end of it. Then we play another quarter and go out for halftime and we still don't know the score. Charlie's hurting, that's obvious; we know that.

But we don't know how much. We set them back, and we don't know how far. We believe that morale's bad, but we don't know how bad. They have problems with resupply. We don't know how severe those problems are. Makes it impossible for us to determine progress . . . "

"That's what the public wants and what it has to have," the President said. "We have to give it to them, we have to give them that dimension, it's so important. It's as if we're playing on an infinite field with invisible goalposts—"

"Their field," Mundelein murmured.

Sam nodded, watching them. They were comfortable translating national security into the language of games. "It's very interesting to those there as well," Sam said. "They—we—live in a world without measurements, except those that we manufacture ourselves. A few of them want to mount an operation to verify what's happening." He paused.

"It's what we need and what we don't have," Mundelein said. "Public confidence. Confidence that progress is being made, and that time is finite."

Sam looked at the President, who was staring intently at the map, or that part of it that was unconcealed by his, Sam's, body. The President made a little motion with his hand, and Sam moved to one side. The Man was hypnotized by the map, as were his predecessors, trying to discover the geographical logic of it, geography that could be reworked into a political solution, a partition of Poland or a Free City of Danzig, a Hanseatic League of Asia. What a success the Allies had made of Trieste, even of Berlin! But there was no symmetry to the ragged lines, the exasperated boundaries of the peninsula. The dragon-shaped pendant attached to the belly of China, an ugly image that told him nothing, not one single thing. God, they were nimble with images, the historians, diplomats, journalists, and soldiers who explained Indochina. They wrote for philosophers and fanatics, not statesmen. It was not a language that a mechanic could understand. The map made no more sense to this Man than to the other Men who had stared at it, enraptured, night and day. It was burned into his memory, but each time he looked at it he found something new, a tuck or oblique angle that he had not noticed before. The place names, An Lao, Bong Son, Plei Me, Moc Hoa, were as familiar to him as St. Louis, Yuma, and Baltimore. But he did not know what these Indochinese towns were like empty of American soldiers. The thing was a puzzle with a mysterious solution. What did they want? All puzzles had solutions, but this one eluded him as it had eluded his predecessors. However, he could not take his eyes from the map and its sharply drawn black and red lines, its longitudes and latitudes and gaudy compass rose. He remembered the first time he noticed it, a geography class in high school or college, part of the dwindling French empire; for a time, he had the capital confused with Macao. He remembered the radio reports of the fall of Dien Bien Phu, and remembered the furious debate at the time. Fathead Dulles wanted to intervene. He himself had played a role, however small . . .

The world was divided then into British pink and French blue. Symbols for rice, copra, rubber, and tin. Turn it, a mirror image, and it could represent California. Indochina was always described in terms of something else, usually French. Apparently too exotic to be discussed in its own terms, Indochina was the Rhineland or the Balkans or a domino whose shadow fell to Waikiki. Where and what was its parliament? Literature, commerce, cuisine, agriculture? Its poets? Its athletes? Its Jews?

At the pause, Sam watched the Man's eyes glaze. He was moving inside again, thinking God knows what. Some other problem, perhaps related, perhaps not; except they were all related. Seattle, the man from Budget, the imprecise telephone call, the meeting at ten a.m. sharp, the artificial snowstorm.

"They say they can depend on technology only up to a point," Sam said. "They say they need good men down there on the ground so that they *know,* and can convince the public. And themselves, too. They say we have to monitor the trails ourselves, and begin to think of new ways to bring the battle to them. I heard that again and again." He recited those words to the easel, conscious only of not wanting to meet the President's eyes. When he turned around he saw that he'd regained the Man's full attention.

"I have fresh statistics every week, and they are always positive."

"Yes," Sam said.

"You are telling me that these are cooked?"

"No," Sam said. "Not *cooked*, exactly."

"Well, then?"

"All of the statistics are accurate, I'm sure."

"That is the point about them," Mundelein said. "They are accurate, of course. Beautiful, in their way. And so numerous."

"None of this is simple," Sam said.

The Man smiled.

Sam hesitated. He did not want to argue the statistics. It was not a situation that was illuminated by statistics. Numbers could not describe a state of mind and it was the state of mind that this Man had to understand. Sam's mission was to portray convincingly the deteriorating esprit of the men on the scene. This was not easy and he did not want to frighten the President. So many Americans had grown comfortable inside the ambiguity, they resembled a regiment of Sisyphuses with stones; the mountain be damned, it was the stones that tormented them. For so many of them it was a life's work, dimensions, radii, and weight; the texture of the stone, its color, composition, and odor. The American proconsuls spoke like moonstruck poets. Were they pushing the stones or were the stones pushing them? To an American no problem was insoluble, and the more ambiguous the context the more comfortable some of them seemed to be. He said, "They are bewitched by the infiltration. The trails, they see the trails as bleeding wounds. They believe that a special force can be sent to monitor the trails and destroy the staging areas. Of course they anticipate casualties, the operation itself is a cloudy area. A twilight zone, a twilight force. Irregulars."

"Volunteers," Mundelein said.

The President said nothing.

"The argument is this," Sam said. "With reliable people on the ground and the technology they're developing now you'd know how much was getting through and you'd be able to gauge the strength of the revolution. No more estimates, no more guesswork. No more helter-skelter weapons counts. You'd have hard intelligence for a change, something you could count on."

"How many would it take?" His voice was scrupulously neutral, almost toneless.

"There are several units already in place." But this was not what he wanted to convey to the Man. It was irrelevant. He wanted him to understand that it was an obsession.

"Uh-huh," the President said. "How many, when you finally get down to it?"

"In the beginning," he said, "a thousand men."

"In teams," Mundelein said.

"Who?" the President asked. "Who would they be?"

"We could get them, Mr. President," Mundelein said, the corners of his mouth turning down.

"You'd have to be damned careful how you did it." He looked at Sam. "The casualties would be so high. Perhaps the Vietnamese could be persuaded to play a role in this thing."

"They are stretched thin, Mr. President."

"But they are so numerous, and if they were convinced—"

"Mr. President?" Sam wanted him to understand this one thing, the key to everything else. "They do not look on the war as we do, for them it's a different kind of war. To them it is timeless, it will go on forever. Because when it is over it will mean that they have lost and they do not know which is worse, winning the war or losing it. It is not in their hands in any case. They see its continuation as our doing and therefore our responsibility. And in an operation of this kind, so hazardous, it's extremely doubtful they would want to participate. They want to survive, you see."

"Uh-huh," the President said.

He had not heard any of it. Sam said, "Most of them are terrified. Time is their enemy, except to the extent that it goes on forever." Or the exact reverse. That was the trouble with the war, you could say any damned thing you wanted to, and it would be true.

"Yes, yes," the President said impatiently. "So weird." Then, "These troopers of ours who could be gotten—"

"We could do it," Mundelein said.

"And who would run it?"

"Langley has the capability," Mundelein said.

"That does not fill me with confidence."

Mundelein said, "This is an unconventional force performing an unconventional mission. I don't believe. It's a mission for the army unaided."

"Uh-huh," the President said. "They've screwed up a lot."

"Yes, sir," Sam said. He did not know which organization the Man referred to now. It was probably the CIA so he added, "You could insist, their best men."

The adviser grunted. "The President and the agency," he began, speaking now to Sam. But he shrugged and did not finish the sentence.

The Man said, "How did you find them generally?"

"Sir?"

"The morale, goddammit."

"In the circumstances," Sam said, "sturdy."

"They're good boys, the best. I get letters, you know, from the parents."

"Yes," Sam said.

"And then from the parents' Congressmen."

"I have, too," Sam said.

"That's the thing of it," the President said. "It makes it tough, these casualties. It's the casualties that they concentrate on, the media people. God damn them."

"I remember," Mundelein said, "first year I came to work here. Looked on it like a campaign, day didn't have enough hours. Sometimes I'd sleep in the office, bought an electric shaver for that purpose, and a change of clothes. I think it was the minimum wage bill, we were fighting that year. It was like a military campaign, that one was. Each day was fresh, and the sense of possibility . . . "

"One of them," the President said, "the father, I think, saw his boy get it on TV. What am I supposed to do about that?"

" . . . and we got it, too, with tenacity and hard bargaining . . . "

"How's the liaison?" the President asked.

"Outstanding, Mr. President."

"They don't like what they see of our allies, the letters are specific on that point. I wish to hell sometimes the dinks were British."

" . . . working with the Congress that year, I was junior man in the Congressional operation. We'd go up to the Hill, it was like negotiating with a sovereign government but, God, we loved it. And we prevailed, eventually! Took a cataclysm to do it, but we prevailed, got what we wanted or most of it, and that's the art of politics, being able to distinguish between 'least' and 'most.' " Mundelein sat back in his chair, lost in memory.

Sam said, "Very close, sometimes you can't tell the difference between them, they're like brothers, the advisers and their counterparts. Ha-ha, there's a mission school near Pleiku. American priest, Vietnamese priest. Known as Father McQueen and his counterpart, they're so close." He hoped the President or Mundelein would follow up, it was the most persistent mystery. The Vietnamese adopted the characteristics of the Americans, but the reverse was never true, except when it came to drafting reports. Was the American the stronger culture? Discourse was always in English, and the Vietnamese army was now organized along American lines. It was so the Americans could assimilate it in the reports. There were some signs lately, however, that the Americans were finding the Vietnamese culture less hostile and alien. This was not an altogether positive development. He said, "We lost an adviser last month. He fell in love with his cook and went AWOL with her to her village, to hell and gone near the border." He watched the President glance at Mundelein. "What made it strange was that the cook was no bimbo, she was sixty if she was a day, teeth black from betel nut, and of course she spoke no English."

"No one can explain what the adviser was doing at that altitude," Mundelein said grimly.

"It's always been high," the President said.

"The morale," Mundelein added.

"It's important to distinguish between the men and their leaders," Sam said carefully. "The men who are running the units,

86

there's dedication and energy. If energy alone could do it, long hours, courage, concern—"

"Dedicated men. We are not to let them down."

"Yes, sir," Sam said. "One difficulty. We're losing so many of our best—"

"You're telling me? I'm the one who gets the calls and letters from the Congressmen, and the parents. The mothers and the fathers, who hold *me* responsible. This thing is a firestorm—"

"Yes," Sam said.

"—and you don't know how hard it makes it here, the burdens."

"I understand that, Mr. President," Sam said. "But our best men. That fact doesn't get into the newspapers, heavy casualties among the best men we have. Casualties not always owing to gunfire, either. Illnesses of various kinds, and of course recklessness takes its toll too. Some of them, it's almost as if they take foolish risks to see if, just once, they could make it yield. Make a difference, one man. They sign up again and again. I talked to one colonel who's been there six years. Can't imagine himself anywhere else, he says."

"That's the kind of dedication I'm talking about."

"Yes, sir. This particular colonel believes the war's lost, has been lost for about two years."

"And he's still there?"

"Just re-upped again."

"Incredible dedication," the President said, "though of course you have to wonder about a man who would voluntarily place himself in the Zone, year after year. You have to wonder about the stability of a man like that."

"A professional soldier," Sam began.

"Uh-huh," Mundelein said. "They're the best we have." Then, "These are the ones carrying the fight to Charlie, and those closest up are most likely to lose sight of the forest, *n'est-ce pas?*" Mundelein cleared his throat. "The proposal we have here involves not only interdiction of the trails but specific targets as well. Vietnamese individuals." He stood and walked to the map, accepting the pointer from Sam. He tapped the pointer first in the south, then west into Cambodia and Laos, finally north to Hanoi. *Tap tap tap.* Then he sat down again. "Of course Langley would want it, if we decided to greenlight it."

"My experience," Sam said, "is that the longer they've been there the more exotic their solutions. This is a paradox. The ones who know the most tend to be extremists. Their solutions tend to be . . . elaborate. They love analogy. Hegel's taken quite a hold on the command." When the President looked at him blankly, Sam explained, "The German philosopher. Believed that quantity was quality. More is better."

"Something bold," the President said. "We could use something bold and imaginative."

Mundelein said, "They'd have to be watched."

The Man peered closely at Sam. "What was the point of the story about the adviser and his cook? I don't get it."

"Well, sir." What indeed? What could he say? It was not any ordinary breakdown. Sam did not know if he could plausibly describe "the point" in these surroundings, the Oval Office flooded now with winter sun, the rose garden drenched in snow, the President, perplexed, awaiting the explanation of American obsession in the damp heat of Asia. A civilian adviser, age forty, had fallen in love with a Vietnamese peasant woman, his housekeeper. In the circumstances it was only a biographical detail to add that the American had a wife and three children, and an exemplary record in the foreign service. Simply put, the adviser had cracked and the note he left behind asserted that the marriage to the peasant woman would materially shorten the war. A ritual marriage binding our two great nations, the note said, his own personal SEATO. Sam said at last, "It was to indicate a certain erratic quality to life in the Zone." Mundelein looked at the President and raised his eyebrows. "It isn't always wise to trust everything you hear from the men on the ground."

"They are often pessimistic," the President said.

That was not what Sam meant. He said, "They work too hard, exhausted, many of them. They're idealists in their own way. There's a scattered quality."

"Uh-huh," the President said. "They are exiled from their

own kind." He bounced his pencil on the desktop. "Was he a drunk?"

"He drank," Sam said. "Most of them do."

The Man nodded, apparently satisfied.

Mundelein said, "It's only money. Trouble is Langley. It's never straightforward with those people. They've got so many cubbyholes. You could have a hundred guys overseeing and that's all they'd do, oversee. You'd never know whether your instructions were being met to the letter, and in a crack you can bet they'd have their ass covered. The damn thing would be done according to their own procedures. And we'd be in the dark. They'd make the mission fit their capability. There's a lot to go wrong."

"Our people need encouragement."

"They've got good heads over there, I'll concede that," Mundelein said. "Better than Hoover."

"Not much gets by Hoover."

"Nothing," Mundelein said. "He runs that thing like a mom-and-pop candy store and he's both Mom and Pop. Knows where all the bonbons are. At Halloween he drags out the skeletons. Skeletons for sale, he says. How much am I offered?" The Man listened to this, expressionless. Sam was fascinated. "Always gets what he asks for and then the skeleton goes back in the closet not to be used again until budget time of the following fiscal year. Son of a bitch thinks in terms of fiscal years, he has special calendars in his office. Tough as a boiled owl, that one. He has his uses, though." The adviser looked at Sam. "Maybe I'll put him on the trail of that sport who eloped with his housekeeper. He can put his gumshoes on that one, find out how it happened, where they are and what they're doing, and how much it's cost the American taxpayer. Maybe he can corner them in a movie theater and gun them down, way he did Dillinger." Mundelein sighed. "Point I'm trying to make is that he's not as good with the operations as he is with the budget at Halloween."

"Hush," the Man said. "That is something else. We have this now."

"It's so seductive there," Sam said. He wanted to give it one more try. "It's easy for a man to lose himself, if he's the slightest bit confused to begin with. All of the best ones are, and that's the paradox. It's not something we're ideally suited for, counter-revolution. I mean, Americans aren't."

"Uh-huh," the President said.

Mundelein looked at Sam. "We have in mind an operation."

"They do," the President said.

"That is correct. It has been presented to us."

Sam nodded, and leaned forward in his chair. They were working like a song-and-dance team, the Man and his adviser.

"There is a unit in place," the adviser said. "As I understand it, this unit would be capable of handling the operation. This one unit, enhanced, augmented." He paused, and read statistics aloud from his notepad. "One thing is certain. It isn't doing anything else." Mundelein looked at him. "You know the one I mean."

"I suppose you mean Sol Henderson."

"There's a lot of fat out there," the President said.

"Yes," Mundelein said. "That one. Ideal man on paper. To control this." Sam said nothing now, aware that both men were watching him. "Respected man, well connected, good reputation, good soldier, Henderson. Wouldn't you agree, Colonel?"

"A fine combat man," Sam said. "He is a very old friend."

Mundelein said, "We could just let them push a button on the computer over there, take the first name on the printout. They've done that before, it absolves them of responsibility. But this case. It couldn't be just any officer. It has to be a hand-picked man, particularly if Langley's involved. As it must be at some level, and most specifically if there were. Not saying there would be, necessarily. But if there were special missions of the kind we've mentioned here."

Sam did not reply.

"Everyone has to pull his weight in this thing," the President said.

"I don't know very much about his background. Tell me about his background, Sam."

"He'll never go beyond colonel," Sam said, "because he never went to West Point. A fine combat man, as I've said. Good with troops, sometimes a little less popular with . . . " He paused. "Brass. Outspoken."

"Family?"

"He's an orphan," Sam said. "Grew up in a foster home in Baltimore."

"The old can-do spirit," the President said. "That's a necessity."

"Langley's very interested in this project in Cambridge." Mundelein looked from the President to Sam and back again. "They believe they can see the trails, as it were. They believe that the fight must be carried to Charlie."

Sam said, "When we have done that in the past they have matched us operation for operation. That's the history of the war. The escalator always accelerating. More this, more that. Always more casualties."

"Uh-huh," the President said. "A heavy weight, that it is."

"The special missions," Sam began.

"Yes," Mundelein said.

"What exactly—"

"They would involve specific targets." He hesitated and leaned back in his chair, staring at the ceiling.

"Vietnamese," Sam said.

"Yes."

"With Sol Henderson in charge."

"It's one option, one option among many."

"It's not a mission for the army," Sam said.

"Yes," the adviser said cheerfully. "And this would require a committed man, wouldn't it? Not your average garden variety infantry officer. Now . . . " He paused. "But you don't think the army's capable of it?"

"It's capable of it," he said. Sol is capable enough. But that's a civilian mission, get Langley to do it."

"Everyone has to pull the weight," the President said.

"Now, Colonel . . . " Mundelein paused. "If you would, please—"

"We place the heaviest burdens on the broadest backs," the President said.

"—tell the President what you told me about the Vietnamese.

The estimate of those with whom you spoke, inside the command and out of it. Just your best estimate, no frills."

"This is so important," the President said.

"The Vietnamese," Sam said. He cleared his throat. "They have been at it even longer than Sol Henderson." He looked at his shoes. Where to begin? "It isn't realistic to expect. Anything of them except that they do what they can to survive. What they *must*. I don't know what your reports say."

"Not that," Mundelein said.

"They are a resilient people," said the President.

"—but whatever they say, it's just survival for most of them. Of course there are others who are psychotic. You have to see them to know how psychotic they are, our people as well. That's what has to be understood and what no one does understand."

"Our medical corps is outstanding," the President said.

"Yes, sir," Sam said. He was talking rapidly, the words coming in bursts. "It's a bedlam and I'm not certain anymore that they know who the enemy is. Each man has a different enemy, sometimes more than one. These various enemies . . . " His voice trailed away. "But it isn't *working*." He sought the correct word. "It's not *advancing*."

"No one said it would be easy," the President said.

"No," the adviser agreed.

"It comes with the territory." The Man sighed. "Every Man who's occupied this office, comes to him sooner or later."

"It's subtle, delicate," the adviser said. "It's not a thing you can paint in broad strokes."

"I've signed on for the course," the President said.

"We all have," Mundelein agreed. There was a little silence while they collected themselves. "Before we get too deeply into it." The adviser lit a cigarette. "Before we decide who actually commands, and the ways and means, how many and who and where." He read again from his notepad, more statistics. "And who funds. And what role Langley plays, if there is a role for Langley. These things will be nailed down in time." He smiled suddenly. "Of course they are just details."

"The reports are so positive," the President said. "Just inches.

We're inches away, if we can hang on."

"They, too," Sam said. "They have to hang with us."

"And they will!" the adviser said.

"Of course it's their war to win or lose, we all understand that."

"Sol Henderson," Sam began. But he did not finish the thought. Sol Henderson was not his brief.

There was a very long silence now, during which Sam heard only the ticking of the clock and the President's heavy breathing. Mundelein held an unlit cigarette in his hand while he stared gravely out the window. "We'll be in touch," the adviser said.

The Man shrugged, as if he hadn't heard Mundelein; as, indeed, perhaps he hadn't. "Of course the whole idea's a long shot." His eyes drifted away. He was smiling again, looking sideways at his adviser. "It's one arrow in our quiver. What was it that you said, Pat? You want to deny them nothing, isn't that right?"

"Yes," Mundelein said.

"Sixty-to-one, probably won't work. Ideas sound better here than there, and we're not in the possession of all the facts. I want you to call the secretary, verify what we have." He picked up the little glass sphere and shook it.

"It's important that we understand exactly what's being said here, Sam," the adviser said. "It's important that we be precise in our language, no fudging. We are talking here of enhanced pacification, a joint operation of the Free World Forces. Us and the ARVN with some input from the Ministry of Revolutionary Development. RevDev is with us on this one, I'm sure they'll be. And Sol Henderson or someone like him in charge on the ground. That is, if we decide to go ahead. There's no green light, we all understand that. This here is just conversation."

Sam Joyce looked from one to the other. Their expressions, pleasant without being in any way friendly, told him nothing. Both men were bent forward, the President over his desk, the adviser rearranging some papers at his feet. Was this all they wanted? Was he dismissed? When neither man said anything, the soldier cleared his throat and stood. He took a step toward the door but the Man raised his hand, a traffic warden at a busy intersection. Evidently there was something further that he wanted to say.

The Man was staring at the map again. He seemed to struggle for a moment. "Maybe we won't even have to do it," he said. "Wouldn't that be something! Maybe we're at the last domino without knowing it." He smiled tentatively. "We've got a big one going now, much bigger than we've let on. *Much* bigger." He rose and walked heavily to the map. "Here and there," he said, pointing. "North and west of Kontum. A total of four infantry divisions, pinching *there* and *there*. More than a thousand helicopters." He patted the waist of the Zone. "The air force in support. Phantoms, Skyraiders, Dakotas with miniguns, B-52s from Guam, A-6s from the *Enterprise*. You should hear the Admiral when he talks about Naval Gunfire. I tell you, Sam, it's a whole new world. The World of Naval Gunfire." He poked his finger at the torso of the country, *boom-boom*. Then he stepped back from the map, looking at it afresh. "Three ARVN divisions in blocking positions, protected by artillery fans and two armored battalions, all U.S. And of course the Naval Gunfire from a battlewagon and two tin cans in the South China Sea, Yankee Station. Do you see it?" He bent forward, his nose almost touching Kontum. "Maybe they'll find COSVN. Capture the headquarters, along with Giap and his suite. Rout Giap from his command post, bring him back to Saigon trussed like a turkey. Oh, the tightest security. Tightest security you can imagine! Long sessions with the boys there, wired for sound so I can listen in. And he will tell us how he has done it. Names, dates, all the details, my goodness their intelligence is so good. Outstanding. They have everything. They make J. Edgar look like a Keystone Kop and J. Edgar's the best we have. Now, when we've learned all that we need to know, and all that we can digest, we'll throw him a press conference. At one of the hangars at Tan Son Nhut. Cocktails for the press, boiled shrimp, fine wines. And a handsome press kit they can quote from, describing the General and his accomplishments. Of course a text will be furnished! He'll be present, in the uniform of a field marshal

---

94

of the People's Army of North Vietnam, chatting with my officers. Having renounced the revolution! All those years, he'll've
had his doubts about old Uncle Ho. He'll defect to our side, become my special representative in the theater of war. And I'll
tell you something else. Listen good now. I'll put him in charge.
I'd put him in charge *tomorrow*, if I had him." He moved forward again, embracing the map; he caressed the waist, running
his fingers lightly down the belly of the country to the Delta. His
fingers lingered there a moment in the tidewater and swamp-
land and twilight.

Then, sighing, the Man went around his desk to the big chair
and slowly eased himself into it. The light went out of his eyes
and suddenly he was any tired business executive approaching a
difficult decision. He said, "Doesn't sound exactly right, this
plan." The familiar voice was now a monotone, directed at the
map itself, as if the map would respond, part like the curtains of
the Wizard of Oz, and give him the answer: Go or No Go.
"They've presented me with an interesting idea, one that's unusual and out of step with these times and I'm disturbed about the
security aspect and the reluctance of the Vietnamese. However,
I don't doubt its political appeal. That guy." He crooked his
thumb at a tiny photograph of one of his predecessors: it was
barely visible in the darkness of the bookshelf. "Would have
laughed you out of here. And it probably won't work. Nothing
else has. Doesn't sound exactly right, does it, Pat?"

Mundelein shook his head.

"I understand perfectly," Sam said. He understood the Man
to be speaking for the record only, opening one more door; a
fresh exit. He was intrigued, but it was important for him to
sound pessimistic. Sam thought that in a way the President had
invented a new language, one that did not define a thought, in
the sense of placing a boundary around it, but the reverse. It was
language in the service of formlessness, of disorder, confusion,
and non sequitur. Sam listened carefully. He assumed that the
interview was nearing its end, and he would shortly be excused.
He paused only to see if the Man had one last word. Any final
note to fling over the wall.

"It's so lonely," the President said.

95

Sam leaned forward.

"Thank God for loyal men such as yourself."

"We would not want to move too quickly," Mundelein said.

"Patience. That's our watchword. We can be more patient because we've never lost a war and we're not going to lose this. History repeats itself, doesn't it, Pat?" Then, "Always liked your father, Colonel." Sam moved back in his chair, alert to this unexpected turn. "Always liked him, the old pirate." The snow had stopped and the sun was full, the garden brilliant now in white light. Sam noticed it had a blue tint, seen through the bulletproof glass. "Always free with advice. Do you know how much advice I get? My daily ration of advice? Advice on the editorial pages and falsehoods on the front page, owing to the generous interpretation of the First Amendment. If a man is in public life the newspaper can print any lie no matter how outrageous and the subject has no recourse—"

"Sir," Mundelein said quietly.

His voice rising: "—except to hunker down and recite in unison Mr. Jefferson's observation that he would rather live in a nation without statesmen than a nation without journalists. Only known evidence that Mr. Jefferson was a fool."

"Sir," Mundelein said.

"That's the advice I get every day. I get advice from official quarters as well. Most of it's to the effect that I do something different from what I am doing."

"Yes, sir," Sam said.

"I always liked him," he said glumly.

"Yes," Sam said.

"And your mother." He searched his memory. "God rest her soul."

Sam swallowed and looked to Mundelein for guidance.

"I'd like to think as we go forward that there'll be some support, some small indication . . . " The President's voice trailed away. He was still looking into the sunny garden. "I never get out anymore."

"This support," Mundelein began.

"It would be good to have someone like Piatt Warden. Piatt

knows his way around, he's an outstanding Representative."

"A man of discretion and wide acquaintance," Mundelein said. "A temperate man, after so many years in the federal city." The adviser smiled.

Sam looked at Mundelein. What was the point of all this? Mundelein looked away.

"You are not married, Joyce."

"No," he said.

"A pity." The Man shook his head.

"Yes, sir," he said. "I think it's better this way. I'm married to the army."

"Cold comfort," Mundelein said, laughing.

The Man did not smile, nor give any indication he'd heard Sam's reply. There was another long silence while he sipped his coffee and the adviser smoked. Sam remained on his feet, knowing that there was something more to come, though the man now seemed completely absorbed in the map. His hooded eyes peeked over the rim of the coffee cup moving to the peninsula, jogged right, and held. He was somewhere in the South China Sea, Yankee Station. The *Enterprise* was there now with its escort of destroyers. Sam thought it must seem to him a Rorschach test, this exercise in measuring the personality traits and habits of a nation; a pretty abstract, drenched now in summer sun, now in rain, now in blood. All so loose, like the soil of Indochina itself; soft, a fluid soil. Turn the map upside down and the great weight of Asia, the immensity of China and of Siberia, hung from it like a boulder on a thread. Sam could imagine the plans that came to this office, plans of every shape, size, and scope. He could imagine the messengers arriving with their black briefcases, the Man and his adviser sitting where they were at that moment, their faces carefully composed, pointedly skeptical—but open and ready for business. The boy assembling the map and the easel, and the charts that went with the map. Supporting evidence and the precedents, as in a court of law. So many of them were lawyers, why not?

A few years before there had been a plan to snatch Vo Nguyen Giap, hero of the revolution, military genius, author of *People's*

War, People's Army. Snatched like the Lindbergh kid, but not killed. They had a time and a place, who and with what means; where he would be taken and by what conveyance. The orders were clear, Giap alive and healthy. The enemy would never acknowledge his death and he would have become a living ghost and legend like a Red Indian chief, forever lurking in the forest, directing events from a concealed command post, now here, now there. Spurious pronouncements over the radio, false sightings, doctored photographs. Unpleasant consequences were anticipated, the Vietnamese were a formidably sly and violent people. And it was unquestionably true that the General would be even more luminous dead than alive. Anthropologists maintained that the Vietnamese believed in ghosts.

Of course it was an elegant scheme, almost literary in its appeal. There would be specially trained teams and exotic hardware and a particular cypher. And that was the trouble, they'd become fascinated with surfaces. They resembled the surrealist artists, finding significance in exteriors: a fur coffee cup, a driping watch, levitating bank clerks, a woman's torso become a countenance; an absurd art to match an absurd war. God knows how much time was spent, days surely, weeks more likely; the Man could talk it for hours. As indeed he had done. It was the infinite appeal of fantasy: he loved yarns, tall tales. An ancient American tradition, was it not? Hilarious lies. Twain, Joel Chandler Harris. Meet Ernst and Magritte. One was beguiled.

The White House diary would never reflect the time spent on that particular scheme, men dreaming. The hardware was *so* fine, a delicious finesse. Then the grinning would stop and there would be no more excitement. He and the adviser would look it over coldly, late at night. They'd turn it over and examine it from all sides and know then that it was a dream and wouldn't work. It would fail not because it was lunatic or untidy but because it was—rational and too neat. The Man and his adviser were familiar with disorder. What was politics but disorder? To understand America you had to understand chaos and have a love for it; and turbulence and have a love for that; and love the power to unleash them both. Or the reverse! To love America and her fabulous destiny was to love the landslide of ambition, tomorrow fashioned from found materials, as it were . . . This scheme, it was too neat and tidy; it had to fail. And when it failed, the President of the United States would look not merely stupid but, worse, unlucky. Star-crossed! That was not a quality that the American people cared for, believing as they did in the glittering prizes of landslide and disorder, a gorgeous fate assisted by the heavens. It was a nation, after all, that was Under God. So they sent a reluctant message to Langley: No Go. Fully recognizing the timidity of the decision, turning down a party that promised fun because of the certainty that you'd drink too much and were in no position to grapple with a hangover the next day. The wonderfully articulated plans! They were exceedingly bright and articulate at Langley; their briefings bristled with metaphors and mighty quotations from great men and read, frequently, like film scripts. No wonder that from time to time the White House gave a green light, the proposal simply too appealing to turn down—again and again, having finished "the scenario" of this scheme or that, Mundelein would turn to his briefer and nod approvingly, barely restraining himself from adding, "good narrative flow." But mostly it was No Go, No Go being the end of it—the studio heads refusing to finance?—except naturally there were pieces of paper in the files. One piece of paper after another. A piece of paper to prove that the scheme existed and a piece of paper to prove that it had been "canceled" and other pieces of paper that were like recondite footnotes to a great work of scholarship.

Sam slipped out of his reverie-room and back to the present. He knew what the Man and his adviser wanted. They wanted Sam to know that they were not interested in first, second, and third drafts. They were not interested in the difficulties of composition. They were interested in results, if results there were. Sam Joyce seemed to them dangerously confused, perhaps he too had been undone in the Zone. Whatever special missions were undertaken, the President did not want to know the details—unless the targets were known to him personally, meaning their names only since he had never actually met a Communist Vietnamese. And if these special missions resulted in failure, he did not want to know that either. These ideas had been back and forth and back and forth and none of them had ever worked out. This one probably wouldn't.

Sam had better commit himself.

The Man stirred and, seeing his lips move, Sam leaned forward. "Sir?"

"It's a good thing to be married to the army."

"Better than living alone, sir."

"How many times have you been married, Joyce?"

Who did they think he was, Mickey Rooney?

"I am a bachelor."

"No one can say that you didn't try."

Sam did not know the purpose of this so he nodded, still at attention in the quiet formal room. His face betrayed nothing. Actually there were a number of people who would say that he didn't try, including Gretchen and her father, along with several close friends and his army mentor, now dead. And Marina Warden would have a word or two to say as well.

"It's hard on a man's personal life," Mundelein said. The adviser turned to the President. "It's as we've said so often, to perform successfully in this city you've got to have stability at home. 'Live like a bourgeois and perform like a demigod.' Flaubert." He grinned. "Concentration and restraint, that's what it is—"

The Man grinned crookedly at Sam. "Pat's not married either."

"I have no complaints," Sam said, irritated now. It was one thing hearing it from the commander in chief, and another thing hearing it from Pat Mundelein. None of it made any sense anyhow. He said to the adviser, "Maybe I'm like that one you were telling me about. Went north to work and never went back home."

"No," Mundelein said, flushing. "I don't think that's it at all, Colonel."

"You've served your country," the President said, his eyes pulling painfully away from the map. Now he seemed to be consciously avoiding it, as one would avoid the embrace of a dear friend abandoned at the moment of need—and indeed, that was precisely the way the Man viewed it. He had been traduced by geography. He stretched in his chair, smiling pleasantly. "You've had an outstanding career." He ticked off Sam's various posts, getting it wrong only once. He mentioned the ease with which Sam worked with civilians. He seemed to have an understanding of civilians. "That must be Ben's training."

"Yes, sir," Sam said.

"And why is that?" The Man answered his own question. They understood the Cold War, having lived with it for so long. This was a war that could not be avoided or abandoned, so much had been put into it; it would be like abandoning a family business at the first sign of recession. No, you dug in and worked even harder. You spent the capital you'd accumulated. He said, "Thank God for men like you." Of course there were those who would discount the effort and devalue the sacrifice. In these times, therefore, it was necessary for a soldier to think in a different way. The Man smiled hopefully.

Mundelein said, "To behave like a soldier it is necessary to think like a diplomat and act like a spy."

Sam stared at the adviser. "No, it isn't."

"So." The Man turned to Sam. "A man like you'd be of great value to us here, this is where the real war is being fought."

Sam opened his mouth, then shut it again.

"This is where the burden is," he said. "The actual operations . . . " He waved his hand in an aimless gesture, wrinkling his nose. "Wouldn't it be a good idea to talk to Max Cather? Informally, nothing specific and nothing on paper. Max is a good head, isn't he? He's had experience and stands outside the network over there. He's played a lone hand before, and his loyalties are firm. I'd hate to see our tit get caught in that wringer. Those files. Max could be helpful in that regard there."

"We think Max has a role to play," Mundelein said.

"You know him, don't you?"

"Yes," Sam said.

"It's always helpful when there's a personal relationship," Mundelein said. "When it's friend to friend there's less chance of error and mix-up." Then, to the President: "He's part of that

Shakerville crowd, Max is. Max, that editor, Piatt Warden, and Sam here."

Sam smiled. It would not amuse Teddy Carney to be described by the adviser as "that editor."

"What the hell is Shakerville?"

Mundelein described Shakerville, its location and inhabitants. The Man listened sourly, nodding at the adviser. "There's a role here for Piatt Warden, too. We'll need some help on the Hill, from the inside." He looked encouragingly at Mundelein, then out the window. "It's stopped snowing."

"Could be," the adviser said. "It would depend."

"I thought it would snow all morning. Looked like it would snow all day long. The city is just tied up to beat hell when it snows like this."

"On the factors. But I would have thought, as we commence the preliminaries, that the particular advice that would be helpful." He glanced at the President, still staring glumly out the window. "Would be Max's."

"Uh-huh," the President said.

"Piatt, too, of course."

"Are they close?"

"They are close friends," Mundelein said.

"I take it you don't think much of the idea," the President said. He was talking to Sam though looking at Mundelein.

"I'm old-fashioned," Sam said. "I like soldiers in uniform, performing the usual roles and missions. What you have in mind here is a bit irregular. It would require an irregular force. Langley's ideal to fund and staff it." He had his hand on the doorknob and now he took it away. He was not certain how to proceed, there were so many salients, and the terrain before him was thick and inhospitable. "I don't think Sol Henderson's the man for the job."

"It's so speculative," the President said.

"This mission," Sam said, "if you're determined to go through with it—"

"Oh, my God!" the President laughed. "*Determined.* Goodness, no. This is preliminary only, and you have given us a very fine report. Things are going well."

"My own view," Sam said. "Is that less rather than more—"

"Yes, of course."

"The other thing," Sam said. "The other part I don't completely understand. Is where I fit in. What is it that you want me to do?" He tried another tack. "The army isn't what it was, there's some demoralization, it's gone on for so long, taken so many resources . . . " He gestured vaguely at the map, realizing that he was perspiring and talking faster than normal. It was obvious what he was saying; it was obvious even to these two, though their expressions were not encouraging. He stopped then, waiting.

"Uh-huh," the President said and turned to Mundelein, muttering something in a low voice. The adviser shook his head and said something in return. They were tête-à-tête, the adviser close to the President's elbow, explaining some matter. It was a moment before Sam understood that they had resumed an earlier conversation and that his business was at an end. Now the dog stood up and shuddered, stretching first one hind leg and then the other. Yawning luxuriously, the animal moved a few paces and collapsed again in the sunlight. Sam experienced a moment of vertigo, the Oval Office dissolved and broke into separate and conflicting parts, the heavy desk, the pictures, the suburban furniture, and the two men tête-à-tête in the shadows, all in opposition. He silently opened the door and slipped out, leaving the desk and the dog in a puddle of brilliant sunlight.

The young woman was standing in the corridor watching him. The corridor seemed to tip, he imagined it a frozen river melting in the sun. In artificial light they faced each other a moment, then she turned and began to walk away. He followed, scrutinizing her hair and the way she moved. She was a beautiful young woman, more beautiful even than Gretchen, or his memory of Gretchen. She wore a coral-colored sweater and a short skirt, the fabric stretched tight across her rear. Her hair swung with each fearless stride. He remembered once in the Zone, driving to the airport to the hotel and watching a delicate young woman on a bicycle thread her way through the murderous traffic, her *ao dai* rippling buoyantly in the breeze, she looking neither to right nor left, supremely, insanely confident that in her innocence and abstraction she would not be harmed; she had power over them and accomplished her left turn without incident, a spirit governing matter. When she had done it, flying into an empty side street without turning her head or otherwise noticing, he wanted to cheer.

Sam was on firm ice now. They moved swiftly down the empty corridor together, only a stride apart, through the private lobby to the back entrance of the mansion. She was hugging one of the distinctive buff-colored folders to her chest, and turning now to look at him. It was a glance of affection and respect, to one who had just come from an hour's private audience with the Man and his adviser. He opened his mouth to say something humorous and provocative but she was holding the door for him, smiling broadly, so he brushed by her into the cold Washington morning. The fresh snow, dazzling in the sun, blinded him. He shut his eyes against the light, the sudden kaleidoscope reminding him of nights on bivouac in the Zone. It was his most intimate connection with nature. Late at night he wandered from his command post to the perimeter to stand and stare at the stars, so brilliant in the tranquil sky. He looked always for the Southern Cross, low on the horizon. It was cool, the heat of the day having been absorbed into the ground. Only the low murmur of his pickets broke the natural noises of the jungle. The heavens located him, he felt, their presence a comfort and balm after the sweat and anxiety of the day. What prayers he had were directed to the Southern Cross. Nights on reconnaissance in the Zone held no terror for him.

When he turned back to speak to her she had vanished. He tried the door and found it locked. Mistinguett, Gretchen, the girl in the *ao dai*, the White House secretary with the buff-colored folder—they were the same woman, forever out of reach. They and the war both, inaccessible, elusive, mocking, savage. Shining surfaces, like his polished shoes and careful explanations.

He tried the door again. Then one of the guards approached and he smiled his official smile and hurried away down the sidewalk to east Executive Avenue, and then to a Chinese restaurant where he would meet Marina Warden for lunch.

Piatt was the first to reach into the glass forest, finding the calvados and pouring generously. Sam sat back for a moment, distracted, toying with the three cigarettes aimed at the demilitarized zone and I Corps. The air was thick with cigar smoke and silence; no one seemed prepared to comment. Max poured a finger of framboise and Teddy sat staring at the ceiling, as if committing what he had heard to memory. Piatt took a swallow at once, his mind racing; he was trying to calculate exactly what Sam had withheld. It had been a circumspect account, a hand carefully played, though played with flair. Well, it didn't matter really. Piatt knew this particular score, better than Sam; probably better than Max.

"A queer interview," Sam said finally. He thought that they used words the way a creative accountant used a balance sheet—assets and liabilities distributed differently according to the reader, one result for the client and another for Internal Revenue. This balance sheet employed accelerated depreciations.

Piatt rose and slipped away, taking his calvados with him. He did not need to listen to the soldier's definition of queer interviews. Piatt closed the door of the bathroom and still he heard Sam's voice, interrupted finally by Teddy Carney. He felt the tension ease. Teddy's voice resembled superior elevator music and now, after a pause, Sam Joyce began a nimble answer. Someone chuckled and he heard the clink of glass against glass. He tried to imagine Sam Joyce, the President, and the adviser in the brilliant egg-shaped room, splendid in gold and green. No one was immune to that room. He remembered the first time he was there with Marina, a signing ceremony in the evening, the President at ease and confident behind his desk. The President had caught him staring at his chair, as if measuring it for size, and had grinned and finally laughed. There were a number of them in the room and no one knew what had amused the President. When Piatt told the story to Marina, she laughed, and laughed again when he'd asked her what was so damned funny. She'd said, "I saw you looking, and I knew that he did, too. And I think you ought to be more subtle about it. It's like an adolescent looking up a woman's dress." He'd been forced to smile at that, Marina was often witty, though usually at his expense. Of course it was easy enough to deprecate, for anyone who had no chance at it or didn't want it. But once anyone of the . . . the *métier* saw it up close, the telephones of various colors, the young marine with the cyphers, the TV consoles, and the aides walking in unannounced to whisper in the Man's ear, the words producing either the shadow of a grimace or the shadow of a grin depending on the information, and a muttered word back, do this, do that. Get me Willy Brandt. Get me David Rockefeller. Get Piatt Warden, tell him to get over here for the signing tonight, tell him to bring his wife, drinks afterwards. . . . It seemed out of reach, until you were there yourself. Then something stirred inside and you began to watch and listen, and weigh.

Piatt put his glass on the basin and buttoned up. The walls of the tiny bathroom were covered with caricatures of the newspaper's foreign correspondents, drawn by the editorial page cartoonist. Tiny heads, large bodies. Plover, the Paris gourmet, dressed in the costume of a chef de cuisine. Sonnemann, the London hipster, carrying a typewriter and a guitar. Charlotte O'Brien, looking like a debutante surrounded by cannibals. And Jessel, the soldier-journalist, his hand tucked in his tunic à la Napoleon. Piatt did not know the men in Rio and Moscow or the woman in Bonn. Directly over the toilet was a caricature of Carney himself, in the guise of a film mogul, wearing a safari jacket and puttees and brandishing a megaphone.

Piatt smoothed his hair, making a face in the mirror. Sam had told his story well, though what he chose to withhold was more interesting than what he said. There was nothing about Piatt or about Max, and they were important players. It was an earful for Carney, though, and would make him think twice, as it was meant to do. Sam Joyce was no dummy, in fact he was quite clever and intelligent for a soldier, certainly clever enough and intelligent enough to appreciate Carney's usefulness. Most soldiers were dumb as posts, army-dumb, dumb in a brutish half-educated polysyllabic way. Sam was screwed up now, though, and at last had been made to understand that the rules applied to him, too. Soldierboys didn't have a free pass any more than anyone else did. Sam Joyce was an awful son of a bitch in some ways, in his arrogance and lack of respect. Really, he was out of place in Washington. It would be a good thing when he went back to the war, to his bivouac where he belonged. One place he didn't belong was the Oval Office, altogether too subtle for a man in uniform. And he was an anomaly in Shakerville, which was entirely too civilized; he was always a little stiff in the civilian culture with its ironies and nuances. Of course dinner in Shakerville was always an opera, two or three plots going on at once, seductions, betrayals, cases of mistaken identity, and worry over the heir to the throne when the king died or was murdered or deposed. There were bits of arcane tribal history too, Mundelein and his old girl, the suicide, and Mundelein's visits to The Farm. Now he heard them through the door talking about her, Marsha and her husband Irv and how crazy Marsha was and how it got to be too much for Irv. The voices in the dining room were louder and more careless. Piatt heard Carney's high-pitched laugh, the prelude to an anecdote concerning Sheila Dennehay; Sheila and Mundelein had had a brief romance, it seemed. Sheila, so much a part of their circle in the old days, seldom seen now except by Max Cather. She worked in another department at Langley but their work often brought them together. And lately, she and Sam . . .

Piatt belched softly. Helen Carney was taking a course in French cooking, although meals at her table had always been rich and determinedly eccentric. Tonight there had been a clear turtle soup followed by cervelles de veau. Nutritious! Carney explained, brains poached in butter and served with capers, parsley, and lemon. The table glittered and conversation was general, the ambience reminding him of the days early in the decade when conversation, serious conversation, was the mark of a successful evening. He had tried to move the talk to high ground, having just returned from Latin America filled with tales of fabulous tyrants, our allies; it was a continent, or incontinent, as weird and tormented as a Bosch triptych, music by Mahler. The visitor was undermined at every turn. But the company listened impatiently, no one was interested in Latin America. It had no resonance, and when he'd turned to Sam and suggested Argentina as his next post, military attaché in B.A. for openers, Argentina a darkness beyond imagining, a monstrous but fertile state of mind, the vastness of the country equaling the spectacular imaginations of the poets and despots who held it in thrall, the Colonel had demurred.

"I prefer the field, with our own troopers."

He had said to Sam, "I'd avoid the war if I were you. It's a wasting asset and it can bust a career, even yours." Sam had not replied to that, though Piatt noticed Marina squirm—in embarrassment?

Piatt threw his cigarette into the toilet bowl. He heard the women coming downstairs and wondered how soon he and Marina could decently leave. There were one or two facts he wanted to know, then they could be gone. No question, Mundelein was preparing some sort of end run, and Sam Joyce and Max Cather were accomplices to it. Mundelein always bore watching, his political instincts were superb and he was not at all the worst of the advisers surrounding the Man. When Mundelein needed help, Piatt was inclined to give it to him. As for Sam Joyce, he would be better off in Argentina. Whatever else Argentina was, it was not exhausted. It was not the end of the line. And it was not the ward of the United States government, either. But Sam was preoccupied with the Zone, devoted to it. Piatt thought it was people like Sam who made the war seem attractive. They were attracted to danger as insects to a lamp. They had never come clean with the committee, had never told what they knew or suspected. . . . The Pentagon could do worse than send all its colonels to Argentina, and Sam Joyce for one would fit right in. Argentina was as reckless, romantic, and violent as he was.

Piatt noticed that the dining room was quiet. He could not hear Teddy's tenor and there were no chuckles anywhere. Opening the bathroom door, he watched the women file by, Sheila first, then Jo, Marina, and Helen Carney. Piatt saw the men stare at Sheila. The women halted in front of the mural; stern women, Piatt thought, exasperated at being made to leave the room and angry that no one had objected. They said nothing for a moment, standing still as statues, except for little Helen Carney, who remained apart from the others, staring at the table, clasping and unclasping her fingers. Piatt suspected that it had been tedious upstairs. Sheila glanced around coolly, her eyes stopping at Max Cather. She said, "I can't imagine what you boys've been talking about."

"Our youth," Teddy said from the head of the table. "Sam and I were remembering all the good times at St. Alban's and NCS. Our friends, one in particular, and all the good things that have happened since."

"We were talking about Marsha Durrell," Max said. "Mundelein's friend. She was married to a man who worked for me. She was a crazy. She killed herself."

"Marsha was a friend of mine," Sheila said evenly.

"I'm sorry," Max said. "No offense meant."

"None taken," she said crisply. "But isn't it odd, we were talking about Marsha, too. Of course our voices don't carry as yours do. So you haven't a clue."

"What's going on in the middle of my table?" Helen Carney said, her voice rising. "What have you done to it?" She pointed at the coffee spoons and butter knives and the crumpled napkins and haphazard condiments.

"It's a battle map, Helen," Sheila said. She moved two of the spoons. "And not very accurate, from the look of it."

"Teddy," Helen said despairingly.

But Teddy was looking at Sheila. "I didn't know you knew her. You didn't go to NCS."

She laughed; it sounded almost like an accusation. "She had a life after NCS, Teddy. Really, her life *began* after NCS. As for me, as you know I grew up in New York and did not attend the National Cathedral School. If I had," she said, "I'd be married to a lawyer and living in Wesley Heights. And I'd be in business because that's what the second generation does in this town. Business or law, or occasionally journalism. That's what we were talking about upstairs, what happens to the second generation. Apart from Marsha Durrell. In terms of career." She was staring steadily at Max, her arms folded; suddenly she reached forward and poured an Armagnac. "It's mostly law because in this town the law *is* the government, isn't it? One way or another the paychecks come from the treasury. Odd, we used to look at money with such contempt. Remember the contempt we had for money, it was fit only for Texans or Republicans or Averell Harriman. We craved power, altogether worthier, even virtuous—"

"Sheila," Max said mildly.

She turned on him and said coldly, "Now, even Max—"

"Why doesn't Max have the right to go into business if he wants?" Jo demanded.

"Why he has every right!" Sheila said. "Maybe he even has a duty. It's just that in the old days money was so déclassé, beneath our attention. There were a number of prizes for winners in Washington but money wasn't one of them. Washington wasn't a great money town then, only a few people made a fortune in it. Sam's father, a few others. As I said, it was déclassé. Then it wasn't so déclassé. What do you suppose happened?"

Marina said, "Deaths and taxes."

"But we were talking about Marsha," Sheila said.

Carney turned to Max. "I didn't know you were thinking about." He smiled behind his balloon glass. "The private sector."

"Let Sheila finish," Sam said.

"That's very surprising news," Teddy said. "You'd have plenty to tell the right client."

"She wrote poetry," Sheila began.

"*You* of all people. It's hard for me to believe, Max in the private sector. Have you actually quit and taken a job?"

"No," Cather said. "Let her finish."

"Some of it was even published," Sheila said loudly. "In magazines no one at this table ever heard of. She'd send me copies of the magazines which is how I happen to know about them because I didn't read them either. Her poems remind me of a fingernail scratching across a blackboard. Not a sound Irv Durrell cared for, by the way." She smiled brightly, draining her glass, looking at Max. "In one of the poems she had a striking image, her fingernail traveled the full length of the board that day. She was describing the Washington Monument at dawn, the sun rising directly over the Capitol. The narrator is standing inside the Lincoln Memorial at the base of the statue, looking dead east and describing the transit of the sun. The sun strikes the monument and the effect on the narrator standing in Lincoln's shadow is of 'a razor blade across the eyes.' "

In the pause that followed, Carney said, "What business exactly, Max. I would imagine a consultancy—"

Marina said, "That's remarkable, Sheila."

"Is it a joke, Max?"

Sheila stared into the middle distance, indifferent to Carney and Cather. She said, "In New York I went to the Ethical Culture school. Part of each day was devoted to ethical conundrums. You know the sort I mean, I'm sure. Three people in a boat, the boat swamping. Who do you throw over the side? You're in an art gallery. An old woman is staring at a Rubens. Fire breaks out. Who do you save, the lady or the picture? We studied triage with the care and devotion to detail that you studied the Periodic Table. I always answered that it was unreasonable to expect children to command vessels or choose between old women and old masters. The director was very cross with me, 'Sheila refuses to commit herself,' the director wrote my father. He said I refused to accept responsibility for my fellow man. Father was extremely upset and I spent a season on East 92nd Street in the care of a renowned psychiatrist, in order that my moral sense be polished to a high shine. Alas, it didn't take.

111

When I arrived here with Major Johnnie after Smith I used to see a lot of Marsha. The conundrums had become more difficult for both of us, and for her they were insoluble. We both looked terribly to our husbands, who did not seem to have those troubles. We thought they were both luckier and wiser than we were." She put down her glass. "Of course as all the world knows, Johnnie had a great war." She looked suddenly at Piatt. "Now tell me. Were there ethical conundrums at St. Alban's?"

"I wouldn't know about St. Alban's," Piatt said. "There were at Springfield High."

"That's right, I'd forgotten. You're like me, a late arrival. Teddy?"

"Roosevelt's third term? The packing of the Court?"

"You can do better than that."

He smiled. "Nagasaki?"

She smiled back. "Of course, Nagasaki. It would be Nagasaki, wouldn't it?"

"The U-2," he went on. "Was Ike correct to lie? Of course that was after my time. I was already an adult by then and it wasn't a question of morals but of possibilities."

"Yes," she said. "That's the way Marsha found it."

Carney flushed but said nothing.

Sheila said, "I have a son in Vietnam."

"I didn't know that," Marina said.

"Civilian or military?" Jo Cather asked.

"Military," Sheila said. "He's a pilot."

"I admire him," Carney said. "For going."

"Do you?" she inquired. "Why?"

"Well," the foreign editor said. He reached for the cognac and poured himself a glass and then tilted the decanter in the direction of Sheila but she smiled, No, and sat down. She was waiting patiently for the answer. He said, "You can't help admiring those who serve."

"Do you have any sons?"

"Let's sit down," Piatt said and there was a general movement toward the chairs. They all sat where they had been sitting at dinner. But no one spoke, waiting for Carney.

"Of course, as you know, they're too young," he said uncomfortably. "They are children, both of them still in school." They were at St. Alban's. "What does your son say about the war?"

"He doesn't say anything about it," she said. "He's not a letter-writer, never was. Sends me pictures instead. I think," she said, looking at Sam, "that he's anxious to come home. That's his frame of mind."

"Where is he stationed?" Carney asked politely.

"He flies out of Danang."

"Helicopters?"

"Yes," she said with a glance at Cather. "SEALs."

"Christ," Carney said.

"He is a very fine pilot," Cather said.

"I don't know," she said. "He doesn't talk about it. And I don't ask. Him or anyone else. Of course there's a certain amount of talk that you can't avoid, so I know more than I want to. Usually I want to know more than I'm entitled to. Not in this case, however. And of course I have the pictures." Sheila was fumbling in her pocketbook. "Here's his picture." She handed a Kodacolor to Piatt. He had not seen her son in years. A good-looking boy, he resembled his father, the major. Piatt passed the photograph to his left. Each guest looked at it and nodded appreciatively. The photograph disclosed a young man in fatigues standing on a beach, his back to the sea. It could be any beach, Jones, Waikiki, or Nha Trang. This one was Nha Trang. Sheila Dennehay's son was hatless, standing listlessly at the seashore, smoking a cigarette, and staring at the camera while the waves curled around his boots. The sea was flat as a prairie and as empty. The boy was as incongruous in green fatigues and flying boots as he would have been in a white dinner jacket and dancing pumps. On the back of the Kodacolor he or someone had written,

Taylor Dennehay 3987627854

in a careful hand. Piatt noticed that the uniform was without markings of any kind.

113

"How long has he been there?" Jo Cather asked.

Sheila gave a little laugh. He looked so weary; he was the weariest soldier in uniform, her Taylor. She stared at the photograph, her son could have been his father, except for the weariness. In the Second World War Johnnie Dennehay was never weary. She said, "Judging from the picture, before the tide came in."

"I mean in the country."

"Yes," Sheila said. "A few months, give or take a year."

"What are SEALs?" Marina asked.

Max Cather answered in his official voice. "It's an acronym of Sea, Air, Land. They perform rescue missions mostly, though some of the work is classified. The SEALs do extremely useful . . . chores. They are an elite, the best men in the navy." He spoke to Marina but he was looking at Sheila. "It's a volunteer unit, of course."

Sheila said, "That's what they used to tell us at Ethical, that we were an elite and had responsibilities. We were a volunteer unit in the war on. I don't know what it was then, bigotry, poverty, stupidity, privilege. I had a teacher who called it fascism, what we were fighting against. But Taylor never had the benefit of ethical culture. Do you think he's disadvantaged?" Then she said, "He loves machines, always has, even as a little boy he loved to take them apart and put them together. Wants to be an airline pilot. Or did. I don't know what he wants to be now, except a civilian. His father was in the air force and flew with Doolittle and once was thirty seconds over Tokyo, but of course everyone knows that. He was just a boy, really. They all were. And they still are." She looked away. "The thing about Taylor is this. He was full of mischief as a kid. An adventurous boy, afraid of nothing except his father. But in this picture he looks frightened. Doesn't he look frightened?"

"Yes," Piatt said. "But he's a fine-looking boy." He knew that was true, despite the abstract expression on the face and the odd sideways tilt to the body. He stood in a queer posture but was apparently unaware of it. But surely she knew who the SEALs were and what they did.

114

"He looks just like his father," Sheila said. "All that's missing is the forty-mission-man hat, and a parade."

But perhaps not. Perhaps she chose not to know. Piatt said, "More Armagnac?"

She pushed her glass toward him, in the manner of a gambler betting the last stack of chips. "You could not tell anything from the uniform because it has no insignia or other indication . . . of *anything*, really, even which army he belongs to. It could be any army in any country, couldn't it? Any branch of any service, navy or air force or whatever. But as it happens he's a lieutenant in the SEALs. And I think this photograph tells us how he sees himself. The camera lens is a mirror, isn't it?"

Max Cather stirred.

"My other son lives in Europe," she said brightly. "With his wife, who's a Roman from Rome. They have two adorable sons and live in Florence. He's an art historian. Did you know that is a very recent discipline, really a product of the twentieth century? You'd like him, Max. He hates modern art just as much as you do. You'd get along famously, you two."

The others were silent, listening to Sheila Dennehay. She finished the Armagnac in a swallow and now held out her glass for a refill. Piatt poured generously.

She stared at him fiercely. "Who would you throw out of the boat, Pi? The youngest? The oldest? The poorest? The richest? The one with the most intelligence? The least? The thinnest? The fattest? The physicist or the plumber? Hemingway or Woolf? Henry Ford or Man Ray? Agee or a Famous Man? The males? The females?" Her eyes burning, she paused.

Piatt did not answer because she did not want an answer.

She said, "Someone's always sacrificed."

"Sheila," Sam said patiently.

"That's right," Cather said. "That's the first thing to understand."

"I gave him a present when he went out there," she said. "Two, actually. A 35-millimeter camera and a movie camera, both. He doesn't write much, as I said, but he sends back photographs and movies. I can't imagine why they let him make motion pictures, I would think if the enemy got hold of them. They would be valuable to the enemy. But that's not my concern. He sends back a couple of movies a month, his billet, the helicopters he flies. Occasionally a panorama of the country, a landscape that often looks like the remote areas of New England. All this in black and white, he refuses to use color film. Stranger than that, the pictures are stills. I mean there is no movement in them. His billet, for example. He sent me a five-minute movie of . . . the room, the bed, the footlocker, the chair, the window. The 35-millimeter and his wallet were on the footlocker, next to a copy of *Playboy*. The bed, neatly made. Glare prevented any view from the window. Five minutes of that and nothing else, black and white and gray. All static and it forces you to observe the details, the ashtray on the footlocker, the fatigues on the chair, the books under the bed, the M-16 leaning against the wall. A paperback book on the bed, the cover down so you can't read the title. A photograph in a frame, facing away from the camera so you can't see who or what it is. A radio on the floor, its antenna awry. That is what he sends me instead of letters. Two films a month, every month."

In the silence that followed, Marina reached across the table and touched her hand.

Sheila seemed not to notice. She said, "We heard you down here, talking about me. Talking about Marsha. Marsha's death, my work."

"You were arguing," Helen Carney said to her husband. She was twisting a napkin in her hands. "We heard all of it. We could hear the arguments in the sitting room upstairs. Why, Teddy? Why tonight? Is the war all we have? Can't we get through one evening—"

"No," Teddy said.

"Mundelein and I were not as close as you seem to think we were, Teddy. But at any event. I should be able to interpret all this, shouldn't I? That's my job. I assemble our psychological profiles," Sheila said. "Ho's, Giap's, Gromyko's, Castro's, maybe even yours, Piatt; though I doubt it. My department has nothing to do with the domestic side, at least not formally. It's a brand-new field and we've made great progress over the years, there are more swamis at Langley than there are at Johns Hopkins and better ones too, I'll bet. Many of them are emigrés and it takes time for them to become accustomed to the American environment—the special ways in which we grow to maturity. But they're drenched in Vienna and top-notch when it comes to their own kind. Of course there's a problem with the translations, literally and figuratively, and that's where I come in. That's my own special expertise. We have the characteristics on file and can put together a profile in under twelve hours. We have them graded according to importance and there are a number of men—almost all of them are men, by the way—who are constantly being updated, a kind of running Dow of the psyche."

Sam smiled at her, "Last I heard, you were in weapons." He turned to the others. "She can field-strip a weapon faster than I can. Or used to be able to."

"I still can," she said. "It's a skill you never lose. It's like riding a bicycle."

"I think that'll do now, Sheila," Max said.

"I was a jack-of-all-trades at Langley," she said. "It was a logical step from weapons to computers. The work now is done by computers, mostly. Stress. We try to predict how they'll behave under stress of various kinds. It's a new and exciting field, and the Director has done wonders with the funding. You'd be surprised to know we even feed in some astrological data—yes, astrology. And why not? Its provenance is respectable, even eminent. Copernicus, Descartes, Yeats, and closer to our own time and space Nguyen Cao Ky. Thieu, too. Even Ho. Once we tried to buy Ky's astrologer, but in the end we could only rent him for an afternoon. His utility was dubious, though he followed our every instruction." She took a long swallow of the cognac. "So I don't have anything to do with weapons anymore, alas. I work with stress. Strained effort, pressure, and forced choice. Cause and effect. How much doctrine, how much psychology, how much hunch, how many stars, and who pays. What were Uncle Ho's relations with Mom? Dad? Was there a sibling rivalry?

117

What is his number? Ky's was 113, but there seems to be some confusion about Ho's birthdate, so we're insecure in that area. So it's rarefied atmospheres and their effect on the people who live and work in them. And the soul of it always comes back to my old classmate at Ethical, the foundering vessel, and who gets pitched over the side. The lady or the Rubens, and the choice between our past and ourselves.

"*Comprenez*, Sam?"

Sam nodded. The French was meant ironically, a private joke, a reminder of her former husband, the bomber pilot with the forty-mission-man hat and the boyish smile, the father of her son the SEAL. He was a war hero at twenty-two and again at twenty-eight, the big war a tremendous thing, the little one an anticlimax. To Johnnie Dennehay nothing was impossible and no reward was excessive. He felt he was entitled to everything he could get, so in the fifties he went to work for an aircraft manufacturer, and like anyone who discovers a fine secret went from success to success, and finally married a French woman.

Now Sam watched Sheila turn inward, her glance falling again and again on the Kodacolor beside her plate. She took another long swallow of cognac and did not seem to hear Piatt and Marina as they made their good-byes. Piatt said, "If you'll give me Taylor's address, I'll write to him. We both will, Marina and I."

"His father sends him tapes," Sheila said.

Piatt said quietly, "He'll be fine."

Piatt smiled but Sheila did not smile back. Instead, she spoke harshly. "I didn't hear your voice when Sam was telling everyone how they were going to win the war. And his interview at the White House, how spaced-out the President was. I thought you'd have something to say about that, some small comment from your vantage point inside the House of Fools." She said, "All those booming voices, artillery traveling at the speed of sound. Not yours. Why?"

"I leave the war to the generals, Sheila."

"Spoken like a sergeant," she said. "On second thought, more like a captain bucking for major." She paused. "You know the data, you've seen enough of them. Enough to venture an opinion, you're in daily touch with those who make and follow opinion." Her speech was beginning to slur. Suddenly she smiled, speaking to Piatt alone. "As a Representative, Piatt, what would you say?"

"I'd say it's late," he said. He thought she was nearing the edge, some edge, although her voice retained its wry timbre. "It's late, we're all tired."

"We're all *friends*, here in Shakerville." She would not let it go. "Give us the benefit of your opinion. All those classified documents, and the closed hearings. The war, Piatt. From your position on the Hill. What are you telling the folks back home on the prairie? Are you being optimistically cautious? Or cautiously optimistic?"

"Yes, Piatt," Marina said, her voice like flint. "You can talk here, it's secure. Teddy's house. It's no different than your office. How do you see it, darling? Tell the lady." Piatt turned away from her voice, the words and her tone so familiar. This was an extension of an argument begun months—or was it years now—before. Of course their son was at its root. Piatt looked at his wife, allied now with Sheila Dennehay.

He said nothing.

"Poor Shakerville," Sheila said in her drawing room voice. "Poor, poor Shakerville, tired of the war, exhausted with the war, fighting it all day in the office and then again at home, and even out at someone else's house. Stuffing ourselves on it, we're fat as geese with reports from the war. Force-fed geese. But we're patient people, aren't we? We won't give up, we're tenacious. And he who is tired of the war is tired of life, right, Piatt? Sam? Max?" She did not wait for an answer but plunged on. "What's Tommy doing?" she demanded.

"He's at St. Alban's," Piatt said.

"Too young for it, what a pity."

"Yes, Sheila."

"Is he still playing the guitar?"

"All day long," Marina said.

119

"What will he do when the draft notice comes?"

"He'll go to Canada," Marina said.

He would not go to Canada, Piatt thought.

"And I'll support him," she added.

He hated arguing with her, and they argued all the time now. They talked about the war in the evenings, he and Marina and Tommy in the study. During these conversations the boy said very little, half listening to them as he plucked away at his guitar. Marina thought it was time that Piatt broke with the moderates and stated his opposition clearly and without equivocation. "Breaking with the moderates": for a year or more their conversation was conducted in the language of the headline,

CONGRESSMAN WARDEN
BREAKS WITH MODERATES,
DENOUNCES "FUTILE WAR"

He wanted it to go away. He didn't know a politician in Washington who didn't want it to go away, disappear somewhere like a forgotten nightmare. He only half believed his own defense: You cannot be a ranking member of the House Armed Services Committee if you are not in the House! His heartland district would never tolerate a politician who refused to support the men in uniform. In the heartland that was the act of a traitor. And that was precisely the way they would see it, giving aid and comfort to the Communist enemy. What he could, and did, "get away with" was an occasional negative vote on a specific defense appropriation bill. This was a vote that could be explained, or excused, on other grounds. It was not enough, or it put money into the wrong hands. Of course there was also his effectiveness inside the committee, those quiet afternoon sessions, all of them sitting around the table taking testimony behind closed doors. He was better briefed than any of them, his questions more persistent and sharper. If he thought for one single minute that by standing in the well of the House and denouncing the war he could bring it to an end, he would. But it wouldn't end. It would mean one less liberal in Congress, come the next election, and that was all it would mean. He wasn't running from the 17th Congressional District in New York or from Cambridge, Massachusetts, he was running from the heart of Illinois. At this point in the conversation Tommy always looked up and stared at Piatt coolly, a long cool stare.

He worked behind closed doors and there was no way an outsider could judge his effectiveness. This scheme aborted, a weapons system scaled down, an appointment reconsidered; questions to the men in charge from one who knew their business as well as they did, better in some instances because Piatt had access to the second and third echelons of the Department of Defense. This was not work that made headlines. All of it was behind the scenes, you could call it sleight-of-hand; that was where the useful work was done, among colleagues who trusted each other. A witness could come clean and you'd work it out, no embarrassment to anyone; they all worked for the same government, after all. But at the end of the session there would be money enough for one wing of aircraft, not two, or two aircraft carriers, not three.

Piatt yearned to go see for himself, a first-hand look, such as Sam Joyce had. He wanted to see what the firebases looked like. He wanted to see an airstrike. They came by with their acronyms and children's slang, RevDev, MACV, Ruff-Puff, PF, Willie Peter, AO, TO&E, Huey, Loach, CAS, CORDS, OCO, GVN, USAID, JUSPAO, ARVN, AIR, ARTY, Little Tigers, Lurps, MIA, WIA, KIA. And a hundred more, all abstractions. But he thought somehow that he ought to keep it at a distance, he had known too many who had traveled to the Zone and become infatuated with it; they were the ones who had a return ticket. He was not immune to their kind of show, the brisk briefings and the casual interviews with those in the field. Give them a day's warning and they'd whistle up a constituent or two, and an army soundman to record an interview and relay it back to the radio station in your constituency, all free of charge. The tours to the hospitals and the pacified villages, then an evening around the bar at the Continental Palace Hotel with the reporters, so cheerful and cynical in their belief that the war could not be won—but somehow had to be fought nonetheless. But then, they too had return tickets.

He did not want to be a party to that. He believed something that he could hardly explain, even to himself. He thought it was a tragedy that would have to be played out, in the sense that water always seeks its own level. In some ultimate sense, there was no one at the controls. The war ran on its own motion. Meanwhile, they would all have blood on their hands; all of them would be drenched in blood. But the thing would not be stopped, because to stop it, simply to end it, would be to repudiate too much. Too many words to eat, too many unforeseen consequences, too much shame, too many unrequited dead. So the war was a force of nature, a wand of the gods. . . . We have all become Orientals after all, he thought, little Buddhas in our search for virtue, and to be at harmony with the universe. It made us terrified—literally filled with terror—to *act*.

Once a month a delegation arrived at his office. There were always two or three university professors or administrators in the delegation, mathematicians, linguists, historians, physicists, and chemists, some of the most eminent in North America. There were always a few men he knew in each delegation, scholars whose advice he sought and who often testified before his other committee. They would ask for him—his signature on a resolution, his promise of support on the floor of the full House—and he would refuse. He gave them the same arguments that he gave his wife, though he reserved his wand-of-the-gods conceit; that was private. They didn't accept them any more than she did. One of them said to him, You are playing a beautiful violin while your people destroy a society. Your music's very pretty, you play a smart fiddle, but it's quite beside the point at this time—don't you think? Irrelevant to the matter at hand? With conditions the way they are? There were 295 KIA last week, and those are just the Americans. Double the figure, triple it, for the civilians. Isn't it time to take a stand, Congressman? Someone has to.

No, he didn't think.

We have supported you in the past, with money and votes.

Thank you for coming by. Come by again.

He was a Congressman representing a particular constituency. That was what he was, had been for ten years and hoped to be for another ten or twenty. They were good people in his district, solid citizens; they were as good people as the country had. Maybe they were better than their government, maybe not. But they required some faith, and they were not to be toyed with; they were people who stayed the course, and expected those whom they elected to stay the course, too. He was a shrewd legislator, an insider; an insider's insider, rated as one of the ten or fifteen most effective legislators in the House. Rarely made a speech, never called a press conference. If Dr. Delft felt so strongly about it, why didn't he encourage his university to refuse the government grants? Did he know that his language department was now teaching several arcane Asian tongues and that the money came from Langley? Why didn't *he* resign in protest, and find another line of work. Piatt loved the House, had always loved it; in an abstract way, he loved his constituents, too. Not made of sugar candy, not them and not him. Perhaps there would come a time when he would want the Senate, its easier work load and its perquisites; and from there, who knew? But that time was not yet.

So he was weary in mind and spirit, he thought, his patience running thin. How much thinner, he wondered, than the lad with the M-16 on the line at Pleiku. Or Sam Joyce, with his practical knowledge of fire and maneuver, and his habit of command. Sam Joyce, who seemed to have no life beyond his profession . . . A simple life, he thought; Sam Joyce had only to believe his eyes and ears, tested against his experience. He, Piatt, lived in a world of shadows and conflicting testimony, and unreliable mirrors. Against this he must fight. He had to fight against the idea that the war was lost, the dream become nightmare, the war and the nation one, a ghastly whirlpool in which all of them were turning.

Finally, late one night a year ago, having fought with Marina since dinner, he could not resist the invidious comparison. He began mildly enough, a straightforward defense of the doctrine of the separation of powers and the ways in which the American system rejected absolutism. The civics books were not wrong, it was a government of accommodation, of checks and balances and continual tension. Then, "You don't like me and my compromises," he said. "My principles. What about Sam Joyce? He's killing them, has been killing them since it began. How many tours has he had now? Four? Five? He can't stay away, he's a drunk in a liquor store. He lives over there, it's his chosen work. He doesn't have to do it, as a matter of fact they'd like him back here. They'd like him to do some liaison work for them on the Hill, he's damn good at that; he's got all those badges and he's his old man's son. So what about him? If I'm a coward, what does that make him? A hero? *He's over there doing it.*" She had said nothing during this, but her eyes never left his face. Her serenity maddened him. "Wonderful Sam," he said bitterly, "the Senator's son. Colonel Sam, the killer. Darling Sam, your great friend. Loyal Sam, my old campmate. What do you say about him?"

She said, "He doesn't apologize for what he's doing."

"Is that what it is, then?" he'd shouted. "His state of mind? Or his public relations? He's a *sincere* killer?"

Her eyes never wavered. "I hate this war," she said. "I hate those who began it and those who prolong it and those who hide behind." She hesitated, and the words were out. "Their own careers, their ambition, and their fear. Who fear this city more than any other single thing. Washington is a city of fear, and you're part of it now. At least Sam Joyce isn't afraid."

He said, "God damn you." But there was something else behind her words, a thing he didn't want to look at or hear about.

"And he's not in hiding, in the Pentagon or anywhere else."

Piatt said, "Forget him a minute."

But she refused to let it go. She said, "You brought him up."

"All *right*," he said, furious now. "I'll bring you some photographs, I have them in my office. They came in a plain envelope the other day. Photographs of severed heads and a bagful of ears, arranged on a plate like figs. Sport for the soldierboys."

She said evenly, "Was Sam in the picture?"

"It's the sort of thing they do, everyone knows that, the place is a charnel house—"

She said, "So it doesn't have anything to do with Sam Joyce, does it?"

He said nothing for a moment.

"*Does it?*"

He stood then, looming over her. She did not move and her eyes were still on his face. He said, "How comfortable it must be on the sidelines."

"No," she said. "You're wrong about that. You're so wrong. It's not comfortable at all. It's the worst place there is."

He opened his mouth to say something else, then didn't. He knew then that the reason she wanted the war to end was that Sam Joyce could then come home. They sat staring at each other for a very long time, and at length he went to bed alone, leaving her sitting in the study; he had an early hearing, and he refused to have this interfere with that.

Piatt stood his ground now, silently facing Sheila Dennehay. In his mind he heard all their arguments, that one and the others; so many of them. He said, "We are all tired of the war." He felt Marina's eyes on him, and the presence of Sam Joyce across the table.

"He's good at it, isn't he?" Sheila said.

Marina said, "Yes, Sheila." Uneasily.

"Plays a nice tune," Sheila said. "I've heard that. I've heard he has a talent."

"Yes," Marina said.

"Does he talk to you about the war, Marina?"

"Not often," Marina said.

"This war will have to end," Piatt said. "All wars do. This one will."

"Don't count on it," Sheila said. "That's what I thought, too. I thought that nothing was forever, not even this war. Now I'm not so sure." She picked up one of Sam's crumpled napkins and dropped it, looking around the table, eyes widening, her irises brilliant in the candlelight.

Max Cather said, "What about you, Sam? Do you count on it?" He did not wait for an answer but turned at once to Piatt.

"So go ahead and tell us what he said, Piatt." Max Cather drew the cognac bottle toward him slowly, as if it were an anchor. He began refilling glasses. "How did he put it? What did he want? And did you find it easy to refuse?"

"Piatt never refuses anything," Marina said. She looked at her husband and they sat down together.

Max said, "Be quiet a minute, Marina."

"It is not my frame of mind to be quiet."

Cather said, "Did you see Mundelein?"

"This isn't the time," Piatt said. Suddenly he began to enjoy himself.

Marina looked into his eyes. "What's this about?"

Teddy Carney said, "Go ahead, Congressman."

Sam Joyce sat quietly, watching Marina watch Piatt, finally turning away. This was one more twist to Piatt's life of which she was unaware. It made her both embarrassed and angry, not for the first time and not for the last. But it was one of the conditions of their life together. It was what he had taken back at the end of their tortured negotiations. He never admitted it but it was what he had done, deciding at last that she couldn't be trusted. Really, he wanted to punish her without seeming to. At any rate he kept his public life to himself. He behaved with his public life as Sam behaved with his private life, and of course for similar reasons.

"No harm done," Max said. "No point in not closing the circle, putting a comma at the end of the clause . . . " Max drummed his fingers on the table *thumpthumpthump*. He was getting his own back now, though Piatt was expressionless listening to him. "He doesn't like to talk much, our Piatt doesn't. He's the soul of discretion. But he likes to listen." Cather was addressing the table now. "He's an expert in other people's opinions, isn't that right? Of course our government is not compulsive and in our milieu Piatt's worth his weight in gems. He's a star sapphire. Depend on Piatt for the straight story and absolute discretion. So fluent, he'll make your case better than you can. I've watched him in committee, he's a wizard. And you'll never hear anyone at my place ask, What's Piatt Warden think about the damned war? He's a man who sticks to his specialty. I'd call it indifference, except I know him too well. It's a talent like any other, golf or steeplechasing or conjuring or poetry. The rest of us have to gather the facts, and then choose among them. We have to choose, and then we have to act. Select one fact, discard another, with only one goal in mind: *What do we know that will help us right now?* That's the essence of intelligence, an unweighed fact is worse than no fact at all—because it can mislead. That's all government is, choosing. If astrology is helpful, we use it. If Hoover is helpful, we use him. And if a Congressional committee is helpful, we use that. And it doesn't have anything to do with whether or not you've got a kid over there, or whether those closest to it are ineffective advocates. This is the government! We run it! Every four years the people have a say but inbetweentimes it's our show, we own it lock, stock, and barrel. They're all our kids, 'our boys,' " he said, mimicking the President. "Each and every one, good boys. Citizens serving the nation. Go visit Walter Reed sometime, the burn ward. Don't always believe that it's better to live than to die. But all of this is by the way, so far as we're concerned. Ten boys in the burn ward, a thousand. It's all the same to us, it's either worth doing or not worth doing. And if it's worth doing, there are those who're going to get hurt. And that doesn't have anything to do with whether or not it's right. War's one long tedious argument, and it doesn't matter in the last analysis which side of it we're on. That's not our business, yours and mine. When you read the casualty lists, understand that these *are* ours, dead, wounded, missing, insane some of them, the casualties, American boys in service to a cause, the Cold War, one I happen to think's worth fighting—"

"Shut up, Max," Piatt said softly. He moved close to Sheila Dennehay, who sat with her hands in her lap, helpless, tears running down her face.

She looked across the table at Sam. "It's all right, it happens all the time." She picked up the Kodacolor of her son and pitched it into the middle of the table. It struck the candelabrum and landed somewhere in the Central Highlands. "For God's sake, let Piatt tell about it. I suppose you mean his conversation with Pat Mundelein. Let's listen. I'm sure it's valuable information we can't do without. I've always been simply fascinated by Mundelein," she said, continuing to cry.

Sam reached across the table to touch her hand, but she pulled away. She was looking at Piatt, challenging him. He had kept that conversation to himself, as he had kept so much to himself. That was the way it was done. An inside man, he could live in no other way. It was the way he was brought up to live, the most valuable work was always done in the shadows. That was the way things happened: a wire pulled, a word in a man's ear, a favor given for one received—all of it inconspicuous. He was so ambitious, and he had studied the milieu of the House with the care of a devoted scholar.

"Mundelein," Cather said.

"Go ahead, Piatt," Marina murmured.

Now he felt Marina's hurt, and as suddenly her dismay and anger. Her anger, Sheila's contempt, Cather's sarcasm, his own frustration—and in the background, Carney's internal tape recorder whirring away. And on the other side of the table, Sam Joyce silent as stone. To hell with them. He wanted to say that it was simple, no mysteries. When Mundelein issued his cheerful summons, Piatt complied. Of course he had. Who wouldn't? When the White House spoke, you were obliged to listen. And Mundelein was one of the best, an acquaintance of many years' standing, and if he had an idea it was worth considering. Except that it wasn't simple at all, nothing was simple in Washington that year.

Mundelein was on the telephone to Piatt the day after Sam Joyce's briefing. He and the President wanted the benefit of Piatt's thinking. He listened to the initial expression of surprise, then brushed the implied objections aside. Tomorrow, he said. And while they were at it they might as well have some enjoyment so if it was agreeable to Piatt they'd leave the next morning at five.

Piatt was half asleep when the adviser arrived in his black Mercury. He loaded his gear into the trunk and climbed in. Mundelein gave elaborate instructions to the driver, then excused himself, turning on the reading light and opening a briefcase. The adviser offered Piatt the morning paper and a cup of coffee from the car's thermos, then bent to his work.

"This shouldn't take more than thirty minutes," Mundelein said as he scribbled on a notepad.

"Take your time."

"Anything interesting in the paper?" Mundelein asked without looking up.

"No," Piatt said. One of Jessel's interviews was displayed on Page One. This was an unidentified colonel, who by the sound of him was at the end of the line. No question, Jessel had an ear for disillusion. "The war is common property," the Colonel said— or was caused to say, with Jessel you never knew—"it belongs to all of us, Vietnamese and Americans, Republicans and Communists. It is bigger than we are and eventually God will decide who will win it. The winners will remain and the losers will be exiled. God will decide, and He will look on all of us with pity. Neither side expected the great magnitude and duration of this war, nor the fact that the cause of the war has ceased before the conflict itself. Who can say what the cause is? That the North invaded the South? That we encouraged the South for our own ends? They are here, and they are all Vietnamese. We are all Vietnamese now." Piatt heard an echo, Lincoln's second inaugural. He wondered if it was conscious or unconscious and decided the former, nothing was ever accidental in a Jessel interview.

They drove for thirty minutes when suddenly the adviser looked up. "Bridge," he said and leaned forward to tap the driver on the shoulder. He glanced behind him, making certain that no cars were following, then said to the driver, "Stop here." They were at the apogee of the great arc of the Chesapeake Bay Bridge. A stiff wind swept across it, rocking the car a little. Both men were silent, bent forward as Mundelein rolled down his window. The adviser listened, smiling. Then he nudged Piatt, "Hear them?" In the distance they heard geese barking, the sound mingled with the wind and part of it. They floated in immense rafts, chattering. Small, scattered flights of ducks moving swiftly in the wind. "What a sound," Mundelein said. "Okay, let's get moving. It's only about forty-five minutes to first light, and we can't miss that." He looked at his watch and frowned.

"Feel that wind?"

"Cold as a bastard," Mundelein agreed happily. "I've just got a few minutes more with this stuff," he said, apologizing and relighting the reading lamp. He leaned forward and told the driver to *move it*, they were five minutes behind schedule. As the Mercury picked up speed, Piatt sat back in the cushions and lit a cigarette. He turned to look at the adviser, bent over his yellow legal pad. He was heavy, his belly strained against the waist of his rubber waders. He had jowls that hung like huge commas beneath an invisible jawbone, punctuation marks to his taut face. Piatt watched him run his hand through his hair, which was cut short and razored in the rear. It was almost a crew cut and gave him the look of an overage, overweight cadet. He had a nose that on a woman would have been called pert but on him was merely small. A familiar face, a Washingtonian

would know it without necessarily knowing the name that went
with it.

   Piatt had been one of those who bought long in Pat Mundelein, knowing his stock would rise. He was what Dennis McDonough would have been if Dennis had lived. Cather thought him
dangerous, Sam Joyce thought him a neurotic. To Teddy Carney he was a "source," neither more nor less. They were all
inside men, but Mundelein's position was the most precarious.
He served men instead of organizations. He had worked for the
chairman of the National Committee, then for a Senate committee as assistant counsel, then as adviser to the dead President,
who in the education of a generation of advisers was Yale and
Harvard. He remained the great enigma of the city, the first
President since Lincoln to inspire public legends—myths, as
Mundelein defined them, fictitious narratives. It would be decades before the historians located him definitely, and when they
did it would be in the light of the following decade. His own
time was lit not by the past but by the future. And irrelevant to
Washingtonians of a certain age, for his example would flicker
always in the memories of those who lived in the capital at the
time of his administration. That was what Mundelein believed,
while freely conceding that analysis of one's childhood changes
the memory of that childhood.
   Alone of the people Piatt knew, Marina had resisted the allure
of that time, and had never been beguiled or undone. Infinitely
more interesting were those on the margins, so eager to be led, so
eager to believe and be of use. So eager to accommodate—does it
not follow (she insisted) that the trouble was not him, it was
you? All of us, she confessed finally, because it was her neighborhood as well. Laughing: We didn't know it at the time but we
rejected Grandpa for Dad. A rakish, devil-may-care Dad. A
randy, cheerful, cynical Dad. Really, not a father at all, she
amended, but a stepfather. He married Mother for her money,
but Mother didn't care. She was happy to give him her fortune,
she was having such a good time and he wanted it so.
   Piatt put these thoughts to Mundelein, his friend at the fac-

tory. Mundelein said he was attracted to the President because of his cynicism and absence of conventional ethics. It was not so much what he had but what he didn't have, and the subtlety with which he carried it. In an old Republican it would have been unforgivable but in a young Democrat it was charming. One trusted the Man's instincts. He was a rarity among professional politicians, a man who seemed to have a life beyond politics. He could as easily have been an actor, sportsman, banker, or criminal. Did he not represent our civilization, refined beyond the point of attitudes? Mundelein smiled as he said that, correctly guessing that Piatt would miss the inversion of Eliot's remark about Boston. Mundelein said he admired the President's emotional frigidity, meaning his unshakable confidence that the reality of life was more agreeable than its dreams, meaning its promises.

He stripped the world clean, Mundelein said, leaving only the bones and offal. He was the United States in its maturity, no longer trusting in God or the two oceans to protect it. A leader on the full-sized European model, transitory, fatalistic, conscious of history and its limits—what was history but a recognition of limits?—and unconcerned with virtue. The world seen with a half-smile and often described with foreboding, as a long twilight struggle with the forces of reformation. In retrospect it was not surprising that this attitude evoked the people's love. The postwar era had finally arrived, new-minted, bright and shiny as a copper penny or a pair of brass knuckles.

Pat Mundelein was a survivor of those years, a man with a career to consider. After the murder, he moved to the State Department, writing speeches for the Secretary. For a time, his thoughts focused on the interruption. He thought of it as that, an interference with history. What if? What if this? What if that? *What would he have done about Indochina?* This Man was not a Man reluctant to cut his losses. Still, the signals were not encouraging; his advisers loved him and emulated him and sought to serve him well. They sought to demonstrate a mastery of events, and as they believed in the war with their whole hearts they could not sanction retreat. They had not inherited the family business in order to liquidate it! After the murder Mundelein read the report with the greatest care, accepting the verdict without truly believing it. He thought it a judgment absolutely necessary to accept, the alternative being too grotesque; the alternative was a horror story written by some dark European radical, a noisy determinist view of existence. Unnamed "interests" employing agents provocateurs. Altogether too weird in its implications. However, it was necessary to acquiesce to the official verdict: a solitary deed, one man "acting alone." An American explanation, though one the Man himself would never have accepted; he would have laughed them out of the room. If this is the best Hoover's gumshoes can do! Hah! Get me MI-5. Get Bond! Mundelein poked and prodded at the underbelly; it yielded to his slightest touch, no resistance anywhere. He never found the spine of it. He had been taught in high school that Princip the anarchist had caused World War I and, far from being comforted, wondered, Was the world so fragile that one man could send it spinning into apocalypse? Ten million dead and a culture destroyed by one man and a gun? And in America how much worse to believe in a conspiracy, a group of men acting together—and by that one profound deed, the metamorphosis of a generation. In the Middle Ages kings and princes were slaughtered wholesale and the world went on as before. Insecurity was now endemic, Mundelein thought, with America the critical mass. Americans believed in chance, a roll of the dice, the mystery of the western frontier, a brighter day . . .

His interest at last waned, slipping away. The administration that he had served with devotion for three years became an episode, contemporary history that one had been privileged to observe first-hand. One day it was in his mind, the next day it wasn't. He was startled one afternoon to discover that he'd not thought of the Thousand Days in a week or more. It was like forgetting about a woman you'd loved deeply. Now you see her, now you don't; a shadow vanished, and became a memory of a memory.

He said, No doubt a mark of middle age.

Piatt said, Come off it.

Mundelein said, I was at that age. It was behind me. I had the memory but it no longer mattered. I was no longer preoccupied with its quality, whether it was a sad or happy memory or whether he was a virtuous or dissolute man. Whether he was good or bad for us. It simply was, this memory. It did not seem to me that a truly malignant figure could evoke so much grief among so many disparate peoples. The experience came back into a kind of balance, so like the others I decided to write a book about it.

He had an outline and a publisher. Then he gave it up. The truth was, he had nothing new to add. He gave his papers to a library and consented to an interview for the Oral History section. The interviewer was a graduate student who asked impertinent questions and then offered to go to bed with him. A year later it did not seem real, his three years in the White House. He felt his memory go out of synch, as if he were a character in some dense and complicated fiction. Later, returning to the West Wing to work for another Man—that was what he did now, advise Men—it was as if he'd never been there before. The Man had changed, the house had changed, he had changed—and after the initial exclamation of astonishment, scrupulously recorded in his diary, there was nothing more to be said about it. Now he kept no personal diary and his confidential notes were filed in the office safe. His telephone calls were taped and sent to the White House archives. He intended to take none of this material with him when he left. If he ever did leave. He was as close to a professional adviser as there was in the American government; he thought of himself as a field grade infantry officer who served a commander in chief, and it did not matter who that commander in chief was. He intended to remain in the White House or close to it for what remained of his working life. The identity of the occupant was not important, he said.

He said to Piatt, As for my ideas and theories about the Man, I wouldn't pay too much attention to them. That period, I'm an unreliable narrator of it.

This was late at night at a party. Marina had gone home. Mundelein kept glancing at the telephone as if he expected a summons. At last he relaxed and began to talk about Washington, his Washington; he loved it as any Southerner loves his birthplace. A layered civilization, each administration building upon the last. "There's a lawyer in the Labor Department who joined the civil service in the last year of the Coolidge administration. Intended to stay for a few years but never went back home. None of us does. When he retires we're going to give him a party. Nice old guy. I talked to him the other day and asked him what he remembered best and he said it wasn't any one thing but the whole thing. He loves the seasons, the suddenness of the summers and the unpredictability of winters. The incapacity of the city to handle snow, or heavy rains, or Republicans. Good gray bureaucrat, he'd stay there forever if we let him . . . "

Sheila Dennehay joined them and Piatt introduced her. Mundelein scarcely paused in his homage to the capital, though his eyes were on her now. To him, the seasons were only a distraction. The city's weather was determined by the news. Nature made no claim upon it, except the inconvenience of clogged traffic or the stink of the Potomac in August. As a city, Washington was benign and almost tepid. It was possible to lead a private life, he said. Difficult but possible. Wouldn't you agree, he asked Sheila Dennehay.

She nodded, amused.

Mundelein said he kept himself remote from private citizens and journalism, believing that his advice to his principal client should be disinterested. I have to know what's going on, but that's different from being involved in it. I try not to let it bear too much. We are removed from the news because we are the news.

Neat trick, she said. Separating the poem from the poet.

The only way, the adviser said.

No, she objected. One way.

But isn't it true, the adviser said. The life is one thing, the poem another. The poem is what matters, isn't that right? The rest is just publicity. The life can be happy or sad, magnanimous or mean, but the poem is what counts. That's what goes into the books, not the interviews. It is a separate thing. The life isn't important. The work is important. Results are important. Publicity is a distraction.

Sheila looked at him slyly, with just a suggestion of triumph. She put her hand on his shoulder, the politician's ancient gesture of affection and complicity. Why? she asked. *Why?* If you're proud of who you are and what you've done.

They left the car and driver under the porte cochere of the big house and walked the quarter-mile through cornfields to the blind. The decoys were in bags beside the blind. Piatt Warden and Pat Mundelein walked slowly over the frozen fields, their waders squeaking. The adviser carried his shotgun and a musette bag with two thermoses, one with coffee and the other with a special mixture of hot tomato juice and bouillon laced with vodka, that to be consumed when the shooting was done. It was still dark with just one streak of gray on the horizon. The wind was dying but the clouds were low and moving, and from time to time a snowflake skidded past their faces. As they approached the blind the cries of the geese grew louder and more insistent. The birds were beginning to move now, restless and noisy as a stadium crowd before a game. The sky seemed to lighten with each step they took, the gray streak widening like the opening of an eyelid. It was a hard flat light from no visible source, its origins as mysterious as its physics.

The blind was well built and large enough for four men. It was thatched front and back with straw and fir boughs; fresh straw, dark wood, it was a very old blind. They stowed the guns and canvas bag on the slatted bench and each took two sacks of decoys, wading into the shallow water to place them. They worked quietly, not speaking, careful that each decoy swung free and did not touch its neighbor. Mundelein took the heavy geese decoys himself, laying them in two prudent lines at an oblique angle to the blind. There were about ten geese in all. Piatt, working to the left of the blind, bunched his ducks in a rough arrowhead. This was cold work. The wind blew into their faces and slightly from right to left, ideal conditions. It was obvious that the two men had different ways of doing things, and if either of them had been impolite enough to call attention to this it would have been a very long morning. Piatt contented himself with a raised eyebrow, unseen by the adviser. Pat Mundelein muttered Oh shit under his breath. Either you placed them in lines or you bunched them, you didn't do both. And any idiot knew that you didn't *bunch* decoys. You arranged them in lines, clean alluring lines, parallel lines as in nature. That was the way a migratory bird perceived its environment. Piatt took the opposite view. He had been bunching ducks for almost thirty years and had seldom failed to get his limit, on the Mississippi, the Rock, or any other river, even the Choptank. It was necessary to bunch them up, disorderly as nature herself. Where the Christ did Mundelein think he was? The Museum of Modern Art?

"Looks fine, those rigs," Mundelein said when they were both in the blind again. They loaded their guns and nodded that it was time. They were both gunners who took elaborate notice of the rules. Never commence before dawn, never linger after sundown, never sugar the blind, never exceed your limit. Mundelein proposed that Piatt take whatever came from the right and he would take those from the left, or the second shot from the right, and vice versa. Most of the passing shots would be from the right, birds flying out of the wind to reconnoiter the decoys.

Hunkered down, they waited. Mundelein described the provenance of the blind. It belonged to the current ambassador to Poland, an old friend of the secretary of state. The secretary held the keys to the blind, and they had done him more good than anything else he held. The secretary used it as patronage with the full knowledge and approval of the ambassador. In this town a good blind's worth its weight in gold, Mundelein said, as if he were telling Piatt something he didn't already know; a weapons manufacturer he knew had a place on the Wye that resembled the Gritti Palace. Of course for a weekend house party, Mundelein continued, the houses go with it. Eight bedrooms in all, guest house, swimming pool, tennis court, putting green. Last time they'd been in Poland together, he and the ambassador, they'd shot the marshes with the minister of agriculture and a gorilla named Druz, who happened to be a major general in the Polish army. Shot in the afternoon following a two-hour lunch with a glass of vodka every five minutes, lucky we didn't shoot each other instead of the ducks. Bagged twenty-five each that afternoon and it could've been a hundred and twenty-five, it was like Stuttgart in the days when Orville Faubus was governor. Still, he had no hesitation recommending the marshes of Pomerania.

"I don't know if you can call it sport," Mundelein said. "But anything to improve relations with the Captive Nations."

Piatt said, "Mark." Five ducks, redheads, were reconnoitering. The two men hunched down even farther, only the tops of their gun barrels showing now above the reeds. "They're moving in," Piatt said. Fast, they were very fast birds and in range almost before he knew it. He shot once and missed, then the birds flared and were gone. There was no chance for a second shot.

"The damned wind," Piatt said.

"We'll get others," Mundelein said easily, then resumed his story about duck hunting in Poland. The party officials had access to the marshes, and ammunition, otherwise in short supply in the People's Republic. "I'll tell you something, though. Druz, who was at that time the commander of the Pomeranian Military District, was one hell of a fine shot. Had with him a set of matched Churchills and a gun case of leather as soft as your granddaughter's ass. Bloody thing could've been made by Guzzi and probably was. Minister of agriculture so nervous he could hardly get his gun to his shoulder he was so busy looking over it. Druz clanking along in his medals—he shot in full uniform—the damned Guzzi gun case slung over his shoulder like a quiver and during the five-second lulls he took the trouble to describe the iron. Polonia Restituta, Cross of Grunwald, and the other badges they give to their all-time favorites. But the ambassador and I were fascinated by the minister. Know what he was shooting? An old Ithaca. We wondered where he got it—"

"Mark," Piatt said.

"—probably from a Sears catalog in '39. *Early* '39. Nice flight," Mundelein said.

There were a dozen or so, high, turning to look at the rig. They began to drop in twos, looking at the decoys. They came around once, seemed to settle, then flared nervously. Nervous suburban women visiting an unfamiliar city street, scrutinizing the doorways, clutching their purses. The two men were motionless but the birds knew that something was not quite right. They moved out again over the water, suspicious, fighting the wind and watching, then returning, circling in tight loops, closer; they were mallards, big ducks, and experienced. Fifty yards out they began to drop, setting their wings into the wind, and coming in big as umbrellas. They looked at the geese but came in over the ducks and when the leader was a yard off the water Piatt rose and fired. One down. Then he and Mundelein fired together and two more were down, one crippled and thrashing the water. It was Piatt's cripple and he aimed carefully at the disturbance and silenced it with one shot. The others were away now and accelerating, climbing, and calling—but they had three good ones and Piatt waded out to get them.

Lovely birds, so heavy in his hands. And they'd come in over his rig, not Mundelein's. It happened so quickly, the speed and sudden violence and confusion. Piatt was happy with his shots. The first duck dropped like a crumpled pillow, the second flew on a little before her wings folded and she, too, tumbled, cannonballing into the water. Two shots, two birds; it couldn't be any more economical than that. Well, there was the third shot to guarantee the second. Piatt lumbered to the place where the cripple had fallen, the water lapping around his thighs. He took a moment and looked across the bay, so gray and cold. An oyster boat made way slowly a quarter of a mile offshore, disturbing a raft of geese. He tucked the cripple under his left arm, holding the shotgun tight against his body. The other two ducks were in his right hand, one of them twitching slightly. Two drakes and a hen. He squinted across the bay at the oyster boat, white against the gray water and lowering sky. God, it was cold.

"Mark."

Mundelein spoke in a natural voice, neither loud nor soft. Piatt froze, bending, his eyes on the water. He calculated that the bird was behind him, probably moving from right to left. Probably a singleton, no flight would decoy with a man in the water. He did not move and felt his bare right hand cramping around the necks of the two drakes. A decoy floated into his vision. It looked to him absurdly artificial, a plastic manikin in a department store window. He remembered that his gun was loaded, on safe. If Mundelein missed, he might have a shot; if his hand wasn't cramped. He thought, Drop the hen first and then the two drakes, swing left and behind. He thought, Get it over with. His back was to the blind, he could not see Mundelein or the bird. He kept his head down, his eyes fastened on the water twelve inches from his nose, and waited motionless for the explosion. His back began to hurt and he was losing his grip on the drakes. Then Mundelein fired two rapid shots and he raised his head quickly to watch a pair of redheads separate and rise, back of him and to his left. It was a long shot and barely possible but he dropped the ducks in his hands and swung, firing over his left shoulder. He did not waver. There was no sense in a second shot. They were gone, out of range. When he turned back, grinning, Mundelein waved at him, gesturing in front of the blind. He'd killed one after all. So there had been three in the flight. He retrieved the fourth duck, his hand limber now, the cold forgotten.

In the next hour Piatt killed two more ducks and Mundelein killed two, their limit. No geese decoyed. Piatt decided that the adviser was a companionable gunner, though he talked more than necessary. Sport in Poland was followed by an account of sport in Algeria. Together they lamented the disappearance of the canvasback, fleetest and tastiest of all American wild ducks. They told identical stories of the canvasback in the days of their fathers, sunless days on the Eastern Shore and in the upper Midwest where there were no limits at all. You shot until you were tired of shooting and the sky was never empty of canvasbacks. It took a century of unrestricted slaughter to bring them to the edge of extinction. But what an aristocrat, this bird native to North America and found nowhere else. Clocked at seventy miles an hour and flying in its swooning, twisting motion, who could ever believe there would be a last can? It was as prolific as the country itself! One seldom saw them now on the Eastern

Shore, though there were still a few in western Canada that migrated down the Pacific flyway. They were there, but you had to look for them; on the Eastern Shore, they were as rare as panthers.

The wind died and by seven-thirty it was almost warm. They'd finished the coffee and now the adviser brought out the special mixture, pouring it into two silver cups. They unloaded the shotguns and stood with their backs to the bay, talking of gunning, drinking a little, and comparing the various methods of enticement.

Mundelein mentioned tolling. Prohibited now of course, it was a common method of killing canvasbacks. A small dog was sent running up and down the shore, a red or white handkerchief fluttering from its collar. The curiosity of the ducks offshore would be roused and they would swim in, whereupon the gunners concealed in ambush would rise and fire in broadside. This led to a long anecdote involving the CIA station chief in a country, this time unnamed, in Latin America. The station chief was a fastidious sportsman, having grown up on a plantation in Georgia, and was appalled at a shoot arranged for him by the head of the secret police. Bloodthirsty devil, according to the station chief. And afterwards his reports could not be trusted because he hated the regime so, owing to the murderous disregard of wildfowl. Killed almost a thousand in an afternoon, and that was slaughter even by Georgia standards. The station chief had to be replaced, Mundelein said.

Piatt smiled and named the country.

Mundelein grunted, peering at him.

"Just returned from down there. Your man's remembered as a *señorito* without *cojones*."

Mundelein laughed; it was neither confirmation nor denial. "Anyway," he said, "we sent him to Eastern Europe. Maybe he even went to Poland. Last one we had in Poland went soft on the Polish. This one, hell, all we'd have to do is get him out on the Pomeranian marshes with Druz, it'd make his former station in Latam look like a wildlife refuge run by Ralphie Nader."

Piatt laughed.

141

"Not difficult to do," the adviser went on, "those bastards all know each other. One session with Druz and his medals and matched Churchills and the beaters in their knickers and cloth caps—'Good shoot, Your Honor,' they'd say. . . ."

Piatt laughed again, watching a flight cruise overhead and begin to decoy, then flare, seeing the men in the blind and hearing the careless laughter.

"We have a problem," the adviser said, as if it were the logical transition from Druz and the Pomeranian marshes and slaughter in Latin America. Piatt did not reply, watching the birds dip and then settle far out on the water. "We need some help," Mundelein said and then smiled.

Piatt was watching the ducks, far out of range now. The adviser was preparing his interrogation and the Congressman could almost hear the barking of the little dog, and see the lure of the bright red cloth. The gunners were concealed, but he knew where they were.

The adviser mumbled something and Piatt leaned forward, straining to hear.

He said loudly, "We have to give them something!"

Piatt said nothing but nodded in apparent understanding. It was always important in conversations of this kind never to betray ignorance. If they thought you were in any way ignorant they would close up and the flow of information would cease.

"They want something and we have to give it to them."

"Yes," Piatt said.

"It's all screwed up over there, but they've got this idea now. This thing of Cather's." Mundelein sighed. "I don't know how far it's gotten but it's gotten pretty far. The command there, some of the people here. It's hard as hell to say no, you want to give them what they need to do the job." He hesitated, thinking. "There's a man over there everyone seems high on, Henderson. I don't know who he is but I had them pull his file and he looks able, though the files never tell you anything you need to know. It doesn't give me a hell of a lot of confidence that he's the one Jessel interviewed in the morning paper, but I won't hang a man because of goddamned Jessel. Shit. The Man wants to put Sam Joyce in charge."

"Yes," Piatt said.

"It can't be Cather. Goddamned Cather's a maniac."

"A zealot," Piatt agreed.

"How well do you know him?"

"I've known Max for years."

"Not Cather," Mundelein said. "Sam Joyce."

Piatt raised his eyebrows. No, they were not close.

"I thought you knew him well."

Piatt shook his head firmly. "Tell me about Cather's thing."

Mundelein waved his hands helplessly. It was too complicated to go into in detail. It was complicated as hell even in the short form, the ideas got more and more complicated any time Langley was involved. . . . He paused and said nothing for a moment, looking across the bay at the oyster boats returning to the shed at St. Michael's. They were so graceful, rising fore and aft, low in the water, white against the white of the sky. "I could go for an oyster right now," he said. "I like the French oysters better than these, though. The *belons*. The *belons numéro deux*. Henry Costello introduced me to them in Paris when we were there straightening out that mess; Henry knows Paris like the back of his hand. They've got a little metallic taste to them." He slowly lit a cigarette and threw the match into the water. "That's one of the troubles with Cather's idea, there's a metallic taste to it. There's heavy metal all over the place. In the short form," he said, his voice dropping a notch. "Cather wants to put some black boxes along the trails and have them monitored by a special force, volunteers I gather. A special force to collect precise intelligence on how much is getting through, men and materials both. Cather and Cather's people think the problem is one of time and accurate data. That's phase one. Phase two is, he seems to have an idea we can target certain individuals. He thinks if you destroy the heads the body will wither. It's hydra-headed, the Cong." He turned to look at Piatt, who was staring gravely into space. "That's the short form, and the Man likes it."

"Max is smart," Piatt said.

143

"He's got himself a laboratory in Cambridge."

"I know," Piatt said.

"That surprises me just a little, Congressman."

"There was some testimony on it. Vague as hell. The appropriation wasn't much, hell they could've hidden it if they wanted to. But Max's smart in that way, he wanted someone else to sign off. So we signed off after about seven minutes of testimony."

"Sam Joyce draws water," Mundelein said.

"He's trusted," Piatt agreed.

Mundelein said, "It's his old man."

"Old Ben hasn't hurt his career any."

"The Man likes him. He likes the idea of a soldier knowing which end is up, which Sam Joyce surely does if he's his father's son. Tell me now, do you think he knows which end is up?"

"I suppose he does. Old Ben and all that."

Mundelein laughed sourly. Old Ben Joyce had come to the law in middle age. Late to law, late to marriage, late to wealth, late to politics, a realist in all things. A man of the nineteenth century, he believed in a government of men, not of laws, and therefore cultivated men. If you knew the men, the laws would take care of themselves. There were two kinds of lawyers, inside lawyers and outside lawyers; those who knew men and those who knew law. He was an inside lawyer who became an inside judge. Then he left Genesee for the nation's capital, the beneficiary of a Senate nomination to counter a scandal in the party. He was the good-government candidate and to the surprise of everyone but himself, he won. He was then over seventy years old, projecting a kind of small-town cunning and common sense—indeed, that was his campaign slogan, "Common Sense"—which appealed to midwesterners anxious to avoid further New Deal excesses in the exhilaration of the great military victory soon to come. After a single term in the Senate he retired to practice law on I Street. Washington was no different from Genesee, according to him; both were river towns of pretty aspect, isolated, prosperous, rich in local legend, a tabula rasa for the clever lawyer who came with no strings attached. Washington was a town where a few men ran things to suit themselves.

144

The play had more characters, he said, but it was the same play. Dubious when his only child decided to become an army officer, he arranged an appointment to the military academy, telling anyone who would listen that the army was not a career for the future. But he did not want any interference in his law firm either. He had seen fathers and sons in the same office and it never worked out, the relationship too close and competitive; someone had to lose and he knew it wouldn't be him, so he was happy enough to see his son at West Point.

"He must be a hundred years old," Mundelein said.

"Close," Piatt said. "He got married very late and then had just the one child, Sam. He's senile now."

"No he isn't," Mundelein said. "The Man talked to him on the phone last night. He was a pirate, tough as hell. The Man told me some stories." Piatt was silent, waiting for Mundelein to turn the corner. "My father is dead," the adviser said quietly, as if that explained something.

"So is mine," Piatt said.

"So this is a private conversation, you understand. Tell me now, between us. What's with Sam Joyce?"

"There are better sources than me," Piatt said. He was looking steadily at Mundelein, waiting for the flicker. And in a moment, it came.

"I'm sure of that. And in good time, I'll ask the same question of them. In the meantime, I'm asking you."

Piatt said in the same toneless voice, "Sam and I don't communicate much."

"I know that, too. And I know why. Now I can do this officially or I can do it unofficially. This is unofficial right here. You better make up your mind which way you want it, because I'm not asking out of any idle curiosity. *I want to know about our Colonel, the Senator's son.* If there's a fall that's going to be taken, Sam Joyce is going to take it. Him and his friend, Henderson. We know two or three things without even having to think about them. Max Cather's not going to take the fall, and I'm not going to take it, and the Man's not. All I know about Henderson is that he talks too much, talks to Carney's man, what's his name? Jessel? Then the television interview, what was behind that? I don't know because I don't know Henderson. I don't understand any of them who're out there, except for a few of the civilians who come and go on TDY. Sending anybody out there for more than two weeks is like sending a kid to Europe to college, you'll never get them back the same way you sent them out. Anyway, I don't have to know about Henderson. I do have to know about Joyce. I have to know if he's smart and I have to know, more than if he's smart, can he be trusted? Is he—?"

"Or what?" Piatt said.

Mundelein looked at him blankly.

"Or what if I don't? What happens if it gets official?" Piatt leaned against the wall of the blind, feeling it give a little. Mundelein did not answer, he seemed to be far away, deep into a private interior.

At last he said, "We've known each other a long time, Piatt. This isn't going into any dossier. It's for me only. And my principal, of course."

"Of course," Piatt said.

"But I have to have it and if I don't get it I'm going to cause trouble."

Piatt smiled. "Not like the old days, though."

"No. It wouldn't be anything you couldn't handle."

"Times change."

"White House can still ring a bell, though. It just can't ring *all* the bells. Time was, you could ring any bell in this town." He picked up his shotgun, broke it, looked through the barrel, and set it down again.

Piatt nodded uncomfortably; the truth was, he felt sympathy for Mundelein. "Sam's been there four tours, maybe five," he said. "And he fell in love, as some of them do. For a certain kind of man it's the great aphrodisiac. Maybe Sam's that kind of man. What's combat but a bloody seduction, it only takes the right combination of moves—"

"Bullshit," Mundelein said.

"You don't buy? Well," Piatt said, hesitating a beat. "He's not afraid, and that's something."

Mundelein laughed softly.

Piatt said, "How are you going to use him?"

"Put him in charge, out there." Mundelein was standing with his back to the bay. Now he turned to look at the water, flat in the windless air. The decoys were motionless in the water and in the distance geese barked. "I don't trust what I hear. What do you hear?"

"Why him?"

"Someone has to be in charge," Mundelein said.

"What makes you think he'll do it?"

"Because his commander in chief will tell him to do it." The adviser turned to face Piatt. "And because he wants to be out there again." He snapped his cigarette into the bay and the cigarette died with a hiss. "I'd say it's goddamned strange, man goes out there four, five tours. What's he trying to prove? But he wants to go out again. It's bloodlust with those people. Talking to some of them over at the Department, they've had some psychological profiles done. You want to scare yourself to death, read those. I don't trust any of them, it's just absolutely necessary to keep the military out of things. God damn them. But they tell me he's better than most." Mundelein looked hopefully at Piatt.

"He's a son of a bitch," Piatt said.

"He came by the other day. Let me tell you, he's got a few things to learn about briefing the President of the United States. It was a shambles. Man couldn't follow anything he said."

"Tell me more," Piatt said.

"I'd like to think I can count on you, if this gets rough."

"Let's see how rough it gets."

"How rough do you want it?" Mundelein laughed, but there was no humor in the laugh. "How the hell rough do you want it?"

"Less rough, Pat. Why can't we at least try to move off the dime—"

"Uh-huh," the adviser said. "It's a bitch, isn't it? It's an end game now and that's a hard place to be. We want out but we can't find the exit. It's no win for us but we have the pride of the country to consider. The dead. Isn't that what it comes down to? And then there are those who are still there, the Sam Joyces. Don't you think they're just waiting for the stab-in-the-back?

Maybe in some ways they even want it. Gives them the excuse they've been looking for." Mundelein nodded vigorously, agreeing with himself. "So it's sleight-of-hand. We're saying one thing and doing another. Yes. You shouldn't make any mistakes, though. My Man is tough. He's tougher than you can imagine. My God, who would want it ended more than we do? And if what it takes is Sam Joyce and Sol Henderson and a special force. If that brings us one inch closer to the end—well then, that's what we'll do. They got us there and now they can get us back, the soldierboys. There are no limits . . ." Piatt listened to the rise and fall of the adviser's voice. How many times had he made this speech? To Congressmen, to editors, to diplomats and moneybags. It was the loneliness-of-command speech. Pat Mundelein could sound sympathetic even while blackmailing you. He said, "I wonder what it is he's got."

What did that mean?

"Women," Mundelein said. "He's going around with Sheila Dennehay now, and she's a hell of a woman."

"I don't know what his charm is in that area," Piatt said.

"Never married, did he?"

"No," Piatt said.

"He says he's married to the army."

Piatt watched the adviser's cigarette, dead in the water, and did not reply.

"He should have a wife," Mundelein said.

Piatt leaned again against the wall of the blind.

"You heard anything?"

Piatt was suddenly alert. It was the second time Mundelein had asked the question. He shook his head noncommittally.

"He had some trouble his last tour, I understand."

"I didn't know that," Piatt said carefully.

"There was a small problem with his command, I thought you might've heard something. I'm glad you haven't, it means it's still tight. The IG has got it now, they say it's been in the pipeline for some time, this matter. His accounts aren't quite . . . straight." Mundelein lit another cigarette. "I've seen some of the raw data, it's not without cause. It's not a wholly bogus investigation. Seems like our Sam was siphoning off funds. Not

148

nickels and dimes either. It's real money and there's a suspicious bank account, uh. That's according to the preliminary report of the Inspector General's gumshoes, a copy of which I have managed to obtain. It's not as easy as you might think, these things get into the system . . . " He shrugged, completing the sentence.

Piatt thought a moment, then answered truthfully. "It's hard to believe."

"No, it seems to be true."

"I'd say, if it was anybody but you telling me this, that it was cock."

"No, it's fairly solid."

"I'd be damned careful, Pat. That's not his speed, and he's a man with a lot of friends."

"Lot of enemies, too, it seems."

"Inside the army?"

"And outside, he's been in the Zone for so long, it makes them uncomfortable. They'd like him to do his tours here, this is where the real war is being fought. His last command, there was something very weird about it. He broke contact with his superiors, and there's a month or more no one can account for. So the gumshoes do what they always do, they go to the documents; in this case, the audit. Really, they want to know about that one month." Mundelein pulled on his cigarette. "I'd like to find some discreet way to get the word to him, all the same. I think he's a fine soldier. Fine reputation, fine family. I'd hate like the dickens to have this get out, have Jessel or whoever get ahold of it. You can imagine what Jessel would do with it, if he had it. Before the investigation's complete. It's by no means an airtight case, and of course it could be innocence itself."

Piatt was silent.

"I'd like somebody to get to him with this preliminary report, give him a little advance warning. I have a pretty strong hunch that he doesn't know anything about it at all. I would think, man in his position, he'd want to engage an attorney, pronto."

"Unless it's all cock," Piatt said.

"It isn't," Mundelein said.

"Any particular attorney in mind?"

"Look at that!" The adviser pointed across the bay. A line of oyster boats crept slowly in the channel, a benign reminder of the ordinary life of the Eastern Shore. Some parts of it had not changed in fifty years. In a few remote estuaries there were probably even canvasback ducks. Above them a flight of swans muscled toward open water, their great wings creaking like hinges. Mundelein raised his arm as if it were a shotgun and followed the lead swan, *bang-bang*. "The ambassador," he said, "the one who owns this place, worst damn shot you ever saw. Couldn't hit a barn with a brick but he looks good missing. He's got terrific form." The adviser indicated the ducks lying in a bloody tangle at their feet. "Good hunting today, couldn't ask for better. So far as I'm concerned, the son of a bitch is ambassador for life." The adviser said softly, "We need some help, Piatt."

"So you said."

"Technology," Mundelein said. "That's what we have. That's our edge, everyone has some edge. That's ours. Machinery."

"Yes."

"There'll be a need for another special appropriation."

"My committee."

"Your committee. We need a reliable man to take the lead." He paused, considering. "This stuff is so new, it's a new world, untried and tested only in the lab. It has to be used under field conditions. The lab is one place, the world's another. All it is, really, is a gigantic wiretap. Max Cather'll give you the details. I'll tell you this: We're not getting anything else out of the war, we might as well use it for something. As for the special missions, I don't think they'll be necessary. I mean the targeting of specific individuals, though you never know what they do with the stuff once they get it out there, that's one of our worries." The adviser saw that Piatt did not completely understand the other remark. "I mean the war. At least it has this use, I'm sure you'll agree. There are spin-offs from it, like the space program. Max Cather's got this little group in Cambridge."

"Yes," Piatt said.

"And as for Sam. I thought you might find that information

helpful, and of course it's for your ears only. Yours and of course your wife's, I know you confide in her completely." He did not wait for Piatt's reaction but rushed on. "As for the attorney, who can say. I myself would recommend—"

"You're going to need more than the testimony of some gumshoe."

"We have documents."

"Of course you do. One piece of paper after another."

"The IG—"

"Come off it, Pat. You know as well as I do, if it comes down to it, a trial or court-martial, Sam Joyce wouldn't have some shavetail from West Bookend Law School the army'd assign him, he'd have a senior man from Joyce & Walsh. You know who he'd have and you know the trouble there'd be. There'd be trouble in the courtroom, trouble at Jessel's end of the avenue, and trouble at mine."

"But there's not going to be any trouble because it's not going to go that far, and I'm sure there's a rational explanation for the discrepancies in the accounts. And of course the missing month, they'd like that accounted for. Their records, the history of the war . . . " He smiled. "But. My interest lies with the Presidency. With this Man now. The administration. My administration. Sam Joyce, good soldier that he is—"

Piatt looked sideways at Mundelein. He had more sides than a geodesic dome. The adviser would be disconcerted now, and morose. How many years ago was it that an adviser could shake any tree in Washington and a dozen enforcers would fall out of it? All of them scrambling to be of use to the White House. It was only yesterday. Now he was hustling a middle-level Congressman, needing help and not certain if that help would be forthcoming. He was being rough, firing the big guns right away.

Mundelein said, "We'll probably turn off the inquiry."

"Is it as easy as that?"

"No," he said. "It isn't. Thing gets into the Inspector General's channels, it's hard as hell to divert. But we will try to divert it, there are ways and means to do that. I know a man who can do it. You ought to appreciate the situation, though. The stuff they have on Sam Joyce is hard as rocks. It would hold up in any court and I don't care who his old man gets as his boy's mouthpiece. I can show you some of the stuff, the man's diverted money and equipment. I don't know why. I don't particularly care why. But I know he has, and I know the amounts. He has some bad enemies."

"Tell me, Pat. Do you like your work?"

He looked at Piatt, surprised. He broke into a grin. "We're government men, and do what's necessary." A sudden chill came over the water. "We'll need luck," the adviser said. "A telephone call can do it, but it has to be the right call from the right phone. The IG has his weapons too, you know; his friends at your end of the avenue and at Jessel's end as well, as you say. It's always a two-edged sword in this town, we know that for sure, don't we now?" He removed his hunting cap and hung it on the blind's overhang. He sighed, rubbing his hands, his belly straining against the waders. "We do some things better than others, and the times are not as they were. I have a friend, known him for years, is president of an outfit we do business with. He's got a place on Long Island and a place in the islands and his company maintains an apartment in Paris. Lives very well, this friend. A company Lear and a contract that'll pay him plenty when he retires, *especially* when he retires. I used to envy him and in a way I still do, except that we have what he has; it's just that it's not *ours*. It's ours to use but not to own, right? We're like renters without a lease, we go from month to month. And of course he has a protection that we don't have." He was silent a moment, contemplating the open bay. "The more public you are, the less protection you have. It used to be the other way around. 'Tolling.' That's what we do now to those we elect, lure them close to the shore with a little barking dog and then blind-side them. No lack of barking dogs in Washington and no lack of firepower either, though it's usually small caliber." He paused to inspect his cigarette, then to snap it into the bay. "Nothing we can't handle. The secret's to remain on the edges, and never raise your voice." He turned to Piatt. "This matter is sensitive and I want to get it over with and behind us so we can move to the important agenda. Now I want you to help us with the appropriation on the inside, if it comes to that. I don't think Cather and his clowns in Cambridge are going to win the war or end it, but there're other pressures on us that you know nothing about. It's one thing we haven't tried and there's evidence that it'll save lives. I'm going to need some help with the IG as well. Sam Joyce needs counsel now. My advice—"

"I know what your advice is."

"—you get him Henry Costello."

"Yes, of course," Piatt said.

"Then have Henry call me. Funny thing." He looked wistfully at Piatt. "Henry can do it quicker than I can. He knows that place inside and out, from the time he worked for the Secretary."

Henry Costello, attorney at law. Piatt said, "I think I know a better man than Henry Costello."

"Maybe, if you were getting a divorce or wanted your will drawn or were suing a doctor because he performed brain surgery on your broken leg. Maybe you could. But you're trying to derail an investigation into the conduct of an army officer so this time you'll get Costello, if you give a damn. He's not cheap, by the way."

No, certainly not cheap. "I know him," Piatt said.

"You'll be doing Sam a favor."

"And you—"

"Oh, this is just personal. I'm not a party to any of this, we're just talking here. This is friendly, friend to friend. I happen to know Henry from way back, he's an excellent attorney. And discreet. Discretion's his middle name," Mundelein said. "I wonder sometimes, when all this is over, won't it be good to get back to business?" He pushed his toe into the breast of the largest mallard. Then he smiled. "Managing the government, making money, gunning for ducks, making the world safe for oystermen and canvasbacks." The adviser picked up his shotgun and broke it. Then he pointed the barrel at the sky, squinting through it. The barrel was filthy with gunpowder. "And have a talk with Sam."

The black Mercury was in the cornfield, its lights blinking. The driver was polishing the headlights with a soft yellow cloth.

Mundelein waved his arms and the driver put away the cloth and began to trot toward them in his black suit and little peaked cap, a comical, formal figure, moving gingerly, his city shoes slipping on the frozen ground. Mundelein said, "He can carry the gear and we'll take the ducks. Can't have Alfred returning to the mansion with blood on his lapels." Piatt offered to wade out to collect the decoys but the adviser shook his head. The ambassador's "guy" would take care of them later in the morning. Another party was due to arrive for the evening shoot.

Mundelein handed the shotguns and ammunition belts and the thermoses to the driver, who accepted them with thanks and began to trudge back to the car. Mundelein divided the ducks between them, giving three of the four redheads to Piatt. Then they climbed out of the blind and tramped across the cornfield to the car. Inside, the adviser opened his briefcase and did not look up for ninety minutes, until the car pulled into the east Executive Avenue entrance to the White House. Piatt read the paper for a bit, then watched the Maryland scenery. Finally he slept. He went to sleep thinking about Henry Costello, Dennis McDonnough's friend, Carl McDonough's attorney, later a special counsel at DOD. Yes, he knew the territory. Piatt had not seen him in years, though his name often came up in conversations where government business was discussed. Now the government business was Sam Joyce, whose accounts in the Zone were irregular. There was a time, he thought sleepily, when you would have laughed Mundelein out of court. But not now, things were weird—though with Sam things were never less than very weird.

When the car stopped, Mundelein touched him on the arm and he came awake with a grunt. "Alfred'll take you where you want to go. We'll do it again soon, maybe in a week or so. A morning at the opera." They shook hands.

Piatt said he'd be in touch.

"No questions then? No loose ends?"

"None that you can answer," Piatt said. Except one.

"None that I would anyway." The adviser smiled.

"Just one last thing, Pat. Why Sam Joyce? All those colonels in the army, how many are there? A thousand? Two thousand? Why Sam?"

The adviser's smile broadened. "The Man wants him, and that's enough. For a mission of this kind, he wants a man he knows personally. Wants that man to have special weight. Wants a man that's insulated, but not a straight arrow, no. Maybe he wants a man with friends, and as we both know every Man wants his own edge. Sam's not an entirely free agent, is he? And along with his many friends, he has many enemies as well. Give my regards to your good wife." He moved heavily away. "Meanwhile, you might want to have a word with old Max. Max has a good head and a sense of direction and people like that are always abrasive. Time's of the essence, isn't it? And you won't forget Henry, okey-doke? And Piatt," he said—irresistibly, it was his inevitable parting shot—"never, *never* bunch your decoys." He waved cheerfully and walked up the driveway to the mansion in his waders and canvas jacket, ducks swinging from his fists, courteously nodding to the guards, an evidently happy man. The waders and canvas jacket made him look twice as bulky as he actually was. One of the guards came forward to relieve him of the ducks and Piatt, watching all this from the car, wondered if the guard called him "Your Honor" when he tipped his hat and bowed slightly from the waist.

There was an awkward silence while the company regrouped. Sam imagined them doing exactly that, retreating to fortified positions. Like a match flaring in the dark, Marina smiled at him, a particular smile between them. Sheila Dennehay sat with her head cocked, her expression abstracted as if she had just heard a dialect story she didn't quite get and wasn't sure whether it was her fault or the fault of the raconteur or the fault of the story. Piatt had tailored his yarn to the audience, only a hint of Sam's troubles and nothing at all about Henry Costello; of course it was a story for men only and Max Cather knew most of it. The objectives were Sam and Carney, and Marina.

Sam smiled. Piatt had done it well, his hint of troubles.

Laughing, he'd said: "Someone over there doesn't like you." Pause. "But Pat's not concerned, overmuch."

"Isn't he now?" Sam had asked.

"As we discussed the other day, Sam. In our conversation. It's often complicated in the Zone." Then he went on to describe the adviser's fascination with the ambassador's form, a good story, everyone laughing, though it had no obvious point.

They made a show of loving what they did, for that was the current style, the exercise of power *joie de vivre* itself. The great commanders displayed good cheer and excellent humor. Melancholia was a prelude to failure. Sam thought the atmosphere resembled the enforced hilarity of a night on the town, roars of laughter while each man secretly consulted his watch and wondered how soon he could decently leave for home. Except of course for Costello, who knew he belonged to the future; the spoils were his for the taking, and he loved the process as a grand master loved the infinite variety of the chessboard.

Now Piatt was retailing anecdotes, Mundelein's stories. Druz,

156

the matched Churchills, the medals that clanked when he walked; the chauffeur in the cornfield. However, he was quick to compliment the adviser's sportsmanship and deportment inside the blind.

Sheila said, "I know what he was doing. He was negotiating one of his insurance policies. That's what Pat is, you know, an insurance man. He's a connoisseur of risk, the Duveen of casualty and liability."

Smart woman, Sam thought.

Carney said, "What did he want really?"

Piatt said, "A friend at the factory."

Indeed, Sam thought. And he got one, too, from the sound of it. God, how could they know so little. They were empowered, obligated really, to run the war, but they refused to learn anything about it. They did not understand the atmosphere of violence, and the difference between fear of the known and fear of the unknown, fear of the present instead of fear of the future. They did not know how high the stakes were. And when they took their inspection trips, conducted through the Zone with the innocence of a high school civics class touring the federal city, they drew all the wrong conclusions from that. They became bellicose and hard as nails at the sight of the coffins, and all the weary young men on the line. Not their sons, either; other mens' sons. The sons of their constituents or their file clerks.

It was not easy to explain, and lost something in the explanation. But he had seen good soldiers moved by Goya's various horrors of war, as well as Anne-Louis Girodet-Trioson's *Ossian Receives in Valhalla the Souls of Napoleon's Generals.* He and old Revdoc Laurence had found that one at the Musée de Malmaison and the Revdoc approved.

Hell, Sam, the Revdoc had said, if that's the way it's going to be. Pretty attractive woman there, the one on her stomach behind the old Irish warrior himself. Looks cheerful enough and well fed. If that's the reward at the end of all this. Well, then. Aren't you glad you signed up? Heh-heh-heh.

He searched his memory, he and Laurence were in Paris briefing NATO officers. That was sometime between the second and third tours, when matters were still somewhat rational. Well, it was before they knew that the war was impossible to win. It was before everything went haywire, and Piatt Warden's information was only the tip of the iceberg. No one knew the full story except Marina, and he hadn't intended to tell her except they were on a drive through the Shenandoah and it seemed the right thing to do. The truth was, he had to tell someone. They had stopped at Manassas and he had given her a briefing on the First Battle there, 21 July 1861, when the Confederates lost two thousand KIA and the Union lost three thousand. Fifteen hundred Yankees surrendered and the Confederates thought they had won the war. It seemed natural enough to describe the various infantry tactics suited to the Shenandoah campaign; the Union generals were almost criminally stupid, the blunders so numerous and so obvious that the troopers thought they had been betrayed. But it was just poor intelligence and stupidity, a foretaste of what was to come later.

She asked him, "Does there always have to be stupidity?"

"Almost always," he said. "It's built-in."

"Because—?"

"Because it is so random," he said.

She was very quiet, driving slowly through the lush countryside, the part of northern Virginia where rich Washingtonians kept country houses. After a long silence he began to describe his own routine in the Zone, the details of his soldier's existence, when he rose in the morning and when he went to bed at night, and what he did in between times. When she asked him what he thought about, apart from the job at hand, his immediate world, he smiled and said he couldn't remember; he didn't think about anything, really, except the job at hand. It had a way of erasing the past and the future both, except when some incident would jog his memory; one way or another, she was always with him, along with the pink house and Mistinguett.

There were forty Americans at Base Fox, of which he was the most senior. They were a mixed bunch, goods, bads, and average individuals in about equal measure. There were ten officers and the rest were noncoms, but all highly trained. Everyone had at least two specialties, weapons, communications, medicine, demolition, psywar. The ratio of one officer to every three non-coms was unusual but no more unusual than the mission. They were running teams across the border mainly to collect intelligence but sometimes to sabotage. Depending on the nature of the intelligence they would either relay it to MACV or act on it themselves. The teams were twelve men each, two Americans and ten Vietnamese normally. There were between sixty and seventy Vietnamese, "indigenous personnel" in the argot, but most of these were not outstanding. Often the Americans would take a mission by themselves, to keep in practice; it was always cumbersome with the Vietnamese because of their slow ways and the language problem. The languages didn't *translate*, he said; he himself had learned some French because it was more precise but his officers and noncoms didn't follow suit. In many ways the war was about language; the reason it was being fought involved language. The meanings of words.

They ran two missions at a time, occasionally three but that was risky because the camp was always threatened. There was no real danger of being overrun because Base Fox was within reach of the artillery fan at Moc Hoa. Also, the approaches were well mined. The camp itself was on the rise of a small hill and commanded a fine view of the countryside. There were only half a dozen ways they could come if they were coming in strength and these were under constant monitor. Still, it was wise to keep a serious force on more or less permanent alert. There were black boxes at the camp, particular machines and cyphers that would have been of value to the enemy. There was a secure room at the command post that was off limits to all Vietnamese, because it was only logical to assume there were doubles in their contingent. The Vietnamese CO was a fifty-year-old major. He had been in the war a very long time. Too long, perhaps; suspiciously long. You wondered how he had survived all those years. But he had beautiful manners and a good command of English and was an agreeable companion after-hours. Anyhow, the secure room was under guard day and night, owing to the special machines and cyphers inside.

He said, I remember the dust. Red dust, it was everywhere, in your hair and under your fingernails. No part of the command untouched by red dust, even the machines in the secure room had to be cleaned every day. We cleaned and oiled our weapons twice a day. When I flew in for the first time I was with a brigadier general from Louisiana, who nudged me as we circled closer. Looks just like home, doesn't it? But it didn't. It didn't look like any place I had ever seen before. From our hill the land fell and then rose again, green as far as the eye could see, filtered through the red dust. Trackless and unbroken, it looked as if it went on forever—which, in a way, it did, through Cambodia and Laos and north to China, none of it charted and all of it mysterious. That was the terrain in which we maneuvered. In the dry season you prayed for rain and in the rainy season you prayed for the sun. They kept explaining the country, its terrain or politics or culture or history, in terms of something else, usually European. And that was a terrible mistake, because Vietnam was, like any other country, sui generis. Metaphors were attractive, but not especially helpful. The Major told me that. I didn't believe everything the Major said, but I believed that. It was very difficult in my CP at Fox imagining what they were doing in the Pentagon or in the national security adviser's office in the basement of the White House. Probably they had the same trouble.

It's very close, you know, he said, just like a family. In this family I was Dad. My XO was Mom. This was Laurence and he was some soldier. We all called him Doctor Laurence or the Reverend Doctor Laurence or just the Revdoc, because his hootch was always filled with the malcontents. He held office hours every day from five o'clock on, a little hand-lettered sign on his door, The Doctor Is In. The great thing about the real army, I mean the professional army, is that it attracts various types of the middle range. Middle-class people as stable as a billiard table most of them, though occasionally you'd get one with a screw loose; that was Laurence. He held office hours every day from five o'clock on, sitting in his director's chair. The troopers would sit on the bed, his favorites were a sergeant from Cape Cod and a lieutenant from the Atlanta suburbs. These two had women trouble, they were both married but had doubts about their wives. The Revdoc had had a good deal of experience with women. He used to describe this experience as "not error-free," but it gave him a salient position from which to judge the experience of others. The Revdoc maintained that however much you knew about women, you could never know enough; and you didn't want to know it all. These two would sit on his bed and smoke dope and discuss the latest letters from their wives. They were always pornographic letters and while they liked to receive them they wondered about the motives. This was not what the movies had led them to expect, and they came to the Revdoc for analysis. He quoted Blake at them. Blake was his all-purpose answer to everything.

You cannot know how much is enough until you know how much is too much, heh-heh-heh.

His observations were always punctuated by the laugh, which was somewhere between W. C. Fields and the grunt of a barnyard animal, perhaps swine. He loved having them there, the sergeant from Cape Cod and the lieutenant from the Atlanta suburbs, or anyone else who wanted his ear. Many of his own problems with women arose from his numerous friendships, the women complained that his house was never empty and that he was—they meant, "they were"—never alone. The charge was true, so having the troopers around his hootch reminded him of home. The only thing that was missing was a complaining woman. No home was complete without a complaining woman. Needless to say, we all loved the Revdoc; he was brave and very intelligent. And for a soldier, he was well read, and almost unnaturally sympathetic. And he had a kind of second-sight, he saw through things to their unexpected meanings. I happened in on one of his after-five sessions once and, looking around the hootch at the men—there must have been six or seven of them inside, all drinking or smoking, but silent suddenly as I entered. I looked at the Revdoc and said, "Men without women."

And he looked at me with his mournful eyes and laughed that laugh. "Oh, Sam," he said. "If it were only true."

We were hit on the fourth of April. They were damned clever about it, they hit in the morning, at first light, and in a heavy rain. We knew something was out there but we didn't know what, and we didn't know how many. The rain confused the sensors and we couldn't be entirely sure that it wasn't a false alarm. We had those about once a week in the rainy season. It was a well-planned attack, the sappers came first to knock out the wire and then their mortars opened up. Well, it was simultaneous, really. They bracketed the camp with six mortars. Their gunners weren't accomplished, though, because it took them a few minutes to get the correct range and by then our big guns from Moc Hoa were knocking hell out of them. Or seemed to be. They stuck, though. I'll give them that. And it was a well-coordinated assault, obviously something that had been planned for some time.

It's hard to know how many there were. I guessed a battalion, maybe three hundred men. They were very determined and disciplined. They breached one section of wire in good order and pretty soon were everywhere in the camp. One of my lads panicked then and blew all the claymore mines at once, and I'd hoped to have at least one string in reserve. So all at once we had a bunch of enemy in the camp. They hit the Vietnamese compound first and did a pretty good job of that. In an assault of that kind, the offensive unit always has an advantage. They scattered most of our Vietnamese, which surprised me a little. I didn't want that to happen and thought it wouldn't happen. I thought the Major could rally his troops. A rout like that can destroy a unit's effectiveness.

It took an hour to get them out, and the thing I'll remember more than anything else was the ease with which they moved around the camp. It was like watching neighborhood kids on their own playground, they seemed to fit into the terrain. Hell, it was supposed to be our camp, our turf. But it was their ground and they seemed to know it intimately. It was raining, remember.

He said, I was taking charge in the CP. The Revdoc was directing a fireteam from the hootches. It was very bad the first fifteen minutes but after the artillery came in and we got our bearings we knew we'd make it all right. Our defense was not error-free, but we'd survive. With Laurence at one end of the camp and me at the other I was confident enough, worried only that we'd lose too many good men. We'd rehearsed this particular drill and everyone knew that they weren't to take any unnecessary risks, though in a situation of that kind it was not always possible to know what was unnecessary. At the end of it we'd lost six KIA and another dozen badly wounded. Not so bad, considering. Considering the force we were facing, and the surprise. It ended slowly, by the way, no sudden silences. They still had snipers on the perimeter, and for the longest time we couldn't be sure whether the relative calm wasn't a feint and once we started to move around they'd fly at us again. So I walked the artillery in as close as I dared and then sent Laurence with his fireteam to reconnoiter. That worked out fine and by noon we were secure or thought we were. He was returning from a second reconnaissance when rifle fire opened to our left. Laurence and his men scattered. He was close enough to my CP to make for that. He was running low and not very fast, the Revdoc was not what you would call in prime physical condition. About ten yards from the CP he fell like a bag of grain, just *flopped*. I knew he was dead from the way he fell and there was so much noise I figured he was hit by a stray slug, though it didn't seem real; the firing was on the other side. I got to him right away but there was nothing to be done. I tried mouth-to-mouth but that didn't work. Our best medic ran the gauntlet to get to him but by then it was obvious he was dead. The enemy pulled out then and the first dustoff choppers landed to evacuate the wounded. They'd been delayed by some screwup at Moc Hoa. The medic was still working on Laurence and at last he looked at me with the most vacant expression. Colonel, he said, there isn't a mark on him.

And in this, he was absolutely correct.

I got on the horn right away and told the chief of surgery at Long Bien that I wanted a complete autopsy. I told him that I had a man killed in action but there wasn't a mark on him. I described the way he ran, including the little skip he gave before he fell. The chief of surgery said nothing but promised to get right on it, and let me know immediately.

We were spooked, but had to go about our business. We collected the dead and put them in green ponchos and carried them to the chopper pad. We had lost three officers and three non-coms. Both the sergeant from Cape Cod and the lieutenant from the Atlanta suburbs survived. We three did most of the carrying, since I'd dispatched a reaction force and thrown up a picket line. It's a bad sight, the bodies covered by ponchos, only their shoes showing. We knew each other so well, and we knew who was who by the look of the boots, their shape, and the way they lay on the pallet. We were very careful with the bodies but they were heavy and as we carried them to the pad we'd occasionally lose our grip and bump them on the muddy ground. It had stopped raining around noon and shortly afterward the sun came out, the first sun we'd seen for weeks. The rainy season was about to end. We stood apart from the bodies, the six. The seventh, Laurence, had gone back with the wounded.

They did the autopsy that afternoon and I got a telephone call that night, and the formal report a week later. It was a heart attack, a myocardial infarction; he had had no history of heart disease or of any other disease. And do you know what the chief of surgery called it? What was listed as the cause? Arrhythmic heart failure. "Irregular rhythms of the heart."

He said, I cried all night long. When I wasn't laughing at the stupid irony of it. Of course I wrote the letters to his kin. He'd been married once and there were two children. They were very long letters and, as I think about them now, unnecessarily detailed. And there was a list of seven or eight women who were entitled to more than perfunctory notification. I mentioned the cause of death in the letters to the women, hoping it would give them a smile as it had given me a smile. But I think they did not see the humor of it or perhaps they saw it and did not feel like laughing. Laurence's women all tended to be what I would call radical personalities. They hated the war, though they seemed to love him. They thought the war wicked and immoral, but did not hold him responsible for it. All but one of the women wrote me back and their letters made hard reading.

My command went to hell when Laurence died. I hadn't thought about it at the time but he served as some kind of moral compass, a way out of the confusion and fear we all felt. He was always willing to listen and to supply answers or to ask the right questions. His answers were not always cheerful but they were consoling. He said to me once that all literature was consolation and in that way he was a living classics course. Mordant, ironical, pessimistic, grieving, humorous, *virtuous*. That was Laurence and I cannot overestimate his contribution, the *necessity* of him to the command. He seemed to see to the heart of the war, the soul of it; and his conclusions were not anything you could print on a bumper sticker or flag. He was sick at heart that it went on, and he knew that we held all the cards. If it was to end, Washington would have to end it; and Washington wouldn't. And the reasons for that had to do with pride, and the arrogance of heredity; the influence of fathers, the wrong fathers. And of course there was the stupidity, and he collected examples of that like a great philatelist with miscanceled stamps. The big thing was not to give in to them. He would never allow us to do a cheap or shoddy thing. He believed there were rules to combat as there were rules to love, and while things didn't always work out well—indeed, they usually didn't work out well or humanely, disorder being endemic to the human condition, as he rather grandly put it—it helped a little to obey a few good rules. It helped *oneself*. Laurence could say that sort of thing and make you believe it. I couldn't take his place, no one could. He was such an unpretentious friend, he seemed to see everything and forgive everything—except the stupidity of our various supervisors who did not understand our life, the conditions of it, and caused us to undertake missions that cost lives. That was the evil thing, carelessness that cost lives; willful ignorance and arrogance by people who did not know how things were but should have. We were able to sidestep many of these orders, thanks to him and thanks to me. He could not forgive those who issued orders without knowing the circumstances in which they would have to be carried out. Of course it was next to impossible to find the genesis of any particular order, go back far enough and you'd find an idiot machine—but someone had to program the machine, didn't they? But that's another story, as much mine as his. The thing about Laurence was this. His own personal life was in terrible disarray, but that did not lessen his authority; it increased it. He knew from personal experience how bad things could get.

My command went to seed. We had a special reputation in the country and it took some time for everything to catch up to us. We were to the back of beyond, to hell and gone near the border, and it was difficult for MACV's investigators to scrutinize us. I could devise a Potemkin village as well as the next man and did, when the brass came to call. At about this time I became close to the Vietnamese Major, reckoning that we might have something to say to each other after all. Previously, I had left him to Laurence, who seemed to have an affinity generally for the Vietnamese. Laurence said he admired the Major's religion, a particular sect called the Cao Dai. Laurence had made an effort to study it, and informed me one night that the Cao Dai's pantheon of saints was worth a look. They were Christ, Buddha, Mohammed, and Victor Hugo. Heh-heh-heh. One evening I invited the Major to my hootch and we had a drink and talked all night, at first in English and later in French. It was the first of many evenings together. I drank whiskey and he drank Coke. Some years before, when he had been a young major instead of an old one, he had visited the United States as part of a delegation. It was something arranged by the Pentagon, a hands-across-the-sea sort of thing; give our plucky little allies a look at the future, and how it was working. They went first to Fort Hood in Texas, where our armored divisions trained, and then to Omaha to see the SAC command, and then to Chicago. He thought the weapons marvelous, more than adequate to win any war in Europe, say, or Australia. Such a large country, he said; so flat and featureless, and so obviously rich. They traveled in a windowless C-135, so he saw nothing from the air and that disappointed him because a friend had told him that the Mississippi bore a striking resemblance to the Mokong. He had never seen so many automobiles, nor so many different kinds of automobile. Was there an automobile for every *penchant*? I said there was, and named a dozen. He said that the delegation had been kept together and did not meet many average citizens. The army escort officers were unfailingly polite and helpful, but stuck strictly to the schedules. Every day they had a briefing on aspects of American defense policy, and the commitment to freedom in Indochina.

There was only a single untoward incident. An official in the defense ministry had brought along his wife, and at Fort Hood she gave birth to twin sons. She had not been fat, as they all thought—or as the army thought—but pregnant. Born in the United States, the twin sons were citizens. He smiled. One more reason for the official to want to win the war. His bets were no longer hedged.

One way of looking at it, I said.

He asked at last if there were very many Communists in the United States and, if so, where they were located.

I said there were very few Communists.

Really?

Yes, I said. Only handful and most of those were treated as a joke.

They are not a threat, then.

No, I said.

Who is their leader? he asked.

Comrade Earl Browder, I said.

And does he hold a position in your government?

I laughed. Certainly not, I said. Mostly he went to international gatherings of Communists. He was the American representative. The FBI had infiltrated the American Communist Party and it was no threat to anyone.

Ah, he said. And that was all he said, "Ah." A subtle man, he felt no need to continue the conversation.

After five or six evenings in my hootch, he invited me to his, in the Vietnamese part of the compound. I brought my bottle of whiskey, but he had arranged for tea. It was served by a woman I took to be his companion, though they rarely spoke. His hootch was spare but comfortable. The only personal touch was a framed photograph of a very old man, his grandfather. I joked that he bore a striking resemblance to Ho Chi Minh and the

Major smiled and agreed; but he was not Ho Chi Minh, he would be many years older than Ho. He died in 1954, the Major said, at the hands of the French.

This was my fourth tour in the Zone, and the first time I had become intimate with a Vietnamese. Strange, how invisible they had become; it was as if we had squeezed them out of their own country, made them anonymous and—trivial. We were silent for a bit, drinking the tea. I was conscious that we were being observed, this was apparently something of an event, the American commander paying a visit to his Vietnamese allies. I was reluctant to ask him anything of his personal life. I had never done so before, and to do so now would be to admit that he had become a human being, suddenly, after a year of acquaintance. But as it happened he began to talk without prompting, as if he read my thoughts and believed it his obligation to tell me some of the truth of his career with the ARVN. He said he owed his commission to a provincial politician, to whom he continued to tithe a part of his salary, like any faithful surrogate son. I condescended to him, until I realized that his situation wasn't very different from my own. In my own way, I tithed to Old Ben. When I told him my father had been a United States Senator, he warmed considerably. Truly, my command was under a special protection. He said that without any obvious sarcasm but he was smiling. He said that his own family was dead, killed in a bombing raid years before. It had been a mistake, the planes had dropped their bombs on the wrong village; somehow, the coordinates had been confused. It was not hard to understand how such a thing could happen, there were thousands of villages, each with a different coordinate. And the maps were not always accurate. So he was a rare Vietnamese, a man without a family; his only loyalty, he said, was to the soil itself. Specifically, the soil of the village in which he was born and in which his family died. It amazed him that he had stayed alive as long as he had, he'd fully expected to be killed as an aspirant.

To what do you owe your good fortune? I asked.

Luck, he said.

Only that?

I have apparently been in harmony with the heavens, he said. Then, after a moment's pause: And of course I have been cautious.

He said there was one thing that he wanted in life, which was to return to the village before he died. There was a family shrine that he wished to visit and pay homage to. When I asked him where this village was, he impassively gave me a name. Of course the name meant nothing to me so I asked him the province. It was near Tay Ninh City in the province of Tay Ninh, not so very far from Base Fox. Cao Dai country, I gathered. He named his parents and his brothers and sisters and his wife and their two children. All dead. He said his family—I gathered he meant his parents—had gone north and then returned to the South. I did not press him beyond that, but suddenly I had a vision of this family as not so different from my own: or from families anywhere, except this family had chosen to live at the junction of unlucky coordinates.

He said, It is too bad about Laurence.

A heart attack, I said.

He nodded gravely.

Irregular rhythms of the heart, I said.

He said, I know.

I miss him, I said. We all do.

We too, the Major said.

I said foolishly, It was so senseless . . .

But the Major, wisely, had nothing to say to that.

So I fixed it up for him to get a ride as far as Tay Ninh City. And if he could find his way through Indian country to his village, fine. Or if not, that was all right too. It sounded to me as if his village was in the center of War Zone C. He said he longed to see Tay Ninh again. He did not care for the climate and ambience of the Delta, and I said I understood that and sympathized with it. I said I felt the same way about Fort Hood. He nodded, smiling and agreeing. I arranged military transport as far as Tay Ninh City and in a week he was gone with no date set for his return. I had cleared none of this through the Vietnamese authorities. It did not even occur to me to do so.

That was the first in a series of inexplicable decisions.

I realized I had to do something for my men, so restless and disoriented after Laurence's death. Now we were only running one short patrol a week and had ceased joint operations altogether. No one trusted the Vietnamese after the attack, and with the Major gone there was no one in charge. They stayed in their part of the camp and there was no fraternization at all; not that there had been very much anyway. I pulled in some chits and got Air America to fly in a dozen girls from Hong Kong. Then from one of the suppliers in Saigon I imported slot machines and a roulette wheel, and extra rations of liquor and beer. There were drugs, too, but I had no connection with that. I was of a different generation. I paid for some of this with my own money and when that ran short I used army funds. None of it was inexpensive. I wanted to deny nothing to the troopers, who had given so much to so little effect, and however pleasant I could make Base Fox it was never so pleasant as any city or town back in the World. Then I shut the place down, effectively breaking communications with MACV. I shut the place down as if it had never existed, as if there had never been a Base Fox. At this time I was trying to figure out what I would do in the war, where it was leading, and whether I wanted to follow. And while I was doing this, I didn't want any casualties.

Like Laurence, I wanted to know how much was too much. At another time, I might've taken two or three men and gone out and got a hostage and evened the score. But not this time. This time, too much was less, not more. So we retired into the worldly world, the place the men called the World.

Fortunately I got word that the IG was to make an inspection, and I cleaned the place up before they arrived. But two weeks later I knew they had evidence of something. One of my men was rotated home and his replacement was an IG stoolie. I issued direct orders that nothing be done to him, and that probably saved his life. We had our own laws and regulations at Base Fox—anyone who wasn't with us was against us, so the IG's man was marked from the moment he arrived. Sometime in July I got wind of something else: my friends from Air America had been interrogated. And in August they decided that Base Fox was redundant. We moved out as quickly as we could, burning everything but Laurence's hootch. It had become everyone's common room and no one could bear to put the torch to it. The sergeant from Cape Cod believed that Laurence still inhabited the place.

My tour was about up but I had a week in Saigon before I was due to go home. I spent the week in Jessel's room at the Caravelle, drinking and carrying on, all the while trying to reconcile my behavior at Base Fox. It seemed like a dream to me, so far away. When the discipline went, it went in a rush, like water out of a bathtub. We were not a command, we were a rabble. I had cause to think again how fragile things were—whether army customs or humor or army life or your own sense of yourself. That place, there was never anything solid to hold on to. Laurence had kept us going, making us believe somehow that we were beyond anarchy; and when he died, in such an absurd fashion, it seemed to take the meaning out of everything. Or, just possibly, it was the reverse. It took the meaninglessness out of our condition and made us understand that we were part of the World after all. The random, throw-of-the-dice world. This was not inspiriting. When Laurence was present we were a cheerful command of good soldiers, doing our duty as we had been trained to do but somehow separated from the larger crime. We knew how much was enough because we knew how much was too much. When Laurence died we all became morose and with that came fear. There is nothing worse than a frightened soldier, unless it's one who gives in. You must never *give in*. You must never be *careless*. I felt it myself, and was ashamed; I had never been ashamed. I was an army officer, responsible for the men in my command and that meant that I lived with certain restraints, and set an example. You rise above pettiness and you rise above ambition and you rise above fear, and that makes it all unnatural. It is the unnaturalness of your condition that you cling to.

Marina had listened to all of this, saying very little, driving slowly through the Virginia countryside so she could concentrate on what he was saying.

Now she asked what happened to the Major.

He returned, Sam said. Walked into the compound one afternoon a month later. He seemed to disapprove. He said he could
hear the laughter of the girls a quarter of a mile away.

I asked him if there were any signs of enemy and he said that
he had seen none.

No enemy?

None, he said, smiling.

I said, We're no threat.

No, he said.

A week later he was gone. I had transfer orders for him, or a
facsimile of what were said to be transfer orders. I don't know
where they came from, or whether they were genuine. It didn't
seem to make very much difference by then. I genuinely liked
him and wished him well. I admired his resilience, he'd been at
it a very long time and had not given in. But I never saw him
again and I only hope to hell that he's stayed alive. But he
cleared out of Base Fox in a hurry, I can tell you that. Base Fox
then was no place for a man who thought he was in harmony
with the heavens, though it was safe enough.

Anyway, Sam said at last, if they want me they've got me.
Careless behavior, dereliction of duty, and embezzlement of
government funds, just like some crooked Congressman or
Washington lawyer.

It's not the same, she said.

Of course it is! he replied.

Your motives—she began.

—are no excuse, he interrupted.

She asked, Will they want you?

They might, he said. It depends.

On what?

On how much they in Washington want to punish—

But in a *war*, she persisted.

That's the *point*, he said. If you don't understand that, you
don't understand anything. The point is, they hate us. They hate
us to death.

She came back to the table reluctantly, pretending to listen
hard to the conversation. But she was looking at Sam and

couldn't focus. He had admitted to her finally that he would return to the Zone, as the only gesture he could make to the future, to convince himself that there was a future. He was but one wheel in a mighty machine, and not the most important wheel; but a wheel he was and would remain and he could not avoid that by resigning or retiring in silence or sitting behind a desk at the Pentagon—or by allowing them to court-martial him, if it came to that. He'd said to her, I know too much.

He looked up suddenly and smiled at her, then as quickly turned away. They were both drenched in memory, more real than the present and sweeter than any future they were likely to have. He winked at her and turned away again. She remembered the time when they could not stop smiling at each other, they had once consumed an entire meal in silence, uncoupling hands only long enough to pour the wine. They loved to eat and drink, loved restaurants, loved each other; they had had so many dialogues and so much laughter, and if history did not repeat itself perhaps it was because it was so well remembered.

Now they were at table together in Shakerville, both remembering. And Piatt, too, across from her, adjusting his tie now. She saw the boy who had become a man, or anyway an adult; he was better looking now as an adult. At last he had come to resemble his father, though there were no lines in his face. It was a face that looked precisely its age, neither more nor less, and in repose it was grave, an official photograph or portrait. There had been so many photographs over the years, thousands certainly, Piatt with constituents, with the Speaker, with the secretary of defense, with the President at a signing ceremony, the President using a dozen pens to ratify the legislation and distributing them later as souvenirs of the occasion; she remembered his handing a pen to Piatt, then holding on to it, so Piatt had to tug, then with a laugh releasing it, Piatt's hand jerking backward. In the photographs Piatt's fingers were on the knot of his tie, it was as characteristic of him as FDR's jaunty wave. In the photograph he was leaning forward to accept the pen. How many had he accepted and given away, in his turn, to important constituents? Piatt rising, he had his own important subcommittee now and needed only a retirement or defeat or death or two retirements or two defeats or two deaths to be chairman of the full committee, the youngest in the House—and one of the youngest committee chairmen in this century, perhaps the youngest. And he was not yet forty.

The table came back into focus. She wanted to shout or throw a tantrum, or dump the bottle of Armagnac in War Zone C. They were laughing quietly now. Carney had said something that made everyone laugh, even Sheila. Watching Sheila now, Marina was surprised at her—forbearance. At the general forbearance of women—Sheila's, Jo's, her own. It would not last, they concealed so much. She knew the tempo of the dance was increasing, they'd have a whirl. Shakerville was no different from Base Fox. They would all go to pieces, men would leave their wives and women their families. Children would disappear. There would be heart attacks and suicides and breakdowns and no one would be as he or she had been. The thin would grow fat, the fat would grow fatter. They were all fighting the same war, in this murderous twilight of the American century. Now she was drawn to Sheila, tired and distraught, her grief worn like a black badge of courage, beguiled and undone as all of them were, or were soon to become. "Beguiled and undone," that was a phrase of someone's. It was Henry James, talking of women traveling in exotic Italy. Siena, Florence, Cadenabbia, Verona, their valises crowded with souvenirs, beguiled and undone by luxurious, smug, languid Italy, and by their virtuous attachments.

Henry James, who had she thought of him? This conversation had nothing to do with Henry James. They were concerned now with Pat Mundelein.

Jo said, "Dennis knew him. I think Dennis was the first to know him, and introduce him around."

"Dennis knew everybody," Max said. "And he had a great eye. He was first to appreciate Henry's subtle qualities. Hell. If Costello had been listed on the exchange back then and you'd bought him, you'd be filthy rich today. And you wouldn't've had to buy all of him, just one itty-bitty piece."

"Pat Mundelein hasn't done badly."

"God no, Pat's managed things very well." Max laughed. "He's IBM to Costello's Xerox."

"A glamour stock, that's Henry." Jo giggled. "Pat's a sturdy blue chip."

Teddy Carney, speaking for the first time in many minutes, said that he disagreed with them both. Pat Mundelein was a dangerous man. A stranger to the common experience, Carney said, and miscast as an adviser. A bachelor in a town of married men, an introvert in a town of extroverts. He never even read the newspapers! He was secretive, you never saw him around. God knows where he spent his time or with whom.

"Nonsense," Sheila said quietly. A few years ago she had had a fling with Mundelein. He enchanted her with his range of acquaintance in Washington. He took her to a jazz club in Southeast; she had not known the place existed. The owner threw his arms around Mundelein and conducted them to the best table. They were the only white people in the room, not counting the jazz band; and that, too, was odd. The owner joined them for a drink and almost immediately the men were tête-à-tête, their voices unheard over the music. She recognized the look between them. The owner was asking for something and Mundelein was giving it, whatever it was. The owner went away and a bottle of champagne arrived at the table. Later, she and Mundelein talked about Communists. She was baiting him, wanting to crack his self-assurance. She asked him why there were no Communists in Washington. Had Hoover scared them to death? There were more Communists in Northampton, Massachusetts, than there were in Washington. Oh Christ, Mundelein'd said finally, I know one, and had taken her to a flat in Adams-Morgan, banging on the door at three a.m. Mundelein's Washington Communist was a painter, his walls covered with old IWW posters. The painter was excruciatingly shy and spoke in whispers, asking Mundelein if he couldn't do something about the telephone tap, and the adviser shaking his head. One of the penalties for advocating the violent overthrow of the government of the capital of the free world, he'd said. The painter had turned to her sadly, Isn't it silly? Yes, she'd replied, embarrassed that they'd awakened the man at such an ungodly hour. Embarrassed that they were tight and playful and that the painter was drowsy and sober. He'd asked her if she was an agent of the U.S. government and she'd answered that yes, she was, she worked for the Central Intelligence Agency. Oh, dear, he'd lamented, she seemed like such a nice person, and when they left he'd presented her with the little red book, Mao's Thoughts, urging her to read it carefully and repent. She did, too; it was now in the bookshelf at the office next to Freud's *Interpretation of Dreams* and her father's signed copy of Upton Sinclair's *The Jungle*. But what she remembered most was the silent street in Adams-Morgan, Mundelein so suave, urbane as any cultivated commissar gone to meet a dissident poet in some anonymous Moscow suburb, the Zil gliding up to the curb, the knock on the door, the commissar producing a bottle of Stolichnaya and a box of sweets. In this case a fifth of Wild Turkey and, from the glove compartment, a tin of caviar, a gift from the Iranian ambassador. Mundelein was not afraid in the usual ways, give him that.

She thought that he understood something that the others did not, namely that he had come into the government at its pinnacle of authority and—honor. The consensus still held, but good men were required to guarantee it. At one time he had seen the government as a kind of patriotic adventure, going to it as his father had gone to war in Europe. This was the substitute for that, not exactly noblesse oblige because there was something quite handsome about the government; it was a rung up the ladder from Wall Street or the Board of Overseers. Still, a rough equivalent to the war—though there were no casualties, were there? No casualties in this war, no deaths or injuries or prison camps. The men now knew it, and were uneasy, and had to prove themselves. It was one explanation for the Cold War, the Cold War validating the hot one. She thought they looked on it as an enlistment and at the end of the tour they could use it, the experience and the badges and the friendships and whatever notoriety they'd accumulated. They could use that in civilian life, for profit. Of course they would never be very far from the government, they would never really leave. It was the subtext of their lives, their literal livelihood, and they stayed on as private lawyers, lobbyists, consultants, analysts, and investment counselors. It was by then a very large family business. Later on, in the seventies and eighties, they would want to be cabinet secretaries or ambassadors.

Mundelein had always intended to make a career of it, seeing himself as the modern government's memory. He had no experience of anything before 1952, when he was a volunteer in the campaign. He knew nothing first-hand of the New Deal or the second war. Sheila thought of him as one of the carpenters of the Cold War. It would be too much to call him an architect. You could call him its archivist, he recorded the actions of the architects, older men, those who had run the show in Europe.

Still—what animated him? He had no antecedents, beyond a vaguely southern accent. No one knew what he read for pleasure or what he ate or whom or what he coveted or whether there were secret vices. It was not clear how much influence he had with the Man or on which subjects. It was enough to keep the staff quiet, though. If it had been anyone else there would have been an assumption of a dirty little secret somewhere. A deliberate cover-up of a life! In Washington, publicity was a sacrament and if one refused its consolation—why, the reason could only be sinister, some combination of shame or disgust. But Pat Mundelein had been around for so long inquiries about him had virtually ceased. He remained secretive and if every man must perforce lead two lives, one private and the other public, the adviser could be said to have arranged the perfect marriage with himself.

Of course Max Cather would defend him. Now he said to Carney, "I can understand your doubts, looking at it from your angle. Me, I don't care if he's Rasputin. If he gets the job done with no doodah. I don't think you understand because you're a civilian without responsibility. No one gets the job done anymore."

"I don't trust him, either," Carney said. A man who lived off the federal payroll but was not responsive to inquiries concerning his life and beliefs, which the public had a right to know in order to judge. Assuming he had beliefs, one was not certain. It was conceivable that Pat Mundelein was another furtive apparatchik, the town was overrun with them.

"Let him run the trains!" Cather brayed. "Call him Mussolini! I don't give a damn, so long as the man does his job promptly. You have no idea of the frustration and difficulty, simply getting the White House to *act*. And he's shrewd, no one ever denied him that. Fox-smart. As for trust, that doesn't come into it. You take your chances in this town, everyone knows that. . . ."

. . . Washington had no lack of them, Carney went on, colorless scoundrels. Not everyone who was colorless was a scoundrel, but most of Washington's worst scoundrels were colorless. They tended to cover up. Their lives were an extended cover-up and of course, naturally, that made a man wonder. Why? What did he have to hide? They tended, men of this kind, to be arrogant, very arrogant, and consider themselves above the process, meaning above the law—

"You mean above the *press*," Cather said.

"The court of public opinion," Carney corrected.

Sheila turned away. Carney's court of public opinion was in permanent session. His court, his public, his opinion, his statutes, his precedents, his judge, and his jury. Carney began an involved anecdote intended to establish the adviser's contempt for the court. Now Marina was staring at Piatt in a Mrs.-to-Mr., her eyes narrowed, one finger soundlessly tapping the table. Piatt shrugged, they were bogged down again and would have to wait for an interval. Carney's gatherings tended to be unbuttoned even by Shakerville standards, but this one was growing increasingly disheveled. Piatt glanced at his watch, midnight, and reached for the cognac. Marina's eyes were on him still, her gaze steady over a tight Not Amused smile.

" . . . point is," Carney was saying, "the press can be useful to anyone in Mundelein's position. Float this, scotch that, deliver the message, set the agenda, settle a score or make one. We can be used as a messenger service which we're happy enough to do, though of course there's time and charges in the usual coin. Nothing's free and everyone knows that. Ma Bell isn't and we're not. Anyone who doesn't know that doesn't know this town."

"Yes, Teddy," Marina said. "But Mundelein apparently doesn't need you. It's just him and the President and maybe he doesn't see himself as an advocate in need of support. Maybe." She smiled. "Maybe he's learned from his long experience as a federal man that there's a more effective way of doing things. Maybe for him it's enough to know what's going on and having a part in that, obscure and unheralded as it may be. Maybe he sees himself as a support, a chef as opposed to a maître d. Maybe," she said sweetly, "he sees himself as a wife. The President's wife."

"The President already has a wife," Carney said.

"Maybe he's like other men and wants two," she said, "one for work and another for show. Pat's the housewife, dusts the furniture and keeps the kitchen clean and well stocked, toting and fetching. Empties the trash, makes the bed, raises the children, pays the gas bill. A manager of the family finances, he takes no credit. He's selfless, back in the shadows, demure, modest, and content to let his Man have all the applause. Hmmm?"

"Marina, Marina," Teddy clucked.

"So you see, Teddy," Marina said. "Pat's in the great tradition of anonymous helpmeets. And at the end of his distinguished selfless service, his Man gives him the Presidential Medal of Freedom. Or maybe it's only a letter of recommendation, 'This man is my friend. And he does windows.' "

"Marina," Piatt said.

"Bravo," Sheila said.

"To the matter at hand," Max said. He was plainly bored with the other. "I wish we knew more. I wish Sheila could tell us more about the insurance policy that Pat Mundelein's offering. I'm interested in its terms, and the premiums and the scope of coverage. Fire? Theft? Casualty? Embezzlement? Interruption of business? Accident? And what's the liability? And who pays?"

They waited, but Sheila did not reply. She noticed Piatt staring into the middle distance, his fists resting on his knees. Sam was as alert as a beast of the forest, sensing danger, or anyway deception. A normal scene in magical Shakerville, whose antique atmosphere often cast a kind of spell. Ancestors rose out of graves and history was close enough to touch. They knew each other so well. Sheila was conscious of the others looking at her, awaiting her reply, some explanation. But when she defiantly raised her eyes she saw that the company was not interested in her at all, but in Max Cather.

Cather had hiked up the sleeves of his dinner jacket and unbuttoned his shirt cuffs and was carefully rolling them up his arms, until he looked like a gondolier or any well-tailored entertainer. He removed his wristwatch and flexed his fingers, shaking his hands lightly, as if drying them. One expected to see drops of water flying into the center of the table, a merry sprinkle on Sam Joyce's parade. Instead a deck of cards appeared in his right palm. He smiled crookedly, raising his eyebrows.

Cather snapped his wrists and transferred the deck to his left hand, his face grave as an accountant's. He cut the cards and flourished both halves. The company moved closer to him, drawn by his assurance. No one spoke. He fanned a dozen cards in each hand simultaneously, displaying them front and back. His fingers were long and slender, manicured, the pink nails buffed to a high shine. He hesitated, then at speed drew a jack from behind Carney's ear, and different cards from Piatt's lapel, Sheila Dennehay's blonde bangs, and Helen Carney's bodice. He turned quickly to Sam and eased a white silk handkerchief from his inside pocket, waving it, then dropping it over Jo's balloon glass, the silk settling like a parachute. They all smiled, a deep hush surrounding them. Cather sat motionless, his right hand poised above the covered glass. The company bent forward, expectant.

"History lesson," he said softly.

Then he snatched the silk away, revealing at the bottom of the glass—an earring, Jo's, as she quickly discovered when she put a finger to her ear, giggling self-consciously. Max began his patter then, while performing rapid-fire a series of tricks, his fingers flying over the surface of the table. Cards were suddenly everywhere, suspended in air, now in Cather's hands, now under Carney's chin, now nestled in the candelabrum, now an ace, now a king; now here, now there. He never fumbled. The patter

180

had to do with Norse and Icelandic traditions of myth and magic, the magic reinforcing the myth, the myth enhancing the magic. Say one thing, do another; promise this, perform that. His accented voice grew louder, drenching them. Rumanian legends. The skills of gypsies. Indian rainmakers and shamans, magicians who shinned a tree to sit astride a branch shaking a hog's hide filled with beads and bones. Civilizations rested on it, governments depended from it. Happy was the man who believed in magic, and happier still the man who could bring it about. Honored, quoted, consulted! *Achtung*, he said, behold the modern attorney! The rainmaker, architect of culs-de-sac, blind alleys, mazes—thickets of words so dense no ordinary human being could find a path through them, a dismal swamp of polysyllables and dead Latin. The magician stood now and stretched his arms to the chandelier, displaying his hairy wrists and forearms, as if suggesting to the company that his very flesh could conceal a red trey or a one-eyed jack. His hands flew together and then apart, now holding the silk handkerchief, and for an instant the crisp silk mesmerized—it became a winding sheet, its folds as disturbing and sinister as the dripping wax that clung to Carney's candles and hung there in creases. Each of them took a step backward in time as the white silk, motionless in Cather's hands, shrouded the present. He was sweating heavily, huge drops coursing down his forehead and cheeks to hang, trembling, on bony precipices, heavy as boulders. The restless motion and performer's patter created a thick, abnormal atmosphere in which no one moved or spoke.

The silk handkerchief disappeared and he dealt each friend a card, face down. Without being told they covered the cards with their palms. Max again began to speak of gypsies, the women; in women was magic, the world conjured from a deck of cards or a glass sphere! The past explained, the future foretold. No wonder gypsies had no homeland, no nation with boundaries, governments, armies, or libraries. They carried their homeland in a deck of cards; they had no written language, all promises were spoken, lasting as long as the sound of the syllables themselves. A queen of spades was a face more final than any decision of president, parliament, or court.

We've learned little from the gypsies, he said, collecting the cards.

Sad, he went on, that there was no tradition of magic in the United States of America. Superstition was society's binder, and the supernatural its dense inner rhythm. Two cogent reasons why the American culture was thin and without mystery, and therefore without resonance.

"Yours," he said to Sam, turning over an ace of hearts. "Yours, yours, yours, yours, yours, yours, mine," he said, turning the cards and naming them before they fell. "Ace, deuce, trey, *quatro*, five, six, seven, and for me, ten." he enumerated in a businesslike monotone. Then he shuffled the cards once, and again, and dealt them back—the other way round the table, but in the opposite sequence. Each of them received the same cards as before, as of course did he, the ten of hearts. "Ten for me," he said. "Do you know what 'ten' means, if you're a numerologist? A perfect one, money and health, love and honor. Good fortune. Benign stars, a safe passage, the wind always at your back, et-cetera. Means the same as 'ace,' " he said, looking at Sam.

The patter was not ended and Sam listened to it, amused. He had watched Cather perform before, all of them had. The performances always came without warning, at odd times and places; the patter varied with the hour and the place and the company and the circumstances of the evening. There were reports that Cather had used his talent to advantage as a field man in Europe in the 1950s. A wallet lifted here, a weapon disarmed there, a compromising piece of paper folded into an inside pocket, a deft exchange of briefcases. Light-fingered Max Cather, the professional dip. It was said (he would not confirm it) that he worked as a magician in Budapest in 1957, a café near the Szechenyi Library, his naturally swarthy skin darkened further by pigment. He performed in white tie and top hat and the patter then was in German, replete with references to Heine, Rilke, Schiller, and Goebbels. The story was not believed by everyone, it seemed derivative of Alfred Hitchcock, among others, but there were intriguing details. He billed himself as "The

Great Cassio," an inside joke; CAS was the field man's acronym for Langley, "covert American services." The job gave him unrestricted movement around the city and familiarity with the best circles, performing as he did at numerous private gatherings. Reliable Americans who knew him then recalled an impressive, dapper figure, dark-skinned, close-cropped black beard, and of course the dazzling hands. He was one of the few (if indeed Cather and Cassio were the same man) who had managed a successful transition from the field to headquarters. The beard came off and he dressed now in sober conventional anonymity, a gray suit and regimental tie, black shoes, a plain white shirt, spectacles in clear plastic frames, a quick indulgent smile; a friend offered to postdate membership in Ivy Club to complete the modern dossier. He performed sleight-of-hand now for friends late at night, when a manic glee overtook him, though there was always something brutal in the performance.

"Jews, gypsies," he said, winding down now. "Cosmopolitan people, slightly suspect. Double suspect if your name was Cather by whim of an immigration officer. Where did you come from? Where did your father come from? Where was your family place? Your schools? The ancestral graveyard? Too often you were untraceable, your past not deliberately buried, like Pat Mundelein's, but obscured by history. You were a man without verification, your credentials never quite in order—you see? So you advanced so far and no farther. They were adept at identifying survivors, weren't they? They did not like to use us as field men; who knew if we had a hostage to fortune out there somewhere in Rumania or Poland or Hungary and if the right mnemonic button was pushed—wouldn't we move on, as we had always moved on, from one dark capital to the next? In a pinch, who knew where we'd jump? Slip away and betray them, pulling on a new identity as easily as they changed a shirt; we had so many loyalties, and so many of them were fragile. And we were attracted to aggressive philosophies opposed to the established order, whatever it was in whatever nation it was not *ours*. Of course that is all passé now, or soon will be; the only ideology that attracts our gypsies is that which comes from the barrel of a gun. In ten years the KGB will be obliged to rely on bankrupt air force sergeants with a wife and a mortgage at home and a mistress two trailers away, or should I say Mobile Home? We have seen the last of the Fuchs and the Rosenbergs, characters from Dostoevsky; our future traitors will seem created by James M. Cain. So—as a rule they used us as analysts, it was well known that we were adroit with numbers. We were good pencil men. Our minds ranged farther than theirs, having a wider acquaintance with the infinite possibilities of men's thinking. However weird it got, it would never get any weirder than we had known. Or more murderous.

"And in an office we could be watched. No surprises that above a certain level the landlords refused to rent. They wanted to keep the neighborhood tight and in the family, people with provable antecedents. The Cold War was a family responsibility, was it not? And it's a mistake to think this is simple anti-Semitism. It's a complex anti-Semitism, there is nothing simple about our capital. It is probably the least anti-Semitic city in America, perhaps the world outside the dear state of Israel itself. And of course the reverse is also true! There is no Semitism either, no Hassidim with sidecurls and black hats, no Seders, no Sabbath, no menorah in the parlor, no ghetto tenements, no *memento mori*, no *Jews*. In Washington we are all feds, neither more nor less. Prejudice owing to creed, region, or fortune does not exist, perhaps because the federal culture is stronger than any other. Race is something else again, it's the one palpable barbarian bias—and how American after all! The truth is, we live in eighteenth-century America, before the crowded boat-loads from Limerick, Leghorn, and Danzig. We live in pre-industrial, pre-urban America. Washington has always been the America of the plantation, and of orderly opportunity—not a westward movement but an implosion. The plantation is a closed world. We operate a service industry, we supervise the pursuit of happiness. We legislate it, then we adjudicate it, finally we administer it. This is where the money is! We decide where it will go and to whom; how much and for how long. So the lure of power—that is what it is, deciding who gets the money—rounds the ethnic and regional edges; in the past there has always been enough for everybody, all you needed was to stake your claim and hire an attorney, sooner or later we'd give you a slice of the pie. There's no room for bigotry or simple snobbery here, not among those of us who are permanents; who are part of the permanent collection, and remain on the walls no matter who occupies the mansion. The isolated islands of bourgeois prejudice, Langley and the U.S. Senate, and the U.S. Army, the U.S. Navy, and the U.S. Air Force are just that— isolated islands. In a generation they will seem almost quaint. Even now we condescend. In Washington we are beyond philosophy or ideology; we are assimilated, Judeo-Christians all. And all far from home." He wet his lips, and when he spoke next it was almost a snarl. "We have taken on the protective coloring of the environment, symmetrical personalities, set at oblique angles. Me no less than you. I meant what I said about Jessel." He looked around him belligerently. "And we are brothers. Except when it comes to supervising the Cold War, so necessary to our unfettered pursuit of happiness. And so fundamental to our concept of virtue. Lucky for me that I have my magic act. Every citizen needs one." He placed the deck of cards carefully in front of him. The others waited, assuming the magician had something further to say. But he did not. He closed his eyes and dipped his head. The bizarre entertainment was over.

For a moment there was dead silence. Then Helen Carney cleared her throat and made a show of offering the cognac.

Jo said, "It's late, Max."

Marina said, "Piatt, we have to go."

Sam said, "Poor Max, they won't let him sit at the top tables. They won't let him play with the tiddlywinks." The Colonel was deeply offended.

Cather smiled broadly, though his glittering eyes narrowed and his fingers commenced to drum on the tablecloth.

Sam said, "You goddamned people at Langley—"

Sheila Dennehay picked it up immediately. "Remember once, Max. We rented that legislature in wherever it was. West Africa somewhere. Cheaper than a purchase, if I recall. The

Director wanted to buy them. You said, 'Why buy? Why not rent them for an afternoon? Let me write the lease!' Remember that?" She smiled.

Jo said, "Max has had a number of offers. The oil companies, the banks. They want him, he knows so much. They always want him to go abroad."

"Always," Sheila said. "They'll give you a vice presidency but you report to the chairman. They like you to base yourself in London or Beirut. Lots of connections both places, nonstops to the Gulf states, Saudi, and Egypt." Sheila smiled warmly at Max. "Of course they're worried that you'll be double-dipping. Then they think about it a little and don't worry so much, it gives them a way into the company when they need help. And they do, all the time. They want to make darn sure where your loyalty is, though. That's why the money's so good. Why they need us is, at the Harvard Business School they don't teach surprises. That's what Max and I specialize in, surprises. God, they're dumb."

"You can't go on forever in that business," Jo said glumly. "It's rosy enough now, but what happens in ten years? It costs money to live in this town, at least the way Max and I like to live." No one replied to that. They all knew that Jo had family money as well as a lucrative business, public relations. She rarely spoke of it, or her clients; she was less a publicist than a censor.

Sam said patiently, "So they've screwed you, is that it?"

Oh no, Cather said. "They've been most kind, though nothing in this town is ever as it appears to be. That's what this decade has demonstrated, surprising results from improbable currences. Even you would agree with that, Colonel. These mysteries ought to remind us of our submission to historical forces, and the simple truth that God is not kind. Also of our own recuperative powers—despite our stupidity and cowardice. We're all friends here of course, in the meritocracy of Shakerville. However, you're cut from a different cloth."

"Say again?"

"You've had all the advantages."

"Provable antecedents?"

"That's one," Cather said. "And it's not negligible, no. You're a Washington aristocrat, one of the cliffdwellers, and there aren't many. It's alluring to the authorities, it makes them comfortable. Your *abba*, didn't he work for Yerkes? Yerkes, think of it. If you were a Red, it would be like heeling for Karl Marx. Tell me. Does he talk about it much? Does he have the original documents?" He turned to the others. "My father knew a man who knew Marx in London, and that makes him close enough to touch. As you touch Yerkes. We've known each other a long time, Sam," Cather said. He poured cognac for himself, then pushed the bottle to the center of the table, somewhere in the vicinity of the demilitarized zone. "Haven't always gotten along, though we've fought for the same things. Now we're struggling with something serious, this city and its processes, and the war and what happens now. *I want this project, Sam.* It means a lot to me, and it'll mean a lot to you, too. The difference between us is, you see it from the inside and I from the outside. But we're both exposed. That's my belief. I think it's Pat Mundelein's belief too, though he's playing it close to the chest. And Piatt knows more than he's said."

Piatt said it was a long story, and classified.

I'm cleared at the highest levels, Max said.

I'm not, Sam said.

"Well," Max said, "it would be need-to-know, wouldn't it?" He foraged among the bottles and came up with framboise. "You and Sol Henderson, you'd make quite a team. You two, you'd just bust their balls, wouldn't you? Of course we'd be in overall charge, that's something that would be written into the contract. But I can promise the widest latitude. We're not timid."

Sam said nothing.

"But I'd have to know what's involved." He tapped the bottle of framboise against his temple, then drew the cork with his teeth. "Why are they so anxious to have Sam?"

"President knows Old Ben," Piatt said. "Likes him, trusts him. Maybe Sam reminds him of Old Ben. And Old Ben reminds him of the good old days."

"It figures," Max said, laughing.

"When things were a lot simpler," Piatt said.

Sam turned away, half amused, half angry. Things were getting disheveled, Max drunk, Piatt sullen, Teddy biding his time. They thought Old Ben was the key to it, but they really didn't know anything. What they didn't know about the world would fill an encyclopedia. What they didn't know about Old Ben would fill the *Summa Theologica*.

What had the President called him? An old pirate, leaning forward and laughing soundlessly. The Man wouldn't let him go, hanging on to Old Ben for dear life. How is he? Remember me to him, grand old guy. Ben Joyce had that effect on people, they wanted to preserve him as evidence of the lusty roguish past, when the country was rambunctious and amused with itself, and was never trod upon. To watch him was to reinvent the past as it was explained in the postwar history books, before the humorless revisionist Marxists seized the academy.

And what had he done, big brave Colonel? He'd nodded and grinned and said, Yes, sir, Old Ben was just fine, never better, fit as a fiddle, implying with his smile that the old bastard had been a dandy dad as well as a living legend.

There was the matter of Lincoln's general. One of the President's generals was an ancestor of his mother's, and in the foyer of the house on Main Street in Genesee was his commission, signed by the Great Emancipator in his bony script, A. Lincoln. It was the first object that caught the visitor's eye, a yellowing parchment encased in a gilt frame. A blundering soldier and a middling farmer but a resourceful land speculator. When he died in the 1880s he owned four farms of about one hundred acres each. This was soybean country, the most productive land in Illinois, and the source of Sam's mother's legacy. Most of it was still in the family, farmed now by tenants who paid handsomely for the privilege. Alas, after her death the commission in its gilt frame was misplaced. Sam knew his father destroyed it. Old Ben hated the general, whom he saw as a rival; one among many.

Your mother's claim to fame, he said contemptuously.

I'd like to have it, Sam said. This was a few years after the war. His father had just retired from the Senate.

It's gone, Old Ben said. Lost.

How was it lost?

What do you care? What's he to you?

My ancestor. And I intend to go to West Point.

You think he'll get you in?

I don't need him, Sam said.

No, Old Ben said. But you need me. It's a Congressional appointment, remember? If I say no, you don't go.

You would, too, wouldn't you?

No, as a matter of fact, I wouldn't. But I could. And would, if I wanted to. But I don't want to. So you'll get the appointment. I'll fix it.

He had become a monument, more stone than flesh, more dead than alive. Lawyers quoted him in their off-hours to each other. A man to be envied for his vitality, inner compass, and vision. Not the career *per se*, they said judiciously, for there was something questionable, not quite counterfeit but not quite genuine either, in his effortless rise from hanging judge to one-term senator to sage and counselor. His rise was both effortless and inevitable, no doubts and no collapse of creed for Old Ben. His greatest achievement was himself, and he gave inside men faith in themselves. His attraction lay not in his ideas, still less his ideals, but in his personality and will and sheer longevity. He had witnessed everything and forgotten and learned much. He forgot that which was inconvenient.

Also, he was rich. He was a pioneer in the practice of law outside the courtroom. His rule: Never litigate. Before the advent of Old Ben the capital had not been a great money town for private lawyers. New York was the mother lode, and at great occasions before the Supreme Court or a Committee of Congress a New York lawyer would be in charge. Litigators were the cream of the profession, and amply paid for their efforts, but a litigator's work was visible: the case was well or badly argued *in the presence of the client*. Old Ben thought he knew a better way. His six years in the Senate had taught him that laws would become more numerous and complex, indeed the more numerous and complex they were the greater the need for a subtle counselor who could suggest additional laws and regulations to correct the obvious abuses and excesses—in short, an attorney who knew the men who wrote the laws as well as the men who administered them. Moreover, he quickly saw that Washington was mysterious to a businessman; it was as mysterious as Hollywood. And the secret was not to demystify, it was to present oneself as a necromancer, a magician. He was the first to see that the government would become the nation's greatest corporation, a great sea of money, greater even than Du Pont or General Motors: he was the first to see, and the first to *act*. And now he was revered for his vision, much in the way modern gamblers revere the breathtaking audacity of Arnold Rothstein in 1919.

Ben Joyce was living proof of the continuity of events. He himself was an "event," knowing everyone worth knowing, his memory reaching back to the nineteenth century: he knew a man who knew Gould, and he himself had worked as a runner for Yerkes. He had been one of Insull's downstate connections, though no scandal ever attached to his name. In Washington his reputation was—immense, though his name rarely appeared in the newspapers. An invitation to his apartment in the Shoreham was considered to be second only to one to the White House itself, among those old enough to remember the days when the mansion was a man's house instead of a fourth branch of government. His birthday parties were civic rituals, the last one held in Mrs. Denver's *palazzo* in Kalorama. Lucy Denver was one of his oldest friends and had invited fifty people, ranging in age from the callow general counsel of the Federal Communications Commission to a retired chairman of the Joint Chiefs of Staff. There was no one there who was older than Old Ben, however. There were toasts and a towering birthday cake with ninety-odd candles and the guest of honor, "the birthday boy," as Lucy Denver put it in her ghastly contralto, in wax at its summit, an effigy. Old Ben sat serenely in an easy chair drinking a Bloody Mary and smoking a Cuban cigar.

Sam described it later to Marina. The old man was in good form. "He passed the cigar box to the Vice President, and was amused when the Vice President declined. And delighted when the box went round to the retired admiral, who accepted."

"So the Vice President disappointed him?"

"That was because the Vice President was afraid of the President, and Old Ben didn't like fear."

That afternoon the talk turned naturally to the war. They were gathered like old Indian chiefs around Old Ben's easy chair, the admiral, Old Ben's law partner—aged eighty, now "of counsel" to the firm but as sturdy as he had been when he worked in the New Deal—and three or four others, a senator, a columnist, a former secretary of state, and in the wings, listening hard, the young lawyer from the FCC. They spoke drolly of the present war, which no one seemed able to win or end. Then the admiral told a story from Two, one that the company had not heard before; it had to do with Montgomery. Laughter followed. The former secretary of state retailed a version of the events of 1957. One could almost hear the cracking of men's spines. At length the Vice President joined in, trying to match them story for story. And that was the idea. The old men listened with a show of respect, veterans to a promising rookie; everything was filed away, current knowledge was always valuable. Then when they knew they had all they were going to get, they returned to their own memories. Guts, bluff, and finesse. The young attorney was soon laughing as loudly as they were, rocking back on his heels, fingers tucked into his waistcoat pocket where they could touch the Phi Beta Kappa key. Sam knew him as a man of the left; that was according to the press. He had no stories to contribute from the Federal Communications Commission so he did not join the raconteurs. They were careful to include him in the laughter, however; communications law was one of the great growth industries of the legal economy.

Now there was contempt in their voices, their country—the "their" was pregnant—couldn't even win a chickenshit war (the admiral's phrase). Couldn't summon up the juice, never should've gotten into it to begin with; even MacArthur knew that, and MacArthur didn't know anything. Sam watched the young lawyer's expression turn from respect to awe. These were the great American proconsuls, having served in the days of empire; their humor and self-assurance made the others feel like novices bowing before worldly popes.

Sam leaned on the mantel, listening. This was not an argument he would join, and it would never occur to them to ask him a question. They needed neither his approval nor his advice.

Old Ben egged them on, and the party was accordingly most hilarious. The admiral and the former secretary of state loved to please him, reveling in his rich, promiscuous laughter. Honoring Old Ben, they honored themselves. This was more than respect accorded a man born a few years after the murder at Ford's Theatre, who had worked for Charles T. Yerkes, married well, read law, was elected a judge and then a United States senator, and finally in what should have been his dotage founded a law firm that was now the city's greatest. Truly, his last years were golden. Old Ben was now beyond politics, as all of them were; they were simply old men together, who for a time had been at the center of events in the capital. It had been the greatest period any of them had known. In that way, they rather pitied the Vice President. It wasn't *that* much fun anymore, the sons having squandered the legacy.

And that was what they had been given, a fabulous legacy, enough wealth and power and authority to last a thousand years. It was clear what had gone wrong. The sons had not wanted it badly enough, being frightened of responsibility. They'd lost their nerve, that much was certain. And they had lost the enterprising spirit, the sheer will to make things go. They had become paralyzed, first by the bomb and then by fear; they did not understand that either you controlled your enemies or they controlled you, there was no middle way. They failed to recognize that the country had an edge. Old Ben maintained that every man had an edge. Once Sam asked him his and he'd shrugged and laughed. And replied finally, "thorough preparation." He knew their secrets. He had represented them before the Commissions and at Congressional hearings and in the offices of cabinet secretaries, as during his years as a senator he had represented them inside the Senate chamber. There was that, and something else. He had prepared their wills and trusts and listened patiently to their most intimate public and private worries. There was nothing so revealing as an asymmetrical last will and testament. Old Ben often boasted that he knew them inside and out—"I know more about them even than J. Edgar"—and Sam, silent at table during those excruciating evening feasts—so reminiscent of his boyhood in Genesee, Old Ben the town crier—would hear menace in his father's voice. One turn of the screw and it was the voice of the blackmailer. Knowledge, the old man would say; knowledge is power. Know the secrets, what they are and where they're kept. To be the custodian of the archives! Washington is a gigantic ossuary, he cried, and I am the curator!

Look, he'd say, warming to the theme. You took a certain pile of bones and went back to discover the provenance, tracing them through a score of transactions. In the beginning the bones were helter-skelter but as you went forward into the past you found the connection each to each and at last, at the moment of a marriage or merger or malfeasance or error of excess or passion or candor, you discovered the shape of the skeleton. What it looked like really, and the closet in which it was hidden. All of life was there: ambition, disappointment, hope, pride, love, hate, *misprision*. Ah, *misprision*. That was the common law of the capital, a high regard for the subtleties of misprision, an ancient conundrum: neglect of duty. But a neglect of duty easy to deny. Misprision: passive misconduct, benign neglect. Then Old Ben, laughing uproariously now, would cite the controlling precedent. As it happened, Oberon's complaint in *A Midsummer Night's Dream*.

> Of thy misprision must perforce ensue
> Some true love turn'd and not a false turn'd true.

Not the action, but the effect of the inaction. A thoroughly modern concept! Then he would laugh and laugh, gaily supplying Puck's dour answer, in falsetto (Old Ben was a talented mimic):

> Then fate o'er rules, that, one man holding troth,
> A million fail, confounding oath on oath.

One man holding troth! There may be such a man in the capital, but Old Ben had never met him. Ha ha!

And that was the trouble with the new men, boys; the boys who were now in charge. They didn't want it badly enough to turn all their guns on the objective. They knew many little things but they didn't know the one big thing. They did not know that you had to grow. Grow always. If you did not grow, you died. Either expand the business or sell it off. There was no middle ground. And when you got into a fight, you won it.

A monster? No, not that. A man rather too attracted to dark corners, and pleased to find so many of them; and so much company when he got there. Especially pleased to find so many dark corners in the government, that unattractive necessity. He remained a man of the Middle West, a resident of the interior, though he never returned to Genesee after he resigned from the Senate. But he remained its representative. Whether judge, senator, or attorney at law, he saw himself as counselor, an adviser. It was necessary to know the facts, and the dark corners from which they came. Any counselor who put his trust in human nature was liable for disbarment. He had a passion to know the facts, and the subtext of the facts, and his power was greater for seldom being used: he suppressed his urge to turn the screw. It was enough that the threat was there. To know was good: to know privately was better. He had taken many things from the interior and his years as a runner for Yerkes, but that was the greatest thing. Yerkes told him that if you had a little power, people thought you had a lot. If you had a lot, people thought you had more still. Never spoil their illusions, it was comforting to them to believe that power was not loose, escaped from its cage, a dangerous and unpredictable beast. Better that it was possessed: men hated uncertainty. Never bring your authority to a test unless absolutely necessary, Yerkes said, because when tested the chances were great that you had less power than you thought and a great deal less than they thought. In a tight spot, therefore, bring all your guns to bear at once. In this context, of course money was power.

Yerkes had destroyed himself. He had let his passions run, he was promiscuous and tireless with women; fundamentally, he was not a serious individual. He had allowed himself to be ruined by lesser men. He had put himself on the wrong side of the fence, and that was a disastrous error. There was no need to do it. There was more money on the right side of the fence, if a man was clever and kept his wits about him; ultimately that was where the power was also. It was important to have a stable reputation.

So Old Ben was benign by his own lights, with something always held in reserve. In that way he resembled his son, except the reserves were different. Old Ben thought it necessary that ordinary citizens not see weakness or confusion. It made them insecure and erratic in behavior; it frightened them. The strength of the country depended on a vision of a prosperous and tranquil future, durable institutions. Sam demurred, believing in clear sight the way an aviator believed in Newton's third law. He had a certain sympathy with the other, however.

Mrs. Denver had brought a friend to Old Ben's birthday party. Sam observed him with care, a stocky, cocky man, under forty, whose most conspicuous features were bright eyes and a growling laugh. In the beginning he seemed out of place, standing politely on the fringes of the group around Old Ben, listening carefully and smiling at unexpected times. He was one of those young men who immediately established themselves with old men, so after the first few minutes he joined the conversation, at first tentatively, then as a full partner.

The admiral and the former secretary of state were mildly irritated at this incursion—who was he, anyway?—but the new arrival was witty with gossip and it was obvious after the first few comments that he was on their footing. How was this achieved? He pointedly refused to refer to Highest Levels by their first names, yet was oddly familiar with their personal lives. The son of one man lost in California, the brother of another in trouble with a federal grand jury in Chicago, the mysterious illness of a third.

The admiral glanced at his hostess and raised his eyebrows.

He had missed the introductions. When Mrs. Denver whispered in his ear, he nodded and bent down to enlighten Old Ben.

"I know who he is," Ben Joyce said testily. He looked at the new man. Of course it was Henry Costello. "You're Costello," he said. "Welcome to my party." Then he turned to his old friend. "How do you know Henry?"

"Ben," Lucy Denver said shyly. "That's indiscreet."

Old Ben nodded, understanding immediately. "Well, you couldn't get a better man."

"It's all so complicated now," she said with a little laugh. "You said yourself, I needed . . . " He put up his hand. There was no need for her to say more. This was a private matter, her own finances and the network of trusts that held them together.

There was a short silence while Old Ben and Henry Costello measured each other.

"I've always wanted to meet you," Old Ben said at last.

"And I you."

They were both smiling as if they shared a secret.

"I admire the job you did," Old Ben said. "My people have kept me informed. We needed another man in the room, man with a different perspective."

Costello smiled. "Optics," he said.

The admiral drifted off, this conversation had nothing to do with the wars. But the young man from the FCC remained, as did Old Ben's law partner and the former secretary of state. Mrs. Denver refilled his glass from the pitcher of Bloody Marys at his elbow.

"Damn fine work," Old Ben said.

Costello stood very still. He was in no way muscular but somehow his stillness and poise suggested an athlete at rest. "I take that as a serious compliment," he said formally. "You have been my ideal for many years."

Old Ben glanced over at Sam. "Young man'll go far," he said, but his smile was only perfunctory. It was obvious that Costello meant what he said.

"I was happy to be of help."

"I trust the matter is proceeding normally," Old Ben said.

Costello looked at his wristwatch. "I think it has already proceeded. As of about thirty minutes ago, that was the plan. But I can check."

"Could you do that?"

"Of course," Costello said. Mrs. Denver indicated a telephone in the corner of the room and then, with another motion, suggested another in a more private place. Costello shook his head and walked to the phone in the corner, dialed, spoke a few words, waited, and then began to speak in earnest. He stood quite straight, his hands in his pockets, the instrument tucked between his shoulder and his ear. It was obvious by his posture and manner of speaking that he was talking to a senior man. After a moment of silence he laughed, signaling an end to the conversation. Then he hung up.

Costello returned to the group and nodded at the old man in the easy chair. "He signed it this morning."

Old Ben smiled, then asked irritably, "Why wasn't I told?"

Costello said that "they" were planning to release the news the next day, along with a cabinet appointment and the itinerary of a presidential journey. "Our news, by contrast, is small beer. In the way that news is measured in our town." Sam, listening, thought of news suddenly as a pet on a leash. Its release depended upon its owner. When it slipped its chain by stealth or carelessness there was trouble all around. But when it was released with other, larger, more conspicuous animals—why, it was forgotten in the crush. Costello now shook his head sympathetically, there'd obviously been a snafu somewhere. It was inexcusable. He'd speak to them. However, he wanted it known that if Old Ben had not asked he, Costello, would've given him the news privately.

"You were the linchpin," Costello said.

"No, I wasn't," Old Ben said. "Nice of you to say so. I'm too old and the matter is too complicated. I *was* very much involved at the beginning, that was—"

"At least ten years ago," Costello said.

The old man smiled. "Much longer ago than that. I was involved then, not now. This is a matter that goes way, way back. But it's good that we've reached common ground at last."

"Everyone's satisfied now," Costello said.

"No doubt," Old Ben said dryly. "Appetites were so ravenous for so long. Perhaps their stomachs commenced to shrink and everyone understood that nourishment was available, if only." He turned to those gathered around his chair. No one had said a word during the exchange with Costello. "Mr. Costello is an attorney," Old Ben said. "But he has devised a new sort of practice."

"Hush, hush," Costello said, laughing soundlessly.

"—amazing that no one ever thought of it before, it's to the practice of law what the invention of the automatic transmission was to locomotion." The old man cocked his head in admiration, his eyes remaining locked on the other. He explained that Henry Costello put himself in service to all the parties. In the present case, he said obliquely, it was a difficulty involving a foreign government, an industrial concern, and the American government. An extremely complex matter, Old Ben said, with political overtones and knotty questions of foreign policy and a certain confusion as to . . . arbitry. A labyrinth, he said.

Costello listened to all this with a fixed smile. He said quietly, "Senator Joyce."

The old man smiled. "My friends call me 'Judge.' " He turned back to the others. "It's breathtaking! Mr. Costello acts on behalf of the matter itself! Not the parties, but the matter! It is as if." Old Ben steepled his fingers and stared into the middle distance, apparently waiting for a revelation. "There was a civil suit involving an idea. Mr. Costello represents this idea. *The idea is his client.* Joyce & Walsh are the attorneys for the foreign government. The industrial concern has its attorneys, and of course we were working in close harmony with them, up to a point. The State Department has its attorneys. The Justice Department is involved, obviously, as is the President's adviser downtown. The Internal Revenue Service has its man in goal, as it were. A committee of the Congress had an interest. Oh, did it have an interest!"

"Counselor," Costello said.

"It is a great moment, Mr. Costello. Let us savor it."

"These matters." Costello fluttered his hands.

"—are by their nature confidential, so no more of them. This is hypothetical, of course. Now." Old Ben's eyes were on his law partner and the former secretary of state, who were both leaning over his chair. "Who is the orphan in this arrangement? Who is without counsel, battered to and fro and hither and yon by the competing interests? It is the problem itself! This infant child, this mere idea, is without voice or definition. Call it—call it an unassembled weapon! Mr. Costello, as it happens, is a friend to all concerned. To the American government, to the foreign government, to the manufacturer, to the Justice Department, to the IRS, to the committee of the Congress, to everyone. He is known to be disinterested. Only Mr. Costello is in a position to cut through this cat's cradle to seek a solution to the best advantage of the *problem*." Old Ben was grinning gleefully. "Indeed, counselor. Optics."

Raising his glass in wary salute, Costello said nothing. But he looked uncomfortable.

"And, of course," Old Ben went on, his voice as deep and untroubled as a mountain lake, "the fees come from as many as four different directions."

"God," the former secretary whispered.

"An interesting concept," the law partner said. Then he laughed. "Why didn't we ever think of it?"

"We did not have the training," Old Ben said.

The former secretary turned to the new man. "What is your background, sir?"

"Mr. Costello," Old Ben said triumphantly, "is a professor of law!"

"On leave," Costello said. He named a great university. "The judge does me too much credit. I am a consultant, no more and no less."

Old Ben's law partner was struggling with a question he did not know how to put. He said, "A valuable service."

Costello took a tiny sip of his drink, so tiny it might have been strychnine.

"Of course it would not be eleemosynary," the law partner said with a nervous laugh. He wanted to know how the fees were split.

200

"No," Costello said softly.

The former secretary of state said, "As a professor of law, would you say there is an overriding principle. To the work that you do, some controlling, ah—" It was the same question, Fowler's elegant variation.

Costello parried. "Only the general principle that the law is anything the majority says it is, Mr. Secretary. It's what is convenient at any given point in time. As Mr. Holmes said, it is the convenience of the majority. The law is."

"Of course," the former secretary said thoughtfully. So it was a negotiated fee, reckoned neither by time nor by percentage; indeed the two were probably fungible. Or, more likely, it was a shrewd combination. Or whatever the traffic would bear.

Old Ben stared at the ceiling, a dreamy expression on his face. He said casually, "Do you remember, Buster?" That was his nickname for the former secretary. "Dear God, how many years ago was it? The taxi zones. Joyce & Walsh was helpful in the negotiations with the District Committee. The taxi owners believed that the zones were drawn for the convenience of the members of Congress, as indeed they were; every zone touched at Capitol Hill. And you'll recall the plan that was worked out. Failing to alter the zones, we devised the group ride." The former secretary nodded vaguely; at that time he had been out of the government and had joined Joyce & Walsh as counselor to the firm. "Ingenious, we thought, and so it was. When there was more than a single passenger it worked as follows. First passenger goes to his destination, pays. Then the flag goes down and a dollar—at that time it was twenty-five cents—is added. Second passenger goes to his destination, pays. And so on and so forth. It did not solve the Capitol Hill problem, but it satisfied the taxi owners." He smiled thinly as the others bent forward, waiting for the point of the story; surely there was one. "Now envision a situation where all the passengers have a similar destination. All pay the same fee on a basis of distance and time, plus of course the usual extras for heavy baggage; as we all know, some passengers travel light and others travel with impedimenta. Now if the ride is comfortable and trouble-free and quick. If the driver is an expert negotiator of the city's many one-way streets, culs-de-sac,

201

roundabouts, and bottlenecks. If the driver is personable and able to soothe the fractious passengers. If the driver *knows where he is going*. Well, then, wouldn't these passengers, in their satisfaction, pool a sum of money for a gratuity? Of course they would! Time is money! Distance is money! The shorter the ride, the more generous the gratuity! Particularly and especially if the destination is important. Those for whom it might be inappropriate to pay in cash might pay in kind, or in future considerations. Or simply in friendship! Mr. Costello has many close friends inside our government."

Henry Costello cleared his throat. He consulted his watch and raised an eyebrow, sighing. He was overdue for an appointment.

"Perhaps you could give me your card," the former secretary said. His own private business dealings were considerable.

Costello said, "I do not have offices here. When I am in town, I stay at the Mayflower."

A lawyer without a calling card and without offices! The former secretary began to smile. He wondered how many years it had been since Henry Costello had looked at a law book. How had he come to be a professor of law? What did he teach? Contracts, no doubt. Was he a popular instructor? No doubt he was, no doubt he was an inside man on the campus as he was an inside man in the capital.

"But the judge would know where to reach me."

The former secretary looked at Ben Joyce's triumphant face, and laughed in spite of himself. Mousetrapped again, he had to admire it. He tried to calculate what the time and charges would be for a minute's use of Joyce & Walsh's switchboard. Whatever they were, it would be worth it.

Then Costello was quietly saying his good-byes, smiles and handshakes all around. He glanced reproachfully at Old Ben, and followed Mrs. Denver to the door.

They watched him glide away, Old Ben and the former secretary and his law partner. Costello had not noticed Sam, or the young lawyer for the FCC.

"He's good," Old Ben said.

The former secretary leaned close. "Which one was it, your 'matter?' "

Old Ben said, "You remember. The arrangement with D."

"Costello did *that*?"

Old Ben smiled. There were limits. "With a little help from his friends."

What was it? It was an arms sale or import quota or export license, an appeal for tax relief, adjustment, or forgiveness. A subsidy, an exemption from a specific regulation. Any of those, or none; or a swaggering variation on them all. Sam, listening to them as they continued to talk, was reminded not of a government but a bazaar. That was the way it was now.

He remarked about it later to Marina. He said, We looked around one fine day and found the city occupied—scientists, economists, sociologists, publicists, weapons manufacturers, journalists, academics of all kinds, all supported by their attorneys. All selling something. The government was now the marketplace, the old Iron Triangle a rialto. The city grew rich from the war, so the universities, the manufacturers, and the professionals would grow rich from the city. No one was excluded from the war economy, since Highest Levels had decreed that there would be both guns and butter. A new weapon, a new use for an old weapon, a trade advantage, a subsidy for this industry, a contract for that, a tax break for the other, a study or a consultancy, any way in. Food, fiber, bullets, books. From the universities and the foundations the academics flocked to the war, and how industrious they were! The government need disguise it only a little, a wink and a nod signaling independence and the integrity of scholarly inquiry. But the contracts were cost-plus. *You remember. The arrangement with D.* He hated to think of his father involved with Henry Costello. But then the butcher Foch considered himself a disciple of the Grand Marshal himself.

Why was it, Sam wondered, why was it that he felt like a child among these men? He had seen more than they, knew more than they, understood and felt more than they. . . . But he was one of the pins on their map. Move a pin from here to there and someone died. Laurence died. At least the Grand Marshal could see what it was he did, Borodino was not *out of sight*. He would always be twelve years old, his father's son, eternally at table listening to lectures on how the world worked.

Marina had smiled then. Welcome to the club.

He knew then that he had become an outsider in the capital, grown comfortable in his anxiety and apprehension. It was not quite pessimism, he always conserved ammunition for the coming offensive. But his desire for the field had an edge of futility to it, almost of nostalgia. That was not where the real war was fought.

Old Ben told him once, You'll never be happy. You avert your eyes from the things you don't like. You don't know how to cut your losses. You believe that things cannot possibly be as bad as you secretly know them to be. Probably it's the fault of West Point and all that bilge, and I don't mean the patriotism; that's all right, in its place. You don't know how the world works. You don't like me because you think I feed on misprision. You think I invented it, but I didn't; I use what's there already. I see things as they are, no controlling theories, only an infinite variety of episodes. I serve them, his father said, in all their variety and humanity. Every man for himself, under God's indifferent eye. Then he laughed. God may not love scoundrels but I do! Life is an entertainment, and the secret is to find out as much about it as you can. Study the drama, son, because that's all there is. See it from the highest mountain, the view's better from there.

Well, he said finally. I wish you luck. You'll need it.

That was his advice on the occasion of his fourth tour to the Zone.

I don't want you lost, he said gruffly.

I don't intend to get lost, Sam replied.

Where you are, he said, you're not in control.

That's *right*, Sam said, furious now. That's exactly correct . . .

And there was a last act to Mrs. Denver's birthday party.

Costello followed her to the door, then paused and looked back. He seemed to make a decision because he returned, avoiding the older men, and shook hands with Sam.

"I haven't seen you for years, since poor Dennis."

Sam agreed that was true, they'd been mainstays at the funeral. He added that Henry seemed to be prospering, "You haven't changed at all." The attorney's face was unlined and there were no traces of gray in his hair. His complexion was almost buttery, the skin of a child. Whatever scars there were did not show. There might be internal wounds, though perhaps there were none or none that mattered. Henry Costello had had a good war. His athletic bearing owed nothing to physique, it was self-satisfaction pure and simple.

"I didn't recognize you at first," he said.

"Do you ever see Jo?"

"Not for years," he said. "Isn't she married to Max Cather now? I never knew her very well. Dennis was my contact, and of course Carl." Carl was Dennis's father.

"Whatever happened to Carl?"

Costello nodded, turning away. His hostess was still at the door. "Living in Chicago, retired. He never got over poor Dennis. He's never been back to Washington, because he never got over Dennis. Really, he's never been the same." Costello put out his hand for a last shake. "You've been away in the wars, but you're not in uniform now. Why?"

Sam said, "This is a civilian occasion."

Costello nodded, understanding. Then he put his hand on Sam's arm. "Tell me, how does it look from there? Do you think we'll make it?"

"No," Sam said.

"Oh, I think you're wrong there. We'll find a way."

"You'd know more about that than I would."

"I don't mean to disagree with someone who's on the scene, but there's much that's happening here. Really, it's here not there. Really, it's Paris. A tremendous effort by those in charge, we're exploring every avenue." He smiled suddenly. "I don't mean to say 'we.' My role's marginal, less than marginal. I try to be helpful, a phone call here and there, an occasional journey. They're pricks, aren't they? But we're going to move them around in ways they've never dreamed of, trust me. Well." He shook hands. "He's something, isn't he?" Costello indicated Old

205

Ben with a nod of his head. "A great man, your father. A great gentleman. A great legal mind."

Sam smiled broadly. "Didn't he cut a little close to the bone, back there?"

"Oh, goodness gracious no," Costello said, moving away now. "The judge, he's one of the great ones. He's earned the right to say anything he wants. Who's to correct him? And, Colonel"—he stopped and lowered his voice, this was just between the two of them—"to those of us in the business, an endorsement from Ben Joyce is like an endorsement from God."

That night he acknowledged to Marina that his attitudes had changed with the years. Perhaps it was Washington, perhaps it was only growing older. No doubt it was growing older in Washington, a city he had come to despise, where conspicuous success was a sign of virtue and character. He was indifferent to their opinions, Old Ben's or Costello's or Max Cather's or anyone's. He told her it was why he must return again to the Zone, and its sovereign failure and neglect. He told Marina that he tried not to judge, that was his father's trick. He was a man of the line, he said; in control of his immediate area only.

She did not like the sound of that and said so.

It's better than God's endorsement, he said.

But she liked that even less.

Henry Costello had no office in Washington. He had his suite at the Mayflower but when he did business it was in the client's office or, less often, at lunch. Joyce & Walsh offered its services for copying or any secretarial service that he might require, but Costello rarely copied anything and boasted that he was his own secretary. His practice did not require that he own a library, only a Rolodex. On those rare occasions when a point of law or precedent was essential, younger associates at J & W were eager to help. It was an education to work with Henry Costello, and a cachet inside the firm. It was like having been law clerk to Frankfurter.

They met in Piatt's office in the capital, at seven when the staff had left for the day. The House was not in session so the building was virtually deserted. This was a few days after Piatt's conversation with Mundelein in the duck blind.

Piatt said without preamble, "Pat Mundelein says Sam Joyce is in trouble."

"That's right," Costello said. "He is."

It would have been better if they had been friendly, but they were not. Piatt said, "Are you certain? Mundelein was a little ambiguous—"

Costello turned away, frowning. Stupid question. Of course he was certain. If he was not certain, he would not be there. Henry Costello did not waste his time on fictitious crimes. "I've seen the IG's report, Congressman."

"And it's not a fake?"

"Fake?"

"Cooked, doctored."

"They don't fake those reports. In fact, it's a pretty good report. Pretty complete, by their standards."

"What are the charges? In outline."

"In outline, he's been stealing money. In specific, it's as follows. Your friend, I assume he is your friend because I wouldn't be here if he wasn't. And Mundelein's friend. Your friend ran a command of roughly forty Americans and maybe twice as many Vietnamese. Reconnaissance mostly, working on the margins; cowboys and Indians stuff, I gather. *Boom boom.* He had a budget, like any branch manager of a large corporation. So much for this, so much for that. It was a flexible budget because his needs varied. He had the authority to make various purchases, food, medical supplies, small construction projects, and a little grease—'squeeze,' it's called out there—when a little grease was called for. This kind of thing. Guard tower in the adjoining hamlet is destroyed or collapses, Sam's authorized to repair it. He had a budget to buy information, though where he was supposed to buy it, I don't know. Base Fox wasn't exactly the Kurfürstendamm. The IG accuses him of siphoning funds for liquor, women, and what they—primly, I think—describe as 'gambling devices.' Slot machines, I gather. A wheel."

"Sam Joyce never played a slot machine in his life."

No doubt, Costello said. "But the men in his command do."

Piatt nodded.

Costello did not wait for the next question. "As to the women. Some were imported from Saigon. On one occasion, according to the report, he brought in a dozen from Hong Kong. Flew them in to Bien Hoa in fixed-wing army aircraft, then transferred them to his airstrip by helicopter. In Friday night, out on Sunday. Odd, they observed the weekend. I wouldn't've thought it would make much difference, way out there. He imported liquor as well. That was plain stupid because as everyone knows the war zone is awash in liquor from the PX system. But maybe the PX didn't have the brand he liked."

"Care for a drink?"

Costello shrugged. "Sure."

Piatt slid the door on the credenza and pulled out a bottle of Scotch. His secretary had filled the ice bucket and there was water in a pitcher. He made drinks and passed one across the desk to Costello.

The attorney said, "They've nailed him."

"Was he stupid? Or was there something else?"

Costello did not answer that directly. "They put one of their people into his command. A stool pigeon. So they have receipts, transcripts of telephone conversations, photographs, and the testimony of a few close friends. And so forth and so on and so forth and so on."

"It doesn't sound as if he was too damned careful."

"He wasn't."

"It sounds as if he didn't care whether he got caught or not."

"That's the way it sounds."

"It also sounds as if what he did was for his command. He wasn't diverting money for his own use. No mistresses, Porsches, or Swiss bank accounts."

"That part isn't clear," Costello said. "The report is ambiguous on that count."

"Then it seems to me that a defense could be built." Piatt thought a moment, then continued. Wasn't this a simple case of a man maintaining the morale of his command? Unwisely, perhaps. Against the rules, certainly. Technically in violation of established procedures, etcetera. But the intent was honorable and it was a wartime command, that was obvious. My God, if the army intended to prosecute every cumshaw artist in the ranks there wouldn't *be* an army—

"Of course that's right. But Sam Joyce isn't 'in the ranks.' He's a full colonel."

Piatt admitted that it was awkward. But still.

Costello sighed. Normally it was not necessary to touch these bases. It was rarely necessary with a Congressman. He listened to Piatt a moment, then raised his hand. "Congressman? I'm not interested in mounting a defense. That isn't what I do. There are a hundred lawyers in this city to do that for you. For you, for Sam Joyce, and for Pat Mundelein. Except that Pat isn't interested in a defense either. We have a problem. We must remove the problem. That's what we focus on, the problem. Not on Sam

Joyce, his guilt or innocence. That's irrelevant to the matter at hand. The problem, Congressman. The *problem*. I'm here to remove it, or try to. Whether Sam Joyce is guilty or not guilty doesn't matter. None of us cares about that. Pat doesn't. I don't. You shouldn't. None of us wants to see this go to court-martial because with court-martial there's publicity and turbulence, and Joyce isn't shy of either of those conditions. If it goes to court-martial my opinion is that he'll lose. The evidence is strong. Or maybe not, I've been wrong before. Maybe by some miracle, he'll win. Maybe defense counsel will mount such a brilliant argument, somewhat along the lines you've suggested, that the court will overturn the evidence. It's possible to argue that the good Colonel was mentally unsound, he'd lost a close friend. But that isn't the point, is it? Guilt or innocence or a skillful defense *isn't the point*. We have to stop the investigation. We have to interfere with the process. We have to put the fix in, Congressman." He smiled, sipped his drink, then replaced it on the desk. He straightened his trouser legs, put his hands in his lap, and looked inquiringly across the polished desk, a challenge.

With some of them he was indirect, almost avuncular. *Let me see what I can do, there may be a way around the problem, just leave it in my hands awhile, it looks to me like a raw deal*. Often he made an effort to sympathize. His client, or his client's client, or his client's friend, was a victim of injustice or a vendetta by political enemies or simply the subject of harassment by bureaucrats who did not understand the complicated problems of aggressive businessmen obliged to make a profit, unlike the federal government which could print its own money, etcetera.

But Henry Costello was not prepared to play Mr. Hypocrite with this Congressman who had been around Washington for years, an inside man whose career was a model of circumspection. Mr. Piatt Warden could play philosopher king at home or on the floor of his House, but not in the office; not in front of *him*. Mr. Piatt Fucking Warden knew perfectly well what was up. He might as well get in on the ground floor and see how it was done by experts. Costello did not like this Congressman, had not liked him from the moment they'd met years ago; he was soft in the wrong places. He did not understand struggle, he with his safe seat and his affordable scruples, and his habit of looking the other way. And his indebtedness, to Pat Mundelein among others; his desire to please, to be of use, to be *on the inside*—

So he would start to squeeze, and watch this statesman sweat a little. "Shall I make a phone call?"

Piatt pointed to his own phone, then slid it across the desk. "Dial 9."

Gauntlet down. Normally, they were no more anxious to hear the conversation than Costello was anxious to allow them to hear, mystification being part of his lawyerly method. Also, his clients did not want telephone calls of that kind originating from their offices. There were too many wires in Washington. They didn't want to know the details of these calls, how many and to whom and the promises. They would tell the story later, at the golf course or around the boardroom table—would *want* to tell the story, how Henry Costello put the fix in, moved the bastards around. Proves the rule, always go for the top talent. Not cheap, they'd say; Henry's instincts are not eleemosynary. But by God, he gets the job done. However, not one client in ten wanted to know the details and none had ever offered his own phone.

Piatt leaned back in his swivel chair, lit a cigarette, and watched. Costello waited a moment and then, forced, picked up the phone and dialed.

"Ed? Henry."

The first few sentences were inconsequential, recollections of an evening together, a bet on a football game. Piatt refilled his drink, stretched, and walked around his desk to the other end of his office to peer at the family pictures framed on the wall. There was a row of pictures above a row of certificates, awards from various service clubs and good-government organizations. He had often been Man of the Year. One year he had been a Man three times, an outstanding year by any measure. He stared at the pictures of himself with the President, the secretary of defense, and the old Speaker. Portraits of a man aging, he thought. He looked hard at the photograph of the secretary of defense, all

confidence and vigor, a stern, board chairman's face; it was the
face of a disapproving father-in-law. The secretary's hands were
clenched into fists.

There were several photographs of his father—Piatt Sr. with
Marina, with Tommy, with his only son. The old man, birdlike
with his cane and fedora. His father was a businessman, the
owner of men's stores in Springfield. When he died there were
six stores, all identical; he thought it was necessary that each
store be welcoming in the same way. The old man had conservative tastes, he specialized in judges, lawyers, politicians, doctors, and automobile dealers. His prices were high by
Springfield standards but he gave good value. Singlehandedly
he had brought good tailoring to the town, handling Hart,
Schaffner & Marx suits, all top of the line, and Arrow shirts.
Clothing made the man. Look the part. Dress quietly. Dress
softly and carry a big stick. In his last years he became something
of a dandy, with his cane and fedora and snow-white handkerchief in three points tucked into the breast pocket just so, unmis-
takable on the streets of Springfield. A good man, Piatt thought.
A genuinely good man, though heartbroken when his only son
decided to enter politics. The old man reckoned it a dirty business; he had known many politicians over the years and they did
not compare to lawyers or Ford dealers; they were slow to pay,
and always seemed to expect a discount.

There was one picture of Piatt, his father, and the old
Speaker. This was made the day Piatt was sworn in. They had a
minute or two of conversation, he could tell the Speaker liked his
father. They were both small-town boys at heart. The old man
complimented the Speaker on the cut of his suit. It was an old
suit, the Speaker said. I know, his father replied, looking at it
with his haberdasher's eye. You can't find that material anymore. It's twenty years old, the Speaker said proudly. All of
that, his father said. Those serge suits, they wear like iron . . .
And his mother, listening to all this at Piatt's side, began to shake
her head. She always said that when he met St. Peter on the Day
of Judgment he'd comment on the cut of the saint's robes. Piatt
stared at the photograph, looking into it, dissolving its frame; he

saw the Speaker's tidy desk in the middle of the ornate chamber, friezes along the crown of the ceiling. The two old men stood close, both the same height, a couple of inches over five feet but radiating authority; they were smiling at each other. Then the picture was taken and they were ushered from the room, there would be a reception later.

There was another picture of Piatt and his mother, he must have been ten; they were standing in front of the family Buick before a motor trip West. And another, a newspaper photograph, taken when he had been elected alderman at the age of twenty-two. Then there were the ritual photographs, he changed them every six months or so, with officials of the Jaycees, the Amvets, the Eagles, Local Number 12, the teachers, the local board of the National Conference of Christians and Jews. He tapped the photograph of himself as alderman, then drummed on it with his fingernail. So long ago, before he had met Marina, before he had run for the House, Washington was just a gleam in his eye—but a steady, persistent gleam. The last photograph was of Marina, alone and pensive in their own backyard. Of the photograph of himself being sworn in by the Speaker of the House he thought, My God, I look twelve years old.

"The matter we discussed the other day, Ed."

Piatt wheeled to look at the lawyer, whose back was to him now. Costello sat perfectly still, his eyes straight ahead, his inactive face reflected in the windows behind the desk. They stared at each other in that way, lawyer to client, at a remove. As was his habit, Costello had the telephone tucked between his shoulder and his ear. His large hands were motionless in his lap.

"The thing that concerns, that's of very substantial concern to all the parties," Costello said, very deliberately, as if he had all the time in the world, "is his connections with our friends in the media." Piatt started, Sam Joyce had no friends in the media except for Teddy Carney; he had never courted publicity. There was a long silence, Costello listening hard, waiting. His eyes were up and watchful and he gave the impression of a hunter waiting for the first bird to break from the flight. He said something that Piatt could not hear and then, "Of course that's understood, Ed. And that's what we come down to. I've talked to those who have the ways and means of analyzing the situation, predicting what's in store, and there's general agreement that he'll try to cut your balls off, the army's, and there's general agreement that he'll very likely succeed. His new friends will be only too happy to oblige—what's it to them? And it's what they're paid to do, with forseeable consequences, particularly unhappy consequences to those who are bearing the real burdens, and so on and so forth." He listened for a moment, then added, "My people are not very happy with the situation, they see it getting out of control . . . " The lawyer smiled at the obvious question. "Well, Ed. For the family naturally, his father, fine old gentleman, and his friends and other concerned citizens. And of course it's political, at this level it's always political." He laughed softly, an encouraging laugh. They were adults, after all. "Mostly, I'm trying to be helpful within the limits of the situation, which wouldn't matter a damn to any of us except for the question of national security and matters getting out of control, to a place where we can't control them. It's in that sense that it's political."

During the long silence that followed, Piatt continued to stare at Costello's reflection in the window behind the desk. He looked as serene and weightless as a fish in a glass bowl. How many years ago was it that they'd met, that ghastly day at McDonough's; it was only yesterday. And what was his prescription that day? *Anger is stronger than grief.* He'd meant, *healthier.* He'd meant, *more effective.* Get mad, then get even. But his voice now was subdued and civilized. Costello was rearranging the file cabinet, encouraging the loss of one piece of paper and the discovery of another.

Now his voice accelerated.

"The army, bless it, doesn't need any additional public relations crises, I think one war is enough, ha-ha, don't you? And the potential here is for a firestorm . . . " His voice softened again, and became inaudible. Then, "The Man wants it, and don't ask me why. You know them. You know the way they are, they get an idea, some burr under their saddle. He wants Sam Joyce for something else, and this is an interference—"

Costello did it well, Piatt gave him that. No threats, and no bombast. His voice was calm and reasonable, modulated according to the note he was striking. Of course the secret was the identity of the official at the other end of the telephone line, a friend, in the Washington sense, from Costello's own days in the government. This was an official, one of two or three, with the authority to turn off an investigation. A nimble official, knowledgeable and respected; a career man, here today, here tomorrow. That was one reason he would be damn sure of himself before getting into it. Sam Joyce was not a problem that occupied him day and night; not a persistent pain, more a nagging ache; he was one of many aches, some days there were so many he could not sort them out. If he could avoid thinking about Sam Joyce, that is what he did. Chicken colonels in trouble were a dime a dozen in the army. It was Henry Costello's assignment to transform the nagging ache into intolerable distress, pain serious enough to cause the official to seek relief. The objective, always, was focus. Get them to focus on this instead of that, impress them with the seriousness of it, and the urgency. And that there would be reciprocity at some unspecified time in the future; favors were never forgotten. Costello was telling him that this particular problem had to be solved immediately, this week; not next week or next month, for the longer it persisted the worse it got. Costello urged preventive surgery.

Piatt watched the lawyer's reflection in the windowpane, a study in concentration. Worthy of Rodin, he thought. Costello's body seemed made of stone, the telephone black and motionless at his ear, his feet flat on the floor, his hands one over the other on his knee. Piatt wondered suddenly what he did with his money. By all accounts he lived quietly, no mansions or limousines or country houses; there was only the suite at the Mayflower. Perhaps there was a woman somewhere whom he draped in furs and gems, a silent beautiful woman. Gems on her fingers, gems hanging from earlobes, encrusted around her neck, on bosom, hip, collarbone, around the ankles wriests biceps, a diamond in her navel . . . Except a woman he knew confided once that Costello was not a gift-giver, depending instead on charm and intelligence; if those were the words. He was indifferent to sex, though he seemed to crave affection. Or perhaps, she'd added thoughtfully, that it was not affection he craved but admiration. In that way he was like a scientist, mind filled to overflowing with the contemplation of the universe and wanting only that others comprehend the beauty of it as he did. He had a very fine mind, she said. It was as bright and shiny and well oiled as a machine, and as heedless of consequence. No limits to its speed or direction, none whatever. Henry Costello was not a man who recognized limits.

Attractive man, the woman had said.

Piatt had heard somewhere that he was a sports fan, and would turn up in distant cities to watch interesting games. The Lakers and the Celtics in Los Angeles. The Cubs and Cardinals at Busch Stadium. The Redskins and Cowboys at Dallas. Once or twice, so the stories went, he had been of use to the Commissioner's office—the NBA, the NFL, major league baseball—as a mediator. Surprisingly, he was said to work *pro bono*; at least, no fee was ever recorded. He had once been quoted as saying that there were "possibilities" in "sports law." Piatt guessed that in his obsession Costello resembled a monomaniacal poet. The only difference was that the lawyer made a fortune and the poet lived hand-to-mouth. Both demanded the highest price for their services, for money was a measure of worth; but both lived in service to the obsession, and it was only a particular feature of the society in which they lived that law paid well and verses paid badly.

Costello was suddenly on his feet.

"Yes, I think that's the best approach." Then, "I want to be able to communicate—"

Piatt lit a cigarette and moved back to his desk, the better to face Costello.

"—a certain movement, of course, that the thing's on track. Obviously, yes," he said, betraying the slightest impatience. "I'll manage that end, a sort of squeeze play, and then I'll be in touch. Or you. Better you be in touch, I'll be at home"—a refer- ence to the Mayflower—"tomorrow and probably Friday, then I go out of town for the weekend . . . " He paused, listening; then for the first time he smiled broadly, and when he spoke it was with casual affability. "I'll know better early Saturday, and I'll call you then. I have your home phone. My hope and belief is that the spread will be six rather than seven but there are some late developments, according to my friends. Injuries. But wait on it a little and I'll let you know." He laughed easily. "That's what I'm here for, glad to be of service." His voice dipped again into the lower register, inaudible to anyone standing more than a few feet away; he was back to the business at hand, expressing his appreciation and the appreciation of his principals, men whose memories were excellent as they both had cause to know. Somewhere in all that he would find a place to remind Ed, "Ed- die" now, of their long friendship and the many occasions on which one had been helpful to the other. Piatt caught the words, "the national interest."

Watching Costello, Piatt laughed. It was an interest that was forever compounding.

Costello shot him a warning glance. Then, his eyes on Piatt, he said distinctly, "If for some reason you cannot reach me, call Piatt Warden on the Hill. That is where I am now. He is with me." He glanced at the telephone. "His private number is—" Costello enunciated each syllable firmly and distinctly. Then he spoke softly into the receiver a last time, and hung up.

He said to Piatt, "I just wanted him to know—"

"I know what you wanted him to know."

"—that you were on board. It's important to him, man in his position. Wants to know that the reserves are there. Wants to know the bench strength."

"I know what he wants to know," Piatt said, "and what you want him to know and why."

"You laughed a minute ago. I didn't like it. What was funny?"

"The national interest."

"Isn't it?"

"I don't know, you tell me. It's Mundelein's and Mundelein's principal's. Maybe it's Sam Joyce's. I suppose it's yours, and I guess it's mine because you're here in this office. I don't know what's national about it."

"If we're involved, Congressman, that makes it national."

"You believe that, counselor?" Piatt refilled their drinks.

"No more for me." He slid his glass to one side. "Am I about to hear a civics lecture? Sam Joyce is a little loco, in case you don't know it. He's about as loco as a man can be and still be walking around loose. Now for some reason his commander in chief wants him to run a project in the Zone. I don't know why he wants Sam and not someone else. But I don't care because it doesn't matter to me. It's enough for me that that's what he wants, and I'm here to help him get it. That's what I do. Sam's a problem, one way and another, and what I do is solve problems."

"Sam'd probably prefer the court-martial, if I know Sam."

"Would he? You better ask him straight out. There are other ways to go about this. But that's idle. That's idle chatter because Sam Joyce is not the issue, not then, not now, not ever. Sam Joyce'll do what is determined for him, he's not in control of this—"

"So you've got him off."

"I think so, yes."

"Mundelein will be grateful."

"Yes, a grateful nation, etcetera. I got him off, with a little help from a friend. Good man, superior bureaucrat. We worked together in DOD a few years ago, he was civil service and I was political. We made a hell of a team, he knew the facts and I knew the people. He introduced me to some of his facts and I introduced him to some of my people. Some, not all. So we both gained, we're quick studies, Eddie and I. And have been friendly ever since."

"Bravo," Piatt said.

"It'll take another telephone call, no more than two."

"Slick," Piatt said. "You're slick, Henry, and I'm envious. You come into town with a bag full of dimes—"

"That's a ten-thousand-dollar telephone call, Congressman.

If there's another, which there will be, that's a second ten. Twenty in all. You can arrange for the check to be sent to me, mark it personal. It's Henry Costello, Inc."

"Who do I tell?"

"I don't care who you tell, but this one is C.O.D. And it's not finished yet."

"At home? The Mayflower? Is that where you want it sent?"

"Why not Joyce & Walsh?" Costello said. "Make it out to Joyce & Walsh, that'll keep it in the family."

"I'll let them know," Piatt said.

"You can call Mundelein and tell him it's done."

"Tell me one thing, Henry. You're so damn good with people, maybe you can explain this to me. What do you suppose Mundelein's real interest is? It's a hell of a lot of trouble they've gone to, just a hell of a lot of trouble."

"Oh, Congressman. You surprise me. You *know* you get into a swamp in this town when you try to be precise about motives. Who knows really? They want him for some project. They want to shut him up. They *don't* want to shut him up. Maybe they're protecting him against himself, or isolating him; maybe, for some reason of their own, they want him back in the Zone. Maybe. Maybe they're setting him up, Congressman. Maybe it's just something the Man wants done for his own reasons, that we don't know about and that maybe he can't even explain to himself. Maybe the Man knows nothing about it and it's just Mundelein. It's Mundelein's caper. Or Max Cather's. Maybe it's just the Man and Mundelein proving that the government still works. And maybe it's *you*, Congressman. Maybe you're the heavy. But really, I think it's Mundelein. Mundelein's quite a piece of work, in our government he's structural steel. You know what they said about that fight promoter. I forget his name, but call him Mundelein. 'Give Pat Mundelein 200 pounds of steel wool and he'll knit you a stove.' "

Piatt smiled. "Then you call him, Henry. He's your client," Piatt said.

Piatt had arranged to meet Sam at Passau's, a neighborhood tavern off Connecticut Avenue, far from the Pentagon and Capitol Hill. Sam had insisted on Passau's, explaining that it was quiet, cool, and dark; Passau left his customers alone. He did not allow fights, drunks, or sponges—except for Surly John, a derelict who appeared every afternoon at three with the first edition of the evening paper. The regulars paid a dollar for the newspaper and Passau gave the old man two fingers of rye at a table in the rear. Derelicts were rare in Washington and everyone felt a responsibility toward Surly John. Sam was more or less a regular, when he was in town. Passau had been a navy chief until his retirement but they never talked about the service.

The place was deserted when Piatt walked in and took a seat at the end of the bar, under the Schlitz sign. Passau watched him suspiciously, he looked like a federal agent in his dark suit and hat. He did not look like an afternoon drinker. But a moment later Sam was at his side, his big hand on Piatt's shoulder, squeezing. Piatt put his hat on the bar and called for drinks.

They said nothing until the drinks arrived. Then Piatt raised his glass, saluting. He said, Glad you could make it. Then, What's new in the war?

An offensive, Sam said.

Another one? Whose? Piatt asked. Ours or theirs?

Ours, Sam said. Multi-division. It is the dry season now, prime time for offensives.

Piatt smiled. The cost is greater in prime time, no?

Infinitely, Sam said.

They had one drink and then another, their conversation in the nature of a reconnaissance. Sam asked Piatt if he was happy in his work on the Hill and he said he was, he was.

Read something about you, Sam said. Was it *Life?*

Time, Piatt said. They did a story about half a dozen of us in the House. We all got two adjectives. Mine were "quiet" and "effective."

In that order? Sam asked.

As I remember, Piatt said.

Could be worse, Sam said.

There were eight or ten of us who came into the House at the same time and stayed. We are all about the same age, with the same concerns, roughly, and the same politics, roughly, and *Time* decided that we were a generation.

This was a cover story, Sam said.

Yes, Piatt said, we were all on the cover. They were going to shoot us on the steps of the Capitol but decided against it, too trite. So they shot us instead in the House chamber. We drew lots for position.

It seems to me there was a bet in the old days, You and me and old Dennis and Teddy and Max. Who would be first on the cover of *Time.* Congratulations then. The drinks're on me.

It seems like a silly sort of bet now, doesn't it? I mean from this distance. But it sounds like the sort of thing we'd do, back then. Odd, I always thought it would be Henry Costello, even though he wasn't in on the bet.

Sam did not answer that. He said, *Life* was going to do something on me and Sol Henderson, but it never did. Perhaps it will now.

They went on in that way for a quarter of an hour. Sam explained that there were almost as many journalists in the Zone as there were in Washington. The Luce people were everywhere, and the networks. You had to get very far away indeed to avoid them, though of course the places he had been were off-limits. Base Fox existed on no map or T. O. & E.

After a little silence Piatt said, "I'm not sure why I'm here. I'm not sure why I'm involved at all, except for Mundelein."

Sam said nothing.

"Costello was in my office yesterday, putting the fix in on your behalf."

Sam nodded. "With the IG," he said.

"I don't know who he talked to. Someone named Ed. Eddie."

Sam thought a moment, then shook his head.

"You don't know him either?"

"With Costello, it could've been anybody."

"You owe him ten thousand dollars."

"Only ten?"

"That's the first installment. It's ten thousand dollars a call. Costello said there'd probably be another call, so it's twenty in all you owe him. It's Henry Costello, *incorporated*. Send the check to Joyce & Walsh."

Sam looked at him. "Is my old man involved?"

"Not so far's I know," Piatt said. "Costello uses J & W as a mail drop, I guess."

"Well," Sam said. "I owe you one."

Piatt ignored that. "You want him to do it, then?"

Sam signaled Passau for another round of drinks. "If I'm to get back there, yes."

"You're going back again?"

"Of course," Sam said. "It's not finished."

Piatt nodded, accepting the drink from Passau. Sam paid. Mundelein was right, they all had a screw loose. Piatt could not imagine volunteering for another tour in the Zone. What did it prove? The thing was finished, anyone with any sense could see that it was finished. But to Sam Joyce it obviously meant quite a lot; he wasn't any ordinary soldier, even as a boy he had a reputation for stubborn behavior. And of course there was his father, no ordinary man; no ordinary father, either. That old man with his massive unsmiling face, hard as iron. Piatt and Sam had gone to the same summer camp in Wisconsin and although Sam was neither strong nor especially athletic he signed up for all the contact sports, never giving less than one hundred percent and enjoying himself hugely; he was a great favorite of the counselors. Giving everything, he said; that was what made it fun. Piatt, quieter, more bookish, almost introverted, was immediately drawn to Sam Joyce. That was the summer after Old Ben had won his Senate race, and it was decided that Sam should have one last summer in the interior; from then on, they would be Washingtonians. That year, they were the youngest boys in the camp, indisputably downstate boys; there was nothing urban about them. They met frequently thereafter, at odd times and places, always unexpectedly, always glad to see each other, having shared summer camp in Wisconsin at a very young age.

"So it's all true," Piatt said.

"I don't know exactly how much the IG has. Or Costello. But it's probably a fraction of the truth. It was much worse than even they can know. I closed down my command for a month, and that's what the IG really wants. That evidence. Some of the men wrote crazy letters home and that's how the word got out. I suppose it is. Someone's pressing the IG, though. There's pressure from somewhere."

"It doesn't sound like you," Piatt said.

"No," Sam agreed. "It doesn't."

"It sounds as if everything went screwy out there."

Sam laughed. Oh, Congressman.

"You of all people," Piatt said.

"You were expecting that determined little chap in short pants and Keds, trying to outrun the older boys?"

"Maybe I was," Piatt said. With all that had happened between them, he was still drawn to Sam Joyce.

Sam said, "I'm a throwback. Retrograde. I used to keep a piece of paper taped to the wall over my bed in my hootch. Oliver Wendell Holmes. 'In the midst of doubt, in the collapse of creed, there is one thing I do not doubt, and that is that the faith is true and adorable which leads a soldier to throw away his life in obedience to a blindly accepted duty, in a cause which he little understands, in a plan of campaign of which he has no notion, under tactics of which he does not see the use.' Isn't that outstanding? True and adorable, my grunts. I kept Oliver above the bed, just to glance at now and then. I like to field-strip him, phrase by phrase. It's like a weapon, that passage. There's a barrel and a sight, a firing pin, a breech, a clip for the ammunition, and a trigger to pull. *One thing I do not doubt.* I think it makes perfect sense, a total misunderstanding of our sacrifices and our pleasures. A cause we little understand, a plan of campaign of which we have no notion, under tactics of which we do not see the use. It was written a hell of a long time ago, but it's as modern as Albert Camus."

Piatt listened and nodded slowly.

"You remember, years ago, Camus. Dennis's memorial—"

"How could I forget?"

"Things went a little screwy that day."

"Yes," Piatt said.

"I don't know if he'd agree with the 'true and adorable' part," Sam said thoughtfully. "I think he would, though." Then, "God, what a day that was."

"I still don't understand how you got into this mess," Piatt said. He did not want to reminisce about Dennis, or the memorial service so many years ago. "It's not like you. You with your principles, your certainties. Your hundred percent. Your blindly accepted duties."

"A close friend was killed. That was the start of it."

Piatt turned away. "I hate getting mixed up with Costello."

"You're not. I am."

"He was in my office," Piatt said sharply. "Sitting at my desk. Using my telephone."

Sam finished the drink in front of him and put the glass at arm's length, nodding at Passau. What could he say to Piatt Warden? Nothing that the Congressman would understand or sympathize with.

"What's at the end of it?" Piatt asked suddenly. "Where does it *end*? You've been there, you ought to know. You're supposed to know everything about the war, God knows you've spent enough time there. You're impatient with the rest of us, you act as if you're the one who understands it. What happens next? What happens tomorrow? Next month? Next year?"

Sam sighed. They did not want information, they wanted sorcery. Washington's eternal question, What do you think is going to happen next? It would give him pleasure to deliver Laurence's set piece, the one he gave late at night to anyone who would listen. I look forward, Laurence had said, and I see nothing but disorder, and all of it in brilliant colors. Not the gray of the parade ground but the kaleidoscope of the circus. Dwarfs, clowns, tumblers, men on stilts, freaks, jesters, lion tamers, and a droll ringmaster to bring the audience to a frenzy. An audience, say, of respectable Washingtonians . . . The thing had lost all coherence. America had invented a whole class of people and assigned them to the killing ground. They were the ones sent off to do the dirty work, and they were supervised by professional soldiers; as the professional soldiers were supervised by the professional federals, politicians and civil servants. He thought it was a far distance from what he had been taught to believe in, the manual, an infantry officer's high ground. A Colt .45 automatic carries seven rounds in its magazine and the muzzle velocity of each round is eight-one-zero feet per second. The length over all is eight and a half inches and the weight is three-niner ounces. Accurate to seven-five yards, maximum range one-six-zero-zero yards. Looks lethal. Keep it clean and it'll last for a hundred years, more. One respected the manuals as Picasso respected his paints. If the label said indigo, he believed it. It was up to him where to apply the paint, which strokes and how many and where, and to what effect. As, knowing the specifications of a Colt .45 automatic, it was up to the individual to aim it. But the targets were no longer obvious.

He said, "I don't know what will happen next. History does not repeat itself in any important way." That did not seem to satisfy the Congressman, so he changed direction. "Do you know what I liked about the military life in the old days? Its privacy and mystery, and its romance. Its exclusivity. We lived by another code and the public didn't have the cypher. We played on a public field but no one noticed. We had an awful lot of idiots but they were our idiots, at least they weren't civilian idiots. Our rule: Do nothing to harm the service. That, and your own self-estimate and the respect of your men. That's what you live with. Or did."

"Civilians," Piatt began, irritated.

"Civilians, that's right," Sam said morosely. "They're different, they like the violence out of sight. And they're a hell of a lot more aggressive than we are because, you know, they won't be doing it. They're directing it but they're not doing it. I'm more frightened of the civilians than I am of the generals, and there're some generals that scare me to death. But most of them, you have to see them up close, you have to work for them, to know how timid they are. How do you think they get to be generals? They never want to go into battle with less than a three-to-one edge. They hate unconventional operations. Unconventional operations breed unconventional units and unconventional units breed elitism. The regular army hates elitism almost as much as it hates Communism. Matter of fact, the way the regular army looks at it, elitism *is* Communism of a special kind: commissars with special privileges and their party connections. Naturally enough the civilian elitists are attracted to the unconventional, not least because it's sleight-of-hand; they think they can run a war the way they've run the country. Now you see it, now you don't."

"Max Cather," Piatt said.

"Sure," Sam said. "Secret wars, secret armies, secret payrolls, confused identities. You don't need a detailed debate to send a specialized team into the swamp. If they're caught you hush it up or deny it; if they're successful you can look on it as a seduction. The accomplishment is enough and a gentleman never boasts. A discreet hint here and there in the right places, only a bounder advertises his conquests, no? We are very far into the woods, farther than we think. Time'll come, we won't be able to see how we got there or where we'll exit. If there is an exit. Of course the trees are fascinating, we're up so close we can see the texture and bark on each tree. There are so many of them, it'll take a lifetime to observe and classify. And you should see the hardware, the scientists've been wonderfully cooperative and ingenious. It's exhilarating the way they perform when you give them a contract. Many of them have free student labor, naturally. Some of the stuff, you wouldn't believe it. It's just dazzling. All the universities. They're on a war footing."

"Cather's lab?"

"The one in Cambridge? The best. I was there a few months ago, they wanted to know what an actual soldier would think of it. A uniformed soldier who actually made his living practicing the military arts and sciences."

"And?"

"I was hung over that morning and it reminded me of an old gothic horror film. Bela Lugosi, bats, creaking doors, rattling chains, screams in the night, metamorphoses under a full moon. You have to see some of the stuff to believe it, it's superb. Technically it's hypnotizing. They think with this stuff they can turn the army into partisans, part Wehrmacht and part civic action with a little of Marshal Tito and Dr. Huer thrown in. They think it'll work against Charlie. With some of this new equipment you can bring into the daylight what you've been doing at night, and of course vice versa."

Bad news, Piatt said.

Most certainly, Sam replied.

That's what you'll be doing?

That seems to be my assignment, yes.

Refuse it, Piatt said.

"They're briefing me," Sam said. "Mundelein is. Then Cather and I are making a little journey to the lab in Cambridge." He looked squarely at Piatt. "They've got to keep the army out of it, though, because the army would never approve. Too many good men lost already. The army doesn't know it yet because there's too little direct knowledge of the field. But in a year or two this army is going to be fighting for its own survival. Its survival as an institution."

"So—"

"So this will be run out of Langley. Has to be. The public won't accept the daylight. It can't object to what it doesn't know, or what it suspects but can't prove. We're great ones at averting our eyes and there's no overwhelming urge to blunder around in dark rooms. This won't be successful at first, unless we score a big hit. But don't count on that. So there will be a bunch of casualties, theirs as well as ours. When the civilians see the enemy dead they'll become very excited, and then the war will take on a fresh momentum. They want to prove they can do it. They want to prove their machines are greater than the enemy's ideals. The machine is more resilient and determined than a man. They want to prove it's not twilight for the West, but dawn. They want to reverse history. You can't blame them, I suppose."

"And you're going to help them do it."

Sam looked at him, surprised. He said mildly that of course he was.

"But you don't believe it."

"Of course I don't believe it!" Sam's voice rose and Passau turned to look at them. "I signed up for the course, Piatt. This is what I'm trained to do, I'm not a soldier anymore; I haven't been one for years. I'm a counter-revolutionary. The thing doesn't have to work completely, just show a potential. Slow the infiltration, annihilate a battalion or two. It's enough. They're desperate for progress." He smiled. "The truth is, they don't know if they're winning or losing or in stalemate. First war we've had where we don't know where we stand."

"Christ, Sam—"

"Look on it as a headlong seduction. It's a seduction in all respects. But I don't think we love her enough to persevere. This is not a passionate affair, it's a one-night stand. Except the nights go on and on. I don't think we have the *passion*. We love her in the abstract, as an extension of ourselves. We don't care about *her*. We're using her for our own purposes. And as we all know, Americans are practical and have a highly developed sense of self-interest. Time'll come when our purposes will change, and we'll become alternately appalled and bored. And then we'll walk out, arguing that we gave her a good time, paid her bills, bought her a new suit of clothes. We'll argue that we paid heavily, and that will be true. But so did she. And it was a higher price."

Piatt turned away. These were queer thoughts from a man who believed data, the Colt automatic that carried seven rounds in its magazine, each round with a range of 1,600 yards and accurate to 75. A man who believed in dwarfs, men on stilts, lion tamers, ringmasters, and clowns. And it did not explain Oliver Wendell Holmes, either.

"I love your wife," Sam said.

Piatt looked at him, astonished.

"Never feed troops piecemeal into battle, that's one of the things I believe in."

"I don't want to talk about it," Piatt said.

Sam smiled broadly. "The heavy stuff always goes first. Artillery precedes tanks, tanks precede troops. Aircraft precedes all, except accurate intelligence. That precedes every single thing except the will to fight."

"I don't want to talk about it."

"I'll give my body to this war but my emotions are my own."

"Then keep them to yourself," Piatt said.

Sam said, "She won't leave you."

"I said I didn't want to talk about it."

"Of course not," Sam said.

Suddenly he felt a nudge. Surly John with the newspapers. Sam handed him a dollar bill and took a newspaper. He nodded at Piatt, "You, too."

"I don't want a newspaper."

"Take one anyway. It's one of the things we do at Passau's, buy newspapers from John." The old man remained at Piatt's elbow, waiting. He was trembling slightly, watching Passau pour rye whiskey into a shot glass.

Piatt dug into his pocket and came up with a quarter.

"John's papers cost a dollar."

"I don't care what they cost."

Sam said, "Don't take it out on John."

"Where the hell do you get off—" Then, "What the hell do you mean, anyway?"

John put a paper in Piatt's lap and waited.

"We've never talked about it," Sam said.

"Look, don't we have enough trouble—"

"It's no trouble," he said.

"My private affairs," he began.

"Pay the man. Pay John."

"Here," Piatt said, thrusting a dollar into the open palm. The old man walked abruptly away to a table in the rear, where Passau had placed his shot glass.

"Nothing will be done about it."

"You're damn right—"

"That was her decision."

"This has gone far enough," Piatt said. The paper fell off his lap to the floor. Sam looked at him in his dark suit and white shirt and quiet tie. Piatt was always neatly dressed. He was neat and anonymous in his clothes. An inside man, as was often said. Sam raised his hand for another round but Piatt climbed off his bar stool.

"Why don't you go back to the war."

"I intend to," Sam said.

"That's all you're good for."

Sam smiled. Some truth in that.

"I'm leaving now," Piatt said. "I wish you luck."

Sam nodded. "The same to you."

"What did you tell me this for? What the hell's the purpose—"

"I'm tired of concealing things."

"We have a fine life together, Marina and I—" He was moving toward the door.

"Bully for you," Sam said.

"I don't believe a word of it," Piatt said, still backing away.

"I always thought it was something you had to know. Good, accurate intelligence is always valuable. It's the most valuable thing there is." Piatt shook his head. He watched Piatt's retreating back. He noticed, inconsequentially, that the Congressman's suit was beautifully tailored, a half-inch of white shirt showed at his neck and wrists; little white cotton nooses. Then he was gone, out the door and into the night. It was dark now. Sam turned back to his drink, slightly surprised to find that he was drunk. It was the wine at lunch with *her*, then the drinks with him. Passau switched on the television set. It was between programs, an ad for the news division of the network. A burning village, and a correspondent moving toward it under fire. Now they were using the war as an advertisement for themselves, as they would use a beauty's smile for the selling of toothpaste. The flames were brilliant in color and the correspondent was attractively resolute as the bullets whined and thumped. He was a good-looking man in a bush jacket and steel pot.

Passau put a drink in front of him. "Look familiar, Colonel?"

He said there was nothing familiar about it. He said he remembered once walking into a *montagnard* village, an immaculate little village, the smell of burning charcoal in the air. No more than half a dozen houses, beautifully built of the plainest materials, mostly wood. The houses were constructed on short stakes, a foot or two off the ground, so simple and formal, quieting to look at. It made you feel good, as if you'd stumbled on a treasured memory. The village appeared to be deserted but they approached with care. He thought he heard voices, a murmuring so subdued it might have been the whispering of women. There was a well beside one of the houses and the three of them took positions around it.

This was before we stopped the patrols, he said to Passau.

His Number Two had a grenade ready to pop as soon as he, Sam, removed the wellcap. This village presented such an austere face to the world that it was easy imagining anything in that well, anything at all. So he slid the cap off in one quick motion. The Two looked, then fell back, retching. The well was crowded with people, men, women, children; it was stuffed with people, but all of them were dead. So he imagined the murmuring to be the voices of the dead, a multitude so vast that it would not be stilled; and this place had been chosen for its renascence.

I thought I should speak to them, the dead.

Passau said nothing.

He gestured at the screen. This thing, it's just something for the evening news.

It's coming on now, Passau said.

There must've been a hundred people in that well, Sam said.

Watch the news, said Passau.

Give me a drink, Sam said.

That's a dumb idea, Passau said.

Jesus, Sam said. *That's my base.*

Which?

That, Sam said, pointing at the screen. The announcer was speaking gravely, something about an extraordinary interview from the war zone. Immediately the screen was filled with the face of Sol Henderson, a severe close-up, the camera panning back slowly to reveal a desolate garrison, wooden buildings surrounded by barbed wire. This, a voice said, is Base Fox. Sol stood with a correspondent, both of them wearing fatigues. The correspondent spoke in a practiced voice, describing Fox, roughly where it was and the mission of the men in it.

The correspondent appeared fit and excited. From the evidence of the screen it was difficult to know which was the journalist and which the soldier, except it was the journalist holding the microphone, and his words flowed more smoothly. Sol was ill-at-ease, a manner that contributed to his authenticity. In the old days he would have been sent on a bond tour or to testify before a Senate committee. Those were the days before cinema verité and the Nielsen ratings, and the inevitable confusion of identities.

Watching, Sam remembered something that Carney had told him years before. The foreign editor had said that reporters were like advertising men. He'd said, They have accounts and when they move from one shop to another they bring their accounts with them. You hire them for their accounts. He said, We hired one man because he had the French account. Good man, but at that level they're all good men. What distinguished this man from some other man was that he had the confidence of de Gaulle's people, and certain permanent civil servants. We took that account right away from New York and brought it to Washington. Carney confessed it was the reason he'd hired Jessel, best war correspondent in the business. Jessel had sources in armies everywhere. "Taking Jess out of the war would be like an agency arbitrarily canceling General Motors. No, we wouldn't do that. Unless of course he asked for a transfer, which he wouldn't do because there's no place else for him, no other assignment that he does half so well."

Sam watched the correspondent, a handsome man with graying hair. He looked nothing like Jessel. But he spoke with authority and now was establishing Sol Henderson's credentials. What was a full colonel doing in Indian country commanding a . . . fort? Then he began to draw Sol out. How many outposts were there? And how did the war look from this particular location on the border?

232

Know that guy, Sam said to Passau.

The soldier or the other one?

The soldier, goddammit, Sam said. Old friend. A bit bats.

Passau grunted noncommittally.

Obviously, Sol said, it was a holding action, stasis. At this location the war was static, still. This was the enemy's territory, after all.

The correspondent moved in closer, his face registering profound surprise, shock even. In the silent interval the viewers heard music, a rag or rhythm and blues; it came from the headquarters building, faint but hot. The correspondent struggled. Why, his eyebrows seemed to say, why, you can't mean— In Saigon he had been told that this zone was secure, cleansed of enemy. It was cited as the place where counter-insurgency was working, the insidious Communist infrastructure rooted *out* and the government infrastructure rooted *in*.

Sol looked at him, then wordlessly pointed to the guard towers and the barbed wire. A platoon of Vietnamese troops led by an American officer straggled out the gate, moving dispiritedly in the heat. The men looked very small, their weapons very large. The camera obediently followed Sol's pointing finger. Does it look secure to you, Mr. Harris?

No, Harris said, it doesn't.

Well, it isn't, Sol said.

The correspondent spoke softly into the microphone. Why then. Why then would Saigon maintain that it is?

Saigon is the New Testament, this is the Old, Sol said.

Harris looked genuinely startled, gaping at Sol Henderson and momentarily speechless. It was obvious what was churning in his mind, he had a religious nut on camera. It was then that Sam remembered the anchorman's proud bluster, *What you will see is* live, *a live interview*, complete and *unedited. From Base Fox via satellite!* So they were not in control. The correspondent cleared his throat and said at last, What exactly do you mean, Colonel?

Sol cocked his head, as if listening to the music. Then he said, Saigon specializes in good news, Mr. Harris. In Saigon there is always progress, a single prophet, and a revelation at the end of the book. Out here, at this particular location on the margins—well, even the most eminent scholars can't agree on the meaning of the Old Testament, whether it's history, myth, moral instruction, or fable. It's an ambiguous document, isn't it? But whatever it is, it surely isn't good news, no.

I see, Harris said.

I hoped you would, Sol replied.

Sam watched the correspondent move to higher ground. It was necessary to wean Sol Henderson from the Bible. It was out of place in this setting, and the millions of American television viewers would think him a religious fanatic. And what he said sounded vaguely sacrilegious, contemptuous of The Word. Harris said firmly, What are your casualties here, at this particular location?

That's classified, Sol said.

Harris turned to the camera, and thus to American living rooms. In a practiced aside, he said, In military language casualties are described as light, moderate, or heavy. He turned back to Sol. Which are these, Colonel?

Obviously, Sol said with a trace of impatience, they would not be light. If they were light, they would not be classified.

So they are heavy.

Sol shrugged, neither agreeing nor disputing.

Why are they classified, Colonel?

Because Saigon believes their publication, exact numbers, would aid the enemy.

Would they, in your opinion?

Any information is helpful.

And how many casualties have you inflicted?

That's classified, too.

Harris went into his why-you-can't-mean-that pose, turning again to the camera with a look of surprise. How can that be? That information cannot possibly affect the enemy. Those are *their* casualties, after all. They know their own casualties, don't they?

Sol shook his head. We don't want them to know that we know.

234

How many casualties they've taken.

Right, Sol said.

Our perception—

Indeed, our perception. If they know that we know what they know, well then. That's a vital piece of information, just vital.

And what of the American people? Harris scowled and moved in closer. The microphone was under Sol's nose now. Don't the American people—

You mean the public in its thirst for knowledge of this war. He moved the microphone back a few inches, grinning widely. Its fascination with the details, and its meticulous attention to the ebb and flow of the battle. Well, then. He leaned into the microphone, the motion suggesting confidentiality. The correspondent stepped backward. Sol said, They're moderate.

That's news, Harris said. Do you have numbers?

Sol laughed. Of course not.

You cannot say with certainty then—

No, Mr. Harris. I cannot say with certainty.

Your own casualties, then. How do they come?

A few each day. A sniper, a mine, a mortar attack, an occasional ambush, sabotage, and from time to time a simple meeting engagement. And there're the usual casualties unrelated to enemy action. Disease, fatigue, boredom, breakdown. Malaria, dysentery, jaundice, fear. A while ago, we even had a heart attack. But I was not in command then.

This camp has been under your command for how long?

Sixty days.

And what has been the progress, then to now?

Progress?

The change. The increment. What has changed, then to now?

It's the same now as it was then, only more so.

I suppose it's the waiting, Harris said.

No, Mr. Harris. The waiting's all right. No one minds waiting.

For something to happen.

Yes, it's that. It's the happening that we mind. No one minds waiting.

Sam and Passau watched this intently, not moving. As Sol Henderson talked about waiting he cocked his head, literally looking down his nose at Harris. It was a pose, a counterfeit; he was acting. Sam moved closer to the screen, leaning across the mahogany bar, pointing out the details. The starched and pressed fatigues, the Colt .45 automatic slung low on his hip, the tousled hair—longer now, it made Sol Henderson look less like a soldier and more like a leading man. His sleeves were rolled up over his muscular forearms, and his hands were tucked casually into the rear pockets of his fatigues. The impression—the image—was one of serenity and authority. His diction was perfect. But the interview moved farther into never-never-land.

So there is progress, Colonel.

There is no change. I don't know if you can call it progress.

Harris turned again to the camera, speaking directly to the audience. Another contradiction, he said grimly. Then he looked at Sol. An official spokesman, General MacVeigh, maintains—

Sol grinned. What do you expect him to do? That's what we do out here, we maintain. We do not go forward. We maintain. Maintenance, that's the stuff of our lives. Get it, Harris?

Well then, Harris said. You have stated the problem. What would *you* do about it? This was apparently the question that Harris considered the essence, the nut's kernel, for his face changed expression while he waited with ominous stillness for the answer. The seconds ticked on, the camera tight on Sol's face.

There's nothing to be done, he said finally. Except nuke 'em.

You wouldn't recommend that?

Oh, Christ, Sam thought. He involuntarily put his hands over his ears.

Sol said, No. I wouldn't recommend it. Somebody will, though, sooner or later.

But meantime, Harris said. We just sit here and lose. Wait for defeat. After the thousands of casualties we've taken.

Our casualties are nothing compared to theirs.

Harris said censoriously, Well, *Colonel* . . .

Sol said, We could try to kill all of them. But it would take a very long time, long's we've decided not to nuke. That's a National Command Authority decision, of course. We've been trying for almost ten years, haven't gotten very far, though I'll grant that there are very many dead souls to our credit. A hecatomb. Maybe we could try it for another ten years, we've been going pretty good—

Harris said, This is your—

Third tour, Sol answered.

Your last?

Oh no, Sol said. By no means.

You mean you'll sign up again, knowing what you know? Believing what you do?

You don't get it, Harris. This is my home. This is where I live, I'm a resident. It's where they send my tax forms and absentee ballot. I'm not a *tourist*, I live here.

But you've said that the war can't be won—

Sol stared at him with a menacing grin. My being here doesn't have anything to do with winning or losing, Mr. Harris.

A little rattle of gunfire erupted off-camera, *poppoppop*. It sounded in no way serious, perhaps only a trooper utilizing the firing range or children playing war. There were a number of small children inside the camp, skylarking near the barbed wire. Neither Sol nor the correspondent moved.

Patrol has contact, Harris said.

Sounds like it, Sol replied.

The correspondent turned toward the camera and commenced a fluent ad lib narration. They, the patrol, couldn't be more than a click from Fox, which Saigon's General MacVeigh had classified "secure," a showcase, a model of intelligent pacification. Harris lowered his eyes and sighed into the microphone, one more dashed illusion. Then he turned back to the Colonel, the spider to the fly. But Sol was no longer there. The camera picked him up walking slowly into the jungle with half a dozen uniformed men, American and Vietnamese. Sol was carrying an assault rifle and was hatless, his height conspicuous. Harris said nothing, leaving the camera to linger on them as they moved down a path through the concertina wire and into the deep blue-green of the forest, brilliant in color on the small screen. Then the camera drew back and the figures diminished, disappearing into the forest.

The war wore many faces, Harris said. He was off-camera now. The screen was dense with concertina wire and jungle. This has been one of them, he went on, the face of Colonel Sol Henderson. An uncomfortable interview, one that took courage for him to grant. Sol Henderson, a professional soldier doing his duty. There are many such in the war. Harris paused and the silence was suddenly interrupted by the sound of distant gunfire. Yet progress comes hard, and even the most dedicated professionals are tempted by despair . . . The camera continued to draw back, revealing a hootch and two figures. Harris said gravely, Many years ago the great jurist Oliver Wendell Holmes—

Sam blurted, Jesus Christ!

Harris continued with the quotation, special emphasis on the "true and adorable." Then, after a solemn interval, the screen went dark.

But Sam did not move or turn away. He was through the looking glass once again. They had rebuilt it, stick by stick. It was now as it had been then. Fox restored, as if it were a historical site, a colonial village or medieval castle. The meticulous artisans of the army! Laurence's hootch was undisturbed. Last summer Sam had ordered it spared, assuming it would disappear into the jungle; sooner or later, the jungle claimed every man-made thing. He laughed out loud, God bless the army. And that was not all, by no means. Standing in the doorway, hand in hand, were Jessel and Sonia McDonough. At the moment the camera lingered, Sonia laughed and did a little swing step; he heard a piano and traps, American blues. It brought tears to his eyes. Her motion was as erotic as a strip-tease. She was dressed in tight blue jeans and a loose olive drab shirt, her hair short and brushed back, and she was deeply tanned. Jessel was in fatigues, tiger-striped for camouflage. They were so vivid on the small screen. It came back to him then, the heat and the damp, the silence and the smell of the place, and the quickened tempo whenever a woman was nearby. Jessel was looking at her sideways; he was making notes as Sol Henderson and the men disappeared into the jungle. Jessel's face was in shadows but Sam could imagine his emotion as he felt the young woman move carelessly in rhythm to the music, her body so supple and trim, unselfconscious in this border zone. They looked as if they hadn't a care in the world and would be together always.

Eyes filling with tears he raised his glass to them both. *Salud!* They deserved what they had. And was it only his imagination but was the Revdoc's sign still there, hanging on the door?

THE DOCTOR IS IN

He smiled, then managed a short laugh. Passau! He wanted to tell the story to someone.

But the barman was serving customers, and Sam did not pursue the matter. It was an insider's story after all, a woman in blue jeans and a man in camouflage. He smiled. And music, the pacification blues. He signaled wordlessly for another round. It was not a story you could appreciate unless you knew the territory.

She saw it all now through a haze, the edges of her vision collapsing then coming into focus, the candlelight unnaturally bright then dull. It was not unpleasant. Lulled by the voices, bored by them, she closed her eyes. Marina did not often drink, a glass of wine before dinner and another during was her standard; none of their crowd drank much except at Shakerville dinners on Saturday night. She liked to drink when she was with Sam. The first time she saw him he had a glass of champagne in his hand and had awkwardly toasted Piatt, then kissed her on the mouth; his mouth was tart with champagne. Their first evening alone together had been at a restaurant, they'd had drinks and beaucoup wine with the meal—his word, "beaucoup," a word from the Zone. They had dined in so many places, in the District and Virginia and Maryland and in Oregon when he had been stationed at Lewis. In Spain of course and in Paris, and one or two other places she was too tired or too drunk to remember. Well, she could remember them all right if she tried. She surveyed the disheveled table, the decanters and bottles, the crumpled napkins, Sam's knives and silver spoons in candlelight, and the mural beyond.

She wished there was music, Amália Rodriguez singing *fados* or Billie Holiday the blues. It didn't matter, the Brandenburgs or anything by Telemann. She tried mightily to summon Amália Rodriguez, discovered by chance in a cabaret in Madrid; she remembered the darkness and the smoke in the room, and the cathedral silence when the singer had commenced her canto, so low and coarse, so sad. But the monologue at the tables interfered and Amália Rodriguez remained a shadow in her memory.

Jo was reminiscing about Dennis, how he'd confided in her and asked her advice, damn rare thing for a man in this town. If

Costello was Xerox and Mundelein was IBM then Dennis was General Motors and U.S. Steel. She was talking to Sheila, saying that it was harder with Max because Max had so many damn secrets. You know, she said, cloak and dagger stuff. Jo was slurring her words and Sheila did not reply, only listened politely. God, we loved him, Jo said suddenly, loud enough for Marina to look across the table at her. Didn't we? Didn't we adore him?

Of course, Marina said. Then something in Jo's tone stopped her and she turned away. Jo was not talking about Dennis but about the former President.

Remember? Jo said, tears in her eyes. He called, that time.

Yes, Marina said.

Now Teddy leaned across the table, a fresh cigar in his fist. The bottles clinked merrily. He tapped Sam on the elbow and began to talk, sotto voce. Max laughed and drunkenly crowded them, a wide leer on his face. No secrets! he cried. Nothing's classified here! We are not *à couvert*!

Piatt said something to Marina and she shrugged. For close to ten years they had come to this table wagering the small change of the government; ten years hence they would be here still. Table stakes, she thought, rising with the general inflation. She stared at Sam's *kriegspiel* with something like hatred. They seemed to allow it to happen; allow things to happen to them with the attractive fatalism so peculiar to the capital city. She could only guess at the truth of what happened between Piatt and Henry Costello, but she had the location firmly in her mind's eye—that thick, heavy building, the formal office, the big desk and the telephone, the glossy photographs on the far wall—it was her history, too—and the lawyer motionless in the leather chair, Piatt prowling. And Sam, the absent party; Sam unconcerned, as if it were nothing very important, certainly not life and death. And Pat Mundelein, an adviser of no fixed motive, who had begun it all. Max Cather was there too, listening in; and she, she also was a ghost in that room.

Marina looked up. Sheila was staring distractedly at the Kodacolor of her handsome son the SEAL. Jo continued to confess, she knew now that she had been loose, far too loose, with Sonia. The world was so different, after Dennis died. Max was good, though; Max had been damned good, understanding that Dennis would be with her always. . . .Sheila nodded automatically, turning to Sam, pleading with her eyes. Helen Carney was out of it. Piatt sat lost in thought. Marina looked across the candlelight at Sam and found his eyes on her. For a long moment, it was as if they were alone.

She winked at him, not very convincing.

He crossed his eyes and she smiled. Teddy was whispering something at him and he was nodding and making faces at her.

Sam's world was so mysterious, more mysterious even than Piatt's. She had never found a way into it, though she had tried. It was like a remote nation with its own laws and economic system and language, as recondite as a special marriage. She would always be a half-hearted tourist in that land because she could not find her way to its heart, and he could not commit his life to her. It wasn't that he wouldn't, he couldn't. He kidded himself about some things but not about that. She guessed part of it had to do with Piatt as much as it had to do with anything outside the service itself. Sam, who had always taken anything he wanted, could not take his friend's wife. Perhaps he remembered the shy bookish midwestern boy who hated games, the boy who seemed as even and uncomplicated as the terrain of the land itself. Sam knew that she was his in every important way and certainly did not consider ending it; but he would not marry her either.

Sam left the table and she heard the bathroom door close. Piatt, animated suddenly, raised his hand. She wanted to tell him to forget it, it didn't matter anymore. The evening was over and it was time they all went home.

"Just to finish it off," he said to Max Cather. His voice was louder than usual and she realized that he was tight. The others turned, conversations suspended. He paused, then spoke in his own patois. "Our fellow fixed it, just as he said he would. He's a real rainmaker, that one, up a tree with a bag full of bones. Rattle, rattle. All charges forgotten. Erased, expunged, purged. No record."

"So he's out of the woods."

"Completely free and clear," Piatt said. "So far as the government's concerned." He glanced casually at the door. "It was a hell of mess, I don't mind telling you."

"Piatt," she said.

"A handy man to have, a rainmaker."

"So he's free to return to the Zone," Piatt said. "That is where he says he wants to be."

Cather grunted. "They're pathological, all of them. Can't stay away from it. The atmosphere, the hardware, the uniforms; it's like a drug and they're all junkies."

Marina looked at Max, then turned away in disgust. That was not the way Sam had described Base Fox; and he was right about the other thing, too. They hated the soldiers, hated them to death. Her attention was wandering again, she had listened so eagerly as he explained his nation, its rules and regulations, customs and cuisine and immigration procedures and medical services, the lot. And when she'd asked him to tell her the one great principle, the virtue of that nation, he'd laughed and said, *Never feed troops piecemeal into battle.* No, she said; be serious. But she was smiling when she said it. Reflecting a moment, he'd added, *Accurate intelligence precedes every single thing except the will to fight.* This was not the first time she'd heard that, he'd told her years ago in Spain. Over some dinner table, the waiters standing silently nearby, watching the performance.

Carney turned to address the table at large. "I think I missed an inning, do you think you can recap for me? Of course it's in the memory only, isn't that right?" He looked at Max, who shook his head. "Or better yet, tell Jessel."

"*Jessel!*" Max snorted. He was pulling himself together with difficulty. "I'd sooner tell Ho Chi Minh. But yes, it's an interesting story. A timely story, yes. A story of the federal city, unique to our own civilization. Wouldn't you say, Piatt?"

"Sure," Piatt said.

And unresolved, Marina thought. Loose ends everywhere. No plausible motives and an unclear objective. And no certain end except that Sam would go abroad to the war again. The war would continue, one part of it under his personal supervision. She was so afraid.

Carney said, "So you'll be going ahead, Max. It's a bit beyond Gethsemane, isn't it? After all."

"It depends on what they want downtown and when. But," he said, "I expect so."

"And you'll run it?"

"Oh, yes," Cather said. He waved his arms expansively, including all of them; his eyes slipped to half-mast but his voice was firm. He reached for the framboise and poured a splash. "It's an intelligence-gathering operation, basically. With some pacification constituents to be sure. And one or two original angles so far's the targeting is concerned. But we would want it in our control, where it belongs. Some warm bodies from the military, that's all we need. My mechanicals will write the programs and all they'll do in the field is push the buttons."

"Let me know," Carney said. He stopped when he saw the shadow in the doorway.

Marina watched Sam leaning against the door, listening to them. His arms were folded, his bulk almost filling the opening. She watched him push off from the door, moving quickly to Cather's side. Max raised his fists in front of his chest, almost childlike in his fear; but then he laughed, his Great Cassio laugh.

Sam said to Sheila, "Let's go."

Marina said to him, "Will you be working for him, then?"

He smiled brightly at her. "Him or someone like him."

"I wouldn't," she said.

He said, "I know."

"I wouldn't follow Max around the corner," Sheila said.

"I don't know what they'll want," Sam said seriously. His hands were on the back of Max Cather's chair and when he tugged the chair moved. "By the time it gets from here to there, who knows what the orders'll be. No one knows how they'll set it up downtown." He glanced at Max. "I doubt if they'll want him, but you never know."

"We saved your ass," Max said.

"Shut up, Max," Piatt said.

"I wish we could have you out there for an afternoon, Max.

You'd find it an eye-opener, the Zone. Your magic act, you'd find plenty of use for it."

"I intend to make frequent trips to the scene," Max said.

"Let me know," Sam said.

Marina turned away. She thought they were, all of them, fixed stars. They were on fixed courses which no one, at this late date, could alter. She couldn't. Sam wouldn't. Not Mundelein, not anybody, except perhaps Costello, the attorney who had problems for clients and a meter with as many buttons as there were passengers and a happy talent for "sports law." When all the rules fell willy-nilly, when results so confounded expectations, the one who survived was the one with no rules at all.

It was as if they were alone in the room, she and Sam. She asked him, "When will you leave?"

"They haven't cut my orders yet."

"I mean," she said irritably, "this week, next? Next month?"

He said, "Soon. Within the month."

"And it will be for one year?"

"The tours are always one year long," Sam said.

"So we can plan on seeing you next year, about this time." She gestured at the knives and spoons and crumpled napkins. "And you can tell us how and where it's changed, because you'll have fresh facts, firsthand."

"It won't change," he said.

"The war won't be over then?"

"No."

"But perhaps you'll know more."

"Yes," he said. "Most certainly I will know more. Max, too. He'll know more. And downtown, they'll know more than anyone."

The others crowded the doorway. Teddy Carney tried to stay the general withdrawal, but Jo and Marina were already on their feet, both of them swaying slightly. Sam was holding Sheila's chair. Conversation was muted for a moment, they they all moved at once. Only Max Cather remained indolently seated. He looked up at Marina and smiled broadly. "I'll save string," he said. "Maybe I'll keep a diary, this project's interesting. So many

---

245

different elements. So many twists and turns, don't you think?"
He laughed, looking at the others, but no one was listening except Marina.

Helen handed them their coats.

"Five tours," Cather said softly, almost to himself.

Teddy whispered something to Piatt, who laughed.

"He must love the life," Cather said to Marina. "It must be about the best life there is."

"Max," Jo said.

"Must you go?" Helen asked.

"Yes," Marina said.

Lovely party.

Great brains.

Lovely . . .

. . . lovely dinner.

Good talk.

It's such *fun* in Shakerville, Jo said.

When it's just us, Helen added.

Who else is there? Teddy cried.

Marina looked around her, all of them were smiling. Suddenly she was convinced that she would never see Sam again, so she stood next to him in the crush at the doorway. Their hands touched briefly, then passionately. No, she thought; he would return to her. He always had before. He's survived so much, he'll survive this. What had he said, so long ago? *It won't be that kind of war for me.* And they had had so much together. She leaned against him, her eyes closed.

Sheila had moved back to the table to collect her Kodacolor. Jo waited impatiently for Max, who was muttering a final word to Carney. He was still at table, his full glass in front of him. Abruptly the foreign editor laughed and gestured at the mural. They all turned to look at it in the flickering light of the candles, the colors ashen and somber in the moving shadows. Beyond the bridge, out of range of the guns, stood the solitary figure in black britches, soft hat, and white scarf, arms folded, watching. He was, as before, slightly bent at the waist, leaning forward. Now, up close, they could see that he was not expectant skeptical inquiring interested at all. He seemed to be laughing, like some comical mortician. Was he leaning on a walking stick or a spade? His right hand was pressed to his temple in mirth, or so it seemed from this fresh angle of vision.

Laughing, Carney said, "That's Jessel."

Marina said, "Where are the women?"

"Out of sight," Sheila said. "The women are out of sight, in their houses, concealed. Upstairs, out of harm's way."

"Ask the man in black," Carney said. "Ask Jessel."

"I'm asking Max," Marina said. She felt Sam's big hand tighten on hers. Piatt was already out the door, standing now in the empty street. It was snowing lightly, Shakerville already shrouded, the hard little flakes brilliant in the glare of the gaslamps. She felt the cold through the open door and her head was suddenly clear. The silent street, the dark old houses so exact and formal in the snow, sent a shiver of regret through her. Or was it only remorse, nostalgia being the capital's drug of choice. Her hand was hot in Sam's. Piatt turned then and looked inquiringly at her. He seemed to shudder, hands deep in his overcoat pockets; then his right hand went to his throat, adjusting the knot of his tie. She moved impetuously against Sam and he held her a moment before helping her with her coat. She did not care what they thought, her lover was going away again. Piatt looked at her, and then at his watch. Snow blew through the doorway.

She whispered to him, It's the second snow, isn't it pretty? Have you ever seen anything so still?

Sam nodded, staring into her eyes.

It's so beautiful, she said.

Very fine, he said. And it won't go away.

Sure about that? she asked.

Absolutely.

I hate it, she said.

Sam kissed her gently.

Carney said loudly, "Tell the lady, Max!"

I'm so afraid, she said.

"I don't know where the women are," Max said comfortably.

247

He was up now, his glass in his hand, and turned to peer back into the dining room and the mural. "Except of course in our minds always. Some say it's the reason we go to war, but I don't believe it. 'Why do men go to war?' " he asked in a mincing falsetto. " 'Because the women are watching.' Rubbish. It's because of the future and the necessity that we guarantee it. I do know this. It's all an end game now." He yawned luxuriously, his back to them. "We never leave an end game, we're a tenacious, patient people. We fulfill our traditions. We never abandon our friends. We never shoot our wounded or leave our dead on the battlefield, *n'est-ce pas*, my Colonel? We always press forward, we're a people that believes in a sunny future, the future always holding the promise of the past. Time is on our side. Sam would never leave an end game, so he'll be in the Zone for some little time. As will we all, in our different capacities. Exercising our various responsibilities. This thing will be concluded one way or another, not to worry. We've so very much up our sleeves, what we've described tonight. What our Colonel described so eloquently tonight. Is just the tip of one little card."

Piatt was in the doorway next to her, listening. She felt physically ill, holding on to Sam, her arm around his waist. His belly felt hard as iron, and she was crowded. There was an embarrassed silence, and Sam turned suddenly, staring at Max, and said something foul. Then, "How much more murderous do you want it?"

Piatt's head came between them.

Max smiled complacently. "It's not what I want. But what the possibilities are."

"And—" Sam took a step toward him.

"And they are almost infinite," Max said.

III

The news of Dennis McDonough's sudden death spread this way through their community. Carney heard it from Cather who heard it from Sheila Dennehay. Sheila was told by a witness, Henry Costello. All this in twenty minutes. Teddy Carney telephoned Piatt Warden at once but Piatt was on the floor of the House, unavailable. The page did not get the message to him promptly because Piatt was in the rear of the chamber talking to a colleague, and the floor was crowded owing to a vote scheduled at the end of the hour.

When he got the message, *Call Mr. Carney immediately*, he delayed. Teddy was always on the phone with idle gossip. He was standing where he always stood, behind the brass rail, watching a debate ramble to its conclusion. He broke away when the majority leader finished talking, vaguely irritated at being interrupted. Piatt loved the floor of the House, its antique furnishings and disorder and seductive atmosphere of compromise. The news mortified him. Dazed, he telephoned his office and told the AA to contact the leadership and arrange a pair. It was not an important vote but he wanted to be with the leadership. Piatt said he would not be available for the next three or four days and if there were any votes the AA should arrange pairs for all of them, and if there was a particular problem he should call; Piatt gave him two numbers.

Then he called Marina. Their telephone was busy so he ordered the operator to break in, an emergency. He had done this before, Marina was a marathon girl on the telephone. Piatt was conscious of the strain in his voice, but his wife misread it and thought he was telephoning with good news. There was so much good news then. She was laughing when the connection was made.

Hello, Pi. What is it now?

He said without preamble, "I have bad news. Dennis is dead."

She did not believe him, right away. People their age didn't die.

"A cab hit him in I Street." He did not add the details Teddy had given him, Dennis crossing I, heedless of traffic as always, knocked into a tree, bouncing off the tree, crashing into a parked car, finally dumped on the sidewalk. He was pronounced dead at the hospital. The ambulance took forever to get there. Teddy called it a freak random accident—but what was random about a man driving fifty miles an hour down crowded I? That was not random, it was specific; and it was not an accident, it was murder. The law would call it manslaughter.

"Dennis didn't suffer," he lied.

"Poor Jo," Marina said. "Poor little Sonia."

"At least he didn't suffer." He said, "I'm coming home right away, get some food together. We should be with Jo. Everyone's going over there now, and I'll be home as soon as I call Sam Joyce."

"I'll call him," she said.

"No, I will."

The McDonoughs lived on the other side of Wisconsin Avenue. Piatt and Marina went first to the delicatessen, then to the liquor store. Coals to Newcastle, Piatt thought, no one ever went thirsty at the McDonoughs. It was a golden October day, the sort of day that showed the city to its best advantage. The common things they noticed seemed overbright, a glittering brass mail slot or a falling leaf acquired an unnatural significance. They walked slowly with their parcels, numb. This death was inexplicable; their world was fast and competitive and sometimes aggressive but it was not violent; Washington was not violent, their neighborhood seemed to them as secure as the Constitution itself. Piatt tried to explain this but Marina only nodded. They had shared much joy and some grievance in six years of marriage, but this was their first encounter with grief. And grief did not seem to unify them. He was irritated with her for being on the telephone, and for misreading his tone of voice. They were plodding up Dent Place now, the houses so familiar. A formal dinner in this house, a reception in that. Someone's parents lived on the corner. The large brick one was a diplomat's, the row house *there* a columnist's.

Oh, look, she said suddenly. Oh, *Pi*. She took his arm and began to cry.

It was Henry Costello's, where they had spent Saturday night. Henry was housesitting for an ambassador, and had given a quiet, formal dinner for ten that had turned into a riot. Carney's stories, then Max Cather's tricks. They had finished one bottle of cognac and begun another. Dennis proposed poker. No one in their circle played cards or gambled in any way except Dennis, who went to Las Vegas once a year with Henry. No one ever knew whether he won or lost but his stories of drama in Vegas were hilarious. None of them knew Henry Costello well. He was Dennis's gambling friend, a lawyer who worked in the Defense Department. Max Cather had just returned from Indochina and was full of enthusiasm for the coming struggle, the test of a great power to engage in counter-revolution. Max spoke of the war as he would speak of a difficult friend, one who had to be explained before he was introduced. A dapper, debonair little war in a land of tigers and elephants! A subtle, elusive, perverse personality, hard to warm to until you got to know it. A thinking man's war in many ways, no Georgie Pattons need apply. . . . Dennis lost the small pots but won the big ones with his reckless play. Suddenly it was dawn and they were on the sidewalk together, all of them tight and vivacious.

On the sidewalk they continued a conversation begun earlier. They had spent the first part of the evening speculating, buying long. Who would be the first to appear on the cover of *Time* magazine? The times were fertile and there were so many candidates, all of them rising in law, politics, journalism, diplomacy, and the army. Washington's critical mass, the chain reaction at hand. Piatt, Max, and Teddy were all permanent; they would remain in Washington as long as there was a government, Piatt in the House, Max Cather at CAS, Teddy Carney at the newspaper. Dennis would be out of a job with a change in administration, though that day was far off; but he would never leave the capital and would return to the government at the first opportunity. And it was Dennis who would appear on the cover of *Time*, everyone knew it; his horizon was limitless. It was hard to know what would become of Henry Costello, Henry was not a man who relished publicity. And Sam—Sam Joyce, captain, U.S.A., was in another category altogether. He was their military friend, and they were proud to know him; it was like knowing a worldly priest. Military men were not as a rule visible in their community, being ever so slightly out of it; of course Sam was the son of Old Ben Joyce, judge, Senator, and sage. He knew Washington well from the inside.

They turned right at 34th Street but did not pause at the little park, where on Sunday mornings Tommy played with Sonia McDonough while the adults read the newspapers and drank coffee from a thermos. Sonia, a few years older than Tommy, always brought a deck of cards. Piatt and Marina had a photograph album stuffed with pictures of the two children playing gin rummy under a shade tree, grave as accountants. They scored according to the Hollywood system and Sonia always won. She was a good winner and generous with her knowledge of the game; she was always a step or two ahead of Tommy, however. They played for a hundred dollars a point, payable in gold in the year 2000. Her father's daughter, Jo said.

A half-dozen people were already there. The first flowers had arrived and been taken to the kitchen, two friends unwrapping them and filling vases with water, taking their time about it. Jo gave a cry when she saw them, half rising out of her chair. She and Marina embraced and Marina began to cry. The others in the room looked away, distraught. Piatt embraced them both, his long arms going easily around their shoulders. He drew them to him until their faces were on his chest. They stood swaying in the middle of the room, a thickness gathering around them. Then as if on signal they broke and greeted the others, all but one of them old friends. The one outsider was Henry Costello. Jo stayed close to Marina. Piatt put the food in the kitchen and the liquor on the sideboard in the dining room. In the kitchen he looked inquiringly at Harriet Cather. Harriet shrugged helplessly. Max was on his way, or so he said. Jo was in shock and should be in bed. Piatt asked, How did she find out? Who told her?

"I did," Henry Costello said. "I saw it happen."

"A cab," Piatt said. "Is that right? A speeding cab?"

"Apparently a stolen cab. Drunk, the driver must've been going fifty. There'd been a robbery, and it's thought that the driver was escaping." He paused. "It's a complicated story. Dennis saw him coming, but . . . "

"A hell of a thing to have to see," Piatt said.

"Yes," Costello said. "I just happened to be at my office window, talking on the telephone."

How strange, Piatt thought. A man who happened to be at his office window, talking on the telephone and looking into the street at the precise moment a friend was struck by a speeding car. Piatt said sadly, "He couldn't get out of the way."

"He didn't," Costello said. He cleared his throat, then lowered his voice, attorney to client. "I know how close he was to you. But the thing is this. His father hasn't been told. He has a brother and the brother apparently hasn't been told either. Someone ought to tell them." Costello seemed to be volunteering.

"Do you know them?"

"Not really," Costello said. "I've met Carl a few times." He added, "Business."

Piatt wondered what business Carl McDonough had with Henry Costello. Mr. McDonough was a Chicago banker. Over the years Piatt had heard numerous references to investments, trusts, various properties, the will that would dispose of them, and the family lawyer who looked after it all.

"You ought to do it, Piatt," Harriet Cather said.

Piatt looked at Costello. "Where is he?" When Costello did not immediately reply, he added impatiently, "Dennis."

"At the hospital. They're waiting for the family's instructions. I went with him in the ambulance. I told them to wait for a telephone call. I've called Wilson's and told them to stand by. Not to do anything until they got a call from Jo. But they're ready to move, Wilson's is." He added softly, "It's the best one."

Piatt turned to Harriet. "Has anyone talked to Jo about any of this?"

She shook her head. "Piatt? Tell her what you're going to do and then do it. Don't ask her. Tell her, and wait for her to object. Do you see?" She put her hand on his arm. "I wish Max were here."

He walked out of the kitchen and into the living room, Costello at his heels. There were a dozen people in the room now, standing in small groups, talking quietly in the tones of the sickroom. The doorbell rang; more flowers. Piatt shook hands with the new arrivals. Most of the women were in tears. He introduced Henry Costello. They took Costello's hand with particular sympathy and attention, recognizing him as the witness. Now that someone was in charge, the talk rose in volume. Jo was on the couch with Marina. Jo: a pretty petite woman who now seemed shrunken. Piatt kneeled on the floor next to her and began to talk. He was conscious of the even rhythm of his words, and Jo nodding. He would call the funeral home and then the hospital. They could discuss the specific arrangements in the morning. In the meantime, with her permission, he would call her father-in-law and Dennis's brother. Jo's own father was dead. He did not mention her mother. So many of the women he knew were on the outs with their mothers; he did not know the particulars of Jo's trouble and was not interested. But it was necessary to handle Jo's mother tactfully because it was important that in the future she have no complaint against Jo. Probably Jo should call her mother herself, but that was a decision they could make later. Jo listened carefully to all this, the funeral home, the hospital, the arrangements, Dennis's family. Finally she said she didn't want him to do it, the telephoning was her responsibility.

"No," he said. He remembered her New England background, more than one Puritan lurking in her past. He believed that she was holding on only with great effort. "It would be better for you to talk to them later, that's when they'll need you." He touched her hand.

She shook her head. "Do you think so?"

"Absolutely."

"I don't know," she said. She looked at Marina. "What about Mother?"

"I can do that," Piatt said.

"Mother," she began, her voice cracking.

"We don't have to do it now," he put in hastily. "Maybe an hour or two, Marina can do it or I can. But let's set that aside for the moment. We'll table it."

"I don't know," she said.

Marina said, "You should do it. You *can*."

Piatt glared at his wife, irritated at her interference. He said, "Trust me. It's best."

"You really think so?"

"Yes."

"You don't mind?" She was caving now. "But if you tell Dad." That was her name for Carl McDonough. "He'll tell—"

"No he won't," Piatt said. "I'll see to it."

She hesitated, then made up her mind, won finally by his sincerity and confidence. "The numbers are in the black book by the telephone in our bedroom."

Marina said nothing.

Piatt leaned over and kissed Jo, then patted his wife on the top of her head. Before Jo had a chance to think and change her mind he heaved himself to his feet—and bumped into Costello, who had been standing silently behind him. Piatt, off balance for a moment, looked back at the women.

Jo suddenly shook her head, focusing. "Wilson's," she said. "Is that the right . . . place?"

Piatt said, "It's the best." He felt Costello's reassuring hand on his shoulder. He moved away from the lawyer, vaguely annoyed. Who was he anyway? But Costello caught him as he reached the stairs.

"You don't have to call the hospital. Wilson's will do that for you."

"I know that, Henry," Piatt said.

"Of course," Costello said smoothly. "But you mentioned it

back there. . . . " He let the sentence hang, then moved in closer. "The other thing. Carl's not well. He had a heart flutter six months ago. He kept it quiet, only a few of us knew about it. So when you talk to him—"

Piatt nodded; he hadn't known. He wondered if Dennis had.

"—act accordingly. Carl's a proud man. He hated illness and he didn't want anyone to worry. But I thought you ought to know about it. So that you can break the news as gently as possible."

"Yes," Piatt said softly. "Perhaps you can tell me how to do that. How do I tell him gently that his son's dead at age thirty-two, hit by a drunk in the middle of I Street."

"First, you make sure someone's with him." The lawyer scrutinized his watch, tapping its face. "Carl will be in his office now. His secretary, with whom he is very close—she's a dear friend as well as a secretary—is called Elaine. I think it would be wise to tell Elaine what you're going to tell Carl, then have her come into the office right away to be with him when he hears the sad news." Costello stared at him with a thin smile. "Second, you tell him that it was a drunken thief who stole a cab, and that the drunken thief is in custody. Anger is stronger than grief and healthier. Isn't that right? We want Carl mad as hell, suing mad. Killing mad, *n'est-ce pas?* His son is dead but there's justice to be done. Justice cannot bring back the dead but it's the next best thing, and we are not without friends—" He touched Piatt on the shoulder. Behind them the talk rose and fell. Several of the women were crying. The telephone rang shrilly. "Or I'll be glad to tell him."

"It's not necessary," Piatt said, turning on his heel and moving up the stairs.

Bonne chance, Henry Costello said quietly, the thinnest edge of mockery in his voice. "Tell him we'll put the nigger away for life."

Piatt turned away, disgusted; it was gutter language, out of place in Washington. When he reached the second floor, Piatt heard the front door close; the lawyer had evidently departed. No loss, Piatt thought; he was not one of the good close friends, and he seemed to be in competition for the body. Or the family.

258

Now he put Costello out of mind as he walked down the hall to the big bedroom. He was familiar with it, occasionally the four of them had watched television there. He knew the location of the telephone and the black address book. Piatt paused at the door, taking in the bed, with its pink spread, and the pictures, three small Hoppers, gifts from Carl. Dennis hated them, Jo loved them. There were photographs in silver frames everywhere, and he went immediately to the one of the four of them on a beach in Bermuda. Last year's picture. There was another of them and the children in the park. They'd asked a passer-by to take the photograph and he'd hesitated and finally complied and his manner was so cool and professional that Jo asked him if he was a camera buff. He'd laughed and said Yes, he was. Jo asked his name and he smiled again and gave it, and Dennis led the laughter. He was a well-known *Life* magazine photographer. He'd joined them for a cup of coffee and they saw him frequently in the park thereafter. There were baby pictures of Jo and Dennis and wedding photographs, bride and groom formal and composed. Piatt and Marina had not known them then, so the attendants were strangers except for Teddy Carney, who had followed Dennis to Washington and was now a journalist of promise. One picture stood out: Dennis at seven or eight, pugnacious in an Eton suit.

Piatt sat down heavily in the chair next to the telephone. Wilson's would not be in her book, so he dialed 411 for the number. The number in hand, he cradled the receiver and sat quietly. He did not feel an intruder in this room, they were all members of the same tribe. Dennis, Dennis—why? For God's sake, why? He heard the doorbell ring and took the telephone off the hook, placing the receiver in his lap. He wanted it free when finally he was ready to place the call. He looked at the bed, the pictures. Who the hell did Costello think he was?

The voice that answered the telephone at Wilson's was lugubrious. Yes, they knew of the unfortunate accident and of course would be honored to assist in any way they could. Had the family agreed on the final arrangements? Of course, of course; there had been no time to do so. Wilson's offered a full range of consulting services and these naturally were at the disposal of Mrs.

McDonough whenever it was convenient for her. Our fees, the voice began—

Piatt cut him off. They could discuss that later, tomorrow or the next day. Money was not a problem.

Did he hear a sigh? The voice said, We will arrange for the deceased to be brought here from the hospital.

For embalming, Piatt said.

Yes, the lugubrious voice said. Will the family want an open casket?

No, Piatt said.

That was what we understood, the voice said. But we wanted to be absolutely certain—

There was no need to ask from whom Wilson's had "understood." Piatt said he would call back in the morning, and rang off. Again he uncradled the telephone and put it in his lap. The black book was thick, its pages soft as cloth. He turned to his own name, the address and the two telephone numbers: home and business. Home and House. Other names in the book occupied many lines, addresses and telephone numbers written and then inked out, and replaced by new addresses and numbers. The book was arranged by city: Atlanta, Boston, Chicago, Las Vegas, Louisville, Los Angeles, Vineyard Haven, New York, Philadelphia. London and Paris were at the rear. He and Marina occupied two lines only, though there was a blank space below; useless, he thought. He and Marina would never move, the address and telephone numbers could be graven in stone. He turned to Chicago and McDonough, Carl. There were three numbers, one in Chicago, one in Winnetka, and one in Green Lake, Wisconsin.

Piatt dialed. A female voice answered on the second ring. He asked if Mr. McDonough was in, and was asked his name in return. He gave it, and inquired if he was speaking to Elaine. She said Yes, what was it about? He said he had bad news for Mr. McDonough concerning his son. He heard her sharp intake of breath. He said he thought it would be wise if she were in the room when Mr. McDonough got the news—

She said, "Dennis or Michael? Where are you calling from?"

"Washington," Piatt said. "Dennis."

She hesitated, apparently composing herself. Then, "I'll put you through." She did not ask for details.

In a moment Carl McDonough's deep voice was greeting him. They'd dined the month before at Dennis's and had had a good-natured argument concerning the economic policies of the administration. Carl McDonough reprised this now, adding the latest unhappy statistic. It was something to do with the capital markets. Your man, that lunatic playboy in the White House, he said, laughing. Driving us to the poorhouse—

He'd thought about it, how he was going to put it. He would not explain everything at once. He would do it in three parts, moving from the general to the specific, and from bad to worse.

He said, "Mr. McDonough." At dinner he had called him Carl and they had gotten on well. Piatt never knew how to address the parents of his friends, but at table they'd been so boisterous that Carl came naturally. The fact that Piatt was a United States Congressman seemed to amuse the old man. Then at the end of the meal they'd begun to talk seriously about a piece of legislation of concern to bankers and the amusement faded and was replaced by respect. But now he said "Mr. McDonough" and his friend's father was instantly on guard. When he said Yes, all humor had gone out of his voice.

"I have bad news."

"Yes, Piatt."

"There's been an accident." He did not wait for a reply. "Dennis was hit by a car this afternoon."

"I see."

"And he didn't pull through."

"Dennis is dead now?"

"Yes." There was a very long silence. He heard Carl McDonough's breathing, then he heard nothing. He said loudly, "Carl?"

"I'm here."

Piatt said, "I'm so sorry."

"When did this happen?"

"At about two this afternoon."

"I see. Three hours. That's one o'clock, my time. Three hours ago." He said it wistfully, as if there was some hidden significance; that if he'd known, he could've prevented it. He said, "How's Jo? Is she there?"

Piatt said, "She's all right. She's resting now."

There was another long silence. "I'd like to speak to her."

He said, "I think it would be better—"

Brusquely, Carl McDonough said, "Of course." Then, with terrible precision, he began to ask the pertinent questions. What? Where? Who? How? He did not ask why. Piatt supplied only the bare outline, pleading ignorance of the details. Carl McDonough was not satisfied but he did not object. He asked Piatt to wait a moment. He left the telephone, then came back on the line with a time and a flight number. Piatt said he would meet him at National. He added that he and Marina would be very happy if he'd stay with them. But Carl said No, he'd stay with Jo and Sonia; that was where he was needed, and where he wanted to be. And there was no need to meet him at the airport, he'd make his own arrangements. And Sonia—

Piatt realized he had not seen the little girl. He mumbled something reassuring.

"Yes," Carl said. Then, "You're sure that son of a bitch is in custody? Sometimes, hell, they just let them go—"

"According to Henry Costello he is."

The old man's voice brightened. "Henry's there?"

"He just left," Piatt said. "But he was a witness."

"Henry *saw* it?"

"He says he saw it from his office window."

"Thank God," Carl McDonough said. "I'll get the straight story from Henry." Then, realizing Piatt could misinterpret the remark, he added, "Thank you, son. I appreciate your calling." After a moment's silence he said, "What about her mother?"

Piatt smiled, then chuckled grimly. "That decision's on hold."

"Why don't I call her?"

He remembered Marina's intervention, and Jo's dazed and hesitant acquiescence. But he did not want to say no a second time. "You know how it is between them. I think Jo's going to do it herself. I think. I don't know."

He said, "As you wish."

"Carl? Christ, I'm sorry. He had so much going for him, everything. He was the best there was."

There was a silence, then the old man's voice broke. He sobbed for a moment, then furiously shouted the first thing that came to mind. "That goddamned town. God *damn* your town. God damn it to hell." With that, he hung up.

Piatt sat listlessly with the telephone in his lap. He supposed Carl would call his younger son, Dennis's brother Michael, but could not count on it and did not under any circumstances want to call the old man back. So he looked through the black book again, found the number, and dialed. It was busy. He waited a minute and tried again. It was free this time and when Michael came on the line Piatt knew he'd talked to his father. Piatt added one or two details to the account, said how sorry he was, and replaced the receiver. He did not offer his guest room to Michael McDonough. The brothers had never gotten on. Then he thought that was mean-spirited so he called back; the phone was busy. Piatt called Sam Joyce at the Pentagon, but Sam was out; he left a message, *Call me immediately.* There were two or three friends who probably didn't know, so he called them. By now everyone in town surely knew. But it was something useful to do, make telephone calls. Dennis McDonough had a legion of friends and he imagined the news moving from coast to coast and abroad. He thought with a smile that there would be mourning in Las Vegas. He tried again to reach Michael but there was no answer at all now so he gave it up. On impulse he looked through the book for Jo's mother's number, quickly dialing it and just as quickly hanging up after two rings. No, the mother was not his business. Carl was, Michael was; her mother wasn't. Finally there were no more telephone calls to make. He thought of the number of calls in Washington that day, where the news would come as an afterthought, at the end of a business conversation.

—Say, do you know Dennis McDonough? Big guy, worked at the NSC, tight with the Man?

—Sure I know him. Know of him.

—Killed this afternoon . . .

After all the telephoning Piatt sat for a moment waiting for the tears to come. But they didn't so he stood up, a little dizzy. The walls with their family history seemed to enclose him; everything looked different now. He took a tentative step toward the door, then with confidence down the hall. He paused at Sonia's door, wretchedly closed. There was no sound within. He debated a moment, then knocked and opened the door. She was lying on her bed, her back to the wall, staring at him.

"Sonia? I'm sorry, baby."

He thought for a moment that she would say to him what she always said to her father, I am *not* a baby. But she said nothing, merely stared at him with wide-open eyes. He moved closer and sat on the floor next to the bed. He said, "We'll never forget your dad." She moved then, shifting her head, revealing a little transistor radio beside her ear. The music was playing so softly he could barely hear it, the velvet beat and the wail, kids' music. *Moo-oo-oon riverrrr* . . . He said, "Do you want to come downstairs?"

She said, "No thanks."

She looked so much like Dennis. "Rather be here?"

"I think so," she said. "I hate it."

"Yes," he said.

"I just hate it."

"Me, too."

She looked away. "If this is the way it's going to be." She brought the radio closer to her ear, still listening hard.

He did not know what to say to that so he patted her head.

"Does Tommy know?"

"Yes," he lied.

"Well," she said. "What did he say?"

Piatt said that his son felt as they all did. He was not as old as Sonia so he didn't understand it completely. But he was shocked and very sad and wanted Sonia to know that they would always be friends.

"Maybe I'll come down later," she said.

"It'll be better," he said, rising to his feet. He wanted to say something more but she had turned again to the radio, fiddling with its dial. He noticed the wallpaper behind her, a Mother Goose pattern, and the stuffed animal at the foot of the bed. A child's room, but a child did not live in it now.

"Uncle Piatt? Is my mom okay?"

He mumbled something reassuring and left quietly, moving swiftly down the carpeted stairs and into the living room. Faces turned toward him with exaggerated respect, as if he were the ship's captain who had navigated heavy weather to bring their vessel safely into port. Jo was sitting rigidly on the couch, her eyes wide and frightened. Piatt went to her, kneeling beside the couch as before, and told her tersely what he'd done. He said he'd looked in on Sonia and she was . . . resting. Carl had taken the news well, and would be with them later in the evening. "He wants to stay with you," he said. "And Sonia."

She said dully, "That's fine." Then, "Piatt? He'll want to have the funeral in Winnetka. I don't want it there, I want it here. Will that be all right?"

"Yes, don't worry about that."

"Well, he'll want it there. But don't you see? Dennis and I don't live there. We live here. This is our home. But Carl hates Washington so, it'll hurt him terribly."

Piatt said, "He'll understand."

He moved closer to her and began to talk, a confident rationalization. It was true, Carl did not like Washington. But this was not Carl's decision. It was hers and Sonia's and Dennis's. What Dennis would have wanted, and it was clear enough that Dennis's choice would have been the capital. This was where he lived and flourished; where they flourished together. It was their town, Washington. When his fluency gave out, Marina supported him, her emotion enhancing his logic. Jo began to nod automatically and he could feel her withdraw and move away from them both, retreating into the interior of her memory. Her eyes clouded over and her lips moved soundlessly. Behind them the noise level rose, everyone was drinking now and low conversation was punctuated by soft laughter; they were remembering

Dennis's escapades. If Jo heard, she gave no sign. Someone turned on the television set in the bookcase, it was time for the news. No one seemed to be paying attention to it but that was usual; in Washington the news was always there, a permanent part of the atmosphere. Now it was oddly comforting, it served to locate them all.

"Please please please don't worry about this," he was saying. "Tomorrow we'll—"

"We can't do everything tomorrow, Pi," Marina said suddenly.

"What?" He looked at her.

"Jo," Marina began.

"My mother," she said.

"Do it now," Marina said.

"I can't," she said.

Piatt shook his head, sometimes Marina simply didn't *get* it. Jo was a woman in shock, her spirit too fragile to make large decisions. He said with authority, "Marina, be quiet a minute. Jo? Let me—"

There was a ghastly silence, so abrupt that Piatt broke off and turned to the little group at the other end of the room. They were frozen in front of the television set, the picture revealing a confusion of people, shouts and auto horns, and the commands of police. Then a stretcher in motion, being wheeled to an ambulance. Dennis's face could be clearly seen, his eyes wide open and locked in an expression of blank outrage. The sheet that covered his body was bloody and one arm hung limply, swinging with the motion of the stretcher. Piatt rose to shield Jo's view but she roughly pushed him aside, standing now. Someone moved to turn off the set but she sharply ordered the offender to stop right there. Jo stepped forward, groping as if the room was in darkness. Piatt watched, motionless. It seemed to him an eternity before the stretcher was in the ambulance and the camera panned away to a reporter, standing on the curb. His voice was calm and matter-of-fact. The victim was Dennis McDonough of Washington, a staff member of the National Security Council.

Jo gave a cry, raising her fists.

The reporter smiled coldly and recounted the known facts. He gestured behind him and the camera obediently swung to a close-up: a young Negro in a cloth cap, eyes cast down in the brilliant sunlight. Two burly policemen in short-sleeved shirts flanked him. Jo was only a few feet away now, and she bent down to peer closely at the tableau. She was looking at the man who killed her husband, but the picture revealed nothing conspicuous or distinguishing. The killer was a perfectly ordinary-looking man, apparently unaware that his picture was being taken. Yet it was unmistakably *him*, a Negro of a certain height and weight and age, a thief who had been at a particular place at a particular time. He had robbed a jewelry store and stolen a cab. That was what Jo was looking at, burning his ordinariness into her memory. The tiny screen filled the room until they all seemed to be part of it, spectators at an immense keyhole. The killer turned then and said something to the policeman on his right. The officer shook his head, an oddly intimate movement; he knew he was on television, the camera's lens was tight on both of them now. The Negro shrugged, looking at the pavement. He gave a little kick, and then was still. What did he want? A cigarette? A toilet? A lawyer?

The reporter said that police had found a half-empty bottle of whiskey in the front seat of the cab, along with a quantity of gems and currency. It appeared the fugitive had done nothing right, had chosen as his getaway route the most crowded of the downtown streets. He'd botched it completely, losing control of the cab at the moment of impact—

Jo sighed, her body sagging. Teddy Carney and one other came to Marina's aid, supporting Jo. She continued to stare at the screen as if hypnotized. Then the camera panned away, disclosing the cab and two men in dark suits leaning on its hood, talking. The smaller of the two had his hand on the other's arm, confiding something—out of the side of his mouth, it seemed. The big man nodded and when he moved, still nodding, he was seen to have a plastic ID around his neck. He was an official of some kind. He looked back at the smaller man and smiled, obviously agreeing to something—all of this in a few seconds. The official gave the other man a sympathetic pat on the back, and Piatt saw that it was Henry Costello. *It's Henry*, someone said.

Jo stared blankly at the screen. Piatt watched him, Costello already oiling the wheels of justice, or of revenge. The official closed on the prisoner. The camera panned away for good now and the cab, the official, the policeman, the prisoner, and Henry Costello diminished, receding. Their expressions faded, they were now but tiny faces in the crowd. Abruptly the set went dark, to brighten again in a studio. Still no one moved to switch it off. The announcer's voice sounded unnaturally loud and insistent. The Yankees won the pennant, the Senators remained in last place. Washington, the announcer said with a smile. First in war, first in peace, and last in the American League.

Someone groaned. That old saw . . .

Piatt stepped forward and turned it off. Marina and Teddy helped Jo back to the couch. The telephone rang. Piatt went to the kitchen, dropped two ice cubes in a glass, and filled it with Scotch. In a moment Teddy joined him. He insisted that Jo go to bed, and a doctor be called for sleeping pills. Good idea, Piatt said. But she doesn't want to go to bed.

Teddy shook his head. Did you hate him?

Piatt drank. Hate who?

Him, Teddy said. Looking at him like that—

No, Piatt said. Yes. He swallowed the Scotch and poured another. I don't know, he said finally.

Mean-looking son of a bitch, Teddy said.

Was he? Perhaps he was. Most of the time, his face was concealed. Just another anonymous, wholly anonymous ignorant bungler who didn't even know how to get out of town or do the job sober.

No, Teddy said. Definitely a mean face.

Piatt shrugged. Who cares? Then Harriet Cather was at his elbow, her face close to his ear. She said, "The White House is on the line." Piatt put down his drink. "The President wants to talk to Jo."

"Let's get her," he said.

"Piatt, she's in no condition—"

"It's the President," he said.

Harriet said, "Shall I call her?" She didn't want to.

"I will," Piatt said. Jo and Marina were on the couch, holding hands; Marina was talking and Jo was listening. Their drinks were on the coffee table, untouched. He leaned down, his arm around his wife. Jo, he began. She looked at him, her eyes brimming with tears. The telephone, he said.

She shook her head.

"The President?"

"Do I have to?"

"No," Marina said.

Piatt said nothing.

"Piatt's right, I should," she said after a moment. "Yes, I really should. He was so fond of Dennis." Piatt walked with her to the kitchen, and the extension phone. Jo said Yes in a faint voice. There was no one on the line but presently a secretary answered and in a moment the President himself was there, the voice so familiar, deep and grave in these circumstances. Jo listened, nodding. Then she whispered, Thank you. There was another pause, she seemed to be listening very carefully. Yes yes, she said. Then, in a clear voice, It was very kind of you to call. She handed the telephone to Piatt and walked back to the living room.

He spoke man to man, as if they'd known and liked each other for years. How was Jo really? Was it true? A thief in a stolen cab in I Street? The President swore softly. Piatt leaned casually against the counter, listening, replying crisply to the questions. Jo was fine, she was tough, full of good stuff; she'd pull through. He listened to the offers, anything they could do, anything at all. Let them at the White House know of the funeral arrangements as soon as they were finalized. In the meantime, chins up, prayers, we'll miss him here, a terrible loss to us and to the country . . . The voice trailed away and the line was disconnected.

Piatt rang off and was surprised to find himself shaken. He stared out the window, crying. It was true, they were a family; he and Marina and Jo and Dennis and the kids. And now the President, he was part of it as well. This government was an extended family, the loyalties direct and uncomplicated. "A terrible loss to us and to the country." That was true, Dennis wasn't just a banker's son who happened onto the government; he worked for the national security of the United States. They all did, in their separate ways; even Teddy, so serious about his journalism, wanting only—only?—to be the capital's amanuensis. This administration, it was their neighborhood, their happy childhood, and rapid coming of age. Too rapid, it seemed to happen overnight. And Dennis, the most promising of them all.

It was dark now and in the house across the street people were having drinks. They were mostly women, the men were not home from work. The lamps cast a secure glow and Piatt watched them laughing and talking, this night no different from the night before. He turned away from the window, alone now in the kitchen. It was damned thoughtful of him to call, his tone worried and concerned; no stranger to deep grief, that Man. Understood it, with an attractive fatalism. No false cheer, just sadness and an offer of help. The country was lucky to have him, Piatt thought. A man of quality, and not all of them were. The President had called him "Piatt," his tone suggesting that he'd remembered the last time they'd met, at the columnist's house down the street . . .

The call had a bracing effect. Jo seemed to respond to his strength. They would all have to be strong now, with a special grace; that was the way good people behaved. She accepted a drink from Piatt, smiling wanly. She turned her head this way and that, like a cat, stretching. She had come into the kitchen with Marina and Teddy Carney, the kitchen so cozy and familiar. They stood leaning against the counters, looking into P Street. Another florist's van arrived, more white flowers. Jo smiled and said she had hay fever and, as if to confirm it for them, she sneezed.

Teddy said idiotically, "The Yankees won the pennant."

Jo looked at him. "Don't they always?"

"Most of the time," Teddy said. "I guess they do. I don't know a damned thing about it."

Jo shook her head firmly, cutting him off. "Dennis didn't care for baseball."

So there was no more talk about baseball. Teddy left and Max and Harriet Cather joined them. They talked about the President and then about the National Security Council, how much

270

Dennis liked working there. A crisis a minute, twelve- and four-teen-hour days were common. Jo was halfway through a rambling account of a memorandum Dennis had been writing when the door opened and Sam Joyce put his head in, then walked shyly to Jo and kissed her on the cheek. He was in uniform, the first time Piatt had seen him out of mufti. On his shoulders were the gold leaves of a major. He looked out of place in khaki and brass buttons, so bright in contrast to their own dark business suits.

He said to Jo, "I came as soon as I heard."

She said, "I'm glad. Fix yourself a drink. That's what we're doing now, drinking."

He turned to shake hands with Piatt and with Max. He kissed Marina and Harriet, each in turn. He said, "I didn't have time to change."

"It's fine," Jo said. "You look good."

Piatt said. "Congratulations. You didn't let us know."

He touched the leaf on his left shoulder and smiled. "The list came out today, and they." He paused. "Had a ceremony at lunch, silly damn thing. They gave me these. But fun, promotion's always a big thing in the army."

Marina said, "It's great, Sam."

He winked at her, pleased. She was the only woman in the room who knew a major from a corporal. No one said anything more for a moment, Sam Joyce's good news had struck a jarring note. He felt it, too, and removed his tunic and folded it carefully away on the counter. He mixed a drink and when Jo turned to Marina to say something, he moved off with Piatt.

"I heard the details on the radio. Are they true?"

"They're true," Piatt said. "Stranger than that, Henry Costello saw it. He was at his office window—"

"He works at the Pentagon," Sam said.

"I know he does but he's a consultant. He has an office there, and his own law office downtown. That's what he told me the other night."

"That's Henry all right," Sam said. "Nothing happens that he doesn't know about. I got a call from him this morning, some-

---

271

how he'd learned—" He gestured at the tunic. "That's how I found out about Dennis, Henry called and left a message."

"You get my message?"

"No, I was at Myers. My office tracked me down there."

"Well, he and Dennis were close."

"How's Jo taking it? And Marina?"

"As well's can be expected," Piatt said. "Marina's all right, she didn't really get it at first. Didn't understand it." He shook his head.

"Marina and Jo—"

"Close," Piatt said. "Very close."

They were silent a moment. Jo had resumed her anecdote, Dennis's memo. Piatt looked at Sam and put a finger to his lips. Jo looked questioningly at him.

"I think that's classified."

"Classified?"

"Probably top secret."

"Can I be prosecuted?"

He smiled. "Sure."

Sam said, "Piatt's joking."

"What's the most I can get?" Jo asked.

"Twenty years," he said. "Life, maybe."

She looked at him. "Is that a promise?"

Tears rose in his eyes but did not spill. They stood looking at each other across a great distance. Recovering, Piatt enumerated the various classification levels; he was being funny and she began to smile. He told one joke and then another. He told a story about Dennis and got it mixed up, but brought it home a winner anyway. Jo smiled, and finally laughed. The tension in the room went slack and they all began to laugh, louder and louder. Throughout the long afternoon and early evening they drank and told stories. There were Chicago stories, Winnetka stories, college stories, family stories, Washington stories, and Las Vegas stories. When Sonia appeared, standing quietly in the doorway, listening, Piatt went to her and held her close, then brought her over to them. He felt almost as if she was his own child. He explained that they were telling funny stories about her father. The laughter died but soon began again. She listened attentively, saying nothing. Some of the stories were rough and she didn't understand them. The early arrivals left, replaced by friends on their way home from work. The living room resembled a delicatessen, hams and roasts, cheeses and French bread and salads, cakes, pies and pastry, and wine. Jo circulated, talking, joining conversations, laughing at some small joke with her low well-bred laugh. Piatt accompanied her, fearing imminent breakdown. She was running on nervous energy and drink. But she seemed to grow stronger and more self-possessed; this was her home after all, her friends. He thought it was her puritan Yankee blood asserting itself, and then he remembered that as a college girl she'd had a treasured nickname, "Icebox."

Piatt stood at Jo's elbow, abstracted. He saw Sam and Marina in the corner, talking seriously. They were sharing a drink and Marina had tears in her eyes. Sam was talking and she was listening, nodding and occasionally looking up at him. Piatt turned away, the soldier still looked out of place in his khaki.

When at last Carl McDonough burst through the front door Jo was frankly drunk. She did not stumble or scramble her words but she was drunk nonetheless. She and her father-in-law embraced in the doorway, both weeping. His hair was wet, a light rain was falling now in P Street. Jo seemed to disappear into his capable arms. Carl was swaying and trying to wipe his eyes. Marina, at Piatt's side now, began to cry. Piatt embraced her, feeling the bitterness of her tears; it was almost a reproach.

She said, "I like them so much. *Why—?*"

He did not answer her then, as he had not answered her the other times she'd asked the question. There was no answer.

"Sam said we all have our memories of him. That's what's left and it's better than nothing at all." When he did not answer, she said, "You won't ever die, will you?"

No, he said, absurdly believing it. Making her believe it, too. She said, "I won't if you won't."

Then Carl and Jo were in the kitchen, smiling through tears. The four of them embraced, and the others backed off to give them room, an island of privacy. Carl looked ten years older than his age, a faded white double of his dead son, a futurity. Jo moved to pour him a drink and at that moment the kitchen door flew open. Piatt looked and smiled broadly, his first genuine amusement that long, dreadful day. He did not know precisely why it was funny, only that it was. The capital was subtle, and it was unusual to find a thing so raw and exact. Henry Costello, sober in a dark suit and vest and black armband, moved heavily through the doorway, bearing Carl McDonough's suitcase. Costello saw the smile and flushed. Piatt stood watching him, his arm around Carl.

Carl said, "Of course you know Henry."

Yes, Piatt said.

Henry Costello smiled, then sighed and turned and shouldered his way out of the room, mounting the stairs with Carl's suitcases, bound for the guestroom. He might have been Dennis himself, so confidently did he climb the stairs. He did not look back, and Piatt watched him disappear from sight.

Carl said, "Poor fellow. He was devoted to Denny."

Jo handed Carl a drink.

"They'd have such fun together, those trips. Funny thing, Henry doesn't gamble. Never has, doesn't like it. He just enjoyed going along." He squared his jaw, then lowered his voice, excluding Jo. "Henry saw the whole thing. He didn't want to talk about it but I forced him. Let me tell you, it was criminal. Thank God, Henry's got friends downtown. But I'm following it every step of the way and Henry and I won't rest until—"

He nodded sharply. Jo was leading him out of the kitchen. There were arrangements to be discussed. He turned back to Piatt and gave a cold stare, his banker's stare; it made things happen in Chicago. Piatt remembered a party a year ago, when Carl was in town unexpectedly. He had come to the party with Dennis and Jo and fell to talking with a young lawyer from one of the commissions. Carl complained of government regulations, the surveillance and interference with businessmen, the administration's vindictiveness toward the steel companies as the prime example. The lawyer looked at him blandly and remarked that the government could not make omelets without breaking eggs. Carl had his banker's stare then, but restrained himself out of consideration of his son. It was Dennis's town, not his. But when the mid-term elections came around, he intended to double his contribution to the other party. And told the story endlessly around the common table at the Chicago Club.

Washington, Piatt thought. There was no place like it, every single move became a purchase on power, no act so small that it did not contain its own significance. Even here, they were in competition for—what?—proximity, intimacy with the family. Still, even by Washington standards, Henry Costello was an aggressive, irresistible force. He had only met Costello Saturday night. Dennis had many mysterious friends. Piatt knew without being told that he was a particular kind of lawyer, one who never saw the inside of a courtroom. He was an apprentice in-and-outer, in the government one year, out of it the next; always on its fringes. Mr. Henry Costello was an inside man, one of the advance guard.

"Piatt, what's wrong?"

It was Marina, looking at him strangely. He thought he was alone, where had she come from? She moved close to him but he shook his head, turning away.

"You look defeated," she said.

What a marriage it had been. You couldn't kill it with an ax, Dennis liked to say. They talked about his work each night at dinner, she, Dennis, and Sonia together at table, even on those evenings when Dennis arrived late. Publicly, Dennis passed off his work on the National Security Council with a joke or self-deprecating comment. I tote and fetch, he'd say, correct their grammar, make the airline reservations, check the Bartlett's for quotations. But in his own house with his wife and daughter he was explicit. He was involved, if only on a tangent, with all the various crises—Berlin, Cuba, Laos, and with many smaller difficulties as well. And just being there, you learned so much. Jo could never get enough of it, details from the inside of national security. The truth was, Dennis wrote an occasional memo and routed paper—innocent enough, any clerk could do it, except the distribution of paper was the heart of the matter. One had to have a precise and subtle understanding of the responsibilities of each member of the staff, and the wit to know when a piece of paper had political as well as national security implications. Then the piece of paper went upstairs. If it was important enough for the President—if there was *any possibility* that the President would want to see it—then it went immediately by hand to the adviser. The President had odd interests, not all of them important by the usual definition; and if he read anything in the newspapers that surprised him, they'd get a rocket and all hell would break loose. The adviser was not forgiving of error. Once or twice Dennis had hand-carried a message to the Oval Office and stood quietly while the President read it, nodding, often smiling mordantly. Once, working late, Dennis had answered the telephone to find the President on the other end wanting to know what was up. He read the President the three most recent cables, one of them an amusing account of an unsuccessful coup in a West African nation. Dennis was halfway through it before he realized its sarcasm and felt he'd blundered until he heard the President laugh and demand to know the author. The President was light; witty, really. Dennis relaxed and they talked for five minutes, the President behaving as if he had nothing better to do.

Dennis replicated the entire conversation for Jo. And when, a few weeks later, the President called Dennis by name, that was news for the dinner table. Twice Dennis and a colleague had briefed the attorney general and done a creditable job and when the AG wrote him a note in longhand the note was passed to Jo and then to Sonia. There were occasional odd jobs of a peculiar nature and he could say nothing of these beyond the fact of them—it was a breach of security to mention even that much— but Jo was glad not to know the details. She was by nature discreet but she did not want to be responsible for a leak, through inadvertence or ignorance. Dennis shared his working life down to the last comma, almost, and Jo was grateful. It meant he trusted her, and so many Washington men did not trust their wives. They were as wary of their wives as they were of prying Congressmen or journalists. When she mentioned this to him, he passed it off; of course he confided in her. That was what marriage was. His own father had kept his mother on the outside and that contributed to their break and all the unhappiness and, for all he knew, her early death. No, of course he trusted her absolutely.

He was one of a half-dozen bright young men who came to work in the White House basement in the early days of the administration, having made reputations at Harvard or on Wall Street, and having put those reputations at the service of the then-candidate. As it happened, Dennis was an alumnus of both places, and delivered his own precinct and his father's as well. For the first time in his life Carl McDonough gave money to a Democrat, though he said nothing about it at the Chicago Club. Dennis wanted it so much. Everyone knew that Denny would be in line for a position of substance in the new administration. He confessed one night to Piatt that he had never had so much fun, had never enjoyed anything as much as working at the White House. Just being there and close to it was a thrill, and so much more than he had expected. Memoranda were his strong suit, Dennis prided himself on being a quick and accurate study. But it would be a while before he could put any stamp on policy. Piatt had smiled at that, unaware until then that Dennis had any strong opinions on "policy." Piatt saw him as an operator, not a theorist. Of course operators were so valuable . . . Dennis did not smile back. I didn't, he said; but I do now. When you're *in* it, he went on, responsible for it—and left the sentence unfinished, forcing Piatt to draw the obvious conclusions, that politicians had too many hostages to fortune, their constituents and moneymen. But members of the NSC were free to observe a single loyalty, as they proceeded to manage a disorderly world—and without benefit of hindsight. Every day there were dozens of matters that required the adviser's attention and decision. Not everything went to the Oval Office. From time to time the adviser or his deputy would assign a memo to him, and he worked over these as carefully as he had worked on his senior thesis, and in a way the atmosphere was similar. The adviser was a hard grader.

As it happened, one of the memos warned against an adventure in Indochina and predicted with clarity the course of events. In time, it became a seminal paper in the Vietnam archive. Much later, when the adventure became a war, Jo had the four original pages framed and hung in her study, the classification stamps—*secret secret secret secret*—a conscious irony. The memo was a profound source of pride to both Jo and Sonia, and only Piatt and Sam Joyce knew that Dennis had written it in an afternoon and sent it to the adviser, who filed it; there was no evidence of its having been read by anyone. Still, he had gone on record; a brave act. Dennis had told them this during dinner at Henry Costello's. He had written the memo on his own motion, freely admitting that he had no special expertise in Asia, beyond the usual Harvard survey course. But he deeply believed that Asia was peripheral and without immediate significance, compared to the various threats to European security. The nation's ancestral ties were West, not East. The East was red, Dennis said, quoting Mao; the essential fact of China was its mystery. It was unknowable, and if China was unknowable after the many years of close, though stormy, relations with the West—why, how much more unknowable was *Indo*china. At any events its purposes were obscure . . . Sam Joyce replied that this was merely the traditional Washington bias, mainly the bias of the State Department whose old Asia hands had been so ravaged in the McCarthy years. Asia was not mysterious at all, but it was poison to a diplomat's career. Europe was a safe haven but it didn't make any difference because the commitment had already been made, *America was going in.* The truth was, Europe was stable and Asia was not; and instability anywhere was a threat to industrialized nations.

I'm going there myself, Sam said.

Dennis was surprised. As surprised as he had been when Sam Joyce, the soldier, was going on about "instability" and "industrialized nations."

As an adviser, Sam said.

A Green *Beret?* Dennis asked. He was impressed.

There's hardly a man in my class at West Point who hasn't volunteered, Sam said. We've got volunteers from here to there, everyone wants to be part of it—

They were talking quietly among themselves, none of this was common knowledge. Teddy Carney was well out of earshot, though Henry Costello was hovering about. Dennis smiled, but did not say out loud what he was thinking, that it sounded like his own class at Harvard, wanting to be part of the administration. Of course it was logical, if you were a civilian you wanted to be in Washington and if you were a soldier you wanted to be in Indochina. The point was to go where the action was. Except he had not realized that plans were so complete, at the Department of Defense. The administration was still not fully committed, or so he had been led to believe. Perhaps this was a plan of the Joint Chiefs, everyone at the NSC had great confidence in the civilians at DOD. He did not want to go against the grain, but believed he had a responsibility—though exactly to whom or to what he could not say. Dennis wrote the memo in an afternoon, and gave it to the adviser a day or two before his death, which was reported routinely.

In Washington:

NSC STAFFER
DIES IN CRASH

In Chicago:

BANKER'S SON
KILLED IN
D.C. CRASH

Jo did not have the will to fight her father-in-law. The service would be in Winnetka. Then, two days later, there would be a memorial service in Washington. Piatt and Marina were obliged to step in for her and insist that burial be in Washington. The old man was heartbroken and almost prepared to trade the service for the burial. He wanted his boy near him. The cemetery by the lake was only six blocks from his house, Dennis's mother was buried there . . . But he yielded at last. There was no thought of Jo leaving Washington, though Carl urged her to do so. She and Sonia would live with him. Her mother tugged in the opposite direction, it was time now for her to return to Marblehead, there was plenty of room for her and Sonia in the family house.

No, she said again and again.

What will you do in Washington? Carl demanded.

I have a job, she said.

Job? It had not occurred to him that she would get a job. Why? There was plenty of money. There was no need for her to work.

Nevertheless, she said, I have been offered a job on the First Lady's staff.

Doing what?

I don't know, she said. Answering letters. Seeing to the press. Buying Brie. I don't know.

"The First Lady." Carl McDonough controlled himself with difficulty. It was patronage and he'd never accepted patronage from anyone. Then, on second thought, he decided that it demonstrated admirable loyalty. At least they remembered their friends. It was loyalty at the taxpayer's expense but loyalty all the same. He had a long talk about it with Henry Costello, who offered to keep an eye on Jo. At last Carl agreed that it was wise for Jo and Sonia to remain in the capital. That was where their friends were and where Sonia's school was. Jo was a Washingtonian, like it or not.

Jo's mother was less graceful about it. She had been the last to know of Dennis's death. She was the last to know the funeral arrangements, made without consulting her. Now she was the last to know of her daughter's plans for life without Dennis. She thoroughly disapproved of the plans and of the fact that she hadn't been told of them. High-handed, she told friends. But I can't reach Jo now, and haven't been able to for years. First the marriage, then Washington. Now this. Poor Sonia.

The funeral would be in Winnetka, but Jo insisted on a memorial service in Washington. It would be held at the Episcopal church across Lafayette Square from the White House, at noon. She would open the ceremonies with a reading from the New Testament. Max Cather would follow with a selection from Hemingway, a favorite of Dennis's. Teddy Carney would read from Emerson's essay on self-reliance, and Piatt would conclude with a collage from Albert Camus. Piatt was surprised when Jo gave him the passages, neatly typed on Dennis's heavy personal stationery. He had never heard his friend mention Albert Camus, so recently dead in a motor accident in the South of France.

He did not want to ask her how she had come to select Hemingway, Emerson, and Camus. Nor the basis on which she had assigned the readers.

Instead, wanting to encourage her, he said, "Perfect. It's just perfect, Jo."

"Not perfect," she said. "But I put as much thought into it as I dared."

He said tentatively, "Odd, how little you know about friends. I didn't know that Dennis was a fan of Camus."

"He wasn't," she said. "I am. I wrote my senior thesis on him. The one I never finished because Dennis and I were married that year."

The first passage: "We are at the extremities now. At the end of this tunnel of darkness, however, there is invariably a light, which we already divine, and for which we have only to fight to ensure its coming. All of us, among the ruins, are preparing a renaissance beyond the limits of nihilism."

It was a puzzling choice. Camus spoke of darkness and endings, but Dennis and Jo lived at the beginning of things. Both of them were unafraid and on the threshold of a sunny, fertile future: Dennis's success was assured. This was not Paris or Oran, faded and exhausted, but Washington, vivid and brimming with energy. It was vulgar to say out loud among strangers but acceptable late at night, among friends. What better place in the world to be? After the long solemn night of the 1950s, new men had come at last to authority. Washington was now a banquet offering every imaginable dish. Of course it was necessary to be close, on the inside, a tomb of secrets if need be. It was not a place for outsiders, not then. The nation would at last enter its golden age of poetry and power, as the poet wrote but could not read in the glare of the winter sunlight on Inauguration Day. It was so obvious even the tired old men conceded it, and seemed prepared to yield. The times were so exhilarating and robust, the mood reminiscent of 1933. That was the conscious parallel, the new men eager to dispel a great depression of another kind. A wise columnist said it plainly one night at Dennis's. This generation would supervise America for years to come. The men at the second and third levels of government would be in the front rank in ten years and elder statesmen ten years after that. American corporations would lose the ablest men to the government, but the nation would gain. Max, Teddy, Piatt, and Sam nodded in unison: the columnist had wanted to get to know them, representatives of the younger generation. Dennis had offered to host a stag dinner, Jo to cook and then disappear. They arrived in black tie and drank too much, owing to nervousness: the columnist was a great friend of the administration. Looking at the text of what he had been given, Piatt remembered the evening with the columnist. Camus was too somber for that year, his strangers, plagues, suicides, and bleached landscapes were European and did not belong in the merry American present.

However, he had meaning for Jo.

The chapel was warm and crowded and smelled of autumn, an Indian Summer day. At the moment Jo rose to speak the attorney general entered from a side door, took his place next to his younger brother, and bowed his head in prayer. The four speakers sat behind a lectern, decorated left and right with white and yellow roses from the Carneys' garden. Jo seemed very small behind the lectern but her voice was strong and sharp with New England salt. They had filed in precisely at noon. Piatt was surprised by the crowd; there were standees in the rear of the chapel, conspicuous among them the under secretary of state and the national security adviser, Dennis's boss. The front rows were occupied by junior men and their wives, personal friends. Most of the NSC staff was there, along with the two Senators from Illinois and, in a back row, the DDP of the Central Intelligence agency. There was a report that the President himself might come but at the last minute he'd left Washington for Camp David. However, his counsel was present and the deputy press secretary and the principal speechwriter.

So there were the great, the almost great, and the would-be great. Carl McDonough sat in the fourth row with Sonia and Jo's mother. A dozen friends had accompanied him from Chicago, solid blue-suited lawyers, bankers, and businessmen. They seemed out of place, ill at ease in these surroundings; their open, substantial faces contrasted with the lean weather-beaten look of the Washingtonians. They were plainsmen in an assembly of seafarers. The businessman at Carl's right craned his neck, turned to his wife and whispered something, then shook his head. She nodded, tight-lipped. Piatt knew what it was, this businessman saw the gathering as political, a rally and not a solemn memorial service for his friend's dead son, the boy he'd known since he was yea-high. But what else could you expect from this crowd? Everything was political, every single thing; spend and elect, rule or ruin. Piatt watched him, his Republican mouth curling in distaste at the anonymous men standing along the side-aisles of the chapel: the secret service. This man remembered Dennis as a hellraising teenager around the club pool, then as a smart aleck at the coming-out parties. Dennis was rebellious, refusing to go into the bank, though a place had been prepared for him. He went instead to a concern in Wall Street, then to the campaign, and finally to Washington—having bought his way in, no other way to put it, with his father's money. And that was galling, Washington was where you were summoned to *serve*, not an end in itself, not a place to which a businessman aspired, as a matter of ambition, but a place he submitted to as a matter of patriotism. Dennis was a young man with Potomac Fever and his father had fed it and fed it in contradiction of his own beliefs and views, going so far as to invite Dennis to lunch on LaSalle Street with the Board to give them a briefing on Vienna . . .

Piatt smiled. He knew them too well.

Carl was drawn but erect. During Jo's remarks he dipped his head and did not raise it again until her peroration, two lines from the President's inaugural address; that had been Jo's afterthought, and it fitted in nicely with the passage from the New Testament. Carl accepted stoically the little murmur of approval. He looked down the row of faces to see how Michael took it. But Michael was staring straight ahead, his expression giving no hint of his own thoughts. Carl's expression seemed to say, This is not his show any more than it is mine.

Jo stepped back and took her seat, and Max Cather replaced her at the lectern. The selections were slow and cadenced and Max read them beautifully. Piatt listened carefully; the passages were unfamiliar to him but the language was so clean and spare, and so precise in its effect, that he felt an immediate affinity. Perhaps it was because they were both of the Midwest, interior men used to monotonous fields and shallow lakes, and the durability of things, the earth abiding forever, and so forth. Max was reading from a novel, something to do with the war. The words were so precise, they cut like razors; but they were of the past, too, serving only to remind him how things must have been, when there was still a frontier to go to. Hemingway was lucky to have lived in that time, and to see it so clearly. Everything was more accessible then. Now he too was dead—and Piatt realized with a rush that it couldn't have been so clear at the end. If the past was prologue—

Now he was speaking of soldiers and in the chapel there was a rustle of embarrassment or recognition, perhaps of sympathy. Piatt unconsciously reached for a cigarette. Dennis knew nothing of war, none of them did. Nor did he know the worst of anything else in life. Piatt put the package back in his pocket, trembling slightly. He and Max had not gotten to bed until five. Talk talk and more talk between mouthfuls of whiskey. They'd exhausted their Dennis stories so they talked about themselves, lying about each other instead of about Dennis. He'd wanted to reach down inside himself but was unable to do so. He made jokes instead. Max was steady as a mountain, reciting the last of his Hemingway. Then he was turning confidently from the lectern, looking smartly at Teddy, winking at Jo, and settling an inscrutable expression on Piatt. Piatt returned a weak smile, raising his eyebrows. He felt suddenly drained, the carousing of the night before; the day before that and the previous night, Chicago and Winnetka and the interminable wait at O'Hare, some unpleasantness with Michael. They all had their special claims, widow, daughter, father, brother, friends, the Chicagoans and the Washingtonians. An undercurrent of mistrust marred the ceremonies. It seemed to him that they'd been burying Dennis McDonough for a week. He looked sideways at Jo. Her head was high and her eyes clear, a deception. She's shed enough tears, she confided the night before, to float the *Queen Mary*. She and Marina and Harriet had urged him and Max to come to bed but they were having none of that. The bottle wasn't empty, and there were a few serious things they wanted to say to each other. Of course these were better said without women present. So the women left, but Piatt had not found what it was he wanted to say, either about himself or about Dennis. Nothing was as Hemingway promised.

Teddy Carney was less successful with Emerson. The irrepressible journalist didn't look the part, and his fastidious drawl wrestled with Emerson's stately cadences. Temperamentally suited to the Gothic South, he found irony where Emerson intended condemnation, arching his eyebrows in the presence of chilly New England. Piatt faced forward, watching the crowd. The under secretary was poised on the balls of his feet, rocking, arms crossed, listening intently. The national security adviser leaned casually against a pillar, his face a mask. The DDP was no longer in his seat, having slipped inconspicuously away after Hemingway. A dozen rows back the attorney general and his brother sat coiled tight as springs, both of them deeply tanned, their faces and tousled hair contrasting with their starched white shirts and tailored suits. They did not look like brothers. It took Piatt a moment to locate the Chicagoans, who were nicely assimilated now, solemn men and women, older for the most part but no longer so conscious of it. Little Sonia had not raised her head once, and now she pressed against her grandfather. To Piatt all this seemed abstract and somehow arbitrary and irrelevant, a ceremony like the legislative morning hour. What did it have to do with his friend, dead now four days—or was it five?

His stomach turned over as he realized Teddy was coming to the end of his excerpt. The journalist was reading slowly, frowning, as if the piece were a wire-service dispatch from the Back Bay of the nineteenth century. Then he was finished and returning to his seat.

Piatt sat a moment, lost in thought. Presently he rose and walked unsteadily to the lectern. There were below him, expectant, hushed and dappled in sunlight. Some of them seemed to be smiling, and he guessed their minds were elsewhere; at home or at the office, far away somewhere. He looked for Sam Joyce, finding him in the center of the congregation. He was wearing his soldier suit, the only one there in uniform. Sam gave him an encouraging smile. In the front, Sonia peeked out from under her grandfather's arm. The attorney general stirred, and his brother looked at his watch. In the rear somewhere, among the standees, Piatt imagined Henry Costello posed still as death itself, his restless eyes patrolling the crowd, counting. The rear of the chapel was in shadows, signified only by an impatient rustle. The government's business waited for him to begin, and then to end. He turned at last and began reading but Camus's rhythms were not his. The sentences sounded stiff and forced. Surely it was the voice of another generation, the one that had given way, parched. Piatt could feel the pressure of the prose, something always held in reserve, a darkness behind the light. The words beckoned as mockingly as any crooked finger, seductive in the off-key. Act, they implored; *act*. But Camus was an exile and they in the chapel were not. They were not alienated from themselves or the nation. They were an official family.

Always beware exiles.

The room began to tilt and slowly spin.

> . . . we are at the extremities now. At the end of
> this tunnel of darkness . . .

A light? His hands were trembling noticeably now, fluttering on the pages. He moved to steady them. He observed the faces in front of him and saw no one struggling, and no preparations for a renaissance "beyond the limits of nihilism." Some of them looked starved but it was not starvation of the belly or of the soul; and it did not result in hunger or melancholy or zealotry or divine madness, it resulted in ambition. It seemed to Piatt just then that they were poised for—more. A surfeit. However much there was, it would never be enough.

He heard a cough behind him, Max. A warning signal, discreetly delivered. He picked up the pace, moving swiftly through the unfamiliar language. It was like navigating a minefield, each word contained its own explosive.

> . . . real generosity toward the future lies in giving
> all to the present . . .

More like it, a sentence of encouragement, justification, and consolation. Listen carefully and you could hear another murmur of approval, a wave of support from the eminent Washingtonians listening critically. He heard it. Camus did not cast a shadow on their dreams after all but a merciless light. He felt the approval of those seated in front of him, yet was no less afraid. Piatt paused again. What did we know best? What had we lost? What did we believe, except that we were on the frontier of a brilliant adventure that nothing could halt or foreclose? As to the adventure itself, there would be portents. Was there something after all to be made of this death, so random and unprecedented? They were unprepared for it, and the fact of it seemed to cause a locked door to open and swing on its hinge. Certainly in every event, however terrible, there was solace—if only the solace of recognition. Piatt was sweating and now his legs began to tremble. He locked his knees but it was no good, they slipped their sockets. He felt himself a shell-shocked soldier jerked by the wires of ghastly memories. He was a man with a happy childhood, and there were many like him; the capital was filled with them. He looked down at Sonia, her little girl's face frightening in its blankness and fury. Piatt was in the embrace of that, a portent of the future, the embrace beginning deep within and growing swiftly, advancing like any undisciplined army—

At the rear of the chapel there was a sudden disturbance. The men stationed along the perimeter hurried to the knot of standees, who drew back. Costello was among them, a dazzling smile on his eager face; he was in the thick of it, taking charge. There was one flash and then another, blinding explosions from no apparent source. Piatt stepped back from the lectern, confused. The congregation stirred irritably. Then Piatt saw him, a photographer; in a moment he was surrounded by men in dark suits. No doubt he was from one of the newspapers, perhaps Carney's own. They were so careless, this was not a public trial. Then the standees at the rear parted, and she suddenly materialized. A man in the last pew stood and indicated his seat but the First Lady hesitated, undecided. Then she took the seat, bowing her head; the congregation stirred again, this time with vitality. The attorney general signaled to a secret service man, who turned to her, but she shook her head delicately, her expression indicating that it would cause too much commotion. The attorney general signaled again, exasperated; finally he walked down the aisle to join her. After a moment's pause, his brother followed. She sat staring serenely ahead. The secret service men relaxed, resuming their silent stations along the side-aisles. Costello leaned down to whisper something to the attorney general, then grinned, unruffled. Piatt glanced to one side. The flashbulbs hurt his eyes but through the window he saw the venerable trees of Lafayette Square, pretty and still in the golden autumn sun, and the stately old white mansion beyond.

Marina said, Where will you go?
I don't know, he said. Somewhere in the boondocks.
And you really want to go?
Of course, he said.
Is it necessary?
That's what they say, he said.
She whispered, You look wonderful in uniform. When I was in college we all wanted dates from West Point because they looked so sexy in uniform. Of course it never occurred to us that the uniform had anything to do with the army, do you know

what I mean? I mean that there might be a war. So I'm afraid. And I hate it.

It won't be that kind of war for me, he said.

How do you know? How do you know that? And what kind of war will it be then?

I don't know, he said seriously. But not that kind.

What's happening back there? she said, turning her head.

An idiot photographer, he said. Then, eyes front again, he whispered: What's wrong with Piatt?

This thing has affected him terribly, she said. And he won't talk about it with me or anybody. He refused to let Tommy come today because Tommy's too young to understand. Doesn't want to "expose" him. Too young to be here, according to Piatt. But he's not too young to grieve, I left him at home in tears. He *wanted* to come and I almost brought him. But I didn't. She looked down at her hands. Then she said, He doesn't know how complicated people are. He doesn't have a clue.

In front of them the attorney general had turned and was motioning. When he left his seat, followed by his brother, Sam nudged Marina. She must be here, he said. That's what the SS was here for; I wondered why there were so many of them. Good of her to come, he said.

Piatt cleared his throat and prepared to speak again. Behind him, Jo whispered something. Her voice sounded angry. Max coughed, a signal, and there was another rustle somewhere in the chapel. Sonia turned away. He did not want to continue, for these words were foreign to him, neither consoling nor flattering nor encouraging. They did not suit the moment and now they furred, turning like a musical figure on the page. He shut his eyes tightly. In the darkness he saw the face of the President's young wife, dark hair, dark coat, a black dress, and an expressionless face like a static portrait.

Piatt's thoughts were everywhichway now, to Dennis, to Jo, Max, Teddy, Marina—where was Marina? He could not locate her in the multitude, the Chicagoans, Carl McDonough, Jo's mother, Sonia, Dennis's colleagues, the various officials of the government. These were unforgiving faces, like the crowd at ringside when the fight is torpid. He finally located Marina, her beautiful face turned to one side, talking to a companion. She was a row behind the attorney general and his brother, their seats empty now. Her hand touched her hair at the base of her neck, a familiar gesture. She looked so much like Tommy. Now he thought she could save him from this panic, from whatever it was that possessed him. He could not escape from himself, could not read the simple words before him or concentrate on his duty. How many times had he spoken before a hostile audience? Told them things they did not want to hear? So many times, he was an expert at soothing unfriendly crowds. He leaned over the lectern, searching for her. He reached, their eyes met, then slid away. She turned first, sadly, seeming to lean on the man beside her, Sam Joyce in khaki.

He saw her in profile only.

He folded the four sheets of stationery, so many lines still unread. The bulk of it was unread. He returned to his seat and after a little silence Jo rose. Max and Teddy rose with her, exiting through the door back of the lectern. Max touched him on the shoulder as he passed silently by. Piatt remained for a moment, distracted and ashamed. Then those in the chapel began to rise and disperse. It was very hot, his shirt was soaked through. The crowd was detained by the secret service, until the President's wife and the attorney general and his brother were gone. She cast one glance behind her, it looked to Piatt almost wistful. He saw them slip away, followed by Henry Costello. Marina and Sam Joyce disappeared, it was odd seeing her next to him, a man in uniform, his childhood friend. Carl and Sonia and Jo's mother stayed where they were, heads bowed, offering a last prayer for the repose of the soul of the dead.

At last Piatt stood, alone and sick at heart. The roses, so fragrant, seemed to mock him. He did not know what had happened, except his nerves had cracked like china against concrete. The darkness had closed around him, and suddenly he was afraid, for he knew that some part of this day would be with him always. Some part of him would always be in this chapel, unable to read simple words. What might he do, poised again at the extremity? Standing now, turning and moving toward the anteroom where the others waited, it came to him that he had been given a warning. One opened one's deepest emotions at a terrible peril to security. Human beings did not adhere, they devoured each other. He turned to embrace Jo.

He said, I'm sorry.

She shrugged and gestured vaguely, her mind elsewhere. Others surrounded them. The talk grew in volume, condolences from friends, assurances that it had been a beautiful service, Dennis would've loved it, Teddy reading Emerson. And it was so good of her to come, she and the attorney general and the others. . . . But very quickly the talk moved along, to matters of current interest. They moved to put Dennis's death behind them. That was the past, this was the future. Consulting wrist-watches, shuffling a little, the crowd began to thin. Men had to return to their offices.

Marina and Sam came forward, Sam shaking his hand and Marina kissing him on the cheek. She said something he didn't understand. Sam was looking over his shoulder, his hands beating a nervous tattoo, one against the other. Then they too were engulfed in the conversation and swept away to a far corner. The attorney general stepped through the door and went immediately to Jo and then to Dennis's father. Henry Costello introduced them. He shook hands with Carl and one of the Chicagoans with him, nodding as if they'd met before; everyone watched. Momentarily alone, Piatt lit a cigarette. He would give it a minute or two, then escape, back to the House. He found Jo and Max standing together in a large group. The attorney general was telling a story, the others leaning toward him, listening carefully. Sam and Marina had disappeared. Piatt moved closer to the center, wanting to hear the story. Suddenly they turned, all of them, looking through him as if he were a pane of windowglass. He might have been dead.

112